To Steve & Paula –
Best wishes to fellow Rotarans!
Happy reading!

And the Wind Whispered

By Dan Jorgensen

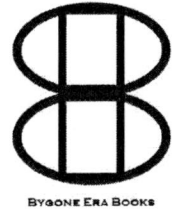

BYGONE ERA BOOKS

Copyright © 2015 Dan Jorgensen

Published by:
Bygone Era Books, Ltd
7665 E. Eastman Ave. #B101
Denver, CO 80231

This book contains material protected under International and Federal Copyright Laws and Treaties. Any unauthorized reprint or use of this material is prohibited. No part of this book may be reproduced or transmitted in any form or by any means, electronic or mechanical, including photocopying, recording, or by any information storage and retrieval system without express written permission from the author.

ISBN: 978-1-941072-19-6

Printed in the United States of America
ALL RIGHTS RESERVED

And the Wind Whispered

PROLOGUE

"What you gonna do with that iron, Masterson?"

Alfred Lewis slid into the booth as he spoke and nodded at the Colt .45 pistol lying on the table. Bat Masterson looked up from his copy of the *New York Morning Telegraph* and blew out a plume of cigarette smoke, glancing in the direction Lewis was indicating. The gun had a dull finish and its weathered wooden handle was decorated with a series of notches.

"Sell it, of course." Bat tilted his trademark bowler hat back on his head, revealing a rapidly receding hairline. He tapped the newspaper. "The money your brother Bill pays me to write for this rag, not to mention all the damn editing I have to do, couldn't keep a foundling alive, let alone a big, strong fella like myself." He gave Lewis a wry smile. "So, I had to get out the old..." he paused as if in thought. "What's that expression you used when you wrote about my lawman days? Oh yeah, 'The Gun That Tamed The West.'" He picked up the Colt, lovingly rolled it over in his hands, then laid it back down. "I'll just have to let it go to the highest bidder. At least then I'll have enough money to buy food and drink for a couple weeks and keep my strength up to write about the ponies and the pugilists."

He tapped the newspaper again. "One of these days I'm going to hit on one of these racing bets and then I can just do my writing as a hobby, instead of a 'profession.'" He snorted and the corners of his salt-and-pepper mustache crinkled up and down. "Professional writer. That's a laugh."

"No, you're good at it. And you were good with that gun, too..." Lewis paused as he pointed at the weapon. "Say, didn't you sell 'The Gun That Tamed The West' a few weeks ago?"

"I might have had more than one you know."

"Uh-huh." Lewis leaned in for a closer look at the gun. "Seems like you might've had quite a few more, now that I think about it. You had a big gun sale last year, too." Masterson glared at him over the top of the newspaper and Lewis shrank back. "Well, whatever gun you used when that was your profession, you could do it again you know. You could go back out West any time. You don't have to keep up this hand-to-mouth shit here in the City."

Masterson took a long drag on his cigarette, stubbed it out on the edge of the booth, and tossed the butt into an ashtray next to the gun. His steel-blue eyes seemed to glint, even in the room's smoky light. "Naw, I told you before, that ain't for me no more." He laughed and his mustache bobbed once again. "Hell, like you said, 'I tamed the West,' or at least me and that damn gun did. That's what all the notches are for. Bad guys who ain't around no more. Sure helps with the sales value." He shook his head. "Now if I could just hit on a bet once in a while, I could 'tame' New York City, too."

Lewis picked up the gun and turned it over in his hands, giving an admiring whistle. "Nice work on this one. Maybe you ought to give up the writing game and just concentrate on refinishing old sixguns."

"Hah, funny!" Masterson snapped the newspaper over indignantly and folded it up, laying it down on top of the gun as the waiter brought over a plate of ham and eggs and re-filled his coffee mug. He leaned closer to his friend. "But just for the sake of saying that maybe I had more than one 'Gun that tamed the West,' I'd appreciate it if you'd keep that sort of talk to yourself." He nodded decisively, leaning back a bit. "Especially if you plan on doing any more stories or that book about me that you keep harpin' about."

"Oh, I'm plannin' on that all right," Lewis answered. "And you'll get your cut from the sales. So the sooner we get it done, the sooner you get some of the cash." He leaned over and tapped Masterson's arm. "I even thought of a book title. I'm going to call it *The Sunset Trail*. Good, huh? And every day you write that newspaper column of yours, it just adds to the energy and excitement. People can't wait to read my stories about you, just like they can't hardly wait to read what you write. My brother is damn lucky to have you, I can tell you that." He pulled the folded up paper over to his side of the table and opened it to a halftone photo of the man sitting across from him alongside the headline: "Masterson's Views on Timely Topics."

"That's what I was hopin' to hear from you, Al. That's why I asked you to come over here and meet me this morning. If I'm so damn valuable to *The Telegraph* then you gotta get Bill to shake loose with a few more bucks each week until that book comes out. I can't keep doing the job, paying the bills, and..." he paused and pointed at the gun, "...and takin' time to fix up a shooting iron every few months just to survive. And I ain't gettin' any younger, either, you know. Hell, I just turned 55."

"No shit, well happy birthday," Lewis said, still pondering the newspaper column. "Hey, this is interesting. I didn't know you knew Texas Jack." He read further. "Jesus, this is great. You know Texas Jack, Lil Marr AND Will Rogers? You're a goddamn gold mine of Old West stories, you know that?"

"Yeah, thanks." Masterson looked glumly at the food, began stirring at it with his fork, and then finally took a bite. "Maybe I can pluck a nugget or two out of that mine to pay for breakfast."

"I'll talk to Bill. I'm sure he can work something out. Okay?" Lewis started to slide out of the booth. He tossed a dollar coin on the table. "For the breakfast. So, when can we talk next? I should write up something about your connection with 'The Texas Jack Wild West Show,'" he said expansively, doing his best show ring barker's imitation. "They're at the Garden tonight." He pointed at the newspaper. "I just read that in your column."

"You going to that show, Bat?"

The woman's voice caught both men off guard and they turned together toward a nearby booth. A handsome, forty-something woman wearing the latest style in hats and walking capes turned around to face them, and Masterson inhaled sharply. "Because I'm planning to take it in," she continued, "so maybe we can go together?"

"Ah, the Widow Seaman. Out slumming with the commoners today?" Bat asked with just the slightest edge to his voice. "I hadn't decided one way or another, but I heard old Jack got Sitting Bull's nephew to sign on with him. That Two Bulls fella we all met." He pondered that information as if weighing the pros and cons. "Sure, why not? Especially if you're buying?"

"My treat," she answered.

"What brings you to this famed eatery?" Masterson asked, gesturing around at the crowded, smoke-filled diner.

"Actually, I came here looking for you," she answered. "Heard you liked the way they fix ham and eggs." She smirked and gestured at his plate before extending her hand toward Lewis. "Hello. I'm Elizabeth Seaman."

He took a few steps over to greet her, and was surprised by her firm handshake. "Alfred Lewis," he replied. "Are you and Bat longtime friends?"

"Eleven years," she said. "And 'friends' might be a bit of a stretch. 'Acquaintances and fellow sojourners,' that might fit our connection a bit more accurately, wouldn't you say Marshal Masterson? We met out West, actually, back in the fall of '94. We met when we were on the same train together going to the Black Hills. Remember all that, Bat?"

"Weren't you going to write about that, Nellie?" Masterson said wryly.

"Yes, I suppose I was," she said. "For some reason I just never got around to it. Too many other things to do, I guess."

He nodded at her ring finger. "Like getting married, burying a husband, and running your own company? Those sorts of things?"

She stared back at him with just the hint of a smile. "Maybe I just wanted to keep that story for another time. I always thought it would make a nice book, actually. Didn't you?"

Lewis perked up at her comment and looked from one to the other, a puzzled expression on his face. "Bat, would that be another book idea ... for us, I mean; you and me? I can interview you about it after we get this first one finished. I have a feeling we're gonna need a second book once *Sunset Trail* hits the market."

Masterson smoothed the corners of his bushy mustache and pulled out a fresh cigarette, lighting it and blowing smoke toward the floor. "Maybe?" he said. "Maybe I need to go over the details with Nellie here before I make any commitments. Eleven years can muddy the mind's waters a bit. And I'd hate to put something out there as a fact when it might be just the way that I remember it."

"Maybe it would freshen up your memory if you'd write a few more of your 'Old West' stories for my *Human Life* magazine. I need something besides my own stories to spice things up in that thing. You can keep writing your 'Timely Topics' for Bill's paper and write some real stories for me. I'll pay you good for 'em too."

"Like that gold, for instance," Nellie said. "You could write about that. You think anyone will ever locate it?"

Masterson shrugged. "I don't worry about things like that."

"Really?" she said. "It's a lot of money and I heard it's still just 'out there' somewhere. Maybe we should go back to the Black Hills and have a look?"

"Not me," Masterson replied. "I ain't goin' any further west than the Hudson River. Haven't you heard? I'm a reborn and bred New Yorker now, through and through. Even some of those wild horses we both knew couldn't drag me back out there."

"You know, that was supposed to be over a hundred thousand in gold, Bat. A hundred thousand...back then. Probably worth twice that by now."

"Could be," he said. "Hell, probably is. Suppose we could at least TALK about it some, although I don't know what damn good it'll do. Besides, what do you care? I'm the one needs money, not you?"

Her face darkened. "I've...our... I mean my business has...suffered a few setbacks recently. That's another thing I wanted to talk with you about." She brightened. "But not today. Today we can talk about the Black Hills, missing gold, and a Wild West Show that we can go and see."

He gestured toward the vacated seat that Lewis had just occupied.

"You had breakfast?"

"I've ordered," she said. "But I think they can put the food down on your table as easily as they can on mine." She slid out of her booth, smoothed the front of her expensive silk dress, and then walked over and slid back in across from him. "Pleasure to meet you Mister Lewis. Who knows. Maybe we'll all be meeting together next time to talk a bit more about OUR book?"

"Sure," Lewis said, realizing that he was being dismissed. He tipped his hat. "Nice to meet you too, Mrs. Seaman." He paused as he looked at her again. "Seaman? From The 'Iron Clad Manufacturing Company' Seaman?"

She nodded.

He gave Bat Masterson another quizzical look, glancing back at the attractive woman sitting across from him. The former lawman turned newspaperman responded with an exasperated "Get Lost Please" expression and tilted his head slightly in the direction of the restaurant door. Lewis started to move away, and then halted as if struck by a thunderbolt. He turned around and walked briskly back to the table.

"Elizabeth Seaman? Nellie? Aren't you...?" she cut him off in mid-sentence, raising one hand.

"Yes, Mr. Lewis. I'm the woman formerly referred to as 'The Amazing Nellie Bly.' Now, if you will excuse us please, I think Bat and I have a bit of catching up to do." She nodded politely in the direction of the door and Bat now gave him a not-so-subtle jerk of his head and shoulder in the same direction.

"Bat Masterson and Nellie Bly together," Lewis muttered as he went through the door. "Who would've ever imagined something like that?"

CHAPTER ONE

"Oh my god! Oh my god! Oh my god!"

Laura Thompson was screaming uncontrollably, backed up against the wall of the cave. Her sister Minnie and friend Alvin Twocrow scrambled toward her voice, carrying one tin-pail style lantern between them and hampered by the narrow walls that seemed to close around them even tighter in their hurry to reach her. The blackness of the cave was almost overpowering and their small light source reached barely beyond their outstretched arms.

As their light merged with Laura's they could see the fearful look reflected on her face. "Laura? What?" Minnie grabbed her sister's lantern, set it on the ground, and wrapped a protective arm around Laura's shoulders. "What's the matter?"

"Look." Laura gasped and nodded off to her right, a look of terror replacing her normally pretty features.

Twocrow took two cautious steps in the direction Laura was indicating and jumped back, startled by what he saw. "Well?" Minnie was getting frustrated. "What the hell? Alvin? Laura? Come on!"

"It's a body," Twocrow gulped. "And I told you. I'm not Alvin any more. I'm Bill. Everybody who's anybody around here is either Bill or Will, so I am too." He paused as if giving it further thought. "You need to call me Bill."

Minnie rolled her eyes. "Okay...Bill. A body? What kind of body? Here, give me that." She reached out and nabbed the handle of his bucket lantern, jerking it toward her. Twocrow clung to it for a few more seconds, let it go and slid closer to Laura and the light of her lantern as Minnie eased on in the direction that had her sister and friend so spooked.

Holding the lantern forward, the suddenly illuminated sight of a corpse met her gaze—a middle-aged man actually—sprawled facedown against a rock formation. The way he was lying against the rocks with his arms splayed to the sides made it appear that he had fallen and hit his head, either dying from the impact or knocked unconscious before slipping into death. It didn't look like he had moved once he had hit the spot where he was lying. Minnie held the light up, trying to see if there was a ledge or something above them from where he might have fallen, but the roof of the passageway about four feet above their heads was all that could be seen.

"Huh?" she said, pushing at the body with her toe. "Guess he didn't fall. Must've been thrown here."

"What are you going on about?" Laura said, now becoming more curious, brave and encouraged by her younger sister's lack of fear. She edged forward to Minnie's side, leaving Twocrow behind them with the other lamp.

"Look," Minnie said, indicating the limp rag doll look of the dead man's body. "The way his body is lying there, it looks like he fell straight down and hit his head. But if that happened, then where did he fall from?" She grasped the pail lamp by its bottom and hoisted it up, exposing the low ceiling. "Unless he fell through a solid rock wall and then it closed back up behind him that probably wasn't what happened. And that means he was already dead when he got to this point and somebody threw him down here. They probably didn't think anyone would be in this passage for a million years."

She paused as if re-thinking her hyperbole. "Well, okay, maybe for a hundred years. Either way, too long to figure how he ended up dead."

Twocrow came forward to join them, adding his lantern to the pool of light and making the area around the body much more visible. Minnie's assessment had to be true because there was no way a body could've dropped into that position without help.

"So somebody killed him and wanted him to disappear," he said. "Wow, this is a great story," he reached inside his coat pocket and pulled out a small notepad. "Who's going to get to write it?" He looked back and forth at the two sisters, who turned simultaneously toward him, Laura looking disgusted and Minnie looking angry.

"Alvin..." she began, then threw her head back and sighed as he pulled up his left forefinger in reproach, "...BILL. What do you mean WHO'S going to write it? Why are you even asking? And, what are you even doing with a notepad? You said you weren't EVER going to ever be a reporter again. That's why you came over here to work at the Cave, isn't it? You said," Minnie reached into her cloth bag and pulled out a small notepad of her own, flipped over several pages, and pretended to read, "and I quote: 'I ain't never, ever, never, for so long as I live, work as a STUPID newspaper reporter again. Ever!' And now that maybe a great story comes along you're suddenly a reporter again? You're unbelievable, you know that?" She huffed indignantly and slipped the notepad back into her bag.

"Well, sure...but...but don't I get...uh...you know...like a second chance? If I change my mind?"

"The Hermosa news," she muttered, referring to a small community that sometimes had news items for her father's newspaper. "You can get your second chance by writing about the Hermosa news." Minnie spun back to the body and reached out to touch it. "Holy crap, Laura and I have been doing this our whole lives. WE are reporters. If YOU want to be one, you have to earn it like we have."

The Thompson sisters had been working with their father on the *Buffalo Gap News* since they were old enough to do their McGuffey's Readers, helping first with the little news pieces from the social events around town; then branching out to cover the small "happenings" stories both in their Black Hills town and in the surrounding ranching community. Minnie, who had just turned 17, was writing for their Dad's paper, but Laura, at the ripe old age of 19, had hired on with the *Hot Springs Star*, a three-times-a-week paper compared to their Dad's weekly edition, something Laura didn't hesitate to lord over her younger sibling.

Laura snorted at her sister's proclamation. "WE are reporters? You wish," she said. "I AM a reporter; you are..." she paused to think of the right term. "Maybe you could be my apprentice and lucky if I would even let you come along with me on a reporting assignment."

"Yeah, lucky me," Minnie said sarcastically. "What would I be learning from you O great and wonderful reporter—cowering in fear against the wall, or standing screaming uncontrollably? Let me know, because I want to use the proper reporting style."

Minnie knelt and pretended to examine the body to mask her disgust with her sister's "holier-than-thou" attitude, which had been grating on her since she and her father had begun moving Laura from Buffalo Gap into the booming resort city of Hot Springs.

Minnie had quickly grown tired of Laura's attitude that signaled she felt she was a step above both her sister and her father in the pecking order of the family journalists. On top of that, Laura, with her natural beauty and outgoing smile, was rapidly becoming the toast of her newly adopted community, something she also played up for her sister's benefit.

"I'm so tired of Laura always in the limelight," Minnie confided to Alvin when he stopped by the boarding house in which Laura would now be residing until she was more settled in her new community.

"Come on, Minnie. She's always been that way," Twocrow had said as he gave Laura a clearly admiring glance. Then, seeing Minnie giving him an odd glance of her own at the response, he had stammered, "You know, you could be, too, if you'd just wear some more stylish clothes and be a little more friendly to everyone. You're pretty, too, you know." He had stepped back as if assessing her. "Really pretty, actually."

Minnie remembered blushing and playfully shoving her friend without responding. She knew in her heart that what he said was a fact, but she just couldn't bring herself to act coy and "fetching," as she'd heard her sister described. She'd make her mark by her work, not her beauty. As for Twocrow, both girls treated him more like a brother than a friend. And, recently he also had been a colleague, since he had worked on the Buffalo Gap newspaper before becoming bored by the paper's daily routine.

The son of a onetime Chief in the Lakota Sioux band that lived east of the small South Dakota town, he had come to The Gap, as it was known, to live with his mother's sister and her white rancher husband after his parents died in the late 1880s smallpox epidemic. Now, six years later, he had been hired to work at Wind Cave, a legendary site for the Sioux and Cheyenne tribes and a developing stop for tourists coming to the spas at nearby Hot Springs.

Twocrow had long been attracted to the Cave. At age 12, Two Crow, as he had been known on his arrival in the Gap, had adopted the first name of Alvin and combined his previous name into a new single last name instead. He had selected the first name after hearing stories of the heroic young cave explorer Alvin MacDonald, who had been courageously entering and mapping Wind Cave's nearly endless passageways and caverns. Thus, the formal name of Alvin Twocrow had been born.

In and out of the Buffalo Gap School, Alvin became fast friends with Laura and Minnie, and started hanging out at the newspaper office where their father eventually thought he might become a permanent member of the staff. By the time he turned 18, he was six feet tall with a muscular upper body and chiseled jawline; good-looking, yet not overwhelmingly handsome. Ranchers and townsfolk alike were used to seeing him with one sister or another, tagging along to gather news or to cover news events and activities. But his failure to complete his writing courses kept him from getting to cover the stories on his own and he was anxious to try something new.

That's when, in late spring of 1894, the MacDonald family began expanding Wind Cave into a tourist attraction and advertised for Indian workers to join the "Wonderful Wind Cave Development Company." Their ad in the Buffalo Gap newspaper was like a magnet for Twocrow. He had marched into the office and pronounced that the life of a journalist wasn't for him. He was leaving to work north of Hot Springs at the sacred Wind Cave and follow in the footsteps of his namesake, Alvin MacDonald, to help explore the mysterious Cave's many caverns and passageways.

The girls pleaded with him to stay on at the newspaper, but he had made his forceful proclamation about never again being a reporter and headed off to take a job at the Cave, where he would get both room and board in Hot Springs and modest wages for his work. Now, after a summer on his own, he was overjoyed to learn that Laura had been hired by the *Star* and would be moving into Hot Springs, too. At least one of his best friends would be close enough to see on a regular basis.

"We should go out and I'll show you the Cave," he had said after helping Laura's father tote up the last of her bags.

"Oh! Can we Daddy?" Minnie had almost sounded like a little girl again in her excited approval of the offer. But her father had demurred saying he had to get back to start work on the next issue of the paper.

"Well, I can bring Minnie home in a couple days...and...she could stay here with Laura," Twocrow said, gesturing toward the buggy in which he had driven up to the boarding house on Hot Springs' north side. "The MacDonalds and Stablers are out in Chicago and then back to Sioux City for a few days doing some promotion, and they said I could use the horse and buggy and do some things for myself until they return. They don't want the Cave operating without them there, anyway. So Laura and Minnie can come and tour the Cave with me. It's only an hour or so from here, you know?"

"And then she can stay over and go to the new Chautauqua Pavilion show with us!" Laura added, excitement growing in her own voice.

"And I can bring Minnie back to the Gap on Sunday!" Twocrow continued. The three had been known for continuing each other's sentences when they were together at Buffalo Gap and this familiar routine just seemed to come naturally now that they were back together.

Their father had hesitated for only a few seconds, especially with the anguished looks on all three of their faces as they stared expectantly in his direction.

"Oh, all right," he agreed as Minnie gave a little yelp of glee and clung to her father's arm in happiness. "But you drive careful up-and-back and get an early start to the Gap on Sunday. It's a three-hour ride each way, you know? I'm putting a lot of trust in you Alvin."

The young Indian, his hair cropped short and dressed in a grey-green shirt and pants that the MacDonalds had adopted as their "trademark" work uniform, beamed. "You know I will sir. They're like my sisters." He looked over to the girls. "They ARE my sisters." They both grinned in return. "And sir," he looked gravely at Mr. Thompson. "I've changed my first name to William, and I want folks to call me Bill."

"Really?" Thompson tried not to look overly amused, but had to glance back toward the street to avoid chuckling at the younger man. "And why's that, I might ask?"

"It seems more manly and important, I think," Twocrow answered seriously. "All the greatest men around now seem to be named William...or Bill ... or Will. Buffalo Bill, Wild Bill, There's even a famous Indian in Buffalo Bill's show called Pawnee Bill. And, did you know that Bat Masterson's real name is Bill? So from now on I'm going to be William Twocrow."

"You do know Wild Bill is dead, don't you?" Minnie said drily, giving him her best fake serious stare as she said it.

"Well, of course," Alvin glared at her. "I was just using him as an example 'cause everyone seems to keep talking about him, even though he died about the time I was born. Look, Alvin is a nice enough name, but I think the MacDonalds aren't happy about my using their son's first name, especially, you know, now that he's gone. They seemed really happy that I was going to change my name."

Both Thompson and his daughters nodded at Twocrow's reference to Alvin MacDonald. The young explorer's death had shocked the entire region. Along with his father J.D., MacDonald had traveled to the 1893 Columbian Exposition —the World's Fair in Chicago —to promote The Wonderful Wind Cave, which he had been meticulously exploring since he was 17. While in the big city, he had contracted typhoid fever, gotten steadily worse and died just days after their return.

"That's pretty understandable," Thompson said, "and admirable of you." He reached out a hand and Twocrow accepted it in a firm handshake. After some quick goodbyes, the newspaper editor headed off in his own buggy, leaving the girls and Twocrow to pack a light lunch and do the ride up to the Cave north of the city.

The day was sunny, not too hot, and calm. The ride was a pleasant excursion through the rolling prairieland surrounded by the majestic Black Hills to the west and north and the smaller foothills horseshoeing on the south and east. Easing the bay horse and two-seater buggy gingerly through the prairie dog towns that dotted the rolling countryside, Twocrow expertly drove them down into the area developed by the MacDonald family as both a home and visitor center for the Cave. A new overnight hotel was under construction, but work had stopped while the MacDonalds were away.

He was thrilled to be working at the Cave, and they were equally thrilled to be able to tell visitors that a "Genuine Sioux Indian, son of a former chief from the original proprietors of the Cave and all of the Black Hills," was part of their operations team. While Alvin and his father J.D. and brother Elmer had mapped out a considerable portion of the eerie-sounding cave as a tourist stop, the largest portion, both mapped and unmapped, remained off limits.

As they drove down to the site, they were greeted by the telltale whistling noise of the wind rushing in and out of the cave's mouth.

"Easy girl," Alvin said soothingly to the horse as she whinnied uneasily. He looked at the girls. "I'll bet we come in and out of here ten times a week and she always acts that way. You and me, we just hear the wind, but maybe she sees Wakan Tanka moving through the air. The Lakota creation story says Wakan Tanka, the Great Spirit, came out from Wind Cave to bring life to the people. It is said that the wind whispered beneath the rolling hills and created our people. My father always believed that it is here Wakan Tanka still resides.

"When the wind goes out from the cave, he is traveling; and when the wind comes back in, he is returning to rest beneath Paha Sapa —the sacred rolling hills." He nodded sagely while gesturing toward the mouth of the cave. Minnie had found herself shivering involuntarily despite the warmth of the day.

"Alvin and Elmer have been working for years trying to figure this place out," Twocrow said as he pulled up to a watering trough and hitching post. He got down and tied up the horse. "I was looking with Elmer at the diaries Alvin was keeping, and he wrote that he thinks nobody'll ever find the end of this place—it goes on that far and that deep. But there's about two dozen passageways and rooms sort-of interconnected up in the front part and that's the area we take people into when they come to get a tour."

He walked into the small entrance building, grabbed a packet of cave maps, and put on a leather belt that held a trenching tool and utility knife. Picking up a canteen, he started pumping it full of fresh water as the girls extricated themselves from the buggy and walked over to join him.

"I'll take some water and the maps; you can handle the lamps." He took two tin-pail lanterns down from a shelf at the door, inserted a huge candle into each one and lit them, turning his back to the cave's opening to prevent the "exhaling" wind from blowing them out. Sliding a glass covering down on each one, he handed them to the girls. "Here." He handed each of them a packet of twine. "Always take some string with you into a cave. You never know if you'll need it."

They slipped the string into their bags as he looped his onto a leather belt and strapped it on. "Okay, let's go. It's almost eight-thirty, so we can spend a two or three hours walking through the areas I know before we eat our lunch and head back to Hot Springs."

They had eased their way inside, the girls' longer skirts swishing and button-up shoes clacking on the hard-rock floors and walls as they slowly descended into the blackness. Along the route, Alvin stopped every 30 or 40 feet to light a wall lantern, leaving a lighted trail behind them. They reached a spot where three distinct trails branched off and he lit two more wall-mounted lamps.

"We call this The Crossroads," he explained. "Let's go to this one." He turned right into a narrow crevice and edged forward and after a few minutes the trail widened. He lit another lamp embedded in the wall and pulled out a long flat strip of metallic ribbon.

"What's that?" Laura asked.

"Magnesium ribbon. We've been using it to light up the bigger spaces. Here, watch." He bent down and lit the end of the ribbon and it flared up and suddenly the room was filled with light. The girls gasped in delight. The room was beautiful and high, soaring almost 30 feet above them and stretching out more than a hundred feet ahead of them.

"We call this room The Garden of Eden," he said as the ribbon continued to burn brightly. "Come on, let's go back to The Crossroads and I'll take you into The Fairgrounds." Minnie held back to study the walls of the big room, light bouncing off glittering crystals in some of the rocks.

"It's so beautiful," she breathed.

"Wait'll you see The Fairgrounds," Twocrow said over his shoulder. "But we'll definitely need another ribbon there because we haven't put in wall lights yet. Just got the lanterns." They reached The Crossroads again and moved across the opening to another gap in the wall.

"We'll go through a really narrow passageway now and then get onto a wide ledge below The Devil's Lookout. That's the Fairgrounds entryway. Stay close together because once we get away from these lights it's really dark. And did you feel how it got so much cooler almost right away. The Cave's temperature always stays the same, no matter what it's like outside. It's always around 45 or 50 degrees in here. That's why I wanted you to bring your shawls." He was definitely acting like a "big brother" now, and he stood tapping his boot against one of the walls as the sisters adjusted the wraps around their shoulders.

"Why is it called Devil's Lookout?" Minnie asked.

"Alvin said the Devil was watching people from the top of this passage." He pointed to one side. "And it looks down over three passages that veer off and down —not straight down, just down and more down. At the end of this one, there's a room called Dante's Inferno. It's a big pit and nobody's ever found the bottom —or tried to go beyond it to explore. Alvin used to say it went three miles down and he still hadn't found a bottom, and as far as he knew it went all the way to hell." He shivered, both thinking about that and from the chilled air now surrounding them. "Look." He held the lantern up and there before them were the perfect images of two pigs made out of stone seeming to guard the passage toward Dante's Inferno. One looked like it had an ear of corn in its mouth.

"There's a story about those pigs, too—about who they used to be before the Devil turned them into stone and put them down here in the cave."

"And?" Minnie asked, hands on her hips as she continued staring at them.

"I didn't say I knew the story, just that there IS one," Twocrow answered. "Ask me next time we come down here. I'll probably know it by then." Laura laughed and Minnie slugged him on the arm. "Ow, Jeez," he exclaimed. Then he grinned at her. "Let's go. I promise to find out about it before you go home so you can tell your dad."

They lit up The Fairgrounds for another spectacular view and then used up most of an hour exploring some of the smaller caverns and easier to navigate passageways that the MacDonalds had accented with the wall lights. As they moved about, they paused to look at the intricate boxwork that seemed to be everywhere, including one whole room called The Post Office because all the boxwork along one wall looked like post office boxes.

Finally, they left the last of the wall-lighted region, extinguishing the lamps as they retreated, and entered a new route that led to a majestic room that seemed to be unending in size. Twocrow took one of the lanterns and made his way out onto a promontory where he suddenly seemed to be bathed in a shaft of light as he stood holding the pail in his arms.

"Wow," Laura exclaimed as she and Minnie stood alongside the wall holding the other lamp. "How do you do that?"

Twocrow shrugged. "Beats me. It's got to be the way the rocks angle around me to reflect the light is all I can figure. I came in here with Elmer and he did this and it was amazing. He's been calling it The Pearly Gates because it's like you're being illuminated by angels. Hey, you can write about that in the *Star* and the *News*. People will want to come to see things like this, even locals, don't you think?"

That had started a conversation about publicizing the wonders of the Cave and that, somehow, local residents needed to get to know it so that they could tell the rapidly increasing numbers of Black Hills visitors, too. They reached another larger flat room and Twocrow pointed them toward a smaller passage with a signature on the wall. "See this. It's Alvin's, dated from last July. His father thinks it's the last one he wrote in here. Alvin was always in here checking new routes and mapping things out or making the openings larger, easier to go through. It would've been nice to know him."

The sisters exchanged glances at their friend's wistful tone and nodded in agreement. "Where does it go?" Laura said, pointing at the crevice veering off from the signature.

"Not sure. It's the one Alvin was exploring when he put his signature up here. He told his father that he was going to have to go back in there later and maybe take some more equipment, because it was both exciting and scary. Elmer told me to stay out of it."

"Sounds like an adventure to me," Laura said. "Come on, let's check it out."

"Well, I'm not....hey!" Laura had already started down the passage, leaving Twocrow and Minnie standing flatfooted. "Laura, don't go off there by yourself. I don't know what's back there yet. Might be years before it's ready to open."

"Don't worry, silly!" she shouted back at them. "Come on! We'll just go for fifty or sixty yards. Maybe we'll find a new space and we can name it Bill." She giggled as she hurried on ahead, her lantern extended in front of her so that she wouldn't be surprised by any holes or sudden drop-offs. Bill and Minnie made slower time, staying together to get the benefit of the lantern they held between them.

"Be careful!" Twocrow called after Laura's retreating figure. "I've never been down that passage and it may be easy to walk where you're at now, but who knows what you'll find in another 25 or 30 feet."

He had barely gotten the words out of his mouth when Laura started screaming.

CHAPTER TWO

"Okay, we need to get out of here, get back to Hot Springs, and get the Sheriff."

As usual, Minnie was taking charge, a habit that made her a good person to have around in a time of crisis, but otherwise—as Laura liked to say—a pain in the butt. Today, though, both Laura and Twocrow were happy to abdicate the take-charge role to her and just concentrate on getting out of the Cave and back into town.

"Maybe we should try to see if there's anything to tell us who he is. The Sheriff might ask that, you know? How long do you think he's been here?" Twocrow asked, moving back to the body. "How do you think he died?"

Laura's investigative reporter mode kicked in and she slipped over to join him, crouching partway down beside the corpse. "We should see if he has any identification," she said, tugging at his coat and pulling it free from beneath his crumpled body. "Let's see if he has any papers or anything that has his name." She directed Twocrow toward his legs. "I'll look through his coat pockets and you check his pants. He looks well-dressed, like he might be a business person, or maybe a wealthy rancher."

Minnie joined them and dropped onto her knees, ignoring the fact that her "dress-up dress," as she liked to call it, was getting covered with the grey-white dust that powdered the Cave's floor. While she liked to dress nicely, she was in no way interested in wearing the fancier things that Laura preferred, instead going for more practical dresses or skirts and blouses that could double-up for her work routine at the newspaper.

Laura, on the other hand, was wearing a new snap pearl button dress with fashionable three-quarter length sleeves and a bell-style skirt reaching about an inch above her lacy petticoat, both covering frilly bloomers. Minnie figured it probably had cost Laura most of her first paycheck, which was why her sister was crouching awkwardly and taking great care not to touch her knees to the ground and risk soiling the bottom of the skirt.

"There's nothing on him," Minnie said, reaching across the top of the man's body. "Let's turn him over. Bill, grab his right leg and we'll turn him toward us. I don't think he's been dead that long, do you?" She said it to both of them and they both responded with blank stares. "If he'd been dead for a while, wouldn't he smell funny?"

"Ooh, that's gross!" Laura exclaimed, standing up after her search of the man's coat pockets came up empty.

"Well, I'm just saying," her younger sister remarked. "You know what something that's been dead for a while smells like. We've found enough dead animals along the trails and roads, and you know how bad that dead cow smelled out by the

Congers' ranch. He doesn't smell like that...or like anything at all. Does he?"

"No, you're right," Twocrow interjected. "But down here, it's so cool and dry; it could be like putting something into an ice box for a couple days." He grabbed hold of the right lower leg, just where the man's shoes met the bottom of his pants. Ready?" Minnie nodded. "One, two, three...uh!" They pulled the man toward them as Laura scrambled out of the way, pulling the bottom of her skirt up against her legs to keep it from hitting the body. Twocrow slipped and fell backward, holding the shoe in his hand as the body settled face up on the dirt and rocks. He turned the shoe over in his hand, started to put it down, and stopped.

"That's weird," Twocrow said, standing and brushing the dirt from his clothing. "He's got some sort of paper inside his shoe." He reached in and pulled out a folded piece of paper and shook it open. "Actually, it looks like some kind of receipt."

Laura gasped as Minnie held the lantern up for a better look at the paper, illuminating the man's face in the process. "Hey, I know him." She paused, contemplating his face. "But how do I know him?" She bent in closer. "How do I know you?" she said to the body.

"Doesn't look familiar to me at all," Minnie said, reaching over to lightly touch a dark red stain covering most of the center part of his chest. "You ever see him before Alvin? Bill, I mean?" She shook her head slightly as if irritated at forgetting her friend's new name.

"I've never seen him," Twocrow answered. "Was he shot?"

Minnie nodded. "There's a hole right here below his heart." She looked back at the place where the body had been. "But he definitely wasn't shot here because even though his shirt is covered with blood, it's totally dry, and there's not any blood on the ground either. He was done bleeding before he was brought here, that's for sure. Must've been shot somewhere else in the Cave."

"So, somebody had to know their way around the Cave in order to bring him here like this," Twocrow said.

"Not one of the MacDonalds," Minnie gasped. "You don't think...?"

"No, no, not them! They've been gone for five days. But, before they went they loaded up a bunch of mineral samples and some of the boxwork pieces, different things like that, to take along with them. Mister Stabler hired some men to come over here from the Mining Company and help us box up the things they were going to take with them. They wanted to sell some of the pieces and use the others to help promote the Cave. There must've been seven or eight men working down here and they had plenty of time to study the Cave when they were going in and out with those crates. And, they would know that the MacDonalds were going to have the Cave shut down for a couple weeks while they were gone."

He looked thoughtful. "On top of that we gave a couple of tours just before they went and we were telling folks we'd be shutting down the cave to tours for a couple or three weeks. So the word was definitely out there that the cave would be empty."

"Yeah, and to know that if they had a body to hide, it'd be a perfect time to stash it down a passageway that no one was going to be exploring for a while," Laura surmised.

"Who's Mister Stabler?" Minnie asked.

"Oh, John Stabler. He's the MacDonalds' partner now for developing the Cave. He's the chief guide when we're open; him and his daughter Katie."

"Honest John Stabler? Is that who you're talking about?" Laura said.

"I guess?" Twocrow replied. "I didn't know people called him that."

"He's pretty well-known in Hot Springs," she answered, "He's been doing some promotional things with the *Star* to attract more investors. They had a story last week about the hotel being built out here, and the fact he plans to run a regular stage line from the Evans Hotel out here every day. I think it's kind of a partnership thing between the Evans and whatever they end up calling the new hotel out here, once it's built. They were printing up some handbills and flyers, things to put up around the area and maybe send back East to reach the 'money' people— that's what he called them, the 'money' people. They're looking for investors.

"Wait a minute!" Laura added, turning back to the body with full recognition flooding over her face. "That's it! That's how I know this guy."

"This isn't Stabler, is it?" Minnie said excitedly.

"No, 'course it's not him," Twocrow said impatiently. "I know Mister Stabler, for cryin' out loud! Don't you think I would know the guy who's been teaching me about guiding people through the cave?"

"Well, Geez, you don't need to get all het up about it," Minnie said crossly.

"It's a man named Irvin or Previn...that's his last name. I think," Laura said, ignoring their exchange. "First name's Alexander...or Arthur, something like that. John," she blushed and quickly corrected herself, "I mean Mister Stanley, the editor of the *Star*, had me working on a story about an event coming up at The Evans Hotel. It was either last Monday or Tuesday. I was working at my desk and this man came in waving one of those handbills and asking to speak to the editor. After he left, Phyllisha...Phyllisha Patrow, she's the woman who works at the front desk and SHE HEARS EVERYTHING that goes on in the editor's office...she told me that this Irvin guy," she stopped as if rethinking the scenario, "no it was definitely Previn, Alexander Previn, I'm sure of it."

"And...and?" Minnie said, growing impatient.

"And she said he had come here to look into buying some property, but this Wind Cave investment might be a better idea, and he wanted to learn more about it. She said Mister Stanley told him what he knew about the Cave and its development and then where he could find Mister Stabler. And, get this, he said he had a lot of money to invest on the spot if he liked what he saw. Phyllisha thought he was just asking for trouble going around with big talk like that."

"How much money? Did he say?" Twocrow asked.

"She said it was a lot. Maybe 50 thousand dollars."

Twocrow whistled appreciatively and Minnie gave a small gasp. "Wow, that's a lot of cash to be toting around."

"Well, that's not the half of it," Laura said. "She said he told John that he might have gold to invest. I don't know if that was the cash he meant, or something more."

"Fifty thousand in gold! Why in the world would anyone travel with fifty thousand dollars in gold?" Minnie asked. "And since he's dead in here, you have to wonder if the gold is even anywhere around here? If he was robbed and killed, it's probably long gone."

"I don't know if there's any gold, but something is still here," Bill interrupted, now studying the paper in his hand. "This is a receipt to Mr. Alexander Previn from The Evans Hotel for two large bags being held in their safe. You think those bags might be full of gold? Or cash?"

"Can't be the gold," Laura said. "It would be too heavy. Wouldn't it?"

The young trio stood silently staring at the body and absorbing what they had just said. Fifty thousand dollars or a pile of gold would definitely be a motive for murder, but only if he had the gold or cash where the killer could get to it. If it was cash and it was still in The Evans Hotel safe, then who had killed him? And why was he here at the bottom of Wind Cave?

CHAPTER THREE

"You say your name is Previn?"

One of the two cowboys on the train seat across from Paulus Previn had asked the question, and now he stuck out his hand. "Name's Jonas McCarty, Mister Previn. And this here's Jake Curley. What brings you to our neck of the woods?"

"Business opportunities," Previn answered. "Meeting up with my older brother in Hot Springs to look over some investment properties."

"That so?" Curley leaned back in his seat and straightened the collar of his Western style blue-checked shirt, tucking the collar's corners under the leather vest he was wearing over it. He had a curious expression on his face. "I'm from around these parts myself and always looking for some good 'opportunities.'" He winked, "If you know what I mean? Anything in particular?"

"Maybe," Previn said. "Expecting to learn more when I get there."

"Usually gotta have hard cash if you want to invest around these parts. Folks ain't so trustin' with them letters of credit and such," McCarty responded.

"If we find what we want, we'll have the money all right."

The cowboys exchanged a sideways glance at Previn's response, and then settled back. They were looking toward the rear of the train while Previn faced toward the front. The train car's seats were arranged in the old stagecoach style. "Heard there's good land options up here, and some new tourist places in Hot Springs? You boys know much about any of those?"

McCarty shook his head, but Curley nodded. "Yeah, that's so, I guess. There's a big-ass new hotel in the Springs, and a new bathhouse or spa—or some such thing—been put up there, too. And that Wind Cave. That might be something to put money into." He looked thoughtful. "If'n I had any, a'course." He laughed loudly and Previn chuckled in return. McCarty remained quiet, pulling the brim of his hat down over his eyes to signal he was tired of the chitchat and planned to get some sleep.

Taking the cue from his traveling companion, Curley pulled his own hat forward and folded his arms across his chest. Previn took out a ledger book and began jotting in some numbers as the train monotonously jounced along. He was coming from Chicago, his first time to the Black Hills where his brother, Alexander, supposedly had struck it rich.

Fifteen years ago, Alexander had gone out to find gold in Deadwood and had now come home to the Windy City with several thousand in cash, about ten thousand more in gold dust, and a flashy young wife, Mollie, who made no secret of the fact that she was attracted to him because he said there would be a lot more gold whenever they decided to return.

That was fifteen years ago, and now they had returned to Windy City after living off the investments made by Paulus, ten years younger than his brother but an expert business advisor. And although Paulus' investing had made them lots of money, Mollie's continuous extravagant spending had kept them from being rich instead of just comfortable. Finally, Alexander had said it was time to go back to the Black Hills to "retrieve some of his holdings"—whatever the hell that meant—and make their next big investment.

Paulus stared at the figures in his book. He didn't see where Alexander planned to get the $50,000 he said he was going to invest in the Southern Hills. But Alexander said not to worry, just come out and meet him in Hot Springs. The money was already there. He yawned, closed the ledger book and pulled his own hat over his eyes. "Must be a buried treasure," he muttered to himself.

Across the aisle, McCarty opened one eye. "What's that?" he asked, staring hard at the bookkeeper.

"Oh, uh, nothin'. Just talkin' to myself," Previn said, lifting his hat brim slightly as he spoke. McCarty gave him an odd look before leaning back again and letting his own hat re-settle over his eyes.

*****

Half-a-dozen rows ahead of the three men, Nellie Bly gave a deep sigh before rolling her shoulders forward and back to keep time with the seemingly endless clack-clack-clack of the train's steel wheels on the rails. Over the years she had ridden on every possible conveyance from ships to mules to a sampan. But she liked to say she'd been on so many trains that she felt as if the "clack-clack" ran permanently through her veins.

And, while some people found train travel "therapeutic," Nellie thought it was boring.

She shifted on the hard leather seat, trying to find a more comfortable position, sighed again and glanced out the window for the hundredth time. The view looked pretty much the same as it had for the last hour and the past day—broad prairieland stretching as far as the eye could see, interrupted occasionally by a few upward thrusts of land forming either small hills or table-top mesas.

Nellie was seated closest to the front on the left-hand side. And since the car was only about two-thirds full, she had her seat and the ones facing her all to herself. She extended her legs and wiggled her toes. Across the aisle a young couple in their early 20s was facing toward the rear of the train, dozing on one-another's shoulders. Facing them, directly across the aisle from her own seat, sat a more elderly man, alternately nodding off and jerking his head back up from time-to-time as if fighting falling asleep.

After transferring from the Chicago and North Western line to the Fremont, Elkhorn and Missouri Valley, Nellie had departed Omaha around noon on the previous day, already the third day on her trip. The FEMV locomotive had steamed west across Nebraska, stopping at communities every 40 or 50 minutes well into the night before rolling into Chadron where it was re-fueled and re-positioned for its northern leg into the Black Hills. After giving the passengers the chance to grab a quick breakfast at the station, the train left before daybreak climbing slowly but steadily toward their destination of Hot Springs, South Dakota.

Nellie was traveling west, away from her newspaper-reporting job in New York City. In the process, she was escaping the heat and humidity New Yorkers had endured for the past two months, still weighing down on Manhattan like a heavy wet blanket. She had just finished another exposé for her newspaper, *The New York World*, and now she needed a break. Joseph Pulitzer, her boss, jokingly said "Go West, Young Girl, Go West." But after thinking about it for just a day, she had shocked him and her editor, Morrill Goddard, by marching in and saying she was taking a few weeks off to travel to Denver and spend time cooling off in the mountains.

Both men had been thrilled. They had already talked about an undercover series on the silver mines and saloon trade near the Mile High City, and if Nellie wanted a break from the heat of New York, they could pay her way "Out West " and probably expect a rousing good round of stories in return.

What she didn't tell them was that first she planned a little detour into the Black Hills—a spot she had been hearing about both before and since a reporting trip she'd taken to the Chicago the previous fall. She had been writing stories about the 1893 Chicago World's Fair—also known as the Columbian Exposition—and working on a series of stories about the Pullman strike affecting rail travel. It was there that she met a man distributing brochures about a new "vacation paradise" called Hot Springs.

"Lady, you'd love it there. The spas, pools, everything. Great place to unwind," he assured her. "And if you're tired of being with the Old Man," he added with a little wink, "it's also a great place to go for a quick divorce. You know, South Dakota has the most accommodating divorce laws in the nation, and we can help you set up residence for a couple of weeks and get you a divorce for a few hundred dollars." He'd winked again, knowingly, as if that's what she really wanted to know.

But divorce was the farthest thing from her mind. She had just turned 30 and the clock seemed to be expiring on whether or not she'd ever get married. And, in fact, she was using the trip as an excuse, of sorts, to end a slowly souring relationship.

After making her famed "Around the World in 72 Days" trek and working on a subsequent series of stories about it, she had rapidly become one of the most-read writers in the country. And with her growing fame came social and romantic opportunities, one being James Metcalfe, a dashing young editor at *Life*—a well-read and highly entertaining humor magazine.

After seeing one another off-and-on for more than two years, their casual socializing had turned more serious, but she was torn between the journalism she wanted to do, and the social life and respectability she craved. She thought she might love Metcalfe, but she also loved the pursuit of a good undercover story, and that led her to explore the sordid lifestyles that both frightened and upset her new beau.

One such story had grown out of her conviction that inmates were being mistreated at the infamous Blackwell Island Mental Hospital. To find out, she had herself committed as "insane" with a plan for Pulitzer to rescue her after several days. Instead, she had been held there as a virtual prisoner for nearly two weeks.

Stripped, roughly "examined," and bathed in icy water in the presence of sadistic guards, she was thrown into solitary confinement. Finally, after 10 days, Pulitzer had figured out where she was being held and brought in help to save her. Her subsequent series of stories uncovered a web of corruption and mistreatment, establishing her as one of New York's leading investigative reporters, and starting a pattern for her of putting her body and life on the line to "get her story."

As she worked to expose corrupt practices and procedures, she never hesitated to use herself as "bait" to trap predators, thieves and corrupt officials, much to Metcalfe's chagrin.

But it was her most recent series on the lives of New York City's infamous chorus line showgirls that closed the book on the relationship with her sophisticated boyfriend. As Nellie prepared to go half-clothed on stage in order to be immersed in the story, she knew she had to be free and unencumbered by any relationship demands.

"I can't have you, or anyone besides my editor, worrying about my well-being," she told him. "And I'm not going to stop taking chances, or going undercover. That's my life. The story's always too important to me." She'd kissed him goodbye and walked away, half hoping he'd call to her to turn around and change her mind. But his silence was all that followed her, and it spoke volumes about where they stood with one-another.

The next day she walked into her editor's office and took on the covert assignment as a showgirl, something she was certain would never be condoned by the "respectable" crowd with whom Metcalfe associated.

After her sensational stories were printed, her encounters with Metcalfe remained strained, and each meeting seemed frostier than the next. Finally, worn out from the demands of her work and the futile relationship attempts, she decided she just needed to get away from Manhattan for a while. Time to "Go West."

She laid her head back, slipped off her feather-laden hat, and closed her eyes for a moment, sighing as she thought again about how tired she felt. Pulitzer may have meant to be flip with his "Go West, Young Girl" remark, but it was the perfect answer. Besides, she wasn't a "girl" any more. She felt old and needed some rest and rejuvenation before tackling her new project. After that, she might go back and see if anything remained of the spark that once flickered between Metcalfe and herself.

She was traveling under her given name, Elizabeth Cochran. Nellie Bly was on vacation, and the only "assignment" she wanted was taking care of Elizabeth.

Opening her eyes, she glanced once more out the window, picked up her bag and extracted a brochure she had picked up at the Columbian Exposition.

"Hot Springs, S.D.—America's Carlsbad. The famous health and pleasure resort in the Black Hills. A most Delightful retreat within easy traveling distance of the principal cities of the Central and Western States. The most beneficial baths known to modern civilization on the site of the famed natural springs so refreshing that two mighty Indian tribes, the Sioux and Cheyenne, fought wars to control them. Relax in the mineral baths and then stay in the splendor of the Evans Hotel, the Finest accommodations west of the Mississippi."

The words accompanied a tintype photo of a beautiful five-story, stone-block building, fronted by a sweeping veranda overlooking a lovely river and backed by bright-white cliff sides. Another photo showed a waterfall and pine tree-covered hillsides.

"Are you staying in Hot Springs?" the older man seated across from her asked, gesturing toward the brochure.

She nodded.

"Ever been there before?" He was speaking softly trying not to disturb the young couple across from him.

Nellie turned slightly in his direction, barely glancing at the couple, who continued to nap. The man was distinguished looking, maybe about 60 years old with a fine tailored suit, thinning white combed-back hair and a well-trimmed mustache. While he was not handsome in the usual sense of the word, she found herself attracted to his warm smile and the twinkle in his crinkly steel-blue eyes, which were accented by wire-rimmed glasses. As one of the world's top investigative reporters, she had learned how to quickly judge those around her and decide almost instantly whether they were friends or foes; something that had kept her out of danger on many an occasion. In the seconds it took to study him, she decided he was someone to be trusted.

"No," she said quietly while holding the brochure open a bit wider in his direction. "But it looks marvelous; at least if their publicity is to be believed." She straightened her shoulders a bit, delicately smoothed down the pleat on the flared skirt of her new silk dress, and looked him over again. "Have you been?"

"Once, for a day on my way out of the Hills after traveling to Custer City. But this time I'm making it my home base for a few days. I'm looking into a business venture at the Evans Hotel, actually, and while I'm out there I want to do a little horse-shopping, too." He extended his hand across the aisle then jerked it out of the way as the conductor opened the car's door that was just ahead of them and came bustling through.

"One hour to Hot Springs!" he half-shouted. The couple jerked awake and the young man glared at the conductor, unhappy at being so rudely awakened. His thin, pretty traveling companion, who Nellie figured to be his wife, held a handkerchief to her lips and coughed, looked sleepily at both Nellie and the older man, before snuggling back onto her husband's shoulder and wrapping both of her arms around his left arm in the process.

The conductor ignored the young man's glare and tipped his short-billed cap to Nellie. "Miss Cochran." She nodded, and he returned his cap to his head and passed on toward the next car. The young man glanced over his wife's head at the retreating figure, while the older gentleman re-extended his hand in Nellie's direction. "Robert Seaman," he said.

"Pleased to meet you Mr. Seaman," Nellie replied, carefully taking his hand in her white-gloved one and giving him a demure look from what she considered her best feature, her oval-shaped hazel eyes. "I'm...Elizabeth. Elizabeth Cochran."

"And what takes you to the Black Hills?"

"Just a short vacation," she answered. "I'm traveling from back East and plan to go on to Denver in a week or so. The Black Hills sounded so...exotic, and Hot Springs so...refreshing." She laughed and he joined her, his deep chuckle accenting her higher-pitched tone. "It's been so hot back in New York, and a busy time for me. So, when I read about the springs, it just seemed like a good way to get, well...." she paused, thinking of the word she wanted to use "...refreshed, I suppose."

"New York? You don't say? That's my stomping grounds, too. I've got a little factory there. We make things like milk cans. Not very glamorous, but it pays the bills."

"And you're out here for both business and horse-shopping? Do you use horses for your work?"

"Well, as a matter of fact, we do," he said putting a matter-of-fact inflection into his voice. "But that's only if I have the time. The main thing is to see about a possible business investment, and then I'll see if I can make a deal on a horse. I've got a little farm outside of the city, up toward Long Island. I've got a few head out there. I want to get a new trotter that might give me a shot at actually winning a few dollars in the next racing season up at Saratoga." He beamed and again she found herself charmed by his warm smile.

The train shuddered slightly and her hat slipped off the seat onto the floor. She reached out to grab for it and Seaman did too, and they bumped heads.

"Oh, Miss Cochran, I'm so sorry!" he reached over and to touch her forehead and a spark jumped from his fingertip, shocking them both.

"Oh my goodness!" she half-exclaimed, holding her hand up to her head, and then starting to giggle.

Seaman looked mortified. "This is getting worse instead of better. I-I. Please, I didn't mean to ... I mean. Oh hell!" he stopped, unsure of what to say next, thoroughly flustered. "Pretty girls always flummox me, and I have to admit I've never 'sparked' one before—especially one I've just met."

Nellie burst into full-blown laughter followed with a more dazzling smile in his direction. "Apology accepted," she said. Seaman blushed and looked away. "And I assume you're talking about horse track betting when you talk about money from the racing season and not from the payoffs from the race itself?"

He nodded. "The race purses are pretty small and hardly pay the bills, let alone make the owners any money. But a good bet or two can set you up for the whole season. If I can find a good horse and bring it back home without a lot of fanfare, I could end up winning a pretty penny or two before the others stop betting against me. And, after that, hopefully, I'll have a good stallion to help build my herd."

The young woman seated across from him stirred and opened her eyes, squeezing the young man's arm while straightening up and smoothing out her traveling clothes all in one motion. She was dressed well; not as elegantly as Nellie, but fashionably. Her curly dark hair was partly covered by a flowered hat that accented her eyes and thin, yet expressive face. The young man also stirred at his companion's movements. He was fuller in the face with dark thick hair of his own. His suit looked as if it had seen better days, but it was clean and well-pressed.

"That's the truth," the woman said, surprising them with both her comment and her somewhat breathy voice. "I grew up in race horse country in Kentucky, and I've heard that said before." Then she hurried to add, "Not that I was listening in on your conversation, but it's pretty hard not too in such cramped quarters as these isn't it?"

She smiled at both of them and extended her right hand across the aisle to Nellie. "I'm Mrs.... " She stopped and blushed. "Sorry, no need to be quite so formal, I suppose? I'm Sallie." She laid her left hand on top of the young man's right hand, "Sallie White. William and I are traveling to the Black Hills for a honeymoon, of sorts, and for me to take in some of the mineral waters at the Cascade Springs and the Hot Springs. I've been feeling a bit poorly now for a couple of months and we've heard they have marvelous healing powers." She smiled brightly as if giving that idea some further thought.

Nellie took her hand. "Elizabeth," she answered. "Cochran." She released the woman's hand, which was offered very limply, and Sallie moved it toward Seaman.

"Robert Seaman," he said, carefully grasping her hand as he realized that she wasn't so much offering a handshake as she was just offering her hand. "So, you're newlyweds, eh?"

"Well, not exactly," the young man spoke up, glancing adoringly at his wife. "We married more than a year ago—almost a year-and-a-half now—but just never seemed to have the time to do a proper honeymoon. And, as you heard," he added, removing his hand from his wife's and first extending it to Robert, then to Nellie, "I'm William. William Allen White."

"Mr. and Mrs. White. A pleasure to meet you," Seaman said. "You were already sleeping when we left Chadron, so I'm glad to finally make your acquaintance. And where is it you're traveling from?"

"Kansas City," White said.

"Really?" Nellie said. "And, in what part of Kentucky is that located?"

Sallie's bell-like laugh was the response and she beamed appreciatively at Nellie for her joke. "I grew up in Kentucky. But Kansas City has been my home for some time now. It's where William and I met and married."

"But once we get back from our trip, I think we'll be relocating," William added. "Sallie loves Kansas City, but I've been wanting to return to my home town of Emporia. That's Emporia, Kansas. It's about halfway between Kansas City and Wichita as the crow flies."

"William is a newspaperman," Sallie said proudly. "He's been writing for the *Kansas City Star,* but he's learned that the *Emporia Gazette* is coming for sale. If we can work out the money part of it, well..." she paused. "Well, I think we're going to get a new start."

"Newspapers, eh? Kind of a risky business, don't you think?" Seaman looked from the young couple over to Nellie to verify his assessment.

"Oh, I don't know about that, Mr. Seaman..." Nellie barely started her response before he held up a hand.

"Robert," he interjected, coughing slightly as Nellie gave him a small nod and another dazzling smile. The Whites exchanged a knowing smile of their own and Nellie hurried to cut off the awkward exchange.

45

"Robert," she repeated. "As I was saying, I don't think it sounds risky at all. People want to be entertained and informed and newspapers certainly have to be at the forefront of all of that, don't they? I think it sounds like a very good idea, indeed. Are you going to work with your husband then, Sallie?"

"Perhaps, but it doesn't seem like such an accepting field for women."

"Oh? Well, I've read many good writings by women. Surely William you would have to agree?" Looking perplexed, White seemed to be formulating what he thought would be the correct response as his wife turned toward him.

"Why, uh..." he stammered "...why, yes...of course." He smiled brightly. "There's the work of Nellie Bly, for example. Exemplary stuff. We studied about her at the University of Kansas, and everyone talks about her all the time at the *Star*."

"Oh, I just love her, don't you Miss Cochran?" Sallie gushed.

"Why...yes. I'm quite familiar with her work...coming from New York and all."

"Well, aren't we all?" Seaman added. "I mean those of us from New York, of course. It seems like her work makes up the majority of the biggest headlines in the *World* these days."

"Oh, the entire world? I had no idea," Sallie said.

"I believe Mr. Sea...Robert...is referring to the newspaper, *The New York World*. It's the newspaper that Miss Bly writes for."

"Oh my goodness! Of course," Sallie said with a bright laugh. "Of course I knew that too. Being from Kansas City, I sometimes get caught up in our own little 'world' out there and forget about the bigger one—especially which newspaper is which back in your big city. Our best news comes to us through William's newspaper, *The Star*."

"Well, that's a fine newspaper, and I'm very aware of it, I must say," Seaman said quickly. "You must be a good writer Mr. White if you have found employment there. Especially someone so young as yourself. And, I'll repeat that I think it takes a great deal of courage to get out there on your own, as you seem to be planning to do, and at your age, too!"

"Well, I AM 26," William said emphatically.

Nellie brought her gloved hand to her mouth to stifle a laugh, but Robert erupted at the response, chortling as he spoke. "Twenty-six, eh? I think I was still learning to button my shoes at that age." He glanced over at Nellie. "Ah, to be 26 and full of optimism again. Those were truly the good old...way, way back... days."

"Oh, surely Robert. You can't be THAT old," Sallie said, studying him more closely. She furrowed her brow. "Can you?"

Robert laughed louder this time. "Yes, Miss Sallie, I CAN!" He looked over at Nellie, and then turned back to Sallie. "How OLD do you put me for?"

She studied him further. "I'm terrible at guessing people's ages, but I'll say..." she paused and brought her right hand to her chiseled chin, her deep brown eyes studying him closely as she contemplated her answer. "Sixty?" His eyes widened and jaw dropped. "I-I, uh, mean, um, 55."

He laughed again, tears coming to his eyes. "In your dreams and mine, too." he exclaimed. "Miss Sallie, you are a delight, and an obvious fibber. I'm proud to say that I'm well over 70."

It was William and Nellie's turns to look surprised.

"I'm shocked," Nellie spoke first. "I don't think Sallie was fibbing to you at all. I, too, was thinking 60." Then she looked over at Sallie and gave her a big smile. "Although when you went to 55, I was a LIT-tle skeptical." She drew out the word little and laughed merrily at Sallie's blushing face. William gave his wife a squeeze and joined in the laughter as Sallie shook her dark curls and then bumped her head playfully on William's shoulder before joining them. "When you're 24, as I'm sure you know Elizabeth, those older than you can look...well, almost any age."

"Twenty-four, yes," Nellie laughed lightly. "Sorry Sallie, but it's been quite a few years since I was 24."

"That can't be true," Sallie said incredulously. "You look my age. Maybe younger."

"Thank you, but since we're all sharing our ages, I must tell you I just recently turned 30. Not being married yet, I think I have officially qualified for Old Maid status." Seeking to deflect the conversation from herself, she looked back toward Seaman. "And Robert, are you married?"

"No-no, I'm quite a confirmed bachelor, I suppose. Just too busy being busy, both as a businessman and a horseman. Not that I wouldn't consider it IF the right woman were to come along." He stopped and looked quickly from William to Sallie, and back to Nellie, all of who had skeptical looks on their faces. "What?" he asked. "Falling in love doesn't have an age limit, does it?"

"No indeed!" Sallie was the first to break the spell. "I think it's wonderful that you're still thinking about it." She looked slyly in Nellie's direction, saw that Seaman was following her gaze, and returned her eyes to him. "IF, as you say, the right woman should suddenly appear." She draped her arm on William's again and clasped his fingers in hers. He gave her a strange look and shook his head ever so slightly as if to discourage her from saying anything more. Before she could utter another word, the engine's whistle pierced the air and the passenger car shuddered as the train began screeching to a stop.

Sallie and William nearly toppled over on top of Robert while Nellie fell back hard against her seat as her bag tumbled away from her. The train jerked violently twice more, throwing Nellie sideways onto the opposite seat while William fell into the aisle. As Nellie started to get up to help him, the train jerked a third time and she lurched headfirst into the window. Then everything went black as she crumpled to the floor.

CHAPTER FOUR

Ten minutes before the train slid to its unscheduled and violent stop, Lil Marr was basking in the appreciative glow of her two traveling companions as she carefully turned her new Winchester .22 caliber rifle over and over in her hands. Its soft buckskin carrying case lay open on her lap.

"It really is a beauty," the youngest of the trio exclaimed, giving a low whistle of appreciation. "And your old man just gave it to you?"

"Yes, Will, father just GAVE it to me. I told you, it's a birthday gift for my 18th birthday."

"I thought your 18th birthday wasn't until November, same month as mine?" Will said indignantly.

"Well he gave it to me early so I could take it with me on this trip?" She glared at him. "In case I needed to shoot one of you for making any 'forward' moves toward me!"

"Forward moves. Who in sam hill'd want to make any forward moves toward an old nag like you?"

Will snorted in response. "I've already got my eye on Polly Baker. Much more my style, if you know what I mean?" He straightened his shoulders, crossed his arms and leaned back with a grin.

"You mean much more your tender age, don't you? I'd about die if a 14-year-old boy made advances to me, so there Will Rogers!" She huffed and put the gun down on her lap. Looking coyly at her other companion, who was sitting next to her. "Now Jack might be a different matter. He's a man!"

"Man? Hah. How old're you Jack? Twenty? Twenty-one?" He eyed Jack's boyish features and the unlined face on which Jack was trying to grow a mustache despite the fact that his light-brown facial hair almost disappeared on his upper lip. Will swung his gaze back to Lil. "And for your information I'll be 15 on my next birthday, which as I clearly said, is in November, same month as yours."

Jack gave an exasperated sigh and half-turned in Lil's direction, his right knee brushing up against the side of her leg in the process. She blushed but did not pull away. Lil had been accused for years of being a tomboy, but ever since Jack had joined her father's ranch as horse wrangler, she'd started paying closer attention to her appearance. She wasn't sure why she wanted to look nice for him, but she knew that she did.

Will, on the other hand, was more like a little brother, since he'd grown up on a neighboring ranch and now was spending the summer helping the Marrs with their horse roundup and sales. Will's sister May was one of Lil's best friends but they were seeing less of each other since the summer began. Colonel Rogers, a circuit court judge and leading member of the Cherokee Nation, had need of a temporary stenographer while traveling the region and May had been pressed into duty.

Thus, taking Will along on this trip seemed only natural to both families.

Lil had already represented her father on horse sales around Oklahoma Territory and North Texas, but this was her first big trip. She was dressed in her finest and most stylish women's ranch wear—a soft pair of deerskin boots coming halfway up her calves where they just touched the hem of her western-style skirt, and a gingham blouse, buttoned to the neck and covered by a soft leather vest that fell below where the blouse was tucked into the skirt. Her black felt cowboy style hat struggled to hold a mop of thick and curly rust-colored hair in place, a job it was mostly failing.

"Twenty-two," Jack said. He was dressed as a western businessman, a neat string tie accenting his pinstriped, high-collared shirt, and a new leather cowboy hat covering his neatly clipped brown hair. Jack had always "looked young," so he hoped his new clothing picked for this trip north would add to his maturity. His boots were gleaming from the polishing he'd given them in preparation for the trip, representing his boss—Lil's father—in delivering a load of mares to the Martin Horse Ranch outside of Buffalo Gap, a booming town north of the Maverick Junction along the eastern edge of the Black Hills.

It was at the Junction that they'd be making a quick stop, since the train would be taking the Fall River Canyon route into Hot Springs, while they needed to continue straight north for another few miles. That meant uncoupling the car carrying their load of brood mares and waiting for the two o'clock Rapid City train to hook them up and take them the rest of the way.

Will was sitting across from them and had started to lean back in Lil's direction as if he were going to make a move to grab her new rifle. Lil grasped the weapon firmly in both hands and pulled it toward her, bumping both knees against his in the process. "Hey!" Will exclaimed. He stopped and looked back at Jack, who had just spoken the two words breaking his silence.

"Huh? What did you say?"

"I said I'm 22."

"See," Lil said triumphantly. "Told you HE was a man."

"Well, he might be a man, but you're definitely NOT a woman." Will sat back in his seat again. "What exactly ARE you anyway?"

"And what's THAT supposed to mean?" Lil slapped the rifle back down on her lap and crossed her arms, blowing a wayward curl out of her eye after it dropped from the front part of her hat down onto her face. She crossed her arms and glared at Will again.

"Can you two stop bickering all the time?" Jack said. "For crying out loud, we're supposed to be on a business trip, and it's beginning to feel like I'm your babysitter. Geez Will I brought you along in the first place because you said you could do this trip like a man. And Lil, your father would be really disappointed if he knew that you were acting like this. I may be his wrangler, but like it or not YOU have to be his business representative up here. If you act like a young girl, you'll get treated like one, so start acting like a woman if you want to get some respect!"

He crossed his arms and moved his legs straight ahead of him, glancing up and down the train's aisle to be sure he wasn't getting in anyone's way. A couple rows back, he saw a bookish-looking man wearing a derby hat writing in a book. Sitting across from him were two cowboys who appeared to be sleeping. He looked back up the aisle. Near the front door a young couple sat facing in his direction talking with an older man and a stylishly dressed woman, who was seated across from them by herself.

Lil settled back on her seat, a hurt look on her face, while Will looked chastened from the scolding Jack had just given them.

"Sorry Mister Omohundro," Will said quietly, reaching up to tug his hat forward on his head and then taking up a rope he'd been knotting into a loop since they'd left Chadron.

"And you don't need to call me that. It's just Jack or Texas, okay? That might be my last name, but I don't like it much. And I definitely don't answer to 'Mister'."

"Okay, Texas...Jack," Will grinned, opened and shut the rope loop in his hands, and then opened it part way and began coiling the rope into a neat pile. "I've been working on those loop ties you showed me." He brightened, already putting the scolding aside. "And I did 19 out of 20 catches on the calves before we left on Friday. I would've had all 20, but that little all-red calf is a sneaky one."

Will pulled off his grey, broad-brimmed hat, wiped his forearm across his wispy brown hair, and put it back on. He was wearing a black, silver-buttoned shirt with a grey bandana that matched the color of the hat looped carelessly around his neck, and a pair of Levi pants tucked into high-topped leather boots. The pants and boots were mostly covered with what he liked to call his "traveling chaps," too nice to wear for ranch work but definitely signifying that he was a true-to-life cowboy—even if he was a half-blood Cherokee and a young teenager, still not quite 15.

When his father had granted permission for him to travel with Lil and Jack up to South Dakota, he had delivered new clothes for Will to wear on the trip. But adding the chaps had been Will's idea, and he liked the way it made him look.

Lil continued to pout; her lower lip protruding and her rifle still lying across her lap outside of its case under her tightly folded arms. After a minute of uncomfortable silence, Jack turned back in her direction and put his hand on the edge of her shoulder. She flinched but didn't pull away or look in his direction.

"Lil, I'm sorry. I need to be more patient, I know. It's been a long trip and we're all tired and anxious to get there and get the horse deal done. I apologize." She remained still, not speaking. "Please?" No response. "Look, what do you want from me? Do I really have to make a move on you? You ARE a pretty girl...young woman...after all. Any man who wasn't your Dad's wrangler and sworn to death if he touched the boss's daughter would be making lots of moves on you by now. Trust me."

"Oh, good grief, give me a break," Will interrupted in a disbelieving voice.

"Will, just shut up and let me continue being forward so Lil can shoot me and put me out of my misery. Okay?" He held his hands out wide as if pleading for Will's agreement or Lil's shot, or both. Lil chortled under her breath, trying to suppress a laugh, and then she grinned.

"All right, you're forgiven. It's just that sometimes Will can be so danged irritating!" She tried to give him the evil eye while putting both hands back on the precious rifle.

"I'm fairly certain that I don't know what you mean," Will said, doing his best schoolmarm imitation as he responded as formally and stiffly as possible.

"You know she can shoot you if she wants, don't you?" Jack asked. "And it would be okay by me."

"Yeah, yeah, she's the Annie Oakley of the Oklahoma Territory," Will answered.

"Well, actually I think she is," Jack said, looking back at the rifle on her lap. "That's a great rifle, Lil, but I don't think your old m...your father...would've given it to you if you hadn't proved that you could handle it." He turned toward Will. "And you know it, too. You just wish you could shoot as good as she can."

"Maybe," he said, continuing to focus on the rope and not looking toward Lil.

"Will Rogers, I could shoot those silver buttons off that stupid shirt of yours and not even tear the material!"

"I guess," he said. "But, you know?" He paused as if formulating what he wanted to say next. "You know I can rope and ride WAY better'n you." He nodded forcefully and stuck out his chin. "So, you own up to that and I'll give you the shootin' part. Agreed?" He laid down the rope and extended his right hand. "Shake on it, and then pinky swear."

She exhaled loudly and stared at his hand as if it were infected.

"Lil?" Jack held his hands apart and nodded toward Will's outstretched arm. "You know he's got that on you."

"The roping part, sure," she said. "But I'm a good rider too!"

Jack rolled his eyes and leaned his head back and groaned. "This is turning into the trip from hell. Why did I agree to have the two of you come along with me?"

"All right, all right," she said with an exasperated edge to her voice. "I'll shake his stupid hand." She reached over and grabbed it with her own right hand, but before they could pull apart Jack clamped both of his hands over theirs.

"And this will seal the deal. Now let's all be good boys and girls and shake hands nicely." He began moving their hands up and down in unison. Simultaneously, they looked at each other, then at Jack and broke into giggles.

"But no stupid pinky swear, "Lil said as Jack started to move his hands away. "We ain't little kids no more." He nodded in agreement. "I better put my rifle back." She slid it into its carrying case and leaned down to put it back under the seat. Her head was bent forward when suddenly the train jerked violently. Lil screamed then went all the way to the floor as Will plummeted across the space above her and smacked his head hard against the spot where Lil had just been seated.

"Aaggh!" the boy said, dropping back toward his own side and grabbing at his forehead as Jack careened off the edge of his seat and sat down hard square in the middle of the aisle.

"What in hell?" Jack started to stand, but the train jerked again and began screeching to a stop, flattening him back down. Lil moaned and rolled onto her side between the seats, her rifle lying half out of its case beside her.

Will pulled his feet out of Lil's way as Jack turned onto his knees toward them. "Lil?" he started. "Are you all right?" Before he could make another move, the conductor opened the rear door and stepped into the aisle, trailed closely by a man with a greasy mustache and a huge scar across his right cheek, carrying a gun in his right hand. "Will," Jack whispered. "Slide her further under that seat and then don't move."

CHAPTER FIVE

Nine cars back, in a freight car riding just ahead of the caboose, Deputy U.S. Marshal Bat Masterson had a big problem—in more ways than one.

The first part of the problem was lying across the floor from him. It was in the form of his traveling companion, a part-time cowboy, most-of-the-time cattle rustler and bank robber, and full-time low-life scumbag named Frank Pasch. Pasch was out cold on a piece of carpet placed on top of one of the freight car's many raw cotton bales, his right arm hooked to an iron chain handcuff that was clamped onto a steel pipe running from floor-to-ceiling alongside the car's sliding door.

The second part of the problem was that Pasch was hurt. The top of his head was swathed in bandages, as was his left arm and left lower leg, and he'd been drifting in and out of consciousness for the past two hours. He'd taken one of Bat's bullets in his leg, while another one had grazed the side of his head in the shootout that led them to this trip in the first place. And, while the Marshal felt empathy for his prisoner's condition, he had no intention of unhooking him from the chain. The outlaw was a proven killer and remorseless as far as he could discern, and getting shot by someone he had been working so hard to transport to justice was the last thing Bat wanted. When it came to outlaws, he could be pretty remorseless himself, and if keeping the chains in place meant Pasch might die, then that was how the chips were going to fall.

But the third part of his problem, and maybe the worst part now that the train had slammed to a stop, was hearing the shouting and shots fired to announce loud and clear that a robbery was underway. Looking out through the slats in the side of the car at the scene unfolding before him, he caught his breath and swore. Bat recognized immediately who was doing the robbing. It was the Doc McCarty Gang, a group of thugs he'd become very familiar with over the past three years as they terrorized much of the territory he was trying to protect.

It was the McCarty Gang connection that had led to the face-to-face confrontation between Masterson and Pasch in the first place, because Pasch was one of Doc McCarty's top lieutenants.

"If the rest of the gang's up here," he gestured toward the outdoors with his rifle while looking at the unconscious Pasch, "then why were you down there by yourself?" He had crossed paths with Pasch at Chadron, about as far east as he held jurisdiction since his law-enforcement center was out of Denver. He pondered that question for a few more seconds, then shook his head and looked back outside where the passengers were being assembled at gunpoint by members of the gang. That would be a mystery to be resolved later, after he got his prisoner to Hot Springs.

Whatever it was that took Pasch to Chadron, it had put him squarely in Bat's path. Masterson had been surprised to see Pasch, but unhesitating in challenging him, taking him down in the shootout, and then getting them both on board this northbound train.

Returning with the outlaw directly to Denver was out of the question, especially in his shot-up condition. But when he talked to Chadron's sheriff about keeping him there, he was politely but firmly told "No." The McCarty Gang had too much firepower for most of the local lawmen and if the gang found out that one of their own was being held in the Chadron jail, it could lead to a confrontation that could end very badly for the locals. So, while he was willing to help Masterson move the captured outlaw, the sheriff had no intention of keeping him locked up there.

After giving it some more thought, Bat decided the best option would be to take Pasch up to Hot Springs where his longtime friend Seth Bullock, a Black Hills-based sheriff, could meet him and help get the prisoner to Denver. The McCarty Gang wouldn't be looking for him or anyone else coming out of Hot Springs, and they could do one of the overnight trains to Cheyenne and get on down to Denver before anyone even knew they were on board.

So, while he waited with his badly wounded prisoner at the Chadron train station, Masterson made arrangements to get his prisoner bandaged and surreptitiously bundled into a freight car during the train's overnight stop. Before departing he sent Bullock a quick telegram.

URGENT NEED OF YOUR HELP STOP MEET IN HOT SPRINGS STOP
BRING YOUR GUNS XXX

Bullock's reply was almost immediate.

ON MY WAY XXX

Once the train got underway, Bat had hunkered down, half-asleep, leaning up against several large bundles of cloth, which in turn held back stacks of boxes and barrels filled with dry goods and grain. He had been cradling his .50 caliber Sharps rifle across his lap when the train screeched to a halt.

Masterson's big rifle had gone flying when he was flung headfirst into a gigantic bag of milled flour, his bowler-style hat crushed beneath him on the freight car floor, and his suit's sleeve ripped. Through it all, Pasch had been tossed from side to side, his arm nearly jerked out of its socket by the force of the sudden stop. Somehow he had not regained consciousness or made anything other than a small moan as the car shuddered to a stop.

"Dammit!" Bat said, retrieving his new hat and working it back into its previous shape before plopping it down on top of his head. Brushing the flour out of his bushy mustache, he peered through the cracks of the rickety train car's walls to see what was happening. That's when the Gang members started shouting and people started being herded out of the passenger cars ahead of him. Now, he watched the unfolding drama of the robbery with one eye while glancing nervously at Pasch, who was still skewed to one side amid cotton bales and bolts of cloth. The outlaw moaned again but did not awaken.

"Christ Almighty!" Masterson swore softly under his breath, talking to himself. "Ya go for a short little trip and get yourself into another fine mess! Why in hell does something like this ALWAYS seem to happen to you?" He took the hat off, glared at it and slapped it against his thigh before putting it back on. "And, of course it would happen right after I get a new hat." He pulled out his revolver to be sure it was loaded, and picked his rifle up from the floor and gave it a careful examination. Satisfied that it hadn't been damaged, he chambered a shell and resumed his conversation, only this time talking to his comatose traveling partner.

"I don't know if you can hear me, you sorry bastard, but if you make one move or one sound, I'll add another crease to that stupid-ass head of yours," he waved the barrel of the long rifle threateningly in Pasch's direction. Pasch obliged him by remaining silent.

"I shouldn't have even been on this goddamned train in the first place," he said, continuing to talk to both his unconscious prisoner and himself. "I should've kept writing sports for *George's Weekly*, then I'd a been home in Denver having breakfast right now."

It was pure coincidence that Bat had been in Chadron at all. He had traveled out to the North Platte area to spend a few days at the ranch of his old friend William F. Cody. Masterson had hoped this would be his last trip out as a lawman. He planned to change careers and become a full-time sportswriter for the Denver newspaper he'd been writing for on a temporary basis.

He had tendered his resignation from the Marshals, but his boss asked him to check on things with the sheriff at the northeastern end of his jurisdiction before he'd let Bat finish his deputy marshal's obligations. After debating it for several days, Bat finally agreed so long as he could first stop to vacation with Buffalo Bill.

After a relaxing visit they went together by train to Chadron before heading in what they thought would be "separate" directions. Buffalo Bill was traveling on to the Black Hills to meet his star performer Annie Oakley for a special exhibition of her shooting skills at the dedication of Hot Springs' new Chautauqua Park Pavilion. Then they'd both see Bat back in Denver where Cody planned to home base his

Wild West Show for the next month while he finalized his winter tour.

At Chadron, they said their goodbyes. Bill stayed on the northbound train, and Bat made arrangements to take the next day's westbound train back to Scottsbluff where he could transfer on into Denver. After a few hours' visit with the sheriff, he bought supper and was walking down Main Street toward his hotel when he spotted Pasch riding toward the livery stable. The shootout that followed left Pasch badly wounded and Masterson with a prisoner he didn't want or need.

Doc McCarty's gang had been robbing and killing in northern and western Nebraska and the Southern Black Hills for several years. Six months earlier Masterson and a posse had tracked them down and shot and killed one gang member, while capturing two more of the gang. But Pasch, McCarty and McCarty's younger brother Jonas had wounded one of Bat's men and escaped north.

They hadn't crossed paths again until the chance encounter in Chadron.

Bat looked out at the robbery underway. "Shit," he said looking back at Pasch. "If they knew you and I were in here, there'd be hell to pay for me putting those bullets in you. But if you weren't here cramping my style, I'd shoot their sorry asses off and send them all packing." It wasn't an idle boast. Masterson didn't carry his big Sharps rifle for show. He was one of the best long-range marksmen around, as several now-dead or wounded lawbreakers had found out the hard way.

"Sorry folks," he muttered under his breath as he watched the passengers removing jewelry and putting money into burlap bags being passed among them by the gang. "I gotta get this scum-bag out of circulation before I go after the other ones."

He thought about his plan. First, get to Hot Springs —now looking a little more problematic — meet up with Bullock, keep his prisoner under cover until his wounds healed a bit, and then travel together to Denver. There, he could turn Pasch over to the federal magistrate and move forward on his new career path—writing about the sporting teams that were suddenly taking center stage in most big cities. He longed to try his luck in New York, and he'd already been there twice to check out the possibilities. But that, he figured, was still a few more years into the future.

Right now he had to get his prisoner delivered, and he needed help.

While he knew this would be a big imposition on Bullock, he'd been encouraging his friend to apply for a Marshal's spot himself sometime soon. "This'll help build the old resume'," he said aloud. Besides, Bullock owed him a favor or two. Twice Masterson had traveled to Deadwood to help him. The first time to break up a gang preying on the Black Hills to Cheyenne Stage Coach Line; and the second to track another gang that had stolen a Homestake Mine gold shipment, killing two guards in the process.

He'd spent weeks on that one, but with no luck. Nearly $150,000 in gold bars was still missing, supposedly hidden somewhere in the southern Black Hills.

He re-checked the leverage on the Sharps and looked back through the slats. It was about 100 yards to where the passengers were being held at gunpoint and if he was counting right, it looked like eight or nine robbers. He knew it would be easy to take out a couple of them with the big rifle. Just as some folks are born poets, others are born shots, and while Bat didn't like to brag, his marksman reputation was well deserved. But, with all those passengers there, it would be tricky at best. There'd be a good chance someone besides the outlaws would end up getting shot, and he didn't want any innocents' blood on his hands.

"I'm getting too damn old for this crap," he said to Pasch, who continued to be the kind of conversationalist Bat most enjoyed talking to: one that didn't respond. "In the old days, I'd of been up on the roof of the cars by now, angling for some sort of way to send those McCarty bastards packing." He walked to the opposite side of the train car and twisted sideways trying to look out the slats on that side. Unable to look forward, he slid a couple of the dry goods boxes out of his way, flattening up against the train car's wall. He peered out, pulled his head back and rubbed his eyes, then looked again.

"What the hell?" he muttered. Laying the rifle down on top of one of the cotton bales, he cupped his hands around the edges of his eyes and looked out for the third time. "Holy shit, you gotta be kidding me! What in hell do they think they're doing?"

Making their way in his direction, creeping stealthily along the back of the train, were two women—one stylishly dressed, looking very cosmopolitan, and holding a Derringer in her left hand. The other, a teenager, was dressed in western style clothing, a cowboy hat covering a mop of rust-colored curls and tied tightly under her chin. She was carrying a small rifle and as Masterson watched, she handed the rifle to her well-dressed companion, grabbed onto the iron bar stairs on the side of one of the train cars, and pulled herself up.

CHAPTER SIX

All around, Nellie and her seatmate's people had been shouting and screaming when the conductor popped his head through the rear door, shouting, "Don't worry folks, I'll find out what's wrong! Just stay calm!" seeming to be anything but calm himself as the train jerked and screeched violently to a stop. Seaman began helping Sallie back onto her seat as William called after the conductor. "We have someone hurt here!" He looked over where Nellie was slumped under the window, starting to re-open her eyes.

Nellie grabbed the edge of the leather seat and tried to pull up, but William slid across and laid a hand on her shoulder. "Please, Miss Cochran," he implored. "Sit still for a few more minutes until we know what's going on." He turned to the window, looked up the track, and gasped. "What in the world?" He glanced at Nellie and looked back at his wife and Seaman, who were staring across at his reaction.

"What is it?" Seaman said, starting to get up.

"Men with guns," he gasped. "I think we've been halted by a band of outlaws."

The screams and shouts of the moments before turned into a confused cacophony of dismayed and bewildered voices as more and more people became aware of what had brought their train to a stop and everyone was trying to figure out whether or not they were going to be safe? White sat down and looked at Nellie's head just as the rear door to their car banged open again and the conductor re-entered, his face blanched a very pale white. Another man, dressed in the gear of a cowboy with a big scar on his right cheek walked closely behind, almost touching him as they moved a few feet up the aisle.

"Ladies and Gentlemen," the conductor began, "We seem to have been stopped by…"

"There's men with guns out there!" a businessman seated four rows behind Nellie half-shouted, standing to face the conductor. "What's going on?"

"Actually," the cowboy said, pushing the conductor into an empty seat and displaying a large pistol, "those men with guns are my men. And so are these two men here." He gestured to the two cowboys across from Previn. Both men unholstered guns and moved into the aisle with the other man. "Just so you know," the Scar-Faced man added, "you folks are being robbed by the Doc McCarty Gang." He took a little bow. "I'm Doc. This here's my brother Jonas." He pointed at Jonas McCarty. "And that's our good friend Jake Curley."

"Jonas, you and Jake check the freight cars!" the Scar-Faced man ordered. "See if they're carrying any cash bags; or if there's a safe of any kind. You," he pointed his gun at the conductor. "Go with them."

William slid back on the seat, took a deep breath and motioned to Nellie to sit still. From her position on the floor she was out of the gunman's line of sight. Sallie looked fearfully across at them but sat frozen in place. Seaman was half-turned in the robber's direction.

"Now everyone just stay calm and nobody's going to get hurt. I want you all to get up from your seats, bring your personal items and come out of the train." He cocked the gun and fired a shot into the roof, eliciting several screams from the passengers. "Do it now!" Nellie sat still. Her head was throbbing but she was thinking clearly. White looked at her and nodded ever so slightly before he stood up and moved a few feet down the aisle as McCarty took a couple of steps in their direction.

"Come on Sallie; let's do as the man said. Mr. Seaman, let's go." He gestured to the aisle and the older man took his hat, stood and moved toward the gunman. Sallie took her bag and she and William followed. Within minutes all had left by the car's back door. Nellie edged herself up onto the seat and looked over the top. The car was empty but through the windows she could see the people gathering together outside, now surrounded by armed men.

Sliding closer to the aisle, Nellie kept her head low and looked for her bag. It was crumpled under the seat. Pulling it up, she jerked it open and extracted a small two-shot Derringer. It didn't have much firepower, but if they came back inside, she could cause some damage before she was taken.

"Ummm." The sound of the groan caused her to freeze and swing the gun from side-to-side. She couldn't see anyone or anything. "Oh. Damn!" This time there was no doubt she was hearing a voice, a young-sounding female voice, coming from several rows back on the opposite side of the car.

"Who's there?" Nellie's voice was more of a hiss than a stream of actual words. "Show yourself. I've got a gun!"

The car went dead silent and Nellie could clearly hear the sounds of the robbers ordering the passengers to take off their jewels and hand over to them any money or watches they had on them. After several seconds, Nellie spoke again, slightly louder, yet still in a controlled whisper so as not to be heard outside. "I said, who's there? Are you a passenger? I'm a passenger!"

Slowly, a mop of red-brown curls emerged above the top of a seat several rows back from hers, but on the opposite side. A teenaged girl sat up, holding the side of her head, which was bleeding. She stared briefly at Nellie and ducked back down behind the seat. Confused, Nellie took a couple of steps toward her, then froze as the girl suddenly reappeared, swinging a small rifle across the top of the seat and aiming it squarely at Nellie's chest.

"Don't move," she said, sighting down the rifle barrel. "Who are you?"

"I'm N...Elizabeth. I'm a passenger. I fell down when the train stopped and they didn't see me. So I stayed on the floor. Who are you?"

The teenager was shaking slightly but keeping her rifle aimed in Nellie's direction. "I'm Lil. Lil Marr." She lowered the rifle a bit seeing Nellie had dropped her hand back to her side, the small gun held loosely in her grasp. "And the only reason I don't shoot you is because the same damn thing happened to me, so I know you ain't lyin'." She scooted sideways without dropping the rifle's muzzle and knelt in the aisle. "What's going on?"

"It's a robbery," Nellie said, ducking back down and edging along the aisle in the girl's direction. "Far as I know everyone else is out there emptying their pockets and handbags." She bent over to look out at the robbery in process before sitting on the edge of a seat on the girl's side of the train. Lil moved out to the aisle, touching her fingers to the blood on the side of her head as she joined Nellie in looking outside. "Geez," she said, staring at her hand and the blood on her fingertips.

"You going to be okay?"

"I guess. I was just showing my new rifle to Will and Jack and was putting it back under my seat." She looked over at Nellie. "Next thing I remember was wakin' up under this seat and you were askin' who was there?" She looked back at the window. "Will and Jack!" She pointed. "My friends are out there." She half stood. "We have to stop this?" She sat back as Nellie made a shushing sound and gestured to the seat.

"Stop this?" Nellie looked incredulous. "I've got a two-shot pea-shooter, and you've got that...that," she gestured at the rifle. "What kind of rifle IS that anyway?"

"It's a .22 Winchester. It's small, but easy to aim and shoot. It'll knock a man down if you hit him right." She turned the gun over in her hands. "And not that I'm bragging, but I ALWAYS hit my targets 'right.'"

"How old are you anyway?" Nellie looked her over as she asked. The girl was small, maybe 90 pounds and about five feet tall, if that. "Do you really know how to shoot that thing?"

"Miss..."

"Elizabeth," Nellie said quickly.

"Elizabeth. I've lived on a ranch all my life and I've been shooting a rifle since I was eight years old, okay? That's more than half of my life because in two months I'm going to be turning 18. So, I can guarantee you that I can shoot this rifle and I can hit what I'm shootin' at!"

Nellie nodded, impressed by the girl's determination. Then she focused once more on reality, which the girl seemed to be missing. "Still, we can't take on all those armed men by ourselves."

"Maybe. But we sure can't if we don't even try," Lil responded. She reached down onto the seat and grabbed a felt cowboy hat with a leather string hanging down from each side. Pulling it over her curly hair, she knotted it under her chin, and turned her face down with a small "Oohh." She leaned back on the seat for a few seconds, crouched in the aisle again, and started moving toward the rear door. "I'm going out to the back side and see if I can get an angle on some of them. Maybe if they think there are more of us than there are they'll skedaddle and nobody'll get hurt. My father says that most thieves don't have the guts to stand and fight, and they'll run before they risk gettin' hurt." She started moving, paused and looked back. "You coming with me, or not?"

Nellie sighed and held her arms wide. "Sure, I guess. But like I said, my gun isn't worth much, being as small as it is. Best it can probably do is nick someone—IF the bullet gets that far after I shoot it."

They crept through the door and turned toward the rear of the train just as its big engine sighed and blew out a wave of steam and smoke that enveloped their car for several seconds. On the other side of the train, the lined-up passengers emitted shouts and screams at the exhalation of the steam cloud wafting over them.

"Shut up!" One of the robbers was yelling. "Stand back up and stay in line!"

"Quick, get off here now!" the girl ordered, and Nellie found herself obeying, slipping down to the ground and partially tearing lose the mock bustle on her dress in the process. She gave it a glance but said nothing, despite the fact that it was a $75 dress in the latest East Coast fashion. The bustle bounced crazily behind her as she hurried to Lil's side.

"Too bad about that," Lil said, looking over at the ripped fabric. "Not the right style for out in these parts, I think." She gestured down at her more form-fitting skirt, blouse and fringed leather top. You should get clothes like these."

"Yeah, I'll do that," Nellie said drily. "Just as soon as we get done shooting our way out of all this, I'll go shopping."

Lil glanced over her shoulder and grinned but kept edging along the side of the train with her small rifle at the ready. They eased past the next three cars —all Pullman passengers —and started moving along the freight cars that followed. The third one, specially constructed with slotted, corral-like slotted sides, was filled with horses, whinnying nervously.

"Those're ours," she said proudly. "Mustangs. The guys and I are bringing 'em up to Buffalo Gap to a rancher friend of my Dad's. They're two-year-old mares, some with foal and the rest ready for breeding."

Nellie looked through the slats at the horses. There were a couple dozen moving nervously around inside the car. One of them, a soft grey with a white blaze on her forehead, pushed her nose partway through one of the gaps in the siding and snorted on Nellie's arm. She jerked back before reaching out and rubbing her hand across the top of the mare's nose. It was fuzzy and soft. The horse nickered and pulled its face away.

"Look," Lil said. "I'm going to climb on top of that next car and see if I can get into a position where I can fire at them if we need to. There's an iron railing and some steps at the end. Can you hold the rifle while I get started and then hand it back to me?"

"Sure," Nellie answered. "But what should I do?"

Lil leaned up against the car as she got past the opening where the cars connected, and signaled for Nellie to come past and join her. Nellie looked around the car's corner, saw no one, and dashed across, flattening as best she could with her bustling dress flouncing out around her. "What do you want me to do?" She repeated. Lil eyed the car they had just passed as the horses shifted nervously inside, several whinnying again.

"I don't know?" She eyed the horses. "You know anything about horses?"

"Yes," Nellie said. "I've been riding for years."

"Well, these ain't for riding, yet," Lil said, gesturing at the carload next to them. "Still need to be gentled down some before they can be used on a ranch." She stared hard at them again. "Geez, he's gonna be mad."

"Who?" Nellie asked, confused.

"My father," Lil answered.

"Why is he going to be mad?" Nellie wasn't sure where this conversation was headed.

"Because you're going to let them all out of that car."

"What? Me? Wait a minute. What do you mean let them out? How can I do that? And WHY would I do that?"

"You ever see a bunch of horses stampede?"

Nellie glanced at the car, starting to see where Lil was going with this. "I can't say that I have," she said softly, "but I can about imagine how crazy it must be."

"Damn right it is," Lil answered, giving Nellie a thumbs-up sign.

"But how?"

"Look I'm going to climb up on top of this car and you climb on that coupling in between the cars. When you get across, you have to go about halfway forward toward the car's door. You'll see it's a sliding door with an eyebolt that has another straight bolt going down through it. That's holding the door shut. You gotta pull that bolt loose; grab the door handle, and jerk it right back toward you as hard as you can.

Then you take that little gun of yours and fire it inside the car."

"Fire inside the car? Are you crazy? I'm not going to shoot at the horses!"

"Not AT the horses. Sheesh. Fire up at the roof of the car...OVER top of the horses. Just do anything to spook 'em and get 'em to stampede out of there. I can guarantee you that once one of them goes they'll all come barreling out of there like a whirlwind—so you get your ass back out of the way if you don't want to have it stampeded off. You gotta do anything you can to get them headed toward that line of people. Understand?" Lil looked so serious that Nellie almost laughed.

"Don't worry. I have kind of a fondness about my..." she glanced back at the puffed-up back of her dress and slapped herself in the rear end "...ass, as you so clearly put it. I'll get out of the way. But are you sure I can handle that door?"

Lil turned toward Nellie and stood facing her, feet splayed apart, and a look of sheer determination on her face. Her eyes were barely at Nellie's nose. "I can do it. If I can do it, you can do it! Okay?"

Nellie nodded. She reached out and gave her young partner a reassuring squeeze on top of her shoulder. Lil handed her the rifle and grabbed the crossbar with one hand and the iron railing with her other. Nellie slid under and gave her a boost, and the girl's boots hooked over the first rung about even with Nellie's head. She looked down and nodded at the gun and Nellie handed it up. "Okay," Lil whispered. "We'll each count to 30, and then I'll go up higher. That should give you enough time to get to the other side and move toward that car door. Ready? Go."

Nellie edged back toward the gap between the cars, counting as she went. The coupling had a straight iron rod extending on either side, almost like steps, and Nellie gathered up her skirt and climbed up on top of it, counting every step of the way. She moved forward, held the skirt tightly bunched at her waist and scrambled down the opposite side.

Dropping the bulky skirt back, she glanced down where the hem brushed the top of her new leather buttoned-down shoes. She sighed in disgust. They were already scuffed. "Oh, hell," she muttered, creeping forward and glaring at the shoes as if the scuffing were their fault, not hers. Her count reached 30. Taking a deep breath, she edged around the corner of the car and walked briskly toward the door.

Ahead of her she could see the outlaws moving from person-to-person with big burlap bags, collecting every item the passengers dropped in, while two men with their backs to her were forcing the conductor into the first freight car. Three others, including the scar-faced man sat on horseback holding guns at ready. One outlaw on the ground handed a bag to the gang leader and started over to where the rest of their mounts were being held by another member of the gang. On Nellie's side, a gunman with a bag came to the end of the passenger lineup. He paused as he looked in her direction, stunned to see her.

His mouth fell open and he gestured in her direction, stepping back just as she reached the door and began fumbling with the bolt holding it in place.

"Hey!" he shouted and took a couple of steps toward her as she pulled the bolt free and flung it aside. Nellie fought with the rusted door handle, pulled it free from the latch and jerked it down, loosening it from the clasp that held the door shut. She grasped the handle firmly in both hands.

"Hey!" he yelled again waving an arm toward her. The two men standing at the first freight car spun in her direction, and one of the horsemen started riding down the line toward them. "What's she doing? Hey, Stop!" One of the men raised his pistol to shoulder height and aimed it toward her. "Stop her!

Shoot her!" the first man shouted. "She's opening that door!"

A second gunman extended his arm to fire and Nellie jerked back on the handle with all her might, nearly falling over backward as the door jumped in its track and slid toward her with a rasping squeak. As the door flew open, the startled horses, whinnying and snorting, shied back against the interior walls of the car. The first outlaw fired a shot and it ricocheted off the door above Nellie's head. Almost in the same instant there was the explosive sound of a rifle from overhead and the man who had fired dropped to the ground grasping his right leg and writhing in pain.

The passengers started screaming, some moving to get under the train, others dropping straight to the ground. The outlaw gang all seemed to be either frozen in place or moving toward her, ignoring the prostrate passengers as they tried to stop Nellie.

"Elizabeth!" Lil was looking over the edge of the train car roof, rifle still in hand. "Get the horses out of the car! Now!" She fired another shot in the direction of the robbers, and they all stopped and began returning her fire. As Lil ducked away from the gunfire and back behind the ridge of the roof, Nellie swung her small Derringer into the gaping opening created by the open door, looked squarely into the faces of the frightened horses and yelled "Hee-yah! Get out of there! Yah-yah-yah!" She fired the little gun into the roof of the car and the mares swirled to their right.

Nellie swung around, heart pounding, as three of the men stood back up and raced in her direction, guns in their hands.

"I thought you said most thieves don't have the guts to stand and fight?" she shouted up at Lil.

"Yeah, well, what can I say?" Lil answered, popping off another round and ducking again as the outlaws leapfrogged forward, firing in her direction as they moved.

As the one closest to them dropped to his knees to take steadier aim at Nellie, she heard another shot from behind her —only this one didn't come from the train car roof. Instead it seemed to come from the ground. The outlaw who had been aiming at her sprawled face first and lay motionless. Nellie dropped to her hands and knees and glanced over her shoulder. Two cars back a tall, bushy-mustached man with a bowler-style hat stood aiming a huge rifle and calmly firing at the gang members, who were now hugging the ground trying to see where this new threat was coming from. One of the men at the side of the train ducked between two cars.

Lil edged forward once more and looked down at where Nellie was crouching. "You've GOT to get those horses out! Do something!"

Nellie looked back inside and the mares returned her look with wild eyes. Then she reached back, grasped the fake bustle on her skirt and ripped it and most of the back half of her skirt off in the process. Swinging it over her head with its decorative ribbons flying, she leaned into the doorway and yelled again. The small grey, its eyes flashing in fear, leaped past her out the door. And, as if a stopper had been pulled from a steaming bottle, the rest of the herd bubbled out of the door as Nellie jumped away and continued yelling and waving the bustle and sending them all directly at the men, who gaped in fear at the onrushing animals before they turned and ran.

"Oh sure," Nellie muttered. "Now they run."

"Come on!" The scar-faced man with the first burlap bag kicked at his horse and galloped toward where outlaws and passengers alike were scattering before the wild-eyed horses. "Let's get out of here!" he yelled at his men. Some of the passengers were screaming and moving further under the train cars for protection.

The conductor leaned out of the freight car from where he had been left alone by the gang, raised a rifle and shot at the scar-faced man. The outlaw swore and grabbed at his left shoulder, dropping both his pistol and the burlap bag in the process. Clinging to the saddle with his now-empty gun hand, he kicked both legs and his horse bolted away. The other gunmen ran to their own horses, mounted and rode after him while randomly firing shots over their shoulders.

Simultaneously, Nellie heard a crack from Lil's rifle, and one more boom from the bushy-mustached man's gun. Another of the outlaw gang tumbled to the ground and lay unmoving in the dirt as his horse raced alone following the rest of the mounted riders, now heading northwest. To the north, the herd of mares kicked up a cloud of dust as they ran alongside the railroad tracks toward their newfound freedom. Three gang members were lying on the ground, two unmoving and the third rolling about while holding his bloodied leg.

Nellie stood up, brushed at her ruined dress and stepped away from the now-empty train car. Then she froze. Directly ahead, advancing with his pistol pointed right at her, was the outlaw who had ducked between the train cars. "Don't move or I'll shoot you where you stand," he yelled, hurrying on toward her. "You're my ticket out of here."

She looked up and saw that the car's overhang would keep Lil from seeing him or getting off a shot. And she was in a direct line between him and the bushy-mustached man, also cutting off any shot he might have. As Nellie slowly raised her hands, she was shocked to see a teen-aged boy wearing a black, silver-buttoned shirt emerge from beneath the train cars directly behind the outlaw. He took two steps toward them and started twirling a lasso over his head as he emitted a piercing whistle.

The outlaw spun around at the sound just as the rope swished through the air and settled neatly around his shoulders. Before he could react, the boy pulled back, tightened the rope and pinned the man's arms to his sides. As the gun fell from the outlaw's grasp, the boy jerked with all his might and the outlaw fell to the ground.

CHAPTER SEVEN

"That was one fine piece of roping," Masterson said admiringly as he finished handcuffing the gang member to the side of the train car. The conductor came out of the car down a ramp he and the brakeman had put up into the doorway and gestured back inside.

"Got that wounded one bandaged up and one of the bodies loaded in the back of the car." He motioned to the brakeman, "Neil and me'll get the other one and their horses loaded in and then we should be ready to roll." He glanced up where Lil was leaning forward at the top of the train car. "Pretty fancy shooting young lady. Where'd you learn to handle a rifle like that?"

"Oklahoma Territory," Lil answered. She nodded toward Rogers. "Will's from there, too. It's our horses that came out of that car." She looked wistfully toward the now-settling dust on the northern horizon. "Was our horses. Guess they're long gone by now."

The Marshal turned back toward Nellie. "Speaking of that. That was a hell of a thing you did there Miss...?"

"Cochran," Nellie answered, extending her hand. "Elizabeth Cochran." She looked up at Lil then over to Will as other people, including the Whites and Seaman, hurried toward them. "Guess you'd have to say it was a team effort, and no small part played by yourself. I assume that you're a lawman of some sort?"

Bat pulled back the corner of his coat to display his Marshal's badge and nodded. "Yes, I'm with the U.S. Marshal's Service out of Denver, transporting a prisoner up to Hot Springs. Name's Masterson."

Nellie started slightly at the mention of his name. "Really? Oh?" She appeared startled but then recovered her composure as he gave her a questioning look. "Hot Springs, you say? I'm going there myself for the mineral water treatment and the spas. I didn't realize they had an incarceration center there too?"

Masterson chuckled. "Well, they don't ma'am. And even if they did I doubt anyone in these parts would refer to it as an incarceration center. We just call 'em jails around here. But, I'm only going to be there with my prisoner for a couple days and then we're transferring over to another train heading out to Denver. That's where he'll be put in a real 'incarceration center.'"

He stared at Nellie again. "Have we met? Seems like we might've crossed paths somewhere, but I can't seem to place it."

"I don't see how," she answered quickly. "I've never been to Nebraska or the Black Hills before." She brushed at her hair and turned slightly.

Bat shook his head, shrugged and looked over at the man handcuffed to the train. He waved to the conductor to come over to join him. The Whites came rushing up just ahead of Seaman, and a young, well-dressed man who Nellie took to be a rancher of some sort also hurried up to the teenage boy's side, clapping him on the shoulder. "Hell of a toss Will," he began, "but what were you thinking? He could'a put a bullet in you."

He looked up at Lil. "And you." He stopped as if at a loss for words. "I can't even imagine what your father's going to do to me when this gets out. They must'a shot 20 rounds at you up there."

Lil grinned. "Good thing they ain't as good at shootin' as me then, huh?"

"Geez, Louise," he muttered. "And the horses are gone too. Come on down from there so we can get you back INSIDE the train instead of on top of it, okay?"

"Well, we had to do something," Lil responded, looking down at everyone. "Elizabeth and me were the only ones left —and the Marshal here. Pop will understand...I hope." She held out the rifle, and Jack extended his arms and nodded. Tossing it to him, she swung her legs around to the iron bar steps and started down.

"Who's your father?" Masterson asked. "When we get into Hot Springs I can wire him about what happened. Maybe it'll help hearing from someone in authority that you had no choice."

"Howard Marr," Lil said, reaching the bottom step and lightly jumping down as Jack passed the rifle over to Will and gave her a helping hand. "I'm Lil Marr, and this is Jack Omohundro, our wrangler. And that pipsqueak over there," she gestured toward Will, "is our neighbor Will Rogers."

83

"Hey!" Will exclaimed, holding the rifle by the barrel as he deftly coiled the rope in his other hand. "Stop calling me names."

"We were coming up here to sell the horses to a Buffalo Gap rancher. Father had a deal for $200 to $250 a head because they were our top-of-the-line Mustang breeding stock. It'll be a big loss, but..." Lil stopped and took Jack's arm, her lower lip quivering as she thought about the loss.

"Well, now, maybe he'll be a bit more understanding when you get the reward money for these outlaws," Masterson said. "I don't know who that one you shot first is, but there's an automatic reward for capturing anyone committing a robbery of a train or stagecoach. Usually five hundred dollars. The dead one they got loaded is a guy named John Silkey. It's a thousand dollars for him because he's been shooting up a lot of places for the past two years, including killing at least one bank teller so far as we can tell. And the one still lying out there is a fella called Robert Ringay. There's either five hundred or a thousand on him, too."

He finished handcuffing the man Will had lassoed and gave him a wry grin. "And this fine young man here is Jonas McCarty." Jonas glared at him in response. "Young mister Jonas here is the brother of the man who heads up this bunch of no-goods, fella name of Doc McCarty. He's the one rode off with a bullet in his shoulder thanks to the fine shooting of our conductor here. And Jonas and his asshole brother," he paused and looked at Nellie and Lil, "if you'll please excuse my French, are each worth five thousand dollars, dead or alive."

"Five thou..." Will said as his two friends and Nellie both gasped. "So, while you ain't got your horses any more, you've got yourself at least six thousand dollars in reward money coming, and I'll make dang sure you get each and every dime."

"But, I'm pretty sure that YOU shot that Silkey character," Lil said. "And that guy out there—the last one—he was pretty far away for my gun to reach. Don't you think?"

"What I think," Masterson said, "is that you deserve the rewards and you're going to get them." He turned toward Nellie. "Although maybe some of the cash could go to this young woman. Seems like she stirred things up a bit too." He chuckled as he gestured toward the now-empty car in which the horses had been riding.

"Oh, no, thank you but no," Nellie replied. "I wouldn't have done anything without Lil here, and besides, I didn't lose anything of value like she and her friends did."

"What about this beautiful dress?" Lil walked over and grabbed the back of the dress and pulled it around. It was shredded from the waist down, displaying Nellie's petticoats and stocking-covered lower legs for all to see. "And your shoes? They're ruined."

"Oh they're repairable. Well, maybe not the dress, but the shoes. Any good cobbler can fix them up in no time."

"I think we ALL owe Miss Cochran a new dress, but it will be my pleasure to pay for one. It's the least I can do," Robert Seaman said. "Thanks to her that burlap bag over there that had all my money and my gold watch is still here and I have everything back."

"Oh, I couldn't..." Nellie began.

"I insist," he said. "When we get to Hot Springs, we're going to the finest dress shop in town and either buy a dress you like or get this one replicated. We are not going to spare any expense on this, and that's the last of it." He nodded firmly. "Now, you may be embarrassed about the display of your underthings Miss Cochran, but I will be proud to escort you back onto the train where you can find your traveling case and change into something else."

They turned toward the car as Bat spoke quietly to the conductor, unhooked the handcuff from the car and pulled both of McCarty's arms behind his back where he locked them together. "Take him back to my car with the other one. I'll be right there."

"Thank you Marshal Masterson," Lil exclaimed. "You saved us." She ran up and wrapped her arms around him in an excited hug. Masterson looked embarrassed at the girl's outburst.

"Wait a minute," Jack said as he turned back toward Masterson. "Did Lil say you were Marshal Masterson? Are you Bat Masterson out of Dodge City?"

Bat nodded. "Yep, that'd be me. But I haven't been in Dodge for quite a few years. Make my home in Denver these days."

Jack looked flabbergasted. Spreading his arms wide he turned in a semicircle as he spoke in an awe-filled voice. "Do you all know who this is?"

"Bat Masterson," Nellie replied in a matter-of-fact tone. "You just told us, you know?" She glanced at Masterson. "Are you famous?"

"Is he famous?" Jack replied. "Holey moley lady. Where you from? Everybody knows Bat Masterson."

Nellie exchanged a knowing glance with Robert Seaman, and they both laughed. "Of course we know about the reputation of Marshal Masterson," she said. "I was just teasing. Even we New Yorkers hear about some of the deeds of people like Bat Masterson."

"Oh, so you're from the big city then?" the Marshal said. "I always thought it would be a good move on my part to get away from here and move back East myself."

"Really?" Seaman said. "Well, I happen to have a little iron works company back there and I'm always in need of good security officers. Based on what I just witnessed, I'd say you would do just fine in such a position."

"Well thank you Mister...?"

"Seaman," Robert answered, extending a hand, which Bat grasped. "Robert Seaman."

"Well, like I said, thank you for the kind offer, but security or law and order of any kind ain't what I figure on doing. I sort-of fancy myself being a newspaper writer and I've been in touch with some friends of mine in Denver about setting up shop and writing some sports stories. Figured if I get good enough at it, they'll consider me back East, too." He paused and chuckled. "It's gettin' a bit tiring always ducking bullets, and I figure even the worst sports fan ain't gonna be takin' potshots at me for what I write."

"Don't be so sure," Nellie started. She paused. "I mean, some fans are pretty intense about their favorite teams—wouldn't you agree Robert?"

"Indeed." He smiled. "Well, whatever, but the offer stands, just so you're aware."

He turned and offered his arm to Nellie and Bat tipped his hat in response as they started toward the Pullman. The other young couple that had been standing and listening moved toward him. Masterson watched Nellie go, a quizzical expression on his face. "Somewhere, I've seen her," he said, more to himself than them, "but where?" He shook his head again.

"Thank you Marshal," the young man interrupted his thoughts. "I'm William Allen White, out of Kansas City, and this is my wife Sallie. We didn't have as much saved from the robbery as Mister Seaman there, but Sallie's wedding ring was in that bag, so we're very grateful." He reached out and shook Bat's hand; then Sallie leaned in and hugged him, causing Masterson to blush for a second time.

"It was interesting to hear you wanted to be a newspaperman," White continued. "That's my profession, too."

"Really?" Masterson was about to turn toward the car where the conductor was now shoving McCarty through the doorway, but at White's comment, he turned back. "Who do you work for?"

"The *Star*," William said proudly. "And I know the sports editor and reporters quite well. But there's a man at the competing paper, the *Times*, who keeps saying how he has connections in New York, including a brother who's an editor there. He's been writing a regular series of stories on the Old West. Name of Alfred Lewis. I know he plans to travel out to Denver soon to gather material for more of his stories. I'd be glad to tell him about your interest and maybe the two of you can meet when he's out there?"

"Well, Mister White, I'd be much obliged," Bat said as the train whistle blew and the brakeman stepped out from the front of the engine and waved his hat toward them. "Listen, I need to get back to those prisoners, but once we get to Hot Springs, let's talk some more." He tipped his hat to Sallie, and hurried over to the conductor's side as the train's whistle blew again.

"Hmmm, that's interesting," Sallie said, grabbing her husband's arm and pulling him toward the passenger cars. "And I wonder why he thinks he knows Elizabeth?"

"Who knows? And, I didn't come on this trip to do any writing," William replied, "But Bat Masterson giving up marshaling to become a sports writer. That might be a story too good to ignore."

CHAPTER EIGHT

Twocrow wheeled the carriage at breakneck speed into the heart of Hot Springs as Laura and Minnie clung to the handrails and their hats, trying to keep the dust from the horse's hooves out of their eyes.

"Whoa!" He shouted and heaved back on the reins as the bay shuddered to a stop, panting and blowing as Twocrow leaped down, pulled the reins forward, and wrapped them several times around the hitching post in front of the Sheriff's office. Two horses, heavily-lathered from hard riding, already stood stamping at the hitching post and their riders were stepping up onto the walkway leading to the office.

"Go in!" Laura directed. "Minnie and me can get down by ourselves. We'll be there in a minute!"

Twocrow nodded and ran across the boardwalk toward the entry, the utility belt with the cave tools attached flapping at his sides. As the girls struggled to get down as quickly and gracefully as possible, Twocrow reached for the door and nearly collided head-on with the taller of the men, a wiry six-footer with intense black eyes and a neatly clipped mustache that drooped over the corners of his mouth. Another shorter and heavier man with wire-rimmed glasses and a bushy brownish-grey mustache of his own snorted with laughter as the first man grabbed Twocrow by the shoulders and held him at arm's length.

"Whoa, whoa, whoa, slow down before you hurt someone young fella!" the man exclaimed. Twocrow gave him a wild-eyed look in return. The second man stepped up beside his partner, staring at Twocrow with a puzzled expression.

"What's going on? You look like you might've seen a ghost there young man." The smaller man snorted again. "So, who died?"

"I need to see the sheriff right away," Twocrow blurted out. "There's a...," he paused and gulped a deep breath of air, suddenly feeling a bit light-headed. "I-I..." he sat down hard on the walkway just as Laura and Minnie hurried up behind him.

"Alvin!" Minnie exclaimed, kneeling beside her friend.

"Young man, you need to get your head between your knees and take slow deep breaths," the shorter man said, joining Minnie beside him. "That's what they taught us in boxing school," he said, glancing up at the taller man as he spoke.

"You went to 'Boxing School' Theodore?" The taller man, who they could now see sported a star on the left side of his vest, emitted a snorting sound of his own. "Out here we just learned as we went along, if you know what I mean?"

"Afraid I do." Theodore chuckled. "But you have to admit that my pugilistic skills have given me a bit of an edge out here, so I've always been glad to have them, if you must know." He patted Twocrow on the back and looked at Minnie and Laura. "Greetings young ladies. I take it you're with this young gentleman?"

They nodded.

"Theodore Roosevelt," the man said, standing back up and extending a hand that Laura reached out to grasp, clearly striving to show that she was the older, more sophisticated of the group. Roosevelt nodded over his shoulder, "And this distinguished gentleman is my good friend Sheriff Seth Bullock of the Deadwood, South Dakota, Bullocks."

Bullock laughed and extended his own hand to Laura as Roosevelt turned his attention to Minnie. "And who might the three of you be?" He looked over at the still-seated Twocrow. "You look like some sort of government official. Maybe you better tell us what all the excitement is that seems to have brought you barreling into the local constabulary?"

"Geez Theodore, do you ever speak regular English?" Bullock asked as he let go of the lingering grasp he had on the pretty Laura's hand. He turned toward Minnie and smiled. "You'll have to excuse Mister Roosevelt. He's from New York City." He said it with a slight touch of sarcasm, accenting each of the words in New York City as if saying something repulsive. "Fortunately, he's spent enough time out here with us regular folks that he can understand us and we can translate for him." He laughed again. "So, what he just asked is 'Who are you, and why are you here?'"

"I'm Laura Thompson, reporter for the *Hot Springs Star*," Laura responded, trying to do her best to look as "official" as possible. "And this is my little..."

"Younger," Minnie interrupted her.

Laura glared at Minnie. "...younger sister Minnie."

"Reporter for the *Buffalo Gap News*," Minnie interjected, with a determined expression on her face.

"And that's our friend Al...I mean, William...Twocrow." She gestured toward the bent-over young man.

"How about you? You reportin' for anyone?" Bullock asked as he reached down and grasped the young Indian under his arms and helped him to his feet.

Twocrow shook his head, still taking slow deep breaths.

"He works up at Wind Cave. And we're coming from there to report a murder," Laura finished.

Both men perked up at her declaration.

"Murder?" Roosevelt said. "I was just joking when I asked you who died." He looked sternly at the three young people. "Now, I'm serious. Who died?"

"Theodore, wait, we should get C.S. No sense in them havin' to tell the story more'n once," Bullock held up one hand.

Roosevelt looked at the three expectant faces staring toward him and nodded. Opening the door he yelled in a shrill, yet forceful voice "Sheriff Eastman. If you could roust yourself, your presence is required in the forward area. Immediately!"

"Like I said," Bullock leaned against the rail in front of the office, "Regular English." Then he roared in a deep voice, causing Twocrow and the Thompson sisters to jump. "C.S., get your ass out here right now! You got a murder on your hands!"

They heard a chair fall onto the floor, and shortly a ruddy-faced, grey-haired bear of a man filled up the doorway, the sixguns at his sides brushing up against the doorframe as he hurried out of the jail.

"What's going on?" he bellowed. He appeared confused when he saw the other men standing there. "Seth Bullock. My god! What're you doing here?" Then seeing the three young people shrinking before him, he mellowed his tone. "What do you mean, a murder?"

"Gene?" Bullock answered, a surprised tone to his voice. "What're YOU doing here? Where's C.S.? Where's the sheriff?"

Gene Akin grinned and jabbed a thumb at the star on his vest. "C.S. went out East to visit relatives for a couple weeks. Brought me back from the Old Folks Home to fill in." He chuckled. "Too old for full-time sheriffin', but I hold down the Sheriff's chair pretty good on a part-time basis." He turned toward the rest of the group. "Name's Gene Akin. I used to be in this office full-time until I got worn out and they put me out to pasture."

Laura stepped forward, taking the lead. "Sheriff, I'm pleased to meet you," she said, holding out her hand. "I'm Laura Thompson, the new reporter at the *Star*, and this is my sister Minnie and our friend William Twocrow. We just came from Wind Cave where William works and we want to report a body that we found there. We believe it's a man who's been staying at The Evans—a man named Alexander Previn."

"That so?" the sheriff gave them a skeptical look. "What makes you think so?"

"Well, he had this—it was in his shoe." She handed him the receipt. Akin opened it and read it through, giving Roosevelt and Bullock an incredulous look as he did so.

"So where is this so-called body?" the sheriff asked, passing the paper to Bullock.

"In the Cave," Twocrow answered. Regaining his composure, he began slowly and carefully explaining what had transpired from the time they arrived at the Cave until their breathless arrival back at the sheriff's office.

Roosevelt glowed with excitement as Twocrow finished his story, whirling around to face Bullock.

"When you got that telegram from Masterson asking you to come down here, I didn't dream it would turn into such a bully adventure as all this! Just Bully!" he nearly screeched in an excited, high-pitched voice. Clapping Bullock on the shoulder, he said, "Thanks for bringing me along Seth. This beats trout fishing and antelope shooting any time of the year. Besides, I can always do that."

He turned to face Akin. "Sheriff Akin, I can be of some help to you with this murder and whatever it is that Bullock and Masterson are doing. I used to be in law enforcement myself out in these parts—back in the '80s."

He looked to Bullock for affirmation.

Bullock turned toward Akin. "Gene, this here is Theodore Roosevelt from New York City. He used to ranch up near Medora and he also served as a Deputy Sheriff up there. He caught a nasty fellow we'd been chasing for over a year, a horse thief name of Crazy Steve. He single-handed brought him and his two no-good hangers-on all the way down to Belle Fourche to transfer them to me. Damn fine job of sheriffin' if I do say so myself." He placed a hand on Roosevelt's back. "We've been friends ever since.

"A couple years back he even stayed with me and my family when he came out here to visit the Reservations."

"I've been serving as U.S. Civil Service Commissioner," Roosevelt explained, responding to the confused look on Akin's face. "Wanted to see first-hand how conditions on the Reservations were coming along. It was good to visit the area again, but that was strictly for work. This time out I was just hoping to relax a bit, do some antelope hunting and maybe a little fishing with Seth before going back to Washington."

"He'll be catching on soon as the new Deputy Police Commissioner up in New York City," Bullock added to Roosevelt's narrative.

"Look, Gene, to answer your question, I got a wire from Bat Masterson yesterday and he told me to get to Hot Springs right away. Sounds like he's got someone pretty important in custody and needs my...our...help. Probably needs to put him up in your jail for a couple days and then get him out to Cheyenne or Denver. My guess is he's on the next train coming in from Chadron, because that's where he sent the telegram."

Akin nodded and looked over at the train tracks that ran just behind his building alongside Fall River—the hot water stream that ran through the heart of town and out Fall River Canyon toward Maverick Junction. "Train should be coming in any time now," he said. He pulled out his pocket watch. "Runnin' behind, but that happens all the time, especially navigatin' those new trestles that switch back and forth across the river out through the canyon."

"Sure. Same thing up by Deadwood," Bullock answered. "Anyway, when I got Bat's wire it was just after Theodore got in, so I deputized him and brought him along." He looked over and spoke directly to Laura, Minnie and Twocrow. "We rode most of the night to meet that train coming in from Chadron. A friend of mine has a prisoner on board that needs our attention."

"Bat Masterson? The lawman?" Laura looked starstruck as she spoke.

"Yeah, that's him. But listen, you and your sister and your friend need to keep quiet about this, okay? We don't know who he's got or even if anyone knows he's on board. So until everything is clear, I'm asking you to cooperate with us. You understand? A man's life could be at stake—hell, maybe several people's lives are at stake."

The young people nodded and Sheriff Akin gestured toward the jailhouse office. "Let's go inside. We can talk more there and figure out what we're going to do next. You think you and Roosevelt here can give me a hand with this murder as well as taking care of Masterson's problem?" he said it quietly to Bullock as they started inside. Bullock returned the receipt to Akin and the two men moved across behind a massive desk to continue their conversation.

"So you've been working with the Reservations sir?" Twocrow asked, directing his question to Roosevelt.

"Yes, I have, hoping to help upgrade the conditions a bit." He studied Twocrow, noting his dark complexion. "Are you from the Pine Ridge Reservation, young man?"

Twocrow shook his head. "Was, but not anymore."

"He's been living with his aunt and uncle in Buffalo Gap," Minnie spoke up. "His mother's sister married a rancher out there. He used to work for my father on the Gap newspaper before he started guiding out at Wind Cave."

"So your parents reside on the Reservation then?" Roosevelt asked.

"No sir, they both died...my sister, too...from the smallpox. My father, he was a chief, but after he died, there was only me, so I came to live at the Gap."

"I'm sorry to hear about that," Roosevelt looked solemn. "I found when I was out here on the Pine Ridge two years ago that health conditions were bad, but improving. Hopefully there won't be any more outbreaks for a long, long time."

"Yeah, I hope so too," Twocrow looked down at the floor as if thinking about the time when his family had died.

A train's whistle filled the air, breaking the brief moment of silence. A big locomotive pulling about a dozen cars rounded the bend in the tracks and steamed along behind the sheriff's office building.

"There it is!" Bullock shouted to be heard. "Theodore, we should get down to the Depot and catch up with Bat and whoever it is he has on board. Gene, you gonna be okay with these three?"

Sheriff Akin nodded. "Sure, but maybe we should come on down there, too. If there's a prisoner to take care of, we're gonna need to bring him back here before we end up with a lot of extra commotion. Better to act quick and get him in a cell. Then we can get back to whatever the hell this is." He looked at the receipt again, then over to Laura, Minnie and Bill as he spoke. "Come on," he said, grabbing his broad-brimmed hat and gesturing for the young people to join them. "We can see what's going on with the train, and then one of us will go with you to check on this receipt that you found. And, I reckon we ought to go out and take a look in the Cave, too." He looked toward Bullock and Roosevelt. "How's that sound to you?"

"Bully!" Roosevelt exclaimed again. His face lit up with excitement and started out the door while Bullock looked askance at his fellow lawman.

"I really like Theodore," Bullock sighed as he watched his friend hurrying away. "But ... Bully?" He sighed again. "Come on. We better get down to the station before he arrests someone."

*****

As the train slowed to a stop at the sandstone-walled depot located across from the magnificent Evans Hotel, Masterson leaned out of the back freight car and signaled to the conductor, who waved back with the rifle he was holding in his left hand. The train shuddered to a complete stop and waves of steam rolled down the tracks.

The stationmaster and his team hurried to set portable wooden staircases into place at each of the Pullman cars and all were greeted by the sound of a brass band playing by the steps of the hotel. The conductor signaled for a staircase to be moved over to his car, climbed down and spoke hurriedly to the stationmaster while gesturing toward the back of the train where Masterson waited.

As the passengers started slowly exiting, a heavy-set man with wire-rimmed glasses wearing a rawhide fringed tan jacket and wide floppy hat jogged toward them, followed by two lawmen and three young people trying to keep up. The stationmaster spoke again to the conductor and hurried to meet them.

"Sheriff, the train was held up," he said, breathing hard as he came up to Akin.

"What the hell? You gotta be joking!" Akin looked from the stationmaster to Bullock.

"What was that? Held up? By whom?" Roosevelt's high-pitched voice caused the stationmaster to turn halfway around in his direction, an anxious look on his face.

Akin gave a little wave and nodded for him to continue. "The McCarty Gang," the trainman said. "Didn't even try to disguise themselves. It was about an hour out, I guess.

"And that ain't all. I just finished taking a wire from Edgemont and their bank got hit first thing this morning. Robbers rode out to the east, maybe headed our way. Sheriff over there thinks it was some of the Curleys."

"How much did they get away with?" Bullock asked. Then realizing that the man didn't know him, he held out his hand. "Seth Bullock. Sheriff from up in Deadwood. I'm here ... assisting Sheriff Akin with a couple things." He pointed to Roosevelt. "This is Theodore Roosevelt." He winked. "Deputy." Roosevelt beamed.

"Um...sure. Okay. Name's Wood. But folks here just call me A.D." The stationmaster shook the men's hands and nodded as Minnie, Laura and Twocrow reached the group.

"They're okay, A.D.," Akin said. "Go ahead."

"Don't know about the bank, but about the train...well, that's the damndest thing. Seems that the gang got driven off without hardly getting a dime. And on top of that, the conductor says they got two wounded outlaws in that back freighter, two more bodies where he's standing, and another prisoner chained up by the door. And get this, the younger McCarty ... Jonas ... he's the main one they captured."

"Whew!" Bullock exhaled sharply. "Good thing we're here. You might want to deputize a couple more of your best shots Gene. Can't figure Doc's gonna let his little brother just sit around in the Hot Springs jail."

"Yeah, that's for sure," Akin said sourly. "Doc McCarty's a bad one, all right. He likes to come in quick and hard, when you least expect it. Had a run-in with him a few years back. Figured I wouldn't have to deal with anything like that again when I retired." He shrugged. "Oh well."

"Really? The McCartys?" Bullock asked. "I thought you shot it up with that bunch of thugs that ran around with those Diamond tattoos?" He glanced over at Wood. "That Curley Gang he just mentioned."

"Well, I did." He looked over at the others. "It was Charley Curley and his main man Frank Diamond got themselves shot and killed out here five or six years back. Frank's the one got them all puttin' those tattoos on their arms. Anyway, the Curleys were ridin' for years on their own, but then he and his men started working with McCarty's bunch—sort-of a Southern Hills branch operation, I guess. Anyway, Doc and Charley's brother Jake and a few of their boys come up here for some revenge after I killed Charley and Frank. But me and some of the Home Guard got the upper hand on 'em and they haven't been back since."

He glanced over at the train. "'Til now. If the McCartys were in on that robbery attempt, then Jake Curley and whoever's still riding with him had to be in on it, too. I was sort-a hopin' they were gone from the Hills for good. Shit!"

"Home Guard? What's that?" Roosevelt asked, his eyes shining brightly behind his spectacles.

"Group of sharpshooters I deputized a few years back after Governor Mellette got worried about the Indians." He glanced over at Twocrow, cleared his throat slightly, and then went on. "After Wounded Knee, the Governor was runnin' scared of the Sioux, so he started up a cowboy militia. Formally, it's the Battle Creek Squad of the Mountain Rangers, but we just call 'em the Home Guard. Got the best shots around and we did some training in '91 and '92.

"But, we never did have to worry about the Indians; it was just the damn outlaws that were runnin' wild. So when McCarty and his boys came up here we 'tested' out our trainin', so to speak." He paused and chuckled. "Them outlaw boys weren't anywhere near a match for my roughriders. Damn that was a good day." He smiled at the thought of routing the gang.

"Roughriders?" Roosevelt said with a quizzical expression. "Why do you refer to them like that?"

"Well, they can handle either a rifle or a pistol and shoot while riding at full gallop over the roughest ground. So, I just call 'em roughriders, 'cause that's what they are."

"Roughriders," Roosevelt said thoughtfully. "I like that. Sort-of signifies the cowboy's 'can-do' spirit I've been writing about in my book about the frontier."

"Theodore's quite the author," Bullock interjected, seeing the puzzled look on Akin's face. "And he's workin' on a new book about ranchin' and such...what was it you're callin' it again Theodore?"

"*Ranch Life and the Hunting Trail*," Roosevelt responded. "And it sounds like your 'Roughriders,' as you call them, would fit right in with the men I rode with when I lived and worked out in these parts." He nodded. "Yes sir, I've long thought it would be just bully to command a regiment or two composed of frontiersmen who have the qualifications of both top horsemen and crack marksmen. I'd be proud to lead such a contingent, wouldn't you Seth?"

Bullock nodded his agreement.

"Yeah, I suppose," Akin responded. "All I know is my boys can ride and shoot with the best of 'em and it's nice to have 'em around when I need some help. Like now." He gestured to the stationmaster. "A.D., can you get word over to Chalky that I need the Home Guard on standby? Whoever he can round up. We should meet at the Sheriff's office." He looked again at his pocket watch, and snapped it shut. "Tell 'em right away."

CHAPTER NINE

Fred Evans smoothed his thick, wavy hair, plucked the few grey hairs out of his beard, and looked at himself in the full-length mirror. His elegant clothing was the latest in men's styles, purchased on his most recent trip to Chicago where he had been striving to drum up tourism business for the Southern Black Hills.

He had invested more than a quarter-million dollars in his new sandstone hotel and another hundred thousand into its furnishings, and he hadn't hesitated to promote The Evans as the finest hotel between Chicago and San Francisco, an elegant option for the discerning upper-class traveler that he and his wife Theresa were seeking to draw. And, Evans saw another possibility—a luxurious "temporary residence" for the movers and shakers of business and industry to take advantage of South Dakota's lenient divorce laws as quickly and painlessly as possible.

Having made many connections in the business and financial world, he slyly let it be known that "residency" was easy to establish in his plush new hotel, a discreet option for his wealthy friends. It was an arrangement that also brought him into further contact with those at the top of the financial pyramid, a couple who had convinced him to invest in their own enterprises.

Unfortunately some of those deals weren't paying off, and now he needed an investor of his own, and he needed one soon. He and Theresa were welcoming dozens of guests daily to their new 100-room establishment, and he was convinced it not only would be a profitable venture, but one destined to put him into the ranks as one of the great visionaries of his time. The problem was, he was cash-strapped at the moment and needed a quick infusion to pay off the last of his creditors or all his dreams would be for naught. The profits were bound to come, but he was running out of time.

The arrival during the past week of a patron named Alexander Previn and his wife Mollie had seemed like a strong possibility. He had met Previn on his recent trip to Chicago, learning that the miner turned entrepreneur had upwards of $50,000 in gold to invest—and he intended to make that investment somewhere in the Southern Hills. Evans hadn't seen the gold directly, but Previn made it clear that it was "at hand," as he put it.

"Why not invest it in Hot Springs?" Evans asked. "And why not in my grand new hotel, a gold mine in its own right?" he had laughed.

Previn seemed unconvinced and continued to speak of putting his gold into ranch land instead. But he agreed to come to Hot Springs and check out the hotel after Evans offered him free room and board while he "explored his options." After just one day in town, Previn said he was impressed but still wanted to converse with his younger brother, who would be arriving on the next train from Nebraska, where he had attended a land development meeting in Norfolk.

"He's got a good eye for new ideas; new ways to put our money to work," Previn explained. He'd reached over and gave his pretty wife a squeeze. "If Mollie here didn't have such rich tastes, we might even have more to invest. That's why I'm glad I have my brother managing things; otherwise we might be out here lookin' into one of them divorces you keep talking about." He laughed a full, booming laugh and shook Evans' hand while his wife gave him a dour look and stomped off across the expansive lobby.

"Look, we'll talk further after Paulus arrives. Who knows, maybe this IS the place to put our funds?" Previn said. "Guess I'd better go smooth things over with the little woman." He laughed again, but looked worriedly at the rapidly receding figure of his wife as she headed past the main desk and out the hotel door.

That had been yesterday afternoon and Evans hadn't seen either of them since, even though the guest register showed they were still checked into the hotel and Alexander had two large bags stored in the hotel's walk-in safe.

Evans knew about having a lot of money to invest. He had made, lost and re-made several small fortunes running a seemingly endless procession of ox teams between Fort Pierre and the Black Hills during the gold rush days, after earning an earlier fortune through the Sioux City Streetcar Company. But, when the railroads arrived, his ox teams were suddenly obsolete and his money had steadily drained away through a number of ongoing obligations. That's when he decided to relocate to Hot Springs and get into the tourism business.

Even before his recent election as Mayor, he had gone to work getting railroads and electricity into the city, the first major steps toward achieving his vision. His next step was to make the community both a vacation wonderland and an entertainment center. The spas and water park he had created—nicknamed Evans Plunge—would be one attraction, and he knew that the developing Wind Cave to the north and Cascade Springs to the south would be two more. Now, the new Chautauqua Park with its grand entertainment pavilion would be the frosting on his cake. Rest and relaxation, first-class entertainment, and exciting natural wonders, a three-pronged draw for his adopted city.

Thus, he had been thrilled during his representation of the community at Chicago's Columbian Exposition to make the acquaintance of the famed Buffalo Bill Cody and convince him and his sharpshooting genius Annie Oakley to come and perform at the Chautauqua. On top of that, he knew that several "moneyed" guests were coming into town—some for vacation and others to start the process toward a divorce.

This week promised to be a huge step toward his regaining his financial standing. All he had to do was convince people like the Previns that their best investment would be right here with him and his hotel. But he wasn't putting all his eggs into the Previns' basket. Another New Yorker named Robert Seaman was also on his way to assess the Evans as an investment, and he had put feelers out to an investment group in Nebraska.

Something, he was certain, would come to fruition.

"Ready Dearest?" Theresa swept into the room, her hair in a stylish mass of curls and pulled up under a Spanish comb. A matching broach held a silk scarf around her neck, topping a beautiful lavender, brocaded dress with puffed sleeves and a wide silk collar. "The train's arriving and our guests will be expecting a formal reception—don't you agree?"

"Yes, of course." He looked at himself once more as she came up beside him. He had told Theresa what he planned to do, but she was unconvinced, just as she had not been convinced to build and open the hotel in the first place. But she'd promised to do her best to help their venture succeed and she was putting her best foot forward.

"You look beautiful," he told her.

She smiled in return and brushed at the front of his suit. "Where's your diamond tie pin?" she asked, frowning slightly.

"Oh, damn! What would I do without you?" He patted her arm and stepped over to the bureau, retrieving a diamond stickpin to hold his cravat in place. "Here," he said, handing it to her. "You do it." She placed the pin, straightened his collar, and nodded.

"Now you're ready." She took his arm and they looked together into the mirror. They exuded confidence and wealth—the perfect combination, he thought, to get the money they so desperately needed.

"Yes," he said. "Let's go do it."

*****

Joshua Dickover and his wife Emma were waiting by the hotel lobby's marble fireplace when the Evans' stepped from the electric elevator—yet another of the fabulous innovations Evans had installed to help put the hotel in the limelight and live up to his boast that it was "Best in the West." Dickover had been Mayor for the past 4 years and then had successfully campaigned for Evans as his successor.

"Fred!" Dickover boomed, striding over. "Don't know if you heard, but the train was stopped by robbers about an hour out, south of Maverick Junction!"

"Oh my word," Theresa Evans said quickly as Emma held out a hand to steady her.

"Anyone hurt?" Evans asked, looking out the window to where the passengers were disembarking to a rousing march being played by a 20-member brass band, another "special touch" he'd arranged just for this arrival

"Not from the train, but the outlaws didn't fare so well," Dickover replied. "Guess there was at least one lawman on board, and a couple of other sharpshooters who helped drive them away. Sheriff just told me that there's two bodies and three prisoners on board and he's taking the prisoners down to the jail."

"Damn, that's all we need," Evans said disgustedly. "Here we are busy promoting Hot Springs as the next best thing to the spa baths of Germany, and a bunch of brigands disrupts everything." He turned to Theresa. "Look, I know you're against me giving away any more rooms or meals, but I want to make an impression on this group because I know that most of them are coming here for Buffalo Bill's show at the Chautauqua tonight. And when they leave, I want them singing our praises to the world."

"What do you want to do?" she said, looking very serious as she reached over with both arms and grabbed both of his.

"I want to give them all a free room and dinner tonight. Welcome them in true Hot Springs style."

"Fred, there must be a hundred people on that train."

"And I think they're going to spend a lot of money in town over the next few days, beginning with that Chautauqua show tonight. I want them to know that this isn't just any backwater hick town, but an elegant resort where they can feel safe ... and welcome —and not just by a brass band playing on their arrival." He gestured through the front window at the band.

"Well," Dickover said. "As you can clearly hear, the Band's doing a bang-up job of welcoming them in style. They've probably forgotten all about the holdup already."

Evans grimaced at the thought and shook his head disgustedly.

"And Fred, I want to know how in the world you got Sousa and his boys to be part of this?" He shook his head admiringly. "You do have the magic touch."

Emma beamed. "John Philip Sousa. Imagine? I think half the famous people in the West are staying here this week."

"Another reason to make sure that whoever's on the train doesn't leave bad-mouthing us," Evans responded. "And, yes, we're fortunate to have Sousa. Just a stroke of luck to get him here. And that makes paying a dollar entrance fee to the show a little more palatable, too, wouldn't you all agree?"

"It IS a grand occasion after all," Theresa Evans interjected. "When Fred learned that Mister Sousa and his band were performing in Rapid City, he just went up there and invited them down to Hot Springs for a couple of days to help us with the Pavilion."

Evans winked at his wife. "And, when I offered them a chance to soak in the baths and stay in the hotel at no charge, I don't think that hurt matters either."

"Yes," she sighed. "Nothing like a free room and board to make the trip more fun." She sported a perplexed look for a fleeting few seconds, but exchanged it for a smile as the band resumed playing, this time breaking into Sousa's famed "Liberty Bell March."

"Makes you want to 'march' on out for the official greeting, don't you agree?" Dickover said expansively, sweeping his silk top hat into place and offering his arm to his wife. "Shall we do the honors?"

"Yes," Evans answered, "Let's." He took Theresa's arm and stepped in front of the Dickovers to lead the way, a subtle reminder to the former mayor that there was new leadership in the city.

The foursome stepped out onto the veranda overlooking the 20-piece brass band being conducted by a dapper young man dressed very much like a German military officer with a well-trimmed pointed beard and sweeping full mustache with curled ends. His military style cap adorned with an eagle emblem and his close-cropped hair added to the illusion. Glancing up toward Evans as he conducted, he nodded curtly and pushed back on his wire-rimmed glasses as the rousing march continued.

"Sousa brought about a dozen of his boys along and they've joined with the musicians from the Minstrel Show to work out a few songs for tonight's event," Evans leaned in to confide to the Dickovers. "I told them welcoming the train would be a great test of how well they can play together and he agreed."

The well-known McIntyre & Heath Minstrel Show with its six-piece band would be performing during the entire weekend's activities at the expanded Chautauqua Park's Pavilion. But for the grand re-opening this evening, Evans was pulling out all the stops. He had both a larger band and a special greeting by Buffalo Bill himself —followed by exhibition shooting by Annie Oakley. Bill and Annie had two of the most posh suites in the upper levels of the hotel; two more "freebies" that Evans was dealing with to make sure his world-class guests were happy.

"Whoo-ee!" Joe Hayden, one of the Evans' black waiters stepped forward from the back of the veranda, clapping and cheering as the band completed its song and the newly arrived passengers joined with the already gathered crowd in applauding the musicians. "Man oh man, with music like that there's gonna be a hot time in the old town tonight!" He laughed. "Yes sirree, a HOT time in old HOT Springs!" He began whistling a catchy tune.

"Hey, you there! What's that you're whistling?"

The question came from a middle-aged man who had been leaning somewhat dejectedly against one of the colonnade-style pillars holding up the veranda roof. He took a step or two toward Hayden as he spoke and Evans eyed both men warily.

Hayden looked startled by the question. "Oh, that? That's just an old tune from my hometown. I was just getting stirred up about all that great music." Hayden looked down at his highly polished shoes. "Sorry sir, didn't mean to interrupt them musicians."

"No, no, you misunderstand. I'm not upset," the man hurried to answer. He glanced at Evans. "Mr. Evans. I don't know if you remember me? Theodore Metz." He extended a hand. "I'm the band leader for the minstrel show. Just watching my boys under *The Master's* baton." He emphasized the words with just the slightest hint of resentment in his voice. "Seems as if he's to be in charge so long as he's in town, right?"

"Yes, that's right." Evans glanced at Hayden and jerked his chin back toward the hotel. Hayden made a slight bow and started to turn away.

"No, wait, hold on a second," Metz held out a hand to halt the waiter. "I was just wondering about that tune and that...expression ... you just said. How was it again?"

"Sir?"

"What you said about 'A Hot Time'?"

111

The young man laughed. "It's from back where I grew up in New Awlins'. When somethin' big was goin' on, we'd say, 'Gonna be a hot time in the old town tonight!'" He laughed again. "My brother and me, we sort-a put together a little tune to go with it." He whistled the catchy tune again.

Metz looked thoughtful. "I like that," he smiled and glanced over at Evans. "Mister Evans would you be upset if your man here were to sit down with me and tell me a little more about that tune? I've been looking to write up a new song for our show, and it seems like 'A Hot Time' is a pretty good description of what we try to provide."

Evans shrugged and turned toward Hayden. "You okay with that Joe?"

"Well sure, I 'spose," Hayden answered. "But it's gonna hafta be before lunch," he turned back toward Metz. Mister Cody and Miss Annie done asked me to show them around the town again this afternoon." He beamed. "Hard to turn down the likes of Buffalo Bill. And after lunch I'll hafta get the dining room set up for tonight's meal."

Metz smiled and extended his hand to the black man, who looked surprised, then smiled in return and took his hand. "All right, I'll meet you in the dining room. Say ten-thirty?" Hayden nodded and hurried back inside as Metz turned back to the street. The musicians were picking up their instruments and music stands as a couple of the hotel employees began moving the chairs back inside.

Evans stared quizzically at Metz for a few more seconds, before moving to the center of the stairs at a signal from his wife. He glanced down at the drummer and nodded, and the man took the cue and did a quick drum roll, followed by a cymbal crash. The crowd quieted.

"Ladies and Gentlemen! I'm Mayor Fred Evans and I want to welcome you all to beautiful Hot

Springs!" Everyone applauded. "And thank you to our distinguished guest conductor, who, like you, has chosen to come to our resort community for both relaxation and entertainment. We are grateful that he was willing to have his musicians 'make some music' for us today and that he'll be leading our band again this evening at the grand re-opening of our wonderful Chautauqua Park! Please thank the March King himself, John Philip Sousa!"

Evans swept his right arm forward to where Sousa was standing near the bottom of the steps, and the band director removed his hat and bowed elegantly as the crowd erupted in loud applause and cheers.

"I was sorry to learn of your untimely stop on the way into our fair community," Evans continued. "That kind of treatment is NOT part of our well-known Southern Hills hospitality. And to try to help make up for it, I want to extend to you all a free night's stay and a free dinner at our wonderful new Evans Hotel—the finest lodging establishment anywhere between Chicago and San Francisco!" He turned back toward his hotel and expansively held out both arms.

The passengers and the locals all gasped at the generous offer, before breaking into another round of applause that grew into a thunderous ovation.

Evans smiled and waved as Dickover stepped forward next to him.

"Should I do my usual welcome?" Dickover asked.

Evans shook his head and spoke again. "Now, if you'll all just come inside, and give us proof you were actually ON the train..." the crowd laughed. "Then we'll get you settled into your rooms and hope you'll want to stay on for several more days to enjoy that true Southern Hills hospitality of which I was speaking.

"And don't forget that Chautauqua show tonight. Seven-thirty. Just one dollar for a great evening of entertainment." He leaned over to Dickover. "People don't mind paying a dollar when they get their money's worth—proved that last month with that big boxing match. No reason why listening to a great band and watching Annie Oakley and Buffalo Bill shouldn't be just as big a draw." He patted Dickover on the shoulder. "Gotta think big Josh. Gotta think big. People like going with a winner!"

Fred and Theresa moved together to the edge of the stairway to begin welcoming the new arrivals as Dickover frowned. Fred started to say something, but his wife reached out and took his arm, pulling him over to other side of the stairs where they joined in the welcoming ceremony instead. Behind them, Metz began whistling the little tune he'd heard from Hayden as he walked back into the hotel.

CHAPTER TEN

"The sheriff wants you to come with me to his office to give our version of what happened out there," Masterson said to Nellie, Lil and Will as he met them and their traveling companions at the base of the hotel's steps. "He's got the prisoners in tow, so I think it'll be okay if we get checked into the hotel first." He smiled. "Don't want to miss out on the free room now, do we?"

Nellie nodded, but the young people looked concerned.

"Don't worry," Bat said, seeing the expression on their faces. "It's pretty standard procedure, especially when someone gets shot. And," he added, "you've got a pretty darned good support person standing here, you know?" And he jabbed both thumbs toward his chest, one pointing directly at his marshal's badge. "Besides, if we're going to put you in for those rewards, now's the time to file the paperwork and get it started."

"I should wire your Dad and let him know what's going on," Jack joined them as he spoke, placing a reassuring hand on Lil's forearm. "And what should we do about Martin?" He paused as Masterson and the others gave him a confused look. "It's the rancher we were going to be meeting today up by Buffalo Gap?"

Masterson nodded. "Well, I'm sure the Sheriff can get word out to him. A good horseman can ride out there and back in no time. Listen, we'll get registered here and I'll put the three of you in two rooms on government expense for a couple more nights if you want to stay on. You can reimburse me when you get that reward money." He looked from Jack, to Lil, then over to Will. "I mean if you two young fellas don't mind sharin' a room?"

"No, no course not," Jack responded. He looked back at Lil. "Listen, you go with the Marshal and get our rooms taken care of and I'll go back into the station and send off that telegram to your father. And don't worry, I can go with you to the Sheriff's office, too."

Nellie smiled appreciatively. "I don't know if that's necessary Mr. Omo..."

"Jack," he said firmly. "I prefer to go by Jack."

"Or Texas," Will interjected. Jack glared at him. "I'm just sayin'..." Will started, and then clamped his mouth closed as Jack's glare intensified.

"Texas?" Nellie looked questioningly at Jack. "I'll just call you Jack." She smiled. "As I was saying, I think I can adequately explain everything to the Sheriff so you can take care of your business needs. He needs to talk to me, too, you know?"

"That's a good idea Jack," Lil jumped in before Jack could respond. "I've been worrying about Mister Martin and our horses. Maybe if the sheriff could send one of his men and lend you a horse, you could ride along? You could let him know personally what happened? He WAS expecting a load of horses after all."

Jack looked thoughtfully from his companions over to Nellie. "All right, but I'll still need to come down there with you—to meet with the sheriff's man, and all—if you don't mind helpin' us with the sheriff and everything?" he added, turning back to Masterson.

"Believe me, it's my pleasure," Bat said. "You two young ladies probably kept me on pace to put a very bad man in jail, and who knows what would'a happened if you hadn't been there. So come on," he held out an arm to each of them. "Come with me into the hotel and we'll get settled. We can meet back in the lobby in thirty minutes." He looked at Jack. "After we get our dealings completed with the sheriff, we can all come back here and get that free meal that just got offered." He looked around at the group. "I hope we can all eat together this evening?" Everyone nodded agreeably.

"Sure," Jack said. "If I can get back from Martin's ranch in time. But let's worry about that later. I'll see you in half an hour."

He turned back to the station as Nellie and Lil accepted the lawman's offer of his arms and headed up the stairs, with the Whites, Seaman and Will following closely behind. At the top of the stairs they stopped on Evans' side of the greeting line as the Whites veered over toward the Dickovers. Fred Evans gave them a quizzical look, seeing Masterson's badge.

"Bat Masterson, Mr. Evans," the marshal said, releasing the women's arms and accepting Evans' handshake. Bat reached down and took Theresa's hand and brought it up to his lips. "And this lovely lady must be Mrs. Evans?"

"Theresa," she said, appearing charmed by his gesture. Nellie and Lil exchanged amused glances. They quickly introduced themselves.

"And I'm Robert Seaman," the older man took the last step up and grasped Evans' hand firmly. "We've exchanged a couple of telegrams Mr. Evans, and I've looked forward to making your acquaintance. I also exchanged some messages with the Ohmer Brothers and I hope to have the chance to stop off in Norfolk to meet them personally on my way back home. I do think we can all work together on this."

"Mr. Seaman!" Evans looked surprised and excited to see his newest arrival. "Why, I had no idea you'd be on this train. I've heard much about your business successes in New York, and I've been anxious to get your counsel when you arrived. A new entrepreneurial effort like this can always stand an infusion from time to time—advice ... and funds." He turned with Seaman, still grasping his hand, and said, "Theresa, dear, this is one of the men I told you about."

Her face brightened and she held out her hand, which he took lightly, then released.

"Let us get you into your room and then perhaps we can dine together this evening. I'd be grateful if you could join us in our private dining room." He clapped a friendly hand on the older man's back and subtly turned him toward the door.

"Thank you Evans." Seaman stopped and turned to Nellie. "But only if you'll agree to have Miss Cochran here join us, too."

"Why... certainly. I didn't realize you had a traveling companion." Evans spoke quickly and looked embarrassed by his earlier lack of attention to Nellie. Masterson had started to take her arm again, but released it and took a half step in Lil's direction, a questioning look on his face.

"I-uh...that is," Nellie had a strained smile. "Mr. Seaman and I are NOT traveling companions." She looked around at the others. "We just met a few hours ago—before all that unpleasantness out in the countryside. And, actually, Robert...I planned to join my other new friends here for dinner, along with Marshal Masterson, of course. So, I don't think I'll be able to dine with you." She gave Seaman a reproving look. "But thank you all the same."

Seaman looked stunned by her rebuff and she could tell that he was not used to having his requests so easily overturned. He reddened slightly and turned back to Evans. "Well, then, I will indeed be delighted to join you and your lovely wife. What time do you eat?"

"Could we dine early, say five?" Evans tentatively suggested. "I don't want to delay getting things started over at the Chautauqua Park, and that's all set for around six-thirty, so Miss Oakley can have some light for her shooting exhibition."

"Five is perfect. I like to eat early, and that Chautauqua thing sounds interesting. I'll have someone direct me to your dining room." He tipped his hat to the rest of the group and strode rapidly into the hotel. Seeing no other customers, the Evans' also nodded and trailed along behind.

Nellie stared after them, and then giggled nervously as she looked back at Masterson and her five new friends. "That went well, don't you think?"

Sallie White watched the door slam shut behind the Evans', then clasped her hand over her mouth, lost her battle to stifle a laugh, and erupted instead into loud giggles. "Oh my!" she gasped as the rest of the group joined in her laughter. "I think I understand now why he's still a bachelor."

*****

The debriefing, as Masterson called it, had gone quickly and smoothly with the exception of Jonas McCarty shouting and cursing at them from his cell in the back. His last threat was that this two-bit jail wasn't going to hold him, especially when his brother and the rest of the gang decided to make their move. Frank Pasch finally had regained consciousness and was being looked at by the local doctor, Doctor Jennings. The other wounded man, unlike McCarty, was lying quietly in a third cell, staring at the ceiling. The sheriff had identified him as Jeremy Franklin, a member of the Curley Gang. It also confirmed that the two gangs were definitely riding together.

The doctor said maybe two more days were required for Pasch's wounds to heal enough for further movement. Then Masterson, Bullock and Roosevelt could take him out on the train to Denver.

Sheriff Akin paced the office deep in thought as Laura, Minnie and Twocrow waited expectantly on one side and Nellie, Lil, Jack and Will on the other. Lil was still dressed in her ranch-style clothing and was twirling her felt cowboy hat from hand to hand as she waited. Nellie had changed into an outfit that reflected the latest "Gibson look" sweeping the nation—her shirtwaist accented by a shirt collar, floppy artist bow and ruffle jabot. Her high-waisted skirt swept down in a bell-like style and Laura was casting envious looks in her direction.

The other men stood together by the doorway leading back to the cells, joined by Akin's two chief deputies—Pete Lemley, a lean and wiry cowboy who also was one of Akin's captains in the Home Guard, and Charles Roe, widely regarded as the "Sheriff in waiting" whenever he chose to try for the position.

"All right, here's what we're going to do," Sheriff Akin looked around his office, glancing at his watch before continuing.

"Chalky?" He called back toward the cells and a young man barely out of his teens hurried past Bullock and Roosevelt into the room. "You got all them horses saddled up and ready like I asked? Oh," he added. "Case you were wonderin', this here's our other deputy, Chalky Burrell," he said by way of introduction to the others.

Chalky touched the brim of his cowboy hat, smiling shyly at the three girls, who blushed in return.

Lil held out her hand and clasped Chalky's firmly. "I'm Lil Marr. Pleased to meet you." She gave him a dazzling smile and Jack glared. "Are you the wrangler, too?"

"Well, not exactly, but Sheriff here does trust me to pick out good horses when we need 'em." He grinned again as the Sheriff harrumphed in response. Chalky pointed out the window. "Yes ma'am, Me'n Star got a half-dozen ready. Picked 'em up from Jensen's Livery." He turned back to the Sheriff. "He said you could figure out a payment later on in the week."

"Who's Star?" Laura asked.

"Oh," Chalky blushed. "That's just my horse." He pointed out the window and the girls all looked to where a beautiful brown and white pinto mare stood swishing her tail. Behind her, in a string all lashed together with a long rope, were several horses of various shades, all broader and taller.

"She's beautiful," Laura said. "I love horses, especially beautiful ones like that."

"Yeah, kind of my trademark," Chalky smiled. "Ya see that horse comin', ya know it's Chalky Burrell and Star. Actually, her full name is Morning Star. Day she was born out on my dad's ranch; I thought she was pure white and she looked just like starlight. But, older she's gotten, the more the brown's come in."

"Okay, okay, you can tell 'em about her lineage another day," Akin interjected, growing impatient. "Mister Omohundro here..."

"Jack," Jack interrupted the sheriff. He looked embarrassed at his sudden reaction. "If you don't mind? I don't like formalities."

"Or you can just call him Texas," Will said brightly.

Jack glared at Will, and Will made an exaggerated key turning a lock motion on his mouth. He grinned at the girls. Chalky laughed and Jack shifted his glare to him as he stepped over to stand between the deputy and the girls. Minnie and Laura exchanged a glance at the wrangler's reaction.

"All right...Jack," Akin continued. "Jack here needs to get to the Martin Ranch out in the Gap. Chalky, I want you to ride with him and then get your butts back here as quick as you can. You two ride the back trails up over the north side and you should get there in about an hour. It's eleven o'clock now, so if you forego the 'formalities' out there," he looked pointedly at Jack. "You should be back here by one-thirty; two latest. And stay up on the north side. I don't want any run-ins with the McCartys or the Curleys."

"Don't you think they'll be coming in from the south, Gene?" Bullock asked.

"Yeah, seems most likely they'd come up Fall River Canyon, but you be careful anyway," he directed the last part to Chalky and Jack, who both nodded.

"Thank you Sheriff," Lil said. "And you, too, Marshal." She said the last part with an infatuated lilt to her voice and touched Masterson's arm. He looked down at her hand, nodded, and eased his arm away as both Bullock and Will grinned. Jack looked perplexed but said nothing.

Akin ignored them all and went on with his assignments. "We also still got that little matter of a body up in Wind Cave to take care of. Seth, that's where I can use your help if Bat's okay with you being away for a few hours." He looked from one man to the other and Masterson nodded yet again. "If Bill Twocrow here can take the lead, you can saddle a couple of those fresh horses and ride up there in less

122

than an hour. Roosevelt, you can go too." Roosevelt looked pleased.

"I'd like to get the body out of the cave and back here to Hot Springs, so young ladies I'm going to need you to take that buggy of yours back up there. By the time the girls get there, you think you could have him up to the entrance?" He directed the question to Twocrow.

"Sure, sheriff. Once we get him out of the passage where we found him, we'll be back on the cave's main pathway. Might take about an hour. Not more'n that. We can put him in the back of the buggy."

"Good. Can you girls handle that rig? I don't want either of you going alone."

"I think so," Minnie spoke up. "I'm the one does the driving whenever we go anywhere, but we haven't handled this horse before."

"She's gentle, but strong," Twocrow said. He seemed unsure. "If you can get the rig up there, then I can drive back."

"How about I drive the buggy?" Masterson offered.

"No, I really need you to stay here with me Bat. I'm not worried about the prisoners so much as I am about the brother of that dirt bag back there trying to come in here and get him out. I don't want to be caught undergunned if the McCartys ride into town." He gestured at Lemley. "And I wanted Pete to pick up a couple other members of the Home Guard and ride out a ways to do some scouting. If that gang's headed our way, I'd just as soon have a little advance warning."

He looked out the window. "So, I'm hoping you'll stay here with Charlie and me. We got our own Marshal down these parts, too, but the bank and a general store over in Edgemont was robbed, and he headed over there to investigate. Name might be familiar to you Seth, because his name is Seth, too. Seth Gifford?"

Bullock shook his head and chuckled. "Helluva good first name, but we haven't met."

"Sheriff, I could help," Will said. "I'm good with a buggy," he turned to Lil and Jack. "You can ask them." His friends nodded their agreement.

"Well, if you can do that young fella, I'd be most obliged." He clapped Will on the shoulder. "That okay with you two?" He looked at the girls. "But only one of you can go with him to show him the way. We'll need that back seat to lay out the body."

"I'll go," Laura said, stepping forward and extending a hand to Will. "We've been talking to each other here for half an hour and really haven't met. I'm Laura Thompson and this is my sister Minnie." Minnie also reached over to shake Will's hand and he responded with a lopsided grin.

"Will Rogers," he answered, taking off his hat and gesturing toward Lil and Jack. "You probably figured out already that I'm with them."

"Let's get going then," the sheriff interrupted. "Time's a'wastin', especially when it gets darker earlier these days. I want everyone back here before 4 o'clock or we'll be sendin' someone out to find out where you're at. I don't need anyone ending up as a hostage for that outlaw gang."

They started heading out the door and Laura stopped to pat Chalky's horse Star on the nose while Lil, Nellie and Minnie looked at one another, then back to the sheriff. Nellie saw that Masterson was staring at her again as if still trying to figure out how he thought he knew her.

Ignoring his stare, Nellie spoke directly to Akin. "Isn't there anything we can do to be of help to you sheriff? It seems like we're all part of this now, whether we want to be or not, so we might as well try to be useful. I'm pretty good at running down information, and Lil's already proven she can handle a rifle." She looked at Minnie.

"I'm a reporter," Minnie said quickly. "Gathering information is what I do!"

The sheriff watched the others getting onto the horses or in the buggy before responding.

"Guess I COULD use some help," he said. "We need to try to figure out if there's anything to this idea that the dead man is this Previn fellow. And if he's really been stayin' up in The Evans like your sister said, then I need to find out more about that, too. You think you three could do some investigating without scaring anyone? I don't need people getting' all panicky over a dead body." He directed the questions more to Nellie than the two younger girls, clearly signaling that because she was older, she would be in charge.

"Consider it done," she said confidently. Nellie felt the stirrings she usually got when taking on a new assignment. "Come on girls." She led her two younger charges out the door and walked over to a nearby tree. Pausing in the shade, she watched as the buggy with Will and Laura rounded the turn and headed north along Fall River. Roosevelt and Bullock finished transferring their saddles over to two of the horses Chalky had brought, mounted and galloped off to catch the buggy.

"I'm glad to hear you're a reporter Minnie. I didn't say anything in there, but I want you to know that I've done some investigative reporting myself— back in New York City. And while I told the sheriff and everyone that my name is Elizabeth—which it is—it's not the name I normally use in my work." Noting the startled look on Lil's face, she hurried on. "It's Nellie."

"Nellie?" Minnie had a puzzled expression of her own. She gasped. "Nellie? New York? Not Nellie

Bly?" Nellie nodded. "I can't bel..." Minnie stopped, at a loss for words, then sputtered, "...you're like...my hero!"

Nellie laughed and Lil's startled face turned a bit darker. "And I can't believe you didn't say anything to me earlier?" She spoke with a slight edge to her voice.

"Well I wasn't coming out here as a reporter," Nellie answered. "I was hoping to just have some time to rest and relax for a few days without everyone wanting to know about going around the world, or fighting off crazy wardens in an insane asylum." She threw up her hands. "But now we've got all this crap going on, and damn it, I want to help. If I'm Nellie Bly, it makes a whole lot more sense for me to do that than if I'm Elizabeth Cochran. You know what I mean?"

She had gotten louder and a bit angrier as she continued and Lil stepped away from her.

"Sure...sorry. Guess I just figured since we dang near got killed together..." her voice trailed off as she looked at Minnie for some sort of understanding of what she was saying.

"Yeah," Minnie jumped in. "That makes sense. I think." She looked from Lil to Nellie and back to Lil. "Hey wait. You just about got killed together? I think I missed that part when we were all inside."

Nellie and Lil glanced back at each other and laughed. Nellie reached out and hugged her young friend. "Come on," she said to Minnie, draping one arm over Lil's shoulders and starting up the street. "We'll fill you in on the way over to the hotel."

CHAPTER ELEVEN

"Definitely shot," Bullock said as they took another look at the body they'd just moved to the main trail inside the big cave. The wall lamps in the open area flickered as he reached down and pulled the man toward him, shook his head slightly and lifted up his coat in the back, holding his lantern closer for another look.

"What are you looking for?" Roosevelt asked, kneeling down beside him.

"Exit wound in the back. But there ain't any."

"Which means?"

"That he was killed with a smaller caliber pistol of some sort," Bullock answered as he pulled the jacket back in place. "Might've been a Derringer."

Roosevelt nodded in understanding. "So he might have been shot by a woman."

"Or a gambler; or someone who doesn't just go around shooting people on a regular basis."

"But if a woman killed him, how'd the body get down here?" Twocrow asked. "He's kind of heavy, you know?" They had just sweated their way out of the narrow passage and the man's body had felt like a bag of lead weights, another reason to stop and rest for a few minutes before making their way back to the entrance.

"Yeah, that's a good question all right," Bullock agreed. "Had to be at least two men to bring him into a place like this." He held the lantern up and looked around. "Sure is a beautiful place though, ain't it?"

"Indeed," Roosevelt agreed, getting to his feet. "This place fits right in with some of the others I wrote about in my book, and just like the others it's the kind of place that every American should see. Definitely a national treasure, Seth."

"Well I don't know about no national treasure Theodore, but it's damn nice I'll say that." He stood up and looked back toward the passage leading to the entrance. "Pretty much a straight shot up there now, right?" Twocrow nodded. "Okay, then you light the path and Theodore and I'll get the body." He reached over and grabbed the man's sleeve to move the body into a sitting position, but the button on the sleeve popped loose and slid backward, exposing his forearm.

"Damnit!" Bullock muttered, now taking the dead man's bare arm and slipping his own hand under it. "Hey," he stopped and lowered the body back to the cave floor. "What's this? Hold that light closer." Twocrow moved in and Roosevelt bent at the waist for a closer look as well. "What's he got on his forearm?"

As the lantern light played across the arm, Bullock sucked in sharply. "Would you look at that," he said. "It's a red Diamond tattoo."

"You mean like the symbol that gang has— that Curley Gang?" Roosevelt asked, instantly recalling the earlier conversation with Sheriff Akin.

"Exactly." Bullock stood. "This man might've rode with the Curleys, or had something to do with Frank Diamond at one time or another." He shrugged. "And maybe that's what got him killed."

*****

"That girl ridin' with you, that Lil? Is she your sister?"

Chalky had been quiet on the ride out to the Martin Horse Ranch, but he had been talking almost non-stop since they started the northern route back toward Hot Springs. They had ridden to the ranch in less than an hour and spent just thirty minutes there, giving their mounts some rest and drinking coffee while giving D.L. Martin a full report on the robbery attempt and loss of the mustangs he had been expecting. The size and beauty of both the Ranch and its existing herd of horses, which Martin had brought in from England a few years earlier, had mightily impressed Jack.

The breeding stock that had been anticipated would have marked a turn toward creating a new line of working horses for the western Dakota ranches, and Martin had been sorely disappointed to learn of the loss. Jack had been thinking further about that when Chalky's question had taken him by surprise.

"No. Boss's daughter," Jack answered.

"She's pretty." He gave Jack a lopsided grin. "You sweet on her?"

"No!" Jack said indignantly. "Even though she's not my sister, she's like a little sister, I guess. Anyway, what's it to you?"

"Nothin', just wonderin' if she's taken, that's all. No offense. But if she's still available, I might want to ask her over to the Chautauqua Park show tonight. I mean," he added hurriedly, noting Jack's face darkening, "if she's not already taken."

"No!" Jack stopped, embarrassed by his own sharp response. "I mean, no," he said in a more normal tone of voice, "she's not taken. But, I heard that it costs a dollar to go to that show. Don't know if Lil'd want to pay so much."

Chalky gave him a curious look. "Sure," he said. They rode on in silence for another minute or two. "But, I was thinkin' if she'd go there with me, I'd just pay…"

"Look, do whatever you want!" Jack snapped, an edge back in his voice. "Besides that would be up to her. I don't speak for Lil."

The two young men rode in silence for another couple minutes, coming up on a rise with a wide sweeping valley to their left flanked by pine-covered hills that were fronted by sandwich-layered rock walls rising a hundred feet or more off the valley floor. To the right, a stream ran up into a series of rocky crags and a long and deep canyon that appeared to alternate between red and gold-colored cliffs.

"They say there's a buried treasure somewhere out in these parts," Chalky waved his hand to the right and back behind them to encompass the surrounding hills and the "gap" through which he and Jack were riding.

"That so?" Jack looked at the panoramic view as they made their way steadily uphill. "So why's it called 'Buffalo Gap?'"

"Well, that's pretty obvious," the young deputy answered. "Back in the day, the buffalo herds had to get up into the hills during the hot summer months and this was the route. It's about the only way they could've gone. Least that's what we've all be told."

Jack nodded. "Sure, I can see that. Too bad there ain't any buffalo left, huh?"

"There's a few, but the big herds ain't been around for years now. You should ask Buffalo Bill about that when we get back into town. He's there, you know."

"Yeah, I know. They say he shot about a hundred thousand buffalo himself—for the railroads. That sound right to you?" Jack half-shouted the question, lightly kicking his horse to have him pick up the pace and keep up with his companion. Chalky had opened up a larger space between them and was having to shout back over his shoulder as he talked.

"One of the reasons I wanted to come on this Black Hills trip was for a shot at meetin' up with him. Heard he was going to be up here. He knew my old man."

Chalky pulled Star to a stop and turned in his saddle. "What? You serious?"

"Yep. My old man was Texas Jack Omohundro, the first. Bill might not want to admit to it, but my I've been told my pop's the one got him started on this whole Wild West Show thing in the first place. They was partners."

"No shit!" Chalky looked impressed as Jack drew closer and they rode on side by side. "What's the story on that?"

"Wish I knew for sure. That's another reason I want to meet Bill. All I heard was how my pop and Bill got this Wild West Show thing going and then my old man up and died. I was barely in britches at the time, but that's what my mother shared with me and until he tells me otherwise, I gotta believe it's true."

"So that's why that Will kid calls you Texas? After your old man's name?"

"Naw, Will don't know nothin' about it. I been callin' myself that, just to keep folks from stumblin' around tryin' to say my last name. Omohundro is a tough one to try'n get your tongue around, so I figured if I got myself some sort-a nickname that'd be better. I grew up down in Texas, so I figured I'd just take on my old man's name, Texas Jack. Plus, when I finally introduce myself to Buffalo Bill, it'll probably get his attention."

"Ya think!" Chalky laughed and urged his pinto forward, re-opening a three or four horse space between them.

Jack slapped the reins on his own horse's flanks and rode up alongside Chalky again. His horse was a lot bigger than Star but the little pinto handled the rough ground much better. "You know, we probably shouldn't be shouting at each other, in case that gang's around here somewhere."

Chalky nodded thoughtfully. He was young, but looked more mature. Jack thought if someone came up and guessed their ages, Chalky would be picked as the oldest, even though he was pretty sure he himself was several years the deputy's senior. Chalky took off his hat and wiped his brow.

"Hot for September," he said, "and for this early." It was already noon and the hot sun was edging to the front of them as they rode west. He looked around, remembering that they should be careful not to cross paths with the McCarty gang. "Good thinking about the yelling. I don't think they'll come this way, but if the Curleys are riding with them, they'll know about this Gap route, too. I heard that a couple of that gang even grew up out in these parts."

"So what's the thing about a buried treasure?"

"Well, back in the late '70s, maybe early '80s, there was two main outlaw gangs operating out of the Southern Hills. One was led by Charley Curley and Frank Diamond, and the other by a guy named Lame Johnny." They rode down a small hill and across a stream as he spoke. "This here creek we're crossin' is a branch of one named for him—Lame Johnny Creek. It runs on out a few miles north of Buffalo Gap—

that's the town, not the gap itself—from up in the hills past Red Canyon and then a bluff called King's Ridge." He waved past some huge old cottonwood trees alongside the creek bed back toward the reddish-gold canyon. "It's all back there."

Jack eyed the canyon walls. "Good place for a hideout, I'd say."

"For sure," Chalky continued. "Lame Johnny was a fairly well-known outlaw who specialized in horse thievin', and they say he had a hideout somewhere right around here. But nobody's ever found it. Not ever. Anyway, like I said, he usually just stole horses and such, but every once in a while he went after a strongbox on various stage routes. Most'a the time he'd just get a few bucks or a couple small pokes a' gold. That was 'til his gang decided to knock off a Homestake Mine shipment."

"Wow. So how much he get?"

"Hard to say, but the story is that it was up over a hundred thousand, and most'a that was in pure gold."

Jack whistled softly and both horses' ears pricked up in response. He leaned over and patted his mount between the ears as Chalky continued.

"The gold was bein' shipped in a special treasure coach that they never figured could be taken, 'cause it was iron-sided and had the guards inside. But Lame Johnny and his partners, they outsmarted 'em. There use-ta be a stage stop up north of Wind Cave on the road toward Deadwood called Canyon Springs. Don't know if it even exists any more, but..." he paused. "I suppose that's neither here nor there, to you, is it?" Jack nodded in agreement, since he had no idea about either the name or the location.

"Anyway, they say Johnny talked a couple of Curley's gang and a 'lady friend' of one of 'em into helpin' him with the robbery. They took her two-wheel buggy all the way from Custer City over to that stage stop. Didn't take much for her to occupy the stationmaster with her charms—if you know what I mean?" Jack nodded once more.

"Anyways, so after she had him 'indisposed,' so to speak, Johnny and the other men rode in took the place over and just waited for the coach to arrive. When the guards opened the treasure coach's back door to get out for water and a privy break, the outlaws come a'barrelin' out of that station and started shootin'. Time they was done, one of the guards and one of the gang was dead and the other two guards was shot up pretty bad."

They rode up to the top of the ridgeline and stopped. Chalky pointed off to the northwest.

"They say the gang made off with seven or eight thousand in cash, about the same in diamonds and jewelry, and damn near 700 pounds of gold dust, nuggets and gold bars. The stage stop manager said he saw four men and that woman load it all on her two-wheeled buggy and drive southeast toward the gap. There's just two ways out from there. One up to French Creek and out and the other right along this here path. And that's the way the tracks seemed to go, too. The Custer sheriff followed those tracks for miles and then, just a coupla miles from here, the tracks just up and disappeared into thin air."

Jack whistled again. "Seven hundred pounds! Holey Moley! And they couldn't catch 'em tryin' to spend it?"

"Nope," Chalky answered, clucking to Star and starting at a trot again. "But the sheriff out of Chadron swore he shot and killed two of the gang down there, 'cause they had some of the missing jewels on 'em. And, just a coupla days later, he and his men captured Lame Johnny himself. Johnny had about a thousand of the cash, but there was no sign of the gold, and never no sign of those other gang members either. Neither the man nor the woman, or that woman's buggy."

"Well, couldn't Johnny tell them more?"

"That's just it. Johnny got put on a stage headed back for Deadwood to stand trial. They were on their way up to Deadwood City when the stage got stopped by a group of men right out by Buffalo Gap where the road we've been on comes out of the hills. The driver said one of 'em told Johnny if'n he didn't tell them where that gold was hid, they'd hang him off the three-trunked cottonwood tree."

He pointed back in the direction from which they'd been riding. "On the other side of the Martin Ranch, there's a big three-trunker that sort-of marks the entrance to the gap, so I'm thinkin' that was the one."

Jack looked at him in disbelief. "You mean they hung him?"

"Sure did, in that big old tree right along the Beaver Creek—that's the main branch of these streams running along here. A couple years later, though, everyone kept talkin' about the north branch of that creek, sayin' that's where Lame Johnny got himself hung. They started callin' that north branch Lame Johnny Creek." He shrugged. "Only, like I said, I don't think he was hung there. It was south, alongside Beaver Creek." He shrugged again. "But, who'd know for sure?"

"But how was he gonna tell 'em where the gold was hid if he was hung?"

Chalky laughed. "Yeah, that's the question, ain't it? Guess you didn't have to be too smart to be in a lynch mob them days. And for damn sure, once Johnny was hung he couldn't talk no more about that gold. To make matters worse, it had been rainin' hard for a couple days, so any chance of re-locating those wagon tracks was washed away, too.

"The Sioux, they say that area where the wagon was headed is protected by Tatanka, a guardian spirit warrior. And that's why the wagon tracks disappeared. Tatanka didn't want any intruders spoiling the land."

Jack looked skeptical.

"Anyway," Chalky continued, "that gold's been missing ever since."

Jack looked over to the north and pointed at a huge ridge topped by a rock outcropping. "Is that King's Ridge?"

"Yeah. But believe me, everyone and his dog has looked around these parts. I think they either buried that gold, or they found themselves a cave—like Wind Cave over to the northwest—and just stashed it in there until they could come back later. Problem is, of course, they didn't come back."

"Except maybe for those two that ended up missing," Jack said. "That would be one of the other shooters and the woman, right?"

"Well, sure, but if they'd come back for the gold, why didn't it start showing up someplace? I'm thinkin' the gang all split up and figured they'd meet again and share the gold. Three of 'em took the cash and some of the gold dust, and the other two took the jewels. Only nobody made it back.

"The missing man might of got himself shot up or thrown in jail somewhere; somethin' like that. And the woman, well it weren't a good time to be a woman around these parts back then—especially if you were one workin' in the 'profession' like she was. She probably ended up dead in some saloon; maybe even back up in Deadwood."

They rode silently for a few more minutes before Chalky spoke up again.

"So that 700 pounds of gold is still out here—just waitin' to be found." They rode over the crest of the next hill and a broad valley, interspersed with sinkholes and clumps of cottonwood trees, spread out before them. Right at the point where the last of the hills ended, a small frame ranch house was built up against the hill. Across a yard to the west of the house stood a horse barn and a haystack.

"That's the Anderson place," he said to Jack. "Usually just Paul and his family this time of year. We probably better warn 'em about the Curleys, just in case they do ride around this way." Jack nodded his agreement as they increased their pace and galloped down toward the buildings.

The ranch appeared deserted.

"Must be out to one of the pastures," Chalky rode into the yard and pulled up near the house. "Usually their old dog raises holy hell as soon as he sees anyone approaching. Hello!" he shouted. "Anybody home?"

The ranch stead was eerily quiet except for a few chickens scratching in the dirt near the barn and a cat lazing inside an overturned woven wood basket lying just outside the barn door. Several ears of corn lay scattered near the basket as if they'd fallen out when it dropped to the ground. The cat, a calico, stretched both front feet out over one of the basket's iron handles and yawned, its pink tongue lolling forward then seeming to reel back in as it half-stood and looked aloofly in their direction.

The ranch house door opened, and a small woman stepped into the doorframe, holding her hands on her dingy white apron. "Hey Chalky," she spoke evenly as if thinking about what she wanted to say. She brushed nervously at a few strands of her brown hair that had dropped over her eyes as she glanced at Chalky's companion. Jack could see that the woman had been pretty at one time, but now she looked a bit worn out; tired; or something else that he couldn't put a finger on.

"Hi Irene. How're things?" Chalky climbed down from his saddle and took a couple steps in her direction, removing his hat and whapping it alongside his leg to get some of the dust out of it. As he walked forward, Star drew back a step or two, tightening the reins in Chalky's hand. He turned and handed the reins to Jack. Both horses shuffled sideways, their hooves stirring up the dust in the afternoon sun.

"Things're good. Where you comin' from?" She gave a questioning look in Jack's direction, making just the slightest nod toward the door as if trying to convey something without saying it.

Chalky gestured towards Jack. "This here's Jack Omohundro. Goes by Texas Jack." He pointed at Irene. "This is the lady of the place, Irene Anderson." She nodded. "Jack's visitin' in from The Oklahoma Territory. We're just ridin' back from Martins'."

"You buyin' horses?" she asked, directing the inquiry at Jack.

"Sellin'... well, sort of," he said, tipping his hat to her. "It's a long story."

"Wish you had time to tell it," she answered, looking over her shoulder and re-wiping her hands on the apron before brushing back again at her wispy hair. Jack's horse whinnied and Star bumped against them.

"Star, what's the matter with you? Easy girl." He stroked the pinto's nose and looked back to Irene. "Might be some trouble comin', so thought I should let you know," Chalky said. "You ain't alone here are you? Paul around?"

"No," she hesitated just a second before answering. "That is, Paul's over to the northeast valley, but he oughta be back by nightfall. Boys're helping out over at the Driscolls for a couple days. What's goin' on?"

"Curley Gang's on the loose and they might be comin' this way. Gene thinks they might'a robbed the bank and dry goods store over in Edgemont and this morning they tried to rob a train down south of Oelrichs—them and some other boys ridin' with 'em outta Nebraska." He pointed to Jack. "Jack here was on board when it happened."

"Well, that's all to the south and west. You really think they'd come up here?"

"Probably won't, but since the Curleys know the area, they might think it's easier to get into town this route. See, we got a couple of their gang in the Hot Springs jail, and Gene thinks they're gonna try to spring 'em. "

"Well, maybe you better get back to town then. No need hanging around here." She gestured toward his horse and looked nervously back into the house.

Chalky looked up at Jack, slipping his hand over to his gun.

"You mind if I get a drink of water before we go?" Chalky put his hat back on.

"Oh. Um. Sure. You wait here and I'll get it for you." Now, she had a frightened look on her face.

" I can just go get a dipper full at the pump by the barn. No need to trouble yourself."

"No! Wait!" she spoke sharply and Chalky gave her another puzzled glance.

"Irene? Everything okay?"

She started to back up, then stopped and sucked in sharply, emitting a little squeak as a shadow filled the door behind her and a six-gun appeared over her shoulder, followed by a heavy-set man with a greasy drooping mustache and a large scar on his right cheek. His left shoulder was heavily bandaged.

"Hey," Jack pointed at the man. "It's one of the guys from the train. One of the robbers!"

"What the hell?" Startled, Chalky stepped back, pulling at his gun as he moved.

The man fired, and Irene screamed and jerked a hand up to her ear as Chalky's face paled and he grabbed his right shoulder. Blood started flowing down his arm and he tottered to his right side, his gun falling to the ground. Jack kicked his horse lightly and leaned in to keep his companion from following the weapon. Irene rushed forward and grabbed for the wounded deputy, helping ease him to the ground. The shooter pushed past her aiming the gun at Jack's face.

Jack dropped the reins on Chalky's horse and raised one hand, holding tightly to his own reins with the other one. In a flash, Chalky's little pinto snorted, wheeled around and raced away past a second man coming toward them from the barn, a rifle in hand.

The horse whinnied loudly and reared up as the second man first tried to stop her, then ducked out of the way. Unencumbered, Star shook her head and continued down the path they had been following before reaching the ranch.

"Get off that horse or I'll shoot you off!" the first man ordered. Jack dismounted, startled to see two more riders descending quickly in their direction along the same path he and Chalky had been on before. He started reaching for his horse's reins and cried out in pain as the second man cracked the barrel of the rifle down sharply on the back of his head. He half-turned toward the man and everything went black as he crumpled to the ground.

CHAPTER TWELVE

The Evans Hotel's main desk area had a long, low ornately carved wooden check-in counter. Along the right-hand side was a tall wooden postbox style cabinet with pigeonholes for each room number and rows and rows of hooks filled with leather tabbed keys. A bright brass bell sat on the end of the counter alongside a sign reading "Welcome to The Evans Hotel. Clerk on Duty: Harry Clark."

Behind the bell and the signs was the doorway to a large safe where patrons could check bags or other valuables during their stay.

On a display table directly in front of the counter was the remnant of a large curved bone. A sign next to it read: "Prehistoric Mammoth Tusk uncovered along Fall River, June 17, 1892." The tusk was starting to disintegrate from people handling it, and bits and pieces of it lay scattered on the tabletop.

Nellie, Lil and Minnie huddled beneath the two large chandeliers hanging from the ceiling over the lobby's plush seating area, eyeing the safe as they talked. Nellie nodded politely to a middle-aged couple who she recognized from the train as they exited off the elevator and made their way over to the leather upholstered chairs and settled in to watch the other patrons come and go. Minnie gestured toward a rack of newspapers that included the *New York World* and both her and Laura's papers—the *Buffalo Gap News* and the *Hot Springs Star*.

"See, we're ALL represented for the patrons' reading pleasure," she said proudly, then frowned as the man who had just sat down stood up and took the copy of the *World* off the rack, ignoring the two local newspapers.

"There's no way the clerk'll let us have a look at those bags," Lil said, seemingly oblivious to everyone and everything except the safe. "But I wonder if we could get into Previn's room?" She looked at the key she'd received earlier when checking into her own room. It was skeleton style encased in a spearpoint-shaped leather sheath that had the room number embossed onto the area above the looped end of the key. "Don't these keys all look alike to you? They sure do to me."

Nellie fished in her bag and pulled out her own room key. Aside from the number, it looked pretty much identical to the one Lil was holding.

"Yes, looks the same to me, too," she said, turning it over in her hands. "But it must be just slightly different?" She looked at the girls. "They wouldn't have all the keys be the same, would they?" They both shrugged. "Although, who would think that they weren't different? Different numbers; maybe even different floors. So, why would anyone even think to try a clearly numbered key in one of the other doors?"

They looked back toward the desk.

"We need to find out his room number," Minnie said, pacing a couple steps as she contemplated the options.

"Hello ladies!"

A man's booming voice filled the lobby. The couple reading the newspapers looked up at the intrusion, and Nellie and her friends turned toward the elevator where William Allen White had just emerged. Beaming, he walked briskly in their direction. "Sallie's next door at the Minnekahta baths soaking in the hot mineral spa, so thought I'd go to the dining room and see about coffee and a pastry. Maybe you'd like to join me?"

"Hello William," Nellie held out a hand to greet him and White shook it vigorously, then grasped Lil's next, as Nellie gestured toward Minnie. "This is our new friend Minnie Thompson. She's a reporter for the *Buffalo Gap News*."

"You don't say?" He extended a hand in her direction and Minnie hesitated before finally reaching over to shake it. "I'm a newspaperman myself. So, a girl reporter. You planning to take after Nellie Bly?"

"But, how did you know she was here?" Minnie turned toward Nellie. "I thought you said..." Minnie stopped in mid-sentence, silenced by the scrunched-up expression on Nellie's face. White appeared stunned at the exchange. "Ummm," Minnie said. "I mean..." she hunched her shoulders down, half-shrank toward the floor, and looked back up in Nellie's direction, hands clasped tightly in front of her while trying to avoid Nellie's glare. "Sorry."

"Nellie Bly? Really?" White half-swallowed the second word as Nellie grabbed him by the arm and dragged him toward the marble fireplace. Minnie and Lil trailed behind trying to set up a bodily screen between themselves and the other people in the lobby. As they pulled up in a scrum near a window, Nellie grabbed both his shoulders and squared up directly in front of him. White glanced back over his left shoulder and found himself looking directly into the faces of the two girls. He turned back to look at Nellie again. "Really?"

"Yes," she whispered. "Really."

"Oh my god!" he whispered back. "Sallie's going to go nuts. She *loves* you!"

Nellie rolled her eyes. "I'll tell her myself, okay? But right now you've got to promise to keep my identity quiet. The girls and I are helping the sheriff, and I can't have everyone knowing who I am. It'll screw things up. Promise?"

White looked around again and the two younger girls nodded in tandem.

"Is it a story?"

"Maybe; maybe not. The only way we're going to find out is if we cannot have everyone all starstruck because they want to meet the 'Amazing' Nellie Bly," she said, accenting the amazing in self-derision. "Now, like you said, you're a reporter, too, so as one reporter to another—please shut up about who I am!" Nellie had been squeezing his shoulders harder and harder as she made her point and as she finished, White reached up and peeled one of her hands away.

"Ow," he whispered, "and okay. Sheesh." He glanced around the lobby, but neither the couple with the newspapers or the deskman was paying any attention to them. "So, what's the story?"

Nellie turned and walked deliberately over to another small seating area in the corner and sat down on one of the ornate leather chairs. White took a seat across from her and the girls plopped down together on a small settee. Over the next few minutes they alternated between what they were doing and what had happened as he edged forward on his chair. "Holy shit!" he finally exclaimed, then reddened a bit as he glanced at the two younger girls.

"Yeah, holy shit!" Lil responded. "And, we gotta find a way to get into that dead guy's room."

"I could try to convince the deskman that I'm here to do an interview with him and if he'd give me the room number I could go there and meet with him." Minnie stopped talking as incredulous expressions formed on the others' faces. "What?"

"You have to be joking," Nellie said. "Either he'll think you're a flake or a prostitute, but either way he's not going to give a young girl a middle-aged man's room number. Even if he IS here with his wife." She waved her hands. "Not in a classy place like this."

"Look, I'm still wanting that coffee and pastry," White interjected. "Let's go into the dining room and talk. We can figure out something there and not out here in front of everyone. Okay?" They looked at one another and Minnie broke the silence.

"Actually, I AM kind of hungry. We didn't eat after we found that man's body—sort of lost our appetite. And all our food is still in the buggy, up at Wind Cave with Laura."

"She's probably having a picnic up there right now," Lil said with a smirk. Then she giggled. "Especially with Will along. He'll eat anything and everything, dead guy or not. He could join Buffalo Bill's show as The Amazing Eater."

"Wait a minute," Minnie had been moving toward the dining room, but she stopped and turned toward her companions. "Buffalo Bill's here, right? And your friend is named Will?" She looked over at Lil who nodded. "And, you're William?" White nodded. "Alvin was right; everyone IS named Will, William or Bill these days."

"Who's Alvin?" White looked confused.

"Our friend. Alvin Twocrow. He's the one who took my sister and me into Wind Cave where we found that Previn guy's body. Only now he wants us all to call him William or Bill." White still looked confused. "'Cause he says everyone important these days is named either William, Will or Bill."

White smiled. "Can't say I disagree with him on that point. Ow!" He reached up and rubbed his shoulder again as Nellie hit his arm, then grabbed him and jerked him through the doorway into the dining room. "Anyone ever tell you that you got a mean streak?"

"Come on, sit down!"

They gathered around the nearest table in the elegant dining hall, which was filled with rows and rows of white linen-covered oak tables accented by napkins folded in bishop hat style at each place setting. High-backed wood chairs with heart-shaped leather seats surrounded each table, and ornately carved pillars were interspersed throughout the room. As White held out chairs for the girls, an older black waiter with a white cloth dangling over his arm sprang to greet them. A second, much younger waiter also was in the room, but he was absorbed in a conversation at a nearby table with a middle-aged white man.

The waiter approached carrying a tray filled with crystal goblets, his highly polished shoes clicking on the glossy cherry wood floor. Minnie and Lil appeared awestruck by the whole scene. "This place also gets a 'holy shit!'" Lil said in a low voice. Minnie clasped a hand over her mouth to try to stop herself from giggling.

"Sir. Madam. Young ladies. I'm so sorry, but we don't serve lunch in the Evans, only breakfast and dinner." The waiter greeted them as he reached the table. "Or we could bring you some coffee or tea." He placed the goblets in front of each of them as he spoke.

"I think we WOULD like some pastries if that's acceptable, and..." Nellie paused and looked to the girls, "...tea?" They both nodded.

"Coffee for me," White interjected.

"Yes sir," the waiter bowed slightly. He gestured at the goblets. "Can I get you some water?"

"Yes, please," Nellie answered.

The second waiter, who looked to be in his late teens, glanced over at the scene, said something to the man he was with and stood up, hurrying over to their table.

"I can help if you want?" he said deferentially to the older man, "Me and Mister Metz finished with our talk." The man at the other table half-saluted toward them, stood and walked out toward the lobby, whistling a catchy tune as he walked.

"Thank you Joe," the older man said. "You serve them some water while I go to get their order." The older man hurried away, the empty tray in hand, as Joe walked to a serving station, picked up a pitcher of water and returned. "This here water comes direct from the Kidney Springs," the young waiter said. "Or, I can bring you some Cold Springs' water if you prefer. Both of 'em are upstream from the Evans Fish Pond, so no fear of getting any 'fishy-tastin' water when you come in here." He beamed.

"Kidney's the spring just across the street and down from the Union Depot where your train came in," Minnie explained. "Water there's supposed to be therpeu...therma-...uh, very good for your health. It bubbles out there beneath that gazebo thing—the one topped with the statue of that naked Indian girl holding an electric light." She blushed. "I'm not sure what she had to do with it, but something I guess."

"Oh! That there was a princess from the Sioux tribe, accordin' to the legend," the waiter said, beginning to fill their glasses as Nellie gestured her okay at the pitcher in his hand. "I been learnin' more 'bout her every time I'm goin' through the passageway over to get the water." He flashed the two girls a brilliant smile and they both blushed in return.

"There's a passageway?" White asked.

"Yes sir. Two of 'em. One runs from under the hotel to the bathhouse just across from Kidney Springs. And there's another one runs up the back side of the hotel to each of the floors. We can get that mineral water any time and take it right up to any room—same thing with food and hot drinks and things folks might order; just like magic, or somethin'. Never have to bother folks by goin' through the lobby."

He smiled and stepped back as the first waiter returned, carrying a tray filled with hot drinks and a platter of pastries. The girls eyed them hungrily, and Nellie motioned for them to start eating as she put a finger to her chin and looked across the dining room toward the street side windows.

"So, no one would see you going back and forth or up and down. Is that what you're saying?"

"That's right, ma'am." The waiter glanced at his companion, not sure if he should say anything more now that the senior waiter had returned.

"How do you know what rooms to take things to?" White asked, taking a huge bite from one of the pastries as he spoke.

The older waiter cleared his throat and the young one stepped back. "Well, you see, our front deskman'll send us messages from the guests and give us their room numbers. So, we can take things any time, either up to a room for room service, or to leave there when the guests is out. We prides ourselves on prompt and quiet service. And sometimes folks'll want somethin' a bit stronger to drink at night—without disturbin' anyone else; you know?"

"Oh, certainly," Nellie answered, sipping from her teacup. She turned toward the girls. "You know what would be fun?" They shook their heads, mouths filled with food, as Nellie looked back at the two waiters. "Getting a chance to go up the secret back passageway. We could go back to our rooms that way. It'd be an adventure!"

She winked at the girls and Minnie squealed. "Oh, Auntie Elizabeth. That would be so exciting!" She clapped her hands and grabbed Lil's wrist. "Don't you think so, too, Cousin Lillian?"

Lil scowled. "I told you...*Cousin* Min...don't call me Lillian no more. Now that I'm grown up I want to be called Lil." She smiled sweetly at the younger waiter while leaning back in her chair to emphasize her figure. "As anyone can see, I'm NOT a little girl anymore." She gave the waiter a sweet smile. "I'm Lil. What's your name?"

The waiter appeared embarrassed. "Me?" She nodded. "I'm Joe. Joe Hayden. And this here is my shift boss, Sam Bass." He smiled broadly as he waved his hand in Sam's direction. He stepped back again as the older waiter gave him a withering look.

"Lil! Stop being so forward," Nellie admonished her. "See, you're embarrassing the gentlemen, and they won't want to take us up through that secret passageway." Nellie kicked her lightly under the table and Lil jerked her leg back, startled by the action. "And you WOULD like that now, wouldn't you?" Nellie glanced around the table. "Perhaps your 'Uncle Will' should go check at the front desk for messages while we finish our pastries and tea, and then we can all go back to our rooms."

William was adding cream to his coffee and glanced around at Nellie's comment.

"Oh!" he finally exclaimed. "Yes, of course. I'll just finish up this cup and then go check ... for any messages and ... and things." He took a drink of coffee and grabbed for the rest of his pastry, starting to stand.

"Sir," the waiter Bass interrupted his movement. "Why don't you just finish up your coffee in comfort and I'll have Joe go check for any messages. If that's okay with you? After he checks for them messages," he paused and looked around while winking at the girls, "he can show all of you that SECRET passageway to the top floors."

Nellie gave him a dazzling smile. "Why, thank you Mister Bass. That's so very kind. It'll be fun for the girls to have an adventure."

Bass nodded. "Now, do you want the bill for the tea and coffee put onto your room charge, or will this be a CASH transaction?" Bass asked, emphasizing the word and glancing back toward where the secret stairway was located.

"Cash, of course!" Nellie spoke up as she followed Bass' gaze. She reached over and took her bag. "We always like to pay for *special* things in cash, don't we girls?" They nodded in unison, seemingly transfixed by what was going on. Nellie opened her bag and took out a five dollar gold piece. "Will this cover...everything?" She waved her arms airily. "And, of course, we would want you and Mr. Hayden to keep the balance as a gesture of our gratitude for our secret passage adventure, and maybe some help with other things in the future."

"Of course. Thank you ma'am," Bass answered. "Joe, you just make yourself available to these fine folks. All right?" He started away, and then turned back, extending the gold piece between his thumb and forefinger. "And I'll make sure you get some of this with your next paycheck." He walked out of the room.

"Make sure you get at least a dollar," Nellie spoke up. "And after we're done with our 'adventure' here, you'll get another dollar from us, too. Okay?"

"Yes ma'am!" Hayden grinned.

"Oh, and Mister Hayden, do you think you could find out the room number of a friend of ours staying here at the hotel? The man's name is Alexander Previn."

"Why sure, ma'am. That shouldn't be no problem. I can even take you to his room." He smiled again and looked up expectantly as Metz reentered the dining room and signaled toward him.

Hayden signaled back. "Listen, I'll be back just as soon as I finish up over there with Mister Metz. He's the leader of that Minstrel Show Band that's in town, and we're workin' on a new song together. Maybe they'll even play it at the Chautauqua tonight." He spun around and began whistling the same catchy tune Metz had whistled earlier. As he walked away, he began singing "Gonna be a hot time in de old town tonight!"

"That IS a catchy song," Minnie said under her breath as they watched the young waiter huddle with the bandleader at a small table near the door. "Wonder what they're going to call it?"

CHAPTER THIRTEEN

"That oughta hold him all right," Bullock panted as he finished tying a hitch knot around the dead man's feet, lashing his body firmly to the back corner of the buggy. He turned to Twocrow. "Do you want to drive him and take the young lady?"

"Laura," she interrupted.

"Laura," he continued. "If you could drive the rig Bill, young Will here could go in on your horse."

"Sure," Twocrow responded. "Besides, I know the countryside. Won't accidentally be drivin' into some prairie dog hole—especially with all these afternoon shadows."

"Yeah, you know any quicker way back to town? I don't think Gene wants any of us out here after four o'clock."

"You bet," Twocrow nodded. "If we go up over that hill there, instead of following the road, we can go right through the Anderson Ranch and save two or three miles. We could probably be back in town in about an hour at most going that way."

"Good idea to warn them, anyway," Bullock said. "There any other ranch folks out this way? Might be a good idea for us to warn them all about the Curleys, just in case."

"Driscoll Ranch is down to the right a mile or two." Twocrow pointed at a series of gently rolling hills to the southwest, backed by a long, wide mesa. "See that big flat-top mountain? Their ranch is down next to the creek that runs along the back side of it. If someone rode straight up through those little hills and across the top, they could get right into their ranch. The main road sort-a splits the two properties."

"I know that place," Laura said. "I rode out there to interview the Driscoll girls about ten days ago." She turned to Twocrow. "You know, when they did so well in that riding competition? We wanted a story in the *Hot Springs Star*." He nodded his recognition. "We could go to their ranch and then cut back to the southwest right into the north side of Hot Springs. Meet you there and head on into town."

"But the buggy won't go up over that mesa," Twocrow answered. "We'd have to go way down the road, then double back along the creek to get to their place. It'd take a lot of extra time."

"Who's talking about the buggy?" Laura walked over to the horse Twocrow had ridden back up to the Cave's entrance, and quickly slid her foot into the stirrup and swung up into the saddle. Her skirt billowed out on both sides but she merely bunched it up around her waist, her bloomers fully exposed as she adjusted her feet in the stirrups. "I'll just take YOUR horse. Which one of you wants to ride with me?" She looked expectantly at Roosevelt and Bullock as she undid her hat, tucked it behind her head, and tied its decorative ribbons tightly under her chin to hold it in place.

"Laura!" Twocrow had seen Laura ride astride dozens of times and had even ridden with her, but they'd never done it in the company of other men. And she usually had on a divided skirt when she rode that way.

"Oh, for crying out loud," she responded. "I'm covered and everyone here is a gentleman, right? Besides, I can ride as good as any man, and you know it, BILL!" She turned the horse toward Bullock and Roosevelt. "Unless either one of you is embarrassed to be seen in the company of a woman riding astride with her bloomers exposed, then I suggest one or the other of you get on your horse and let's get moving. Otherwise, I'm going without you."

"You and Lil have a lot in common," Will half-sighed. "And, I'm reckonin' that this means I'll be ridin' back to town in the buggy with old Bill here." He climbed dejectedly into the passenger side of the buggy, took off his hat and put it on his lap.

"I'll ride with her Seth. I like your gumption, young lady," Roosevelt said, tipping his big floppy hat in her direction as he mounted up. "I have a ten-year-old daughter of my own, Alice, who would probably want to do the very same thing." He looked over at Bullock. "At least I hope she would. Maybe best that you stay with our murder victim Seth, even if we both ARE officers of the law." He winked.

Bullock nodded his agreement, walking over to Roosevelt's horse. "I was just gonna suggest the same thing Theodore. But you keep your old .40-.90 at the ready," he added, tapping the Winchester rifle in the buckskin-fringed rifle case alongside Roosevelt's saddle. "And don't take any chances with anyone who don't seem right."

Roosevelt pulled up his right hand into a salute and turned his horse in quick pursuit of his pretty young companion as Laura kicked her horse in the flanks and galloped up the hill.

"All right, let's get movin'." Bullock gestured toward the cross-country direction Twocrow had pointed out earlier and the young Indian flicked the horse's reins in response, turning the buggy off the road and heading in a southeasterly direction toward the Anderson Ranch.

Caught off guard by the sudden start, Will flailed around with his right hand, searching for something to stabilize his body, while snatching at his hat as it started to blow away. Chuckling, Bullock climbed onto his horse, took out his own rifle to make sure it was loaded and ready, then chirped to his horse, who responded by breaking into a quick gallop after the rapidly receding rig.

"Is this the same direction as the Martin Ranch?" Will shouted over the clatter of the buggy's wheels.

"Kind of," Twocrow kept the reins in his right hand and pointed with his left. "The Anderson Ranch is about two miles dead ahead, and from there we'd have to veer to the east and follow the creek on down through the gap. Martin's Ranch starts a couple miles up into the gap from the east side of the Hills."

"So, we might run into Jack and that deputy, Chalky?"

"Maybe, but if everything went okay for them, they should almost be back to Hot Springs by now. But ya never know, I guess." Bullock came galloping up alongside them and they all rode in silence for the next half mile.

"How's the body ridin'?" he yelled.

Will turned around in the seat and looked back at Previn's corpse, which was jouncing up and down on the buggy's rear seat as they sped over the rough terrain. Aside from straining mightily at the ropes across the chest and those holding his legs taut against the corner, he seemed to be sleeping instead of dead.

"Looks okay," he said, glancing up just in time to see a buckboard pulled by a team of huge horses crest the hill to their left coming from the northeast. "Hey, who's that?" He pointed up the hill, and Bullock rode around to the front side of the buggy, holding up a hand for Twocrow to stop. He extracted his rifle from its case and chambered a bullet as the man turned his team and drove toward them.

"Howdy," the driver half-shouted in their direction. He was middle-aged, dressed in a linen work shirt and denim pants with suspenders and wearing a large, floppy black hat. He was unarmed except for a rifle of his own, which remained in its scabbard hooked onto the back of the buckboard's wooden seat. The big horses—a pair of huge Belgian Percherons—snorted and shook at their harnesses as he reined them in and stared at Previn's body. "What's goin' on?"

Bullock edged his horse closer to the driver's side of the buggy, his rifle still at the ready. His sheriff's badge glinted in the late afternoon sun. "Howdy back to you," he answered. "Name's Seth Bullock. I'm the sheriff up in Deadwood. Been down here helpin' out Sheriff Akin with a killing out at the Wind Cave." He pointed the rifle at the body and nodded toward the two young men. "Driver here, Bill Twocrow, works up at the cave. The other one, Will Rogers, is visiting in from Oklahoma Territory."

The rancher nodded and took off his hat. "You boys are a long way from home, then." He gestured at Twocrow, "'Ceptin' for you." He eyed him. "Don't know if we've met. I'm Paul Anderson. Me'n my family own this here land you're ridin' across."

"I think Mister MacDonald and me talked with you one time, a couple months back, when we brought up some boards from Hot Springs that he was using on the Cave's new entryway. You and your sons were drivin' in a few head of calves at the time."

"I remember," Anderson said, nodding his recognition in Twocrow's direction. He touched the brim of his leather hat toward Will, and turned back to Bullock. "So why're you comin' across my ranch instead of takin' the main road?"

"Well, we were tryin' to save some time. And Sheriff Akin has some other problems—another reason we thought we maybe should head over your way and let you know, too. If you don't mind, we can keep movin' and I'll fill you in?"

Bullock reined in alongside the buckboard and they continued on with the buggy trailing behind. By the time they reached the top of the next hill, he had explained everything that had transpired and Anderson had a concerned look on his face. "My two boys are helping out at the Dricolls' Ranch for a few days, so my wife's to home by herself," he said. "Maybe we oughta get her and head into town for the night? Boys'll be fine where they're at."

Bullock nodded. "You want us to wait? We could ride on in together."

"Maybe." He thought about it for a few more seconds. "Yeah, I think that'd be good."

They crested the hill, saw the ranch stead in the distance and started toward it. Anderson stopped his team. "Hold up," he waved an arm back at Twocrow, who reined in the buggy just below the top of the far side of the hill. "Somethin's not right."

"Whad'ya mean?" Bullock asked, staring intently at the ranch buildings, which were a good half-mile away. Everything looked calm.

"What can you hear?"

Bullock listened carefully, but all he could hear was the heavy breathing of their own horses and the sound of a meadowlark singing off in the gully to their left. He shook his head questioningly.

"Nothing?"

"Exactly," the rancher replied. "Too damn quiet. There ain't nothin'. My dog should be raisin' hell by now seein' more'n just me up here on the ridgeline. He's a smart one." He wheeled his team around and Bullock followed as they made their way back across the hilltop and halted next to the buggy. "Somethin' wrong down there," he said as Rogers and Twocrow gave him a puzzled look.

Anderson had an anguished expression as he turned and looked back at the hilltop where they had just stopped. "Geez Sheriff. I'm scared as hell. You think them outlaws are down there?"

"I don't know," the big lawman answered, joining him in looking back to the crest of the hill. "But I know for sure we don't want to go racin' down there hell bent for leather. If they are there, we'll be cannon fodder and your wife won't be any better off either. Any chance she got herself into some sort of hidin' place?"

"Maybe," Anderson answered. "We've got a door out the back side that leads underground to a root cellar in the hillside—over to the northeast side of the house. We keep vegetables and ice stored in there pretty much year-round. If you don't know it, the door looks like a closet off the back room. She might've gone there to hide, I suppose?"

Bullock turned his horse back toward the buggy. "I want you boys to take the rig and cut back to the main road. See if you can meet up with Roosevelt and the girl and get on back into Hot Springs as fast as you can and let the Sheriff know what's going on. Tell Theodore I could use a hand back here." He gestured toward Previn's body. "And don't worry about him. He's dead anyway. Just keep the buggy in one piece and make the best time you can.

"Soon as you get into town tell Sheriff Akin that it looks like the Curleys and McCartys might be comin' in the north way, so whatever he's gotta do to be ready, he oughta be doin' it right now!" Twocrow raised the reins. "Wait!" Bullock pulled his rifle from its scabbard and handed it across to Will. "Take this, too. Just in case. Now get going!"

As the buggy raced away just below the ridgeline heading west, he climbed down and signaled for Anderson to join him, kneeling in the powdery dirt. "Any other way to get closer to your place without anyone seein' us?"

Anderson reached out and broke off a sagebrush branch and began drawing in the dirt. "Here," he said, making a circle. "Here's the house on the northeast and the barn over to the west." He pulled the stick back toward them and made a squiggly line. "Here's the ridgeline where we're at. It leads to a draw that opens up wider from the north to the south as you come down toward the house.

"But here," he drew another squiggly line on the northwest. "This is another set of draws that drain off to the north toward the Lame Johnny Crick. If we head back north a quarter mile and then go west, we can take a draw just below that ridge," he gestured toward a sharply jutting hilltop where the sun was descending. "We'd come up only a couple hundred yards from the back side of the house."

Bullock stood and looked at the hilltop. "And," he added, "by the time we get there, the sun should be straight at our backs."

"So, even if they see the buckboard, it'd be hard to see a rider coming in, too, especially with the barn between us and the house," Anderson said, already climbing back onto the wagon seat. "Riding right behind me, you'd be damn near invisible."

Bullock nodded and mounted up. "My thinkin' exactly."

CHAPTER FOURTEEN

"Room 417—the Governor's Suite. Almost right on top of the secret passageway, and you'd never know it," Hayden said cheerily as he led Nellie, William and the girls through the hidden doorway at the back end of the hallway onto the fourth floor. The door to the suite that they had identified as being Previn's was on their right, indicating the suite backed onto the interior courtyard, giving the occupant both a view of Battle Mountain and the serenity of an inside room.

Hayden pushed the doorway closed, and it was instantly hidden, turning into a floor-to-ceiling painting depicting a waterfall and the hillsides through which they had ridden on the train down Fall River Canyon into the city.

"Your friend, Mister Previn, he must be somethin' special, gettin' into the Governor's Suite?"

"Oh," William answered after several seconds of uncomfortable silence, finally realizing that the young waiter was addressing him. "No, no, nothing special." He looked inquiringly at Nellie.

"Oh don't be so modest," she said, pushing at the same shoulder she had hit before. He leaned away slightly to avoid direct contact. "Alexander is a very successful businessman," she bragged. "I'm sure Mr. Evans wanted to recognize that when he arranged for the room."

Hayden nodded. "Maybe I shouldn't be so forward 'bout things like that. Don't mean to offend. I'm still learnin' the ropes here and sometimes I talk outta turn, sir."

White tried a nonchalant wave to show he wasn't offended, but it came across as someone swatting at a mosquito. Lil and Minnie struggled to keep from laughing.

Joe touched a windowsill next to the hidden doorway and lifted the window. "This here window looks straight down to the hotel's wine cellar," he told the girls. "Take a look. It's quite a drop."

Minnie and Lil leaned out alongside him and stared down, gaping at the view.

"You ain't gonna believe this," Hayden laughed, "but old Frank Crabill's horse got loose last week and wandered back there and fell right into that cellar. It took half-dozen of us and two other horses to pull that sonofagun outta there." He laughed harder and the girls joined him, enjoying the adventure of looking straight down for nearly six stories and out at the top of the rim of the hidden rock wall that backed the hotel.

"Well," Hayden said, turning and walking over to Room 417's doorway. "I'll just leave you here then," he smiled shyly at the girls, "unless you'd like for me to escort the young ladies off to their own room?"

White gave Nellie an inquiring look.

"Oh, thank you Mister Hayden, but the girls are going to stay here with us for a time before they return to their room." She smiled sweetly. "And, we're so glad to have been able to learn about this secret passageway." She leaned over toward him with a conspiratorial glance down the empty hallway while slipping him a silver dollar. "And we promise not to tell anyone else. Don't we girls?" They gave vigorous nods of assent. "Perhaps we'll see you tonight in the dining room, or maybe tomorrow morning."

She offered him her hand and he looked surprised, took it and bowed slightly before heading off down the hall. He smiled back over his shoulder and gave a friendly wave to the girls, who both waved and giggled in return.

"Okay, knock it off!" Nellie admonished them. "Stop flirting and let's see about getting into this room. Which key you want to try first?"

"Might as well try mine," White said. He pulled the leather-encased key from his pocket. "What happens if none of the keys work and we can't get in?" He held the key toward the door, his hand shaking slightly. "I've never broken into someone's room before."

"Oh, give me that!" Nellie exclaimed, grabbing it from his hand and pushing it toward the lock. She slipped it into the keyhole, then sucked in her breath as the big oak door creaked and clicked open even before she could try the key. She glanced at her companions and gave the door a push. It creaked again as it swung open.

"It wasn't even completely shut!" She gaped at the half-open door, "Let alone locked." She stepped back away from the door, motioning to the girls and White to move to the side. Stepping back to the opposite side, she pushed it further open and looked around the corner.

The room was big and plush with a piano topped by a fringed cloth off to the right, backed by a beautiful painting depicting members of the 17th century French court. An immense canopied bed was to the far left sitting alongside an ornate fireplace, while a loveseat framed the fireplace's other side. Just inside the door and further to the left, they could see a stately hand-carved chair alongside a wrought iron writing table.

"Look at this place," Lil said under her breath. "Holey moley!"

Nellie pushed the door open wider so they all could get a better look.

"Hi there, looking for something?"

The man's voice shattered the intense silence. The girls and Nellie screamed and White flattened back against the hallway wall, holding one hand up to his heart. Bat Masterson's face peered around the edge of the door and he smirked at them.

"Like I said, looking for something?"

"Are you crazy!" Nellie exploded, stepping into the room and pushing him back with both hands. "You scared us all half to death." She looked back at White. "Maybe some of us three-quarters." The girls rushed forward to each take one of White's arms and keep him from dropping to the floor. "What are YOU doing in here?" she added.

"Catching up with an old friend," Masterson answered, a slightly puzzled look on his face as he stepped back to allow the girls to help White into the plush sitting room of the suite and onto one of the overstuffed chairs sitting next to a marble fireplace. "My turn. What the hell are YOU doing here?"

"We came over to the hotel and figured out that there was no way we were going to find out what it was that Previn had checked into the safe, especially since no one knew about him being dead. So, our next move was to get into his room." She looked exasperated. "If we'd known you were going to come over here, too, we would've just come along with you in the first place, since you have a badge and all."

"Umm, I suppose," Masterson gave all of them a perplexed look in response. "Okay, but why are you HERE, breaking and entering into...?"

"Probably the same thing as you!" Nellie interrupted him, frustration in her voice. "We're looking for clues about what happened to our famous Mister Previn. Are we not on the same page here? And we weren't 'breaking and entering'," Nellie said. "The sheriff told us to see what we could find out, and since nobody but us, you and the sheriff knows about Previn being dead, we just couldn't walk up to the clerk and ask for a key, now could we? And since we didn't have either a badge or a famous lawman's name to go with it, we figured we'd just have to use whatever means necessary to get in here and check things out."

"Okay, I get it, but then why come here?" Masterson persisted. "I mean, if you want to go into Previn's room, then you should go to Previn's room, but this room belongs to..."

"Me!" A booming voice from the doorway silenced the rest of the room as everyone turned toward the sound. Minnie stood frozen, her mouth open wide in shock.

"It's Buffalo Bill!" she exclaimed. Nellie was stunned to see the famous western showman filling the doorframe.

"And me," a young woman with long, flowing brown hair, topped with a huge red bow, lifted up Buffalo Bill's left arm and peeked underneath. "Don't forget me." She smiled.

Masterson took a step away from Nellie in the couple's direction. "Hello Annie," he said warmly, a big, crooked grin covering his face. "Great to see you again."

Lil shrieked and jumped to her feet nearly knocking William off his seat in the process. "Annie?" she gasped, pointing at the woman, before rushing toward her. "You mean like in Oakley?" She waved her arms wildly. "It's Annie Oakley!"

She half-pushed Buffalo Bill out of the way and threw her arms around the diminutive woman. Lil looked around excitedly and then back at Annie. "My name's Lil Marr and I want to be a sharpshooter just like you!" The words were tumbling from her mouth in rapid fire. Not letting go of Annie, she looked back over her shoulder at the others. "Annie Oakley! She's my hero!"

"No kidding," Nellie said drily. "Who would've guessed?"

Buffalo Bill rolled his eyes at Masterson. He peered back at Nellie. A glint of recognition came over his face he smiled a huge smile. "Well, well, well, if it isn't Nellie Bly." He strode over toward her as he was speaking. "It's been a few years, Miss Bly, but you haven't changed a bit. What're you doin' out in these parts?"

"Nellie...Bly?" Masterson stammered. He stopped advancing as Buffalo Bill walked right past him and clasped Nellie's small hand in his own oversized one, seeming to swallow up her hand in the process. "You mean the New York writer?"

She shrugged. "Yes," she answered meekly.

"Bat," Cody interjected. "You mean you didn't know who she was?"

"Apparently not," a chagrined Masterson answered, "although I did think there was something familiar about her. And our paths have sort-of crossed before." He cut off the statement as soon as he saw a somewhat embarrassed expression cross Nellie's face.

Cody's booming laugh re-filled the room. "Miss Bly interviewed me back in '88 in the big city itself. Hard to believe it's already been six years. Say, " he added, "why didn't you come and see me in Chicago last fall? I heard you were there and Annie and me were there, too. We were sort-of expecting you, weren't we Annie?"

"You bet," she untwined herself from Lil's grasp and came toward them, holding out her own hand. "Pleasure to finally meet you after all these years. I've heard a lot about you."

Nellie snorted. "You've heard a lot about ME?" She shook the famous sharpshooter's hand. "Umm. Likewise."

William sat limply on the big chair and Minnie plopped down beside him, shoving him over with her hip. Buffalo Bill laughed again and walked across the room, extending a hand to each of them. "You know who I am," he said. "So who are you two? And, by the way, what're you all doin' in my room?"

"William Allen White," White answered, reaching into his vest pocket to take out a small piece of folded paper as he spoke. "I work for the *Kansas City Star*."

"I'm Minnie," the girl added, realizing that White wasn't going to introduce her. "Minnie Thompson. *Buffalo Gap News*."

"Oh-oh, surrounded by reporters," Buffalo Bill grinned at Nellie, back at his friend Bat Masterson, and finally at Annie. "We gotta watch ourselves every step of the way today." He glanced back at White. "But, you still ain't answered my question."

"We're here, sir, because we thought this was the room of a man named Alexander Previn," White said. "The sheriff thinks he's been murdered and he asked Nellie here to see if she could find out more about him. We thought we were going into his room. Obviously, we got some wrong information."

The sound of a throat clearing drew all of their attentions toward the door. "Um, I was just comin' back here to tell you all that." Joe Hayden was standing there, several pieces of paper in his hands and a puzzled expression on his face as he took in the occupants of the room.

"Joe!" Buffalo Bill walked over and clapped the young waiter on the shoulder. Looking back at the others he said, "Joe's been a great help to me and Annie down in the dining room and with whatever else we needed."

"So this is YOUR room, then, Mister Cody?" Hayden asked with a frown.

"Yes, it sure is Joe. Why do you ask?"

"Girls," Nellie interjected, stepping up to Joe and Buffalo Bill and gesturing to Minnie and Lil. "Why don't you take Mister Hayden here out into the hallway and explain what's going on. Can we trust you Mister Hayden?"

"With what, ma'am?" He looked suspiciously at her and the others in the room, glaring at everyone except Annie, who gave him a warm smile. He smiled in return before resuming his glare at the rest.

"Listen...Joe is it?" Masterson walked over and pulled back his coat, showing his marshal's badge on his vest. Hayden gave him a slight nod as he stared at the badge. "These folks are all working with me to help figure out what might've happened to a guest here who turned up dead. Man's name was Alexander Previn. Did you know him?"

Hayden shook his head. He pointed toward Nellie and William. "I thought that Mister Previn was y'all's friend? Ain't that what you told me? That's why I brought you to his room in the first place. Maybe I ought'n go get Mister Bass again. He'd know more about what we oughta do."

"Joe, you can't do that. We need to keep this very quiet until we figure out a few more things about Mister Previn and what might've happened here," Nellie spoke up. "The sheriff asked us to try to get some information about him, so that's why we wanted to get into his room."

"Well that's why I come back," Hayden said. "He's in 471, not 417. I got the wrong information from the front desk." His frown changed to a smile as he walked into the room and over to the window. "The room you're lookin' for is a suite all the way across the courtyard on t'other wing," He pointed out the window and across the central courtyard. "It's a twin to this room, directly across from us." He pointed. "It's that one, right there. The one with the gentleman and lady standing by the window."

Buffalo Bill leaned in to look to where Joe was pointing, cupping his hands around his eyes. "Joe, you see that?" The waiter nodded and they both stood up and turned toward the others.

"Bat, we might want to go over there," Buffalo Bill said. "Couldn't swear to it for sure, but it looks to me like that woman over there is pointing a gun at that man."

*****

"Did you really live and work out here before you got into politics back east?" Laura asked Roosevelt as they rode along the top of the mesa and started winding their way back down toward the main road into Hot Springs. They had ridden quickly to the Driscoll Ranch to warn them of the outlaws' possible arrival—their own arrival garnering a lot of attention from the big ranch's cowboy contingent, who seemed very amused at both Laura's exposed bloomers and Roosevelt's leather-fringed riding outfit.

Her skirt billowed out on both sides as they picked up the pace and she reached out with one hand, then the other, to bunch up the material and scrunch it up under her legs. It made her thighs look big and bulky while her bloomer-covered lower legs dropping down to the stirrups seemed almost like a pair of spindly toothpicks in comparison.

"Yes I did," he answered. "Lived out here in the early '80s, but it was up in Medora, North Dakota—before the states split and it was still Dakota Territory. Did some ranching and served as deputy sheriff. And one spring I worked as a cowboy down here, outside the Badlands. I brought a couple of outlaws from Medora to hand off to Sheriff Bullock, and decided to stay on for the roundup."

He paused as if thinking about that time. "Guess I got my fill of cowboyin' during that month." He exhaled long and slow. "That month seemed like it lasted for half a year."

Laura smiled. "Yeah, I've heard the cowboys in these parts say the same thing and they do it year-around, full time." She glanced over in his direction. "No offense, but you don't look much like either a cowboy or a lawman. Your outfit looks a bit like a city dude's, and with your glasses, well, I'll bet you take a lot of grief, huh?"

He sighed. "I happen to like the way I dress. And if I didn't wear these spectacles, I couldn't see ten feet. You know I could say the same thing about you. You don't look much like a western newspaper reporter either, you know?"

"Exactly what my sister's always saying," Laura laughed. "She thinks I waste my money and dress too 'prissy.' But I just like to look nice. Who knows, maybe someday I'll go off to the big city. And, if that happens, I don't want to go there looking like a country hick...or a western newspaper reporter, whatever that is?"

"Hah, well said. And as for me, all I want is to wear clothing that I find comfortable, and if that makes me look like a 'dude,' as you put it, then so be it," Roosevelt said. "This buckskin tunic was made special for me, and it fits like a glove and wears like iron. And this big hat of mine may look strange, but I'd burn myself to a crisp out in this high plains sun if I didn't wear a big, broad hat." He pulled it off and waved it at the sun and his horse snorted and leaped forward. Chuckling, he quickly replaced it on his head and brought the animal under control.

"As for my spectacles, I've been called 'four eyes' so many times, I'm beginning to think Theodore is just my nickname. But I assure you I can handle myself just fine."

"I don't have any doubt, Mister Roosevelt. You know, I should write a newspaper story about you; I mean, once we get through all this mess with the body, and this outlaw gang and all. You're an interesting man."

"Well...bully for that!" he grinned. "I'm going to be starting a new job soon as Deputy Police Commissioner in New York. How about you come East and do your interview? We could do a sort-of comparison piece—the law out East versus the law out West, so to speak." He waved his arm, "After we finish up with all this, of course."

Laura nudged her horse over near his and held out a hand. "Deal." They shook and she moved her horse back into the lead. "Watch yourself over this next little ridge. There's a bit of a drop off there and we need to jump 'em across." As she finished speaking, she rode up and over and disappeared. Roosevelt urged his own horse forward and saw that she'd already jumped the small ravine and was smoothly moving ahead.

He followed her lead and rode faster to catch up. "You're a fine rider, young lady."

"Laura," she answered. "Well, I dress up nice, but I'm a cowgirl at heart, even if I am from 'in-town.' Grew up on a horse, just like a lot of girls my age. That's why we all want to ride astride and not be treated like we're from some back-East finishing school. You know, out here cowgirls are actually able to ride smoother than most cowboys because they're slender and lithe. And we're tough too. Two weeks back a group of four cowgirls brought a huge herd of cattle all the way up from Cheyenne. Just four of 'em.

"I got to write the story about that one for the *Star*," she said proudly.

"Guess I'm getting to be known as the reporter who writes about unorthodox women. Did the cattle drive story, then a story about the Driscoll girls and that young women's riding competition sponsored by the Evans. We had women riders from all over the Hills for that one, but our local girls did real good."

"Did you ride in it?" Roosevelt asked.

"No. Couldn't. I was the writer, after all. Couldn't be both rider AND writer now could I? Wouldn't be very objective."

Roosevelt's laughed. "No. That's why I think you'll do a bully story about me."

"AFTER I write about this murder and all the stuff that's been goin' on with these outlaw gangs. I told my sister Minnie that going to work at the *Star* would be good for my career."

"I saw the *Star*'s office in that big stone building right next to the Evans Hotel," Roosevelt said. "Have you been a reporter there for very long?"

"Only about a month. My father owns the *Buffalo Gap News*, which is where I cut my teeth on newspapering. Minnie's still out there. And our friend Bill. He used to work for the paper too, before he took on his work at Wind Cave."

"I thought he seemed pretty well-spoken for an Indian lad," Roosevelt responded. "I know that sounds racist, but like I said back at the sheriff's office, I was out here to the reservations once before, and I never met anyone who talked or acted like him. Most didn't even speak English."

Laura explained about Twocrow's background as they crisscrossed their way alongside the hill and down toward the road. "But the Cave was a powerful draw for him. His people see it as sacred."

"Well, I can see why. It's a thing of wonder all right...and beauty. I've got to bring my family out here to see it too—and explore it further myself of course. There are places all over this great country like that, and we'd be smart to set them up as national parks or monuments. Future generations ought to have the same chance to see them that we have today."

"Sounds like another part of my story about you," Laura laughed. "I like your style, Mister Roosevelt."

"Look, if I'm going to call you Laura, then you better call me Theodore," he answered. He reined in his horse and pointed to a small pasture alongside the main road. A brown and white pinto mare was grazing there, despite being encumbered by a saddle, halter, reins and a bit. "That horse seem familiar?"

Laura dug her heels into her own horse's sides and galloped up to the paint. The little mare snorted and shied away. "Star," she said. "It's okay girl." The horse eyed her suspiciously but stopped moving. Laura dismounted and handed her reins back to Roosevelt. "Easy Star, easy girl," Laura continued, holding out a hand. The mare stuck her nose forward to smell at the hand, then stood quietly as Laura reached over and patted her neck.

"It's Chalky's horse Star," she said over her shoulder. "And, look, his rifle's still in the scabbard. That can't be good."

Roosevelt pulled his own rifle free from its buckskin carrier and pointed it back to the northeast. "Quite a cloud of dust being stirred up over there.

And it's getting closer. What do you think? Should we be riding faster toward Hot Springs?"

Laura took Star's reins and handed them up to Roosevelt. She climbed back up on her own horse and cupped her hands around her face to blot out the sun's glare as she looked toward the dust cloud.

"I'm not for sure on this," she said, "but it looks like that dust is being stirred up by my friend's buggy. And he's coming toward us way faster than I've ever seen him go before!"

CHAPTER FIFTEEN

Jack stirred and opened his eyes, struggling to get oriented. Not only was his head pounding but he was dizzy and tied up tightly against the corner post of a bunk bed that had been built into the wall alongside a wood-burning stove. As his eyes finally started to focus, he could see he was in some sort of multipurpose oversized pantry that jutted off the ranch house kitchen; one that was used both for storing food, and as a sleeping area.

Through a doorway leading into the kitchen, he saw Irene Anderson sitting on the floor binding up Chalky Burrell's shoulder. The young deputy was unconscious and covered with blood as was Irene, who kept wiping away more blood as she worked the bandages around the wound at the juncture of his right arm and shoulder.

"He'll need a doctor," she said, finally seeming to get the blood flow stopped.

"Yeah? Well I need one, too, Goddamnit!" The Scar-Faced man spat the words at her as he walked into Jack's line of sight and glared at the ranch woman across the top of a table, his own left shoulder heavily bandaged. "That's why once your old man gets back, he'll be taking a nice little trip into Hot Springs for us." He lit a cigarette and blew the smoke at her, pointing the cigarette at Burrell. "If your old man helps get a doc and get us in and out of Hot Springs, you and your deputy friend here will be just fine."

Looking up, he waved the cigarette in Jack's direction and Jack snapped his eyes shut.

"And him, too, whoever the hell he is?"

It was quiet for several seconds so Jack partially opened his eyes again and tried to see what was happening. Another man with a scruffy red beard wearing a blue-checked shirt had stepped between Irene, Chalky and the table, his leather vest-covered back facing in Jack's direction. The two men were speaking in low voices while filling the air around the table with their cigarette smoke. The checker-shirted man turned and started away from the table and Jack realized he had seen him earlier in the day on board the train.

Jack opened his eyes wider and tried to get his bearings. As far as he could tell it was a typical ranch house. The part of the kitchen he could see had shelves lined with heavy crocks along the back wall just beyond the second man's left shoulder. The small wooden table had four spoked wood chairs around it, and now the two men settled down into two of them, facing one-another as they continued to talk.

A black-bearded man wearing a dark grey hat and blood-red bandana draped over his dark grey flannel shirt stood at the latticed kitchen window holding a cup of coffee and cradling a rifle as he kept watch. He turned toward the table, jerking his neck toward the window. "Charley's back."

"Tell him to get his horse into the barn and come inside," the Scar-Face man said. He turned back to the other man at the table. "Hicksy and the rest of our boys oughta be ridin' in on the south side by nightfall or just after dark. By then the sodbuster oughta be back. Then we can decide what to do about getting in AND out of Hot Springs. I need that doc." He grimaced. "AND I want my brother back!"

Checker Shirt nodded and said something Jack couldn't understand, sitting up straighter and completely blocking his view of Scar-Face. The man at the window walked out of view and Jack heard the front door open and close.

Irene patted Chalky's shoulder, got to her feet and walked toward Jack, a small knife that she had been using to cut strips of bandages off her sheets still in her hand. Jack leaned back slightly as she held a finger to her lips.

"Hey!" the Scar-Faced man stood up. "What're you doing?"

"I thought I should check on him," she said, starting to kneel beside Jack. "His head didn't look too good when you tied him in here, and he's still out cold."

"Tough! Get away from him until I tell you it's okay." Jack closed his eyes again as the man lurched around the table and came toward them. Irene coughed and dropped the knife down alongside her leg and onto the floor as she stood, turning abruptly to meet the incoming outlaw.

"He's still unconscious," she said. "Probably another one for the doctor to check as hard as your friend hit him."

"Yeah, then let's have the doc do that—once he takes care of ME! Gotta have our priorities straight now, don't we?" He coughed hard, then snickered and slapped Checker Shirt on the back. They both laughed before Scar-Face broke into another series of coughs. He leaned heavily on the edge of the table. "Now, get back in here and get us something to eat." She hesitated, glancing at Jack, who fluttered his eyes slightly. "Now!"

The knife was lying about a foot in front of him in plain sight. Jack glanced at it, then up at Irene's face and nodded. He groaned loudly and thrust out both legs, placing one directly on top of the knife.

"Mister..." she began, pretending to turn back toward him.

"Listen lady, I'm not telling you again. Leave that sonuvabitch alone and get your ass back in here; or I'm going to come in there and put a bullet between his eyes." He stepped toward the doorway and pulled out his revolver.

"No, no! Don't!" she said fearfully, hurrying past him and on into the kitchen, where she started pulling out pans and food from the cupboards. The man eyed Jack who groaned softly again and slumped back against the bedstead, his eyes closed tightly. Scar-Face watched him for several more seconds, holstered his weapon and turned around as a clamor at the doorway signaled the entry of Black Beard and another wiry-looking man wearing a beat-up brown hat, faded blue shirt and denim pants.

He said something to Scar-Face and laughed loudly, displaying a mouth nearly devoid of teeth. Chewing tobacco juice dribbled from the corner of his mouth, and he swiped at it with the back of his wrist as Checkered Shirt stood up to greet him. Jack quickly slid his leg back, pulling the knife to his side with his upper thigh and butt. Stretching around with both hands, he strained at the rope binding them, relaxed slightly as the rope shifted, and stretched again, looping his pinky finger across the top of the knife handle. Taking long, slow breaths he began edging the knife along his backside and up into his right hand.

"Anything at the Telegraph's?" Doc asked.

The man shook his head.

"You find that caretaker's hut okay Charley?" Checker Shirt asked the next question as Doc sat drumming the fingers of his right hand on the table. "The others ain't never been in there before."

"Yeah. We rode up around the north side of Cold Brook Canyon, met up with Tom and Harvey, and then came down along the Hot Brook through Bradley Flats. Nobody there, Jake, just like you thought, so they can wait there until we get back. Then we can go find a doctor and bust our boys out of jail at the same time."

The man Checker Shirt had called Charley was speaking as he walked to the doorway and stared in at Jack, who played possum again until Charley turned back toward the kitchen and continued talking. "Seems like they're gettin' ready to do somethin' big at that Tent Pavilion on down the road from that hut. When I rode into town to check the Telegraph Office, I went right past there and it's all gussied up. Lady, you know what's goin' on at that place?"

"There's some sort of grand re-opening show," Irene's voice was interspersed with a clanging sound as she answered while putting pots and pans on top of the wood cook stove. Jack heard water splashing into a pan as she operated the hand pump. "Supposed to be lots of entertainers in town for it, too. Even Buffalo Bill."

"That so? Didn't you know anything about that Jake?" Scar-Face asked.

"Me'n my boys ain't exactly regular visitors into the Springs," Checker Shirt answered. "Jake Curley, Charley Johnson, Harvey Logan and Tom

Ketchum ain't on the invite list for many of them fancy doin's—especially out at that Chaw-taw-qua Park." Curley guffawed loudly as he emphasized the park's name. "So, to answer your question Doc, 'No, I don't know nothin' about that.' But who gives a shit?"

He turned back to Charley. "How about Grace? You get a message to her?"

Charley nodded. "Yeah, she's going to come out to that hut by two o'clock. She'll meet you there."

Scar-Face sank down into one of the chairs and Jack could see him grimace again in obvious pain as he spoke. "I don't like it," he said. "I can't ride any further all shot up like this, and now we got some special event goin' on right in the middle of the town where they're holdin' my brother and one of your boys, too."

"Well, it's not in the middle of town Doc..."

Doc cut him off. "Goddamnit Jake, it's been one fuck-up after another since we joined up with you to hit that train. I don't fucking care if that Pavilion is in Custer City or right next door to the jail in Hot Springs. I just don't want any more surprises or any more to go wrong! You told me there would be a lot of rich people ripe for the pickin' on that train. Instead, we got nothin'. Hell! We got less than nothin'!" the Scar-Face man ranted. "Couple'a my best men killed, another one shot, my brother's taken prisoner, and there's nothin' from those passengers. Nothin'!"

A wracking cough interrupted his rant and he put a hand onto his wounded shoulder. "For your sake, I hope your boys did better'n that over at that Edgemont bank."

"Sure Doc, they got a couple grand there," Curley whined. "But you really can't be blamin' me for things goin' wrong on the train, ya know? There WERE rich folks on the train. A guy Jonas and me were sittin' next to, he talked about meetin' up with his brother and that they had a lot of gold to invest. You know, maybe..."

Doc exploded out of the chair in anger and the other man abruptly stopped talking. Doc's chair tumbled to the floor and Irene gave out a small yelp of surprise. As Charley retrieved the chair, Jack took advantage of the noise to shift upward alongside the bedpost and start slowly moving his right hand up and down, sawing at the rope as beads of sweat formed on his forehead.

"Jake, you dumb-ass!" Doc yelled. "Do you really think some yahoo would be travelin' on a train with a bag full of gold?

"And where in hell is Pasch? You sure there weren't no telegram from him? He said he'd case that Chadron bank, then let us know."

"No Doc, there weren't no word from him one way or t'other," Charley answered, stepping away from the table.

Blood started seeping through the bandage on Doc's shoulder. "And this!" He said as he sank back onto the chair and pointed at his wound. "I can't ride any further," he paused and pointed at Irene, "so we can't wait for her old man to come home. You gotta go back into town now.

"Soon as you get there, go get me that doctor. And while you're at it Jake, go get my brother out of that tin can jail so we can get the hell outta here and back to Nebraska! If not, Jake, then you better have a good plan to get your ass outta Dodge, because I'm going to personally shoot it off! You got that?"

"Yeah, sure Doc." The response came meekly from the big man as he nervously tucked in the back of his checkered shirt as if trying to add padding to his rear end.

Jack could not see the big man's face, but he imagined how it must look. It was at that second that he felt one of the rope strands give way to his persistent sawing. Jack wriggled his left hand and the rope gave some more. He opened and closed his right hand, clasping the knife handle tighter, then continued the effort. He grimaced as a sharp pain ran through the top of his left hand and blood started wetting the rope where the knife blade had slipped. Biting down hard on his lip to take his mind off the pain in his hand, he wiggled the knife around, got it between his thumb and forefinger and renewed his sawing.

"All right," McCarty groaned in a lower tone of voice. "So, change of plan. Jake, you go get your friend Grace to help you round up some horses or another wagon, or whatever you need and take your boys in there and find that doctor. Then get my brother and anyone else they're holdin' out of that jail. Ringay, Franklin and Silkey are all missing, so they're either dead or in that jail. If they're in there, I want them out."

He gestured toward his left as if pointing to a place. "Packard's leading five of the boys over from the east side through Fall River Canyon, so if the local Sheriff gets wind of them comin' that way, I figure he'll head down there with his deputies to try to stop 'em from getting into town. If he does, that should leave things wide open for you coming down from the north side, right?"

Jake nodded. "What if he doesn't go after Packard?"

"Then I guess it'll be a little tougher job for you won't it Jakey boy?" Doc said derisively. "You told me this Grace, whoever the hell she is, could help you get around town. So get her to help you already!" He slid his chair back a few inches and pointed at Charley.

"Charley, you're in charge here. Wait out in the barn for her old man to come home and bring him in here once he gets here. We're gonna need him and his wagon to take us out of here as soon as I get patched up. And if any of the boys Jake brings back from Hot Springs are hurt, they can ride in the wagon, too. I want to get out of here tonight so that if they come looking for us tomorrow we'll be long gone."

He looked up at Curley. "Good plan, huh Jakey? Now you better get your ass back into Hot Springs before I decide on a plan that doesn't include you."

CHAPTER SIXTEEN

Bat Masterson walked briskly down the hotel's hallway and stopped in front of the door of Suite 471. Buffalo Bill, Nellie, William and the girls had been following closely behind him. Now, they all halted and moved over closer to the inside hallway wall as Bat pulled out his revolver and stood to one side. He reached over with the barrel of the gun and rapped loudly on the door. After several seconds with no response, he repeated the action and this time a man's voice replied.

At the sound of the voice, Nellie inhaled sharply and moved forward to Masterson's side. "That's Robert Seaman's voice."

"What? You sure?"

"Positive. I talked with him for two solid hours on that train."

Masterson pushed the barrel of the gun up to the brim of his hat and scratched his forehead with the weapon. "So what the hell's he doing in Previn's room?"

Nellie shrugged and glanced back as Buffalo Bill came up behind her, a questioning look filling his face. Now, a second man's voice responded from the room.

"Who is it?"

Cody stepped around Nellie before either she or Masterson could respond. "It's Buffalo Bill Cody, sir. Sorry to disturb you. Is Mister, uh...?" He paused and held up both hands, palms up.

"Previn!" they both hissed back.

"Previn in? I was hoping to talk to him."

They could hear a sudden excited exchange between the occupants. The second man's voice, now closer to the door, responded again. "Just a moment." Cody, Nellie and Masterson exchanged a quick look and then Nellie and Bat moved away from the door as the key turned in the lock and the handle started to move. Cody held his ground, filling the doorway.

A well-dressed younger man with a thin face and mustache to match swung the door part way opened and emitted a slight gasp as he saw that it was, indeed, Buffalo Bill at the door. "M-Mister...Cody! Good heavens. Um...Alexander is not here at the moment. What were you...?"

Before he could finish the question, Masterson stepped in front of the showman, leveled his gun at the man and swung the door open wider. The man reacted with a shocked yelp, echoed by a woman's scream and Robert Seaman's angry voice exclaiming, "What's going on?" Seaman stood from the small table where he had been sitting, his face registering both anger and shock. "Marshal Masterson? What are you doing here?"

As Masterson pushed the man back into the room, Buffalo Bill and Nellie hurried in behind them, greeted by a second scream from a stylishly dressed brown-haired woman sitting on a plush settee by the window holding a small pistol in her hand. When Seaman saw Nellie, his face changed to a look of dismay. "Miss Cochran? What on earth?"

"Mister Seaman, are you okay?"

He looked puzzled until he saw that her gaze was directed at the middle-aged woman with the gun.

"Oh, her?" He laughed. "Of course."

Before he could go further, the younger man broke into the conversation. "What are you doing? Why have you come barging into our room?"

"Your room?" Masterson responded. "We were under the impression this room belonged to Alexander Previn."

"Well," he sputtered, "of course it does. And I'm his brother Paulus." He looked indignantly from Masterson to Nellie. He gave an accepting half-smile to Buffalo Bill. "And you Mister Cody? You came to talk with my brother? Whatever for?"

Cody looked helplessly to his two companions for assistance.

"Mister Previn, as you heard Mister Seaman say, I'm U.S. Marshal Bat Masterson."

"Yes, Masterson. So what do you...?" Paulus began before Bat interrupted him again, turning a hand in Nellie's direction.

"...And this is Nellie Bly."

Previn spun back toward Nellie. "The famous newspaper reporter?"

She half-nodded as Seaman's jaw dropped. "What?" he said in a stunned voice.

"Robert, I can explain, but first we need to make sure that you and Mister Previn are all right and not in any danger from whatever that woman is doing with that gun. And, I'm afraid Mister Previn that we also have some rather bad news to share with you about your brother Alexander."

"THAT woman..." Paulus Previn spat at them, "...happens to be my sister-in-law Mollie, and that gun happens to be a collector's item that she was about to sell to Mister Seaman here."

He glowered at Nellie, who shrank back, chagrined by his response just as Minnie, Lil and Joe came up behind her in the doorway.

"Now what?" Previn asked, appearing even angrier by the growing number of strangers coming into the room. "Who's this bunch?"

"And what do you mean, bad news about Alexander," Mollie said, standing up and taking a couple of steps in their direction. "What bad news?"

*****

"No, no, listen to me!" Twocrow interrupted Roosevelt, who had been laying out a plan on how to get the buggy and Chalky's horse returned to Hot Springs while he headed back to help Seth Bullock.

"You don't know your way around here, and I do. You can go back to help them. But I'm going too!"

"And so am I," Laura added, her jaw set firmly as she eyed her friend and the others.

Will sat helplessly on the passenger's side of the buggy, threading and unthreading the noose of the coiled rope in his lap as he waited for the others to make some sort of decision. He pulled the rope into a tight loop just barely larger than his fist and waved it at the western sky. "Time's a'wastin' you know?" He spoke quietly and matter-of-factly and they all stopped talking to look at him.

"He's right," Laura said, "and one of us has to help take that buggy back into town because we're the ones who know the best way. And you drive way better than me Alv...Bill... and you know it. Sheriff Roosevelt and I can go back to help."

"Will can drive the buggy. And besides, you don't know the way across the Anderson Ranch," Twocrow responded. "And, damnit! I do!"

"And you're so stubborn you'd stay out here arguing until nightfall just to get your way, wouldn't you?" Laura stood toe-to-toe with her taller friend and they glared at each other. Twocrow took Laura's arm and pulled her aside, ignoring the frustrated expression on Roosevelt's face.

"Laura, you've got to let me do this," he spoke quietly as he turned his back to the others, looking into the sun, an anguished expression now filling his face. "I'm always the one helping out, or filling in, or learning how to do something new. This is something I KNOW I can do. He reached up and took her other arm and looked her squarely in the eyes. "You and Minnie, and your Dad, and the MacDonalds. Everyone always figures I'm the one who can be the 'helper,' not the leader.

"Ever since I came into the Gap, I've been that little Indian kid who needed someone else's help to get along. But you know my father was a tribal leader before he died. He had the respect of his people; MY people. Now, I can be a leader, too. Laura, I need to DO this!"

Laura had been angrily glaring at her friend, ready for an argument, but now, seeing the pleading look in his eyes, her face softened and she finally nodded. "Okay." She lifted her arms under his, wrapped them around him and hugged him fiercely. "But if you get killed, I'll never forgive you. You got that?"

He gasped as the air was squeezed out of him, following up with a small laugh. "Got it. Don't get killed. Sounds like a good plan."

He grinned, hugged her back, and turned around to face Roosevelt and Rogers. "So, this is what we have to do," he began as he walked over and took

Star's reins and led her toward the buggy. "Will, you gotta drive the buggy." He looped Star's reins around Laura's arm and reached over and pulled Chalky's rifle out of its scabbard.

"Laura can ride Star and guide you back into town," he said to Will. She nodded in agreement, slid her foot into the stirrup and swung effortlessly up onto Star's back. The little paint stepped back in surprise as the girl's skirt billowed above him, but she calmed down immediately as Laura leaned over the pinto's neck and gave her a reassuring pat while whispering soothing words of reassurance in the horse's ear.

Twocrow gestured with the rifle. "I'll take this rifle, and you keep the one the Sheriff Bullock gave us." Will looked down at the rifle under the buggy seat and put one foot on top of it. "You better get going." He climbed up on the horse Laura had been riding. "Let's go Mister Roosevelt." He swung the horse's head back in the direction from which they had come with the buggy and started riding. Roosevelt tipped his hat to Laura, clucked to his own horse, and galloped after Twocrow.

Laura swallowed hard as she watched them ride away. She looked over to Will, who had put down his rope and picked up the reins. "It's about 30 minutes back to the edge of town if we take a little shortcut I know. You can handle that rig, right?" He nodded. "Okay. Let's get moving."

*****

"Do you believe her for even a minute?" Nellie panted as she strained to keep up with Masterson as he strode down the street and up to the door of the Sheriff's office. Her skirt was bouncing along at the tops of her button-up shoes, and she held one hand on top of her bell-shaped felt hat to keep it from blowing off as she hurried along.

"She hardly flinched when I told her that her husband had been shot," Masterson agreed. "And I was surprised that she asked about getting access to the bags he has stored in the hotel's safe. Not usually the first thing a grieving widow asks about."

"That fake crying on her brother-in-law's shoulder." Nellie scoffed. "I mean, come on. She knows something about her husband's death, or I'm not Nellie Bly."

Masterson took his hand off the door handle and turned to face her. "Speaking of that, MISS BLY." He held out his hands. "What the hell?"

"I was undercover," she responded.

"Oh yeah! For what?"

"My sanity," she glowered at him. "I'm supposed to be on vacation, and this time in Hot Springs was supposed to be a nice, relaxing side trip before I go to an assignment in Denver. I didn't want to deal with everyone interrupting me every five minutes to ask about meeting Jules Verne or what it was like to be trapped inside an insane asylum!"

"Oh, and our shootout at the OK Corral this morning didn't get you to thinking that maybe this wasn't going to be such a 'relaxing' trip after all?" his voice filled with sarcasm. "I mean, after all the fireworks out there on the prairie, it would've been nice to get the real story about who you were, ESPECIALLY for me!"

"Marshal Masterson. I've always been grateful for your assistance in helping protect my train on my Around the World trip," she said, laying a hand on his upturned arm. "I'm sure that we came through eastern Colorado and western Kansas as smoothly as we did because you had cleared such a good path for us; and I greatly appreciated it."

Masterson seemed taken aback by her response. "Well...all right then," he said. "I guess I was just a bit hurt when you didn't identify yourself earlier...especially after all that earlier connection we had...I mean, after what you just said. Right?"

"Yes," she said, "and I truly hope you'll accept my apology. But, I also hope you can see my point about traveling incognito. You yourself have been held up as an icon, and I know you also have had to take on an assumed identity from time-to-time."

He nodded in agreement. "Well...that's true, I understand about that all right." He reached back toward the door. "But Elizabeth Cochran? Couldn't you have been more imaginative in coming up with a fake name?" He snorted derisively as he spoke, then paled as she pulled both hands to her hips and glared up at him, her face turning red.

"I'll have you know that Elizabeth Cochran happens to be my REAL name! And I like it!" She pulled down on her floppy hat, brushed his hand out of the way, and yanked open the door, stomping into the Sheriff's Office as Masterson stood frozen in place for several more seconds before timidly trailing behind.

Akin stood up behind his desk at their entry and gave an inquiring look toward the Marshal as Nellie paced angrily back-and-forth. Masterson shrugged.

"Everything okay?" Akin asked.

"Yes!" Nellie exclaimed, overpowering a lower-voiced "Sure" being emitted by Masterson, who shrank back as she shouldered past him up to the desk. "We found out something down at the hotel you need to know."

"Your dead body might have a wife," Masterson spoke out. "And a brother..."

Nellie stepped to the side and gave the Marshal a withering look. He quickly closed his mouth and waited for her to tell the rest of the story.

"And we think she knows something about her husband's death," Nellie went on.

"What about the brother? You think they were in on it together?"

"I don't think so," she continued. "He just came in on the train with me and he seemed genuinely shocked to learn that his brother might be dead. The wife acted like she was surprised, and yet..." she paused as if thinking over how to express what she wanted to say next. "And yet, there was something in her eyes. I don't know. I've been an investigative reporter for a long time, and she just wasn't coming across as..."

"Wait a minute!" Akin interrupted. "A what?"

Now it was Nellie's turn to go silent and after a few seconds of awkward silence, Masterson spoke up. "Uh, Gene, let me 'officially' introduce you to Miss Nellie Bly."

The sheriff slowly shifted his gaze from Masterson to Nellie. "You mean, the New York newspaper writer? THAT Nellie Bly?" She nodded. He continued to stare at her as if formulating what he would say next. Nellie spoke up first.

"Yes, that's me," she hurried on. "Okay, so we've got that out of the way, and now we need to talk about something else, don't we?" she said brightly. "As I was saying, I think his wife...or widow, if the body IS his...is involved somehow or other, and once they get the body back here, you need to go have a look at those bags he has in the hotel safe—before she gets her hands on them. Right now, until it's a 'for sure' thing that he's dead, she can't see them, right? But if..."

"Miss Bly...," Akin interrupted.

"Nellie," she said quickly. "Now that about half the town knows who I am, no sense in being formal about things. Don't you agree?"

"Oh, uh...sure," Akin answered. He gave Masterson a "Help me please" look and the Marshal came back into the conversation.

"Nellie's right. Something's not on the up-and-up, but I don't know if the grieving widow is the problem, or just involved somehow. When we asked her why no one seemed to know that she was traveling here with her husband, she told us that she had been visiting family members up in Deadwood and she just got into Hot Springs on this morning's BN train out of Custer City.

"Apparently, Mollie—that's her name—met Alexander Previn back in the late '70s when they were both up in Deadwood."

"I thought the brother seemed totally shocked that his brother might be dead," Nellie added. "He said Previn came here to make some sort of investment, either in land or a business, and one of those business opportunities was in the Evans Hotel. He and Mollie went with us to talk to Mister Evans and we all found out that Previn had been talking about investing—as part of a larger group out of Kansas and Nebraska. Another man I met on the train is thinking about doing the same thing, and he was just as surprised to hear about Previn."

"So Fred Evans is thinking about selling his hotel?" That information seemed more shocking to the Sheriff than the details about the possible widow and the brother.

"More like selling shares," Masterson said. "Seems like he's getting it set up like some Back East business corporation, and that's what got Previn and some of the other potential investors out here in the first place."

Akin sat down and leaned back in his chair. "So that fifty thousand dollars that Laura Thompson heard about. That might be sitting in those bags in the Hotel safe? That what you're thinking?"

They both nodded.

"Did you ask the wife and the brother about that?"

"Not directly," Masterson said. "But we did tell them that if Alexander Previn is dead, he might have set himself up as a mark by making a lot of big talk around the community about all the money he had to invest. His brother jumped right in on that and said he didn't know where that fifty thousand was going to come from because he didn't see that kind of cash on their company books.

"He asked Evans to open the safe so they could look at his brother's bags and Evans refused. He said he had a signed document from his guest stating that he was the only one who could get those bags. Now, if he's dead, of course, then the wife will get custody of his belongings, and that will be the end of that."

"What about the wife?" Akin asked. "How'd she strike you when she heard that?"

"She didn't seem surprised," Nellie said. "Just irritated that we knew about some of the things we were asking. And she and the brother had a really strange exchange. She said, 'I told him not to talk about that gold. Sometimes Alexander can be the biggest idiot about things like that.'"

"And the brother looked completely baffled and he just said. 'What gold?'"

"And she said, 'Oh, Paulus, you know?' Then she told him they could talk about that later."

"Why is that strange?" Akin asked.

"Well, I don't know about Marshal Masterson, but I could see written all over Paulus Previn's face that he had no idea what she was talking about."

CHAPTER SEVENTEEN

"Annie Oakley! Can you believe it?"

Lil tossed her hat into a chair in the corner of her room as she spoke. "It's just amazing! She's who I want to be some day! Oh my God!" She hugged herself and gave Minnie a lopsided grin hoping the other girl shared some of the excitement she was feeling over meeting her long-time idol.

Instead, Minnie flopped down on the bed and sighed as she lay back on the featherbed coverlet. "Wow, a girl could get used to this." She spread her arms wide and bounced on the bed. "I've heard a lot about the Evans Hotel but I never thought I'd be in one of their rooms."

"Well, we weren't planning on being in here, either, but then that robbery changed everything and we got the rooms for free," Lil answered. "I get my own room, of course, but poor Jack has to put up with Will in his."

"You could always trade," Minnie snickered as she spoke.

"Minnie!" Lil had moved over in front of the room's washbasin and continued talking to Minnie's image as she eyed herself in the oval-shaped mirror. She saw herself blushing at the suggestion of rooming with Jack, and reached over to pour some water into the basin to cover her reaction.

"What?" Minnie said, sitting halfway up and resting on her elbows with her feet dangling over the edge of the bed. "You don't think Jack's dreamy? I only saw him for half an hour, and he looked like a great catch to me. And, besides, anyone could see he's got googoo eyes for you."

"No!" Lil exclaimed, wheeling around and turning an even brighter red. She took a couple steps toward the bed. "Do you think so?"

"KNOW so," Minnie said. "Like I told the sheriff, I'm a reporter. Uncovering things is what I do." She laughed. "I thought he was going to go have words with that Chalky character after he smiled at us. I think the only thing that kept him from doing it was he wasn't sure if Chalky was smiling at you, me, or Laura." She sat all the way back up and let her feet go down to the floor, ignoring the fact that her skirt slid up as she did so, exposing her lower legs. "And if he saw the way you were flirting with that Joe Hayden, he'd go ballistic!"

"Flirting? Wha...?"

"Oh come off it Lil. 'As anyone can plainly see I'M NOT a little girl anymore'," Minnie mimicked while sticking out her chest and tossing her hair back.

Lil turned even a brighter red and giggled. "Well, I get tired of always being 'The Little Girl' if you know what I mean? Don't you?"

Minnie nodded. "Yeah, I get it." She stared over at Lil. "You do like him, though, don't you? Jack, I mean? 'Cause if you don't, well..."

Lil walked over to the window and looked down at River Street and the top of the hotel's front veranda. "Yes, I like him a lot," she said to the window. "I just didn't think he felt the same way about me." She turned back toward the center of the room. "I've been afraid he only saw me as a little sister, or that 'little girl.' You know?"

"Well, I saw the way he glared at you when you were shaking Chalky's hand. Trust me, He sees a LOT more than that...*Cousin Lillian!*" She provocatively posed once more then broke into laughter as Lil shrieked and grabbed a decorative pillow from the foot of the bed and began pummeling Minnie with it. Minnie rolled toward the top of the bed and grabbed feather pillows in each hand, wheeling back to retaliate. Laughing and screaming they soon had the air filled with feathers before a loud knock at the door brought them to a breathless halt.

"Oh crap!" Lil exclaimed, tossing her pillow back onto the bed and hurrying to brush at her now-disheveled hair while Minnie stuffed the feather pillows back under the coverlet and struggled to smooth it back into shape. The knocking came again. "Coming!" she called, stifling a laugh as Minnie turned away toward the wall to avoid looking at her.

Lil stepped over to the door, turned the key and opened it. William Allen White and Sallie were standing there with Joe Hayden, the younger of the two waiters, puzzled expressions on all their faces. "Oh, hello," Lil said, trying to be as nonchalant and polite as she possibly could without laughing. Behind her, Minnie snickered again and Lil glanced back over her shoulder and then lost control. The Whites peered past her as Minnie's laugh cascaded over top of Lil's.

"Uh..." White began as Minnie stepped into view. "Sallie came back from her visit to the spa, and she had some interesting things to share, especially when I told her about our little adventure upstairs. I thought we'd better come and find you, since the Marshal and Nellie went back to the Sheriff's office. Mister Hayden here was kind enough to show us the way to your room."

"You can just call me Joe, sir," Hayden said quickly, embarrassed by White's remark. "My father is *Mister* Hayden."

"Sure," White grinned. "And you just call me William." Hayden smiled in return.

"Hi." Minnie extended a hand in Sallie's direction. "I'm Minnie Thompson." She struggled to keep a straight face as she spoke. "Lil and I were just getting to know each other better, weren't we Coz?"

"That's right...Coz," Lil answered. She looked over at Hayden. "Hey how come you knew where our room was located?" she asked. "You keep track of all your guests like that?" Hayden blushed and stared down at the tops of his shoes, but before he could respond she tapped him playfully on the shoulder and turned back to the Whites. "Did William tell you about the lady with the gun and how we found her with Mister Seaman?"

"He did," Sallie said. "And I told him I was especially interested when I heard that her name was Mollie." She gestured toward the room and looked up and down the hallway. "I think we should talk in private. Can we come in?"

"Oh...sure." Lil stood away from the door.

"I was at the next door spa soaking in the hot mineral baths and I dozed off in one of those private rooms. It's so relaxing there," Sallie began as they came into the room. "But I woke up when I heard women's voices coming from the next room. I'm sure they didn't know I was there because I hadn't been moving around, or anything." She paused and looked at the others who quietly waited for her to get on with the story.

Sallie nodded, more to herself than the others and cleared her throat before continuing. "Anyway, one of them called another one Mollie. And then they started talking about someone finding a body. I was trying to maneuver around to hear better, but I guess that's when they heard the water sloshing and they left. I heard a lot of footsteps moving away and a door going shut, then everything got real quiet. When I met William in the lobby after your room-search adventure, he said that Mollie was the name of the woman you found in Mister Previn's room."

"Who was this Mollie woman talking to?" Minnie looked to be in full reporter mode now, an earnest look on her face as she asked the question.

"Well, I don't know for sure, but it sounded like Mollie called one of them Grace."

An audible "Oh!" brought everyone's attention back to the doorway where Hayden was still awkwardly standing as if waiting to be dismissed. He made a face. "Uh, sorry," he said quickly, starting to step back from the doorway.

"Wait! Do you know her?" It was William's turn to ask a question.

Lil lurched over to the doorway, grabbed the young waiter by his forearm and half-dragged him into the room. "You're staying," she said firmly. "Like it or not, you're helping us now. You're part of the team." She looked at the others as if daring them to contradict her. None did.

Hayden gulped and stepped awkwardly into the room as Lil looked back out into the hallway to make sure no one was there before jerking the door shut behind her. Minnie moved over beside the Whites, curiosity filling her face as the couple settled onto two of the chairs.

"Well?" William continued. "You acted like you might know this Grace?"

"Yes Mister...I mean, yes William..." he paused. "Hey, what's your real last name anyway?"

"White," William responded. "William Allen White." He glanced over at Minnie. "And like Miss Thompson here, I'm in the newspaper business."

"Please, just call me Minnie, okay?" she said quickly. She turned back to Joe. "So, who's Grace? Spill."

"Well, I can't be certain, but I'm thinkin' it's a woman name of Grace Franston. I saw her and a couple of her, um...friends...come into the hotel lobby right after I got back there from all that business with you folks. I thought it was real curious that they met up with that other woman we saw upstairs...that one with the gun...and they all went out toward the bath house." He pulled out a small pocket watch and glanced at it. "It was 'bout an hour back, because I was gettin' set to take my break. It was right after I got back from break that I ran into you again," he gestured at White then eyed the watch. "You know, I'm 'sposed to be back in the dining room by now. That's gonna be trouble for me, I can guarantee it." He looked worried.

"I'll talk to your manager," White responded. "So, who's this Grace Franston?"

Joe made a wry face as he looked quickly to the girls and Sallie. "Well..." he paused. "I ain't the kind to go talkin' 'bout things like this...in polite company."

"Oh for cripes sake!" Lil interjected, causing Sallie to jump back in her chair. "Talk!"

Joe grinned at Lil's reaction. "Well, she's our leading lady of the night, if you know what I'm talkin' about?" He raised an eyebrow and smiled slyly. "Got a house right up the canyon road about two streets to the west. Miss Grace Franston and her...Kittens."

Minnie giggled, Lil looked confused, and Sallie pulled up a hand to cover her mouth. "Kittens? You mean she's a Madam?" William asked. Joe nodded. "Meeting with the wife of our dead man. Well, I'll be damned."

"William!" Sallie said in a disapproving voice, and White shrugged in response.

"Madam...?" Lil started, then stopped. "You mean she...sells sexual favors?"

Everyone else in the room nodded.

"Well, her AND her kittens," Joe said. "Can't say from first-hand experience, a-course," he added hurriedly. "But I hear tell that she has half-a-dozen of them cats hangin' out with her up at that big house."

Minnie giggled again and turned abruptly to face Sallie.

"So, now it's your turn to spill. What were 'Miss' Grace and our friend Mollie talking about before they took off?"

"Well, that woman Grace said something like 'Mollie, why are you so upset?' and another woman's voice—I figured it must be this Mollie person—said she had just come from her room and some people had barged in and told her that they had found a man's body. And it might be Alexander's. Then there were several confused-sounding women's voices all talking at once before one of them said 'Oh my God, Grace! If they found his body, what are we going to do?' And that's when I moved in the tub and they must've heard the water splash, because they all got real quiet. And, the next thing I heard was the sound of footsteps walking away."

"We need to go tell Sheriff Akin about this," Minnie said.

A knock at the door caused them all to go quiet.

"Who is it?" Lil broke the awkward silence.

"Lil? It's Annie Oakley. I was wondering if you...?" Her voice was stopped in mid-sentence as Lil jumped past Hayden and jerked open the door. Annie stood frozen in the doorway, startled by the response. She glanced at the roomful of people, then raised a hand and gave them a little wave. "Hi," she said in a small voice. "I'm sorry, I didn't mean to interrupt..."

She half-swallowed the sentence as Lil reached out and pulled her into the room. "Interrupt! Don't be silly." She beamed at Annie, then at the room. "Annie Oakley," she said, pointing at Annie as if no one else could see her. "What are? I mean, why are? Oh, crap!" Lil stammered. The others, including Annie, burst into laughter.

"You've got to get over being star-struck if you're ever going to be a performer yourself," Annie said, beaming as she looked around the room. Spotting Hayden by the back of the door, she gave him a friendly wave. "Joe?" Annie seemed both surprised and glad to see Hayden. "I didn't expect to find you here. I just talked to your manager and said I was hoping you could take Bill and me over to the Park? Bill's got our rig rented out for all day and your manager said it would be fine if you continued to show us around."

She turned back to the others. "Joe's been sort-of our 'unofficial, official' guide around here." She looked back at him. "I think I kept you out of trouble with your boss, by the way. He figured you were still with us and that's why you hadn't come back to work. I told him you were helping us, and could we have you to help us some more? That okay with you?"

Hayden looked pleased. "Why sure Miss Annie. I jus' need ta pick up my hat, and we could go right on over."

Sallie extended her hand to the famous shooter. "Hello, I'm Sallie White, William's wife. I know I don't look as star-struck as Lil there, but believe me I am. You're probably used to having people act a little..." she glanced over at Lil "...impressed by your celebrity. Right?"

"Yeah, I get that all the time," Annie laughed. "And believe me, it ain't so much deserved. I'm just a down-home girl who happens to be a pretty good shot."

"Pretty good?" Lil started, then stopped as she realized Annie was grinning as she spoke. "Okay. Well, someday I hope to be 'pretty good' like you."

"Sounds like a plan," Annie answered. "Look, I just came by to see if you and your friend..." she paused and pointed at Minnie, "...might want to go with Bill and me over to the Chautauqua and practice a little shooting for tonight's exhibition? I think we could all squeeze into that rig, don't you Joe?"

Hayden nodded.

"Oh my! Yes, yes, yes!" Lil looked like she was about to faint. She leaned back and Hayden stepped forward to put a hand on her shoulder and help steady her.

"Fantastic!" Annie beamed. "How about you...Minnie, isn't it?"

Minnie nodded.

"Would you be interested in seeing what goes into planning for a show?" She turned and gestured at the Whites. "All of you are welcome, of course. We just need to find another rig to get everyone over there."

"I'd love to go," Minnie said, "but we have to go down to the Sheriff's office. William and Sallie have some information that Sheriff Akin needs to have."

Lil's face fell. "Oh, yeah." She turned to Annie. "We probably should..."

White stepped forward, raising a hand as he moved. "Listen, there's no reason we all have to go down to the Sheriff's office. Sallie and I can go there and fill him in, and then once we're finished we plan to take a buggy ride out to Cascade Springs. Sallie's going to try their therapeutic mineral water treatment, too, and we need to get started with that." He squeezed his wife's arm as he spoke.

"What's Cascade Springs?" Annie asked.

"Cascade's another big mineral water resort about 5 miles down south. Part of the reason for our trip here was a chance for Sallie to try the all the area's special waters—both bathing and drinking. We don't want to miss it while we're here." He smiled. "But we can stop at the Sheriff's before we head out there. Besides, you don't need a ton of people standing around while you're trying to get ready for your show."

He turned to Lil. "And you, young lady, the way I've seen you shoot, you really need to go and show Annie here what you already know how to do."

Lil reddened at the praise, but Annie nodded in agreement. "So I've been hearing from a number of people who were on that train with you, including Marshal Masterson. I'd love to see you shoot."

"Look," White interjected. "Sallie and I will head down to Sheriff Akin's office and we'll stop over to the park later, or come to the show, after we visit Cascade Springs." He patted Lil on her shoulder. "Now you go with Annie. That's all there is to it!"

Sallie nodded vigorously in agreement. "Spending time with the Show Queen of the West in Hot Springs' Chautauqua Park. It sounds like something right out of a book, doesn't it? Girls, I'm sure this is going to be an afternoon that you'll never forget!"

CHAPTER EIGHTEEN

Jack felt another strand give way to his relentless sawing and suddenly he could move his hands around inside the ropes. He shifted ever so slightly so as not to attract attention, pulled his hands together, and felt the rope slide away.

He shrugged and bit down on his lower lip to keep from crying out as his arms and shoulders were wracked with stabbing pain from being immobilized for such a long period. He leaned back against the bedpost and carefully inched his arms forward, feeling the blood flowing back into his lower arms. His hands felt like bees were stinging each finger, and his forearms were throbbing.

Flexing his fingers, he let the knife settle onto the floor and felt the warmth of blood flowing out of the cuts he had made in his own left hand. He hoped none were too deep.

In the ranch house kitchen the men were finishing up the food Irene had prepared and were back on their feet heading for the door.

"You want someone to stay in here with you Doc?" Charley paused at the door and stood with hat in hand waiting for McCarty to reply. The Scar-Faced man shifted in his kitchen chair, groaned, and waved one hand toward the other side of the room where a large bed sat in the corner.

"Have Whit take over the road watch from Georgie and send Georgie in to get something to eat. He can help me into that bed, tie up the woman, and wait here with me while you get the other boys ready to take down her old man when he comes back."

"What about him?" Charley moved back into the room and walked over to the doorway leading into the room where Jack was tied. Jack continued leaning back against the bedpost while peering through the bottom of his eyes, trying not to open them wide enough for the men to see. Charley turned back toward his boss.

"I don't know yet," McCarty rasped. He suddenly sounded very tired. "I haven't decided. But we need to get him gagged in case he comes to. I don't want him making any noise and spooking the husband."

McCarty stood and leaned heavily on the edge of the table. "You and the boys wait for the rancher in the barn and take him when he gets back." Charley nodded and pulled open the outside door. "And don't fuck it up. We need that rancher alive, you understand?"

"Sure Doc. Of course. No problem, okay? I'll take care of it." Charley swallowed hard, slapped on his hat and exited quickly, slamming the door behind him.

"You fucking well better or the next bullet I shoot will be into you," McCarty said to the door as

Irene stepped over to the table and started taking the dishes away. The outlaw swung around at her movement, pulling out his gun. She made a small yelp and staggered back in response. "What're you doing?" He glared at her.

"Just clearing the table," she said, shaking slightly.

"Leave it!" he ordered. "We got another man coming in to eat now. Just set up something for him." He sat back in the chair with a sigh.

Irene nodded, retrieved a bowl from the cupboard and began ladling the contents of a pot that was steaming on the cook stove into it just as the door re-opened and a new man entered. He was almost as tall as McCarty, but considerably leaner.

"Georgie. Seen anything out there yet?"

"Not a thing Doc. But it's early. Her old man probably won't be rolling in much before sundown, don't you think?" Like the other outlaws, he had a scruffy beard and very dirty boots and Levi jeans. And, like the others, he wore a gun belt and leather vest, covering a stained grey shirt. A black bandanna was slung carelessly from his neck, knotted just below a very prominent Adam's apple, which jutted out every time he spoke. Surprisingly, he was well spoken and seemed to carefully choose his words. He started to sit as Irene placed the bowl on the table directly across from where McCarty was seated.

"Yeah, probably," Doc responded to Georgie's question. "Look, before you start eatin', can you check on that deputy and then help me over to that bed? My shoulder's killing me, and I'm feelin' real tired. Maybe if I rest for a while it'll feel better. And go in the other room with the woman and have her put a gag on that cowboy. When he comes to, I don't want him making any noise that might scare the rancher off. Okay?"

"Sure Doc." He stood back up and walked over to Chalky's side, kneeling down beside him. He moved him around and put his hand on his wrist, then his neck. Standing, he glanced at Irene, and looked over to Doc. "Deputy's dead Doc."

Irene gasped. "Shit!" McCarty spat. "Well, ain't nothin' to be done for that. Just leave him for now and we'll get him out to the barn once the boys come back from town."

"Okay," Georgie stood and looked sympathetically at Irene as tears began streaming down her face. She was standing by the table staring in Chalky's direction.

"Get me over to that bed now, and put a gag on that cowboy. Then you better eat."

Georgie walked around to the gang leader's side, gingerly helped him to his feet and offered a shoulder to lean on as they started across the room. As the two men moved out of Jack's sight, Irene glanced his way, swiping at her cheeks. Jack slid his right arm around in front of him and held out some strands of the rope, nodding as he did. Irene's eyes, still filled with tears, grew wide. Giving him a slight nod, she stepped back and busied herself at the stove.

The sound of a cloth ripping filled the air, and Jack quickly stuck the hand behind his back as the outlaw came into view, handed Irene a piece of what looked like a torn off bed sheet, and walked her ahead of him into the pantry. He had his gun drawn. "Put that in his mouth," he ordered.

Irene leaned down and gently pushed Jack's face back, stuffing the cloth into his mouth. Jack groaned in response but kept his eyes shut tight and his arms firmly behind him. Georgie pushed at Jack's shoulder with the gun, and Jack slumped back toward the floor. Satisfied that he was still unconscious, Georgie grunted and motioned Irene toward the table, slipping the gun into his holster as they returned.

He dug into the food, noisily eating a couple of bites and slurping at a mug of coffee Irene brought over.

"Thanks ma'am," he said. "Good food." He gave her a half-hearted smile that showed off a mouth missing a front tooth. The other front tooth glinted from a silver cap. "What you call this?"

"Shepherd's Stew," she answered, swiping at her eyes and shifting around to Jack's side of the table effectively blocking Georgie from seeing past her to where Jack was seated. Jack quickly moved both hands around in front of him and spit out the cloth while shedding the pieces of rope. He gave his left hand a quick once-over as blood dripped from the fingertips. He could see at least two prominent gouges in the fatty part of his palm.

He picked up the cloth again, stuffed it onto the palm of the injured hand, and wrapped part of the rope strands around it to hold it in place. Assured that he had the wounds covered, he carefully moved his legs and slid upward using the bedpost as a brace.

Just as his hands had reacted before, his legs now internally screamed at him for moving after such a long period of inactivity. He bit his lip again to keep from gasping, then reached down and retrieved the knife before taking several halting steps in the general direction of the kitchen door. As he shuffled forward he began to feel his legs loosening up. The room spun around for a few seconds, and he put his bloody hand up to his head and closed his eyes, waiting for the dizziness to pass.

"Do you have any bread?

Jack's eyes popped back open as he heard the outlaw's question to Irene. He had to get out of the line of sight. He took one more step, felt the dizziness return and crouched down, finally letting his knees ease all the way to the floor. He'd have to crawl.

"Um..." Irene was stalling to give Jack time. Jack crawled to his left, leaving the safety of the cover of Irene's body, which still blocked most of the doorway into his room. He could see just past her left shoulder where the outlaw continued scooping up the stew. A moan from across the room where Jake was in bed drew Georgie's attention and he stood up and walked over to the outlaw leader. "You gonna be okay Doc?" he was speaking as he walked.

Jack scooted completely out of the line of sight as Irene moved from the doorway toward the area where she had been cooking. "Yes, I think there's some over here. I'll check," she said, answering Georgie's earlier question.

Jack forced his body upward and flattened himself against the wall. Georgie spoke quietly to McCarty, but their voices were too muffled for him to hear what they were saying. Irene's figure re-filled the doorway, her back to him once again. Jack edged closer, then reached over and touched her in the small of her back. She gasped, then recovered her composure and continued standing where she was, obviously waiting for the outlaw to return to the table.

"I found some bread," she said as his footsteps retreated to the table area and he slid a chair out and sat down. "Can I get you more coffee?"

"That'd be real nice ma'am," he replied, once again his polite voice seeming out of place based on everything else Jack had been hearing from the group. Irene moved away from the door and Jack peered past the doorframe's corner where he could see part of the table, the front door of the cabin, and, across the room, the bed where the Scar-Faced outlaw was lying with his hat now covering his face, one leg up on the bed and the other draped partway onto the floor.

"I'm going to have to ask you to sit down on one of these chairs so I can tie you up," Georgie continued, this time speaking with his mouth full of the bread she had just brought him. "Sorry, ma'am. And sorry about your friend." He waved at Chalky's body and took another bite as she remained where she was standing.

"Can I just sit in this chair, then?" Irene asked, pointing down at the one on her side of the table.

"Don't really matter, I guess," he answered. "And I'll be putting a piece of cloth in your mouth, too. Can't have you shouting to your man when he rides in." He slid his chair back and got to his feet. "Might as well get it over with." Another moan, this one lower, came from the bed. "Looks like Doc's gonna be out for a while."

Irene choked slightly as if she were going to cry again. She nodded. "Okay, I'm ready." She reached down and pulled the chair from under the edge of the table, the back facing Jack's room. She sat down as Georgie stood. Jack tensed, grasping the knife tighter in his good hand as Georgie's footsteps approached. The corner of his shoulder budged into the doorway and he knelt behind the chair, a rope in his hands and a piece of bed sheet draped over his shoulder.

"This might hurt and I'm really sorry to do this ma'am," he began looping the rope around her wrists. Jack took a quick step forward and stuck the knife up into the inside corner of Georgie's ear while grasping the man's left shoulder with his bloodied hand. The outlaw flinched and started to rise.

"Don't!" Jack hissed. "One word or one wrong move and this knife's going straight into your brain." The outlaw tensed but remained still. "Take his gun."

Irene slowly stood, glancing across at the unconscious form of McCarty. Turning, she reached down and pulled the gun from the man's holster, then edged back as quietly as possible while keeping it pointed at Georgie's face. Jack grasped Georgie's shoulder hard with his bad hand, forcing him back to his feet, while never moving the knife's blade from his ear.

"Into this room with me!" he ordered, still whispering. "And quiet as a church mouse or it'll be the last noise you ever make...or hear. Got it?" He was still directly behind the outlaw and now half-pulled backward while using the motion to stabilize himself in the process. Two steps brought them closer to the bunk bed, and he nodded at Irene to stay with them. She advanced with the gun now leveled at the outlaw's chest.

"Get down on the floor and get those boots off," Jack eased Georgie to the floor, never flinching with the knife and seeing a bead of blood rising from where the knifepoint was pushing into the man's ear.

"Take that rag?" he whispered toward Irene. She looked around, saw it on Georgie's shoulder and snagged it with her left hand while keeping the gun leveled directly at him. She held it out. "Take it," Jack said to the outlaw, his voice deadly calm. "Take it and put it in your mouth, then get those boots off and slide back up against that bedpost where I was tied."

He extended a hand toward Irene, signaling for the gun as Georgie filled his mouth with the cloth and began working on the boots. "Get something to wrap around his face," Jack continued whispering, "and bring me those ropes." He jammed the barrel of the gun up against the nape of Georgie's neck. "If you plan to keep on living, be VERY quiet." Georgie had a scared look in his eyes now. He gulped and his prominent Adam's apple bobbed up and down.

Irene walked quietly into the kitchen, grabbed a linen towel off the cupboard and glided back to Jack's side. "Pull it around his mouth and tie it in the back." She did so as he jerked Georgie's arms behind the bedpost.

"Grab your right hand with the left one," he directed as he put more pressure on the gun up against the man's neck. Georgie meekly complied as Irene finished knotting the towel behind his head. Jack nodded at the gun and she quickly took it from him, keeping it pressed against the man's neck. Jack dropped to his knees and wound the rope around and around the outlaw's hands and the bunk bed post.

Satisfied that the knots were secure, Jack stood and stared at Georgie for a few seconds. He reached over and jerked the top part of the towel up from his mouth to also cover his nose and eyes. Without speaking, he pointed at his own eyes and looked toward the door. Irene edged back over to look at McCarty, looked back and nodded.

Jack pointed toward Chalky's motionless body lying next to the sink and tears suddenly re-filled Irene's eyes. She shook her head. "We have to leave him," she whispered. Jack inhaled sharply. The thought of the young man being dead was still a shock. He glared down at the blindfolded and bound robber and pointed the gun back at him, suddenly very angry. He turned back toward the kitchen, extending the gun.

Irene moved as quickly as she could from where she was standing and put a hand on the gun, shaking her head again and mouthing the word "No!" She pointed at the pantry door on the other end of the room, put a finger to her lips for silence, and slipped past Jack.

Tiptoeing across the room she very carefully opened the door. Jack stared in surprise as she walked in and disappeared from sight. Reaching over to pick up Georgie's boots, he moved as noiselessly as possible to the door, stepped inside and pulled it shut behind him.

Irene was standing about ten feet ahead holding a newly lit lantern and pulling back a nearly invisible burlap curtain that covered another opening leading toward a pitch-black passageway. Jack turned slightly and glanced back, unsure what he should do. He felt Irene's hand on his shoulder. "We have to go," she whispered. "Chalky's dead, and if we don't get out of here now, we will be too. That McCarty is a cold-blooded killer, and if he wakes up he and the others will shoot us. We can't take a chance."

"What about your husband?"

"This tunnel leads to a little cave we use for storing food and ice," Irene said. "It's away from the house on the northeast side. Out on its back side is another entrance. So, if we just keep going, we'll get up into the hills in the direction where Paul was working today. If he comes back along the route he usually takes we should meet him on his way in. Then we'll all be together, and safe."

*****

Paul Anderson and Seth Bullock had looped all the way around the base of the mesa to the northwest side of Anderson's ranch when Roosevelt and Twocrow galloped up from the southwest following the Hot Springs road. Seeing Anderson's buckboard, the riders cut off toward them, picking up their pace. Anderson pulled his team to a stop and reached for his rifle.

"It's okay," Bullock held up one hand. "That's the Indian kid from the buggy, and my... deputy." Anderson leaned back on the buckboard seat as the pair rode up, dust swirling around them. Roosevelt tipped his hat to the rancher.

"Theodore Roosevelt," he said as the sun caught the corner of his spectacles and sent a small beam of light in Anderson's direction. The rancher's team shied away from the sudden flash of light and he pulled back on the reins, clucking to them to be calm.

"Paul Anderson," he answered. "Careful with them specs of yours. Don't wanta spook my team...or whoever's over to my place, either." He gestured in the general direction of his ranch stead. Roosevelt grimaced and pulled his big hat down further to shade the top half of his face.

"We didn't think you'd be way over here," Twocrow glanced around as he spoke and pointed Chalky's rifle, which he continued to hold in his right hand, toward a row of hills almost due north. "I told Mister Roosevelt we'd be meetin' you over on the other side of that ridgeline there. You must have a better idea, huh?"

"Yep. Go in with the sun direct behind us," Bullock said. He looked at the rifle. "That don't look like the rifle I gave you before. Where'd you get that?"

"I think it's Chalky's. We found his horse running loose and grazing alongside the road about two miles back."

"Chalky? You mean that young Hot Springs deputy?" Anderson asked. "Why would...?"

"The sheriff sent him and a visiting rancher out of the Oklahoma Territory out to the Martin Ranch to let them know about the train holdup," Twocrow interrupted. "It's kind of a complicated story, but there were a bunch of horses on the train that were supposed to go to the Martins. Instead, they got run off during the robbery. Sheriff sent the two of 'em out there about the same time we went up to get that body out of Wind Cave."

Anderson turned his gaze back toward the direction of his ranch stead. "Well, then they would've been riding right past my place. Shit!"

"Yeah, that don't sound so good," Bullock said. He glanced over at Roosevelt, who gave him a slight

"Don't know?" shrug in response. "Any blood on the deputy's saddle?"

"Not that we could see," Roosevelt answered. "Could be the horse just ran off and the deputy is on the ground somewhere. Or he and that young rancher could be pinned down some place. Hard to say."

"I think they're at our ranch," Anderson said, his lips pursed determinedly. He took off his hat and wiped a forearm across his brow, then settled it back on his head. He looked back over to Bullock. "How you wanta handle it?"

Bullock nodded to the buckboard. "If they're in there and took over your place, they'll be expectin' you to come back driving that rig. If a bunch of us come riding in on horseback, they'll know right away that we're onto them and that could be trouble for your wife...and the other men if they've got them. So, I'm thinkin' we need to go in slow and easy. Make it look like you don't know they're in there." He got down off his horse, picked up a stick and cleared off a spot with his boot. "Draw this out for us Paul. Where we headed here?"

Anderson climbed down and joined him as Twocrow and Roosevelt shifted their horses around to look down on the spot. The rancher took the stick and made several quick swipes, drawing a couple of boxes to represent the ranch stead, and outlining the path from the Hot Springs road going past the buildings and heading east. Then he made an X further to the north and west.

"We're here," he said. "The path Chalky probably was riding is over there. There are two natural draws going down past my buildings on this side. One is that path they were probably ridin' on, and the other is straight ahead of us. Nobody usually uses this one, but it wouldn't be unusual for me ta be comin' home this way since it's a lot more direct."

He looked around at the others and they nodded. He pointed back to the main path. "If we came that other way, they'd see us a half-mile off 'cause it's a lot more flat. But coming here, where we are now, they wouldn't see us until we come out of the end of the draw; maybe 50 or 60 yards at best." He pointed back at the sun. "And like we talked about Sheriff, the sun'd be pretty much fillin' up our backs when we did come out. They'd see me coming, but all they'd see would be the horses and my rig."

"So if we left the saddle horses here and were lying flat in the back of your wagon, they probably wouldn't see us until we pulled up. They'd be planning to take you by surprise," Bullock said. "But what if we surprised THEM instead?"

Twocrow edged his horse around, jumped down and pointed the rifle at the drawing in the dirt. "Isn't there a ridgeline on the south side of your place Mister Anderson? I seem to remember a creek running alongside that road and then some rock walls going up to a flat ridge. What if someone got on up there to provide some crossfire? Seems like a rider could get up there from off the Hot Springs road—a 'high ground' route, right?"

Anderson stood and nodded. "Yeah, you're describing it right, but if you rode past that way they could see you as soon as you came into view on the top of the ridge. You'd be a sitting duck. Way too risky."

"Unless the rider wasn't a threat." Twocrow said as he studied the drawing then extended the rifle toward the rancher. "Hold this, will you?"

Anderson took it from him, a puzzled expression on his face as Twocrow pulled off his shirt, his bronze skin gleaming in the late afternoon sun. He took the utility knife from his belt, sliced into the shirt's bottom front corner and ripped a strip off all the way around. As the others stared at him as if he'd gone crazy, he tied the strip across his forehead and knotted it in the back. Reaching down, he picked up two hands full of dirt and dusted the top half of his body, streaking some across his face.

He went back to his horse, uncinched the saddle, swung it down to the ground, and straightened the saddle blanket. "Give me a hand up, will you?" Anderson formed a bucket with his hands and boosted Twocrow up onto the blanket. "Easy now, boy," he said soothingly to the horse as the animal whickered nervously at this unusual riding style. Twocrow held out his hand for the rifle.

The rancher cautiously handed it back to him and looked at him with amazement. An Indian brave now sat on the horse in front of him.

"My people still ride through this area all the time, right?"

Anderson nodded.

"And I'll bet they ride the ridgeline, don't they? Stay away from the ranches. You ever pay them any mind?"

He shook his head. "Not much. We don't worry about them no more. These days they're more of a nuisance than any kind of problem. No offense." Twocrow shrugged. "They don't bother us, we don't bother them, so long as they're just ridin' through and especially when they're away off the road..." he paused. "Yeah, just like you been describin'."

"Exactly." Twocrow nodded. "They're invisible because they're not a threat." He turned his horse to the south. "Give me fifteen minutes and then head in. I'll be hiding in plain sight on the south side of your place when you get there."

Anderson reached over and tapped the rifle, now lying across the horse's mane in front of the boy. "You know how to use this?"

"Twocrow swallowed. "Yeah, I can shoot if I need to. See you at the ranch." He grabbed the reins with his left hand, kicked the horse lightly and galloped away.

"You think he'll be any help to us?" Roosevelt asked as he watched the horse disappear over the ridgeline.

"Don't know," Bullock said as he climbed into the back of the wagon. "But even if he fires off a couple rounds and makes some noise, that might be enough to draw the gang's attention away from us; get us close enough to do some damage of our own."

Roosevelt pointed to the north. "If I go up and around to the north and east of that hill will I be on the path back into your ranch stead?"

Anderson was climbing back up to the buckboard's seat and paused to look where Roosevelt was pointing.

"Yeah, that'll give you a line straight in from the northwest side of the barn," he agreed. "It flattens out pretty quick once you get off the side of that hill. You'll be out in the open."

"Then you and Seth better keep the attention focused on yourselves and off me," Roosevelt said with a twinkle in his eyes.

"In other words, draw all their fire right down on us," Bullock grumbled. "Thanks Pard, you're all heart."

"Just glad to make that clear," he chuckled, tipping his leather hat slightly before wheeling the horse away.

"Hey!" Bullock's shout caused the Easterner to rein in and look back. "How'll we know when you're coming in?"

"Don't worry. You'll know." He gave a two-fingered salute with his right hand and galloped off.

"Sort-of a strange dude, ain't he?" Anderson said as he watched the dust settle.

"Yeah, but damned if I wouldn't want to follow that man anywhere he wants to lead me. I'm not sure what it is, but he's definitely a man to follow, and I'm glad he's on our side." He nodded toward the trail. "But for now, I guess we better take the lead."

CHAPTER NINETEEN

Laura dug her heels into Star's side and reined in the little mare. They were on a ridgeline overlooking the north slope leading down into Hot Springs, and after veering west off the main road they were stopped at the edge of a large grove of aspen and pine. Shadows were starting to stretch to the east and a pair of trails lay just ahead of them, one leading back to the road, the other going around a small hill further to their west.

Will pulled the buggy up next to her and Previn's body bounced back and forth before settling. "Why'd we go off the road? And why're we stopping here?" he asked, glancing back at the body.

"Somebody's coming up fast behind us," Laura replied, signaling for him to move the buggy further under the cover of the trees. "I saw the dust a few minutes ago and it's been growing. It might just be Bill and Mister Roosevelt, but I want to make sure before whoever it is gets to where they can see us."

Will moved the rig into the deeper shade, pulled back on the brake handle and stood up on the seat, shading his eyes to get a clearer look.

"Lots of dust all right, but I think it might be just one rider," he said. "One very fast rider, but just one."

"That's probably why so much dust," Laura said. "I'm going to tie Star out of sight further under the trees. You get out that rifle." She nodded and Will sat back down and reached under the seat for the weapon. She rode away into the deep shade, returning in less than a minute and climbing up alongside him. He extended a hand and helped pull her up as the sound of horse's hooves approached. Their buggy horse made a soft grunting sound in response and shifted around. Will and Laura exchanged a startled look, and then Will handed her the rifle and jumped down, moving up to the horse's head. Taking off his shirt, he draped it over the animal's face.

The big mare snorted, stamped one foot, and stood quivering, unsure what to do now that her vision was impaired. Laura gave Will a thumbs up and turned back toward the loud hoof beats coming from the bend on the main road about fifty yards away. Suddenly, a big man on a large red horse galloped past, his wide-brimmed hat dangling from a leather thong and pushed back on his head by the wind being made from his own fast riding. The horse and rider, dust swirling behind them, crested the ridge and disappeared.

Laura and Will stood frozen, not speaking as they listened to the hoof beats fading. As the dust finally settled, a bird in the grove began chirping and Star nickered in response. Laura nodded, laid the rifle down on the seat and started climbing off the buggy as Will removed his shirt from the horse's head.

"We better hurry and get into town," he said as he walked toward her, buttoning the shirt as he moved. "That was one of those outlaws."

"What?" She had started toward the spot where Star was tied, and now she turned back to face him, startled by his comment. "How do you know?"

"He was one of the men on the train car with us. Pretty hard to forget somebody like that." He nodded as if reinforcing his own statement.

"Oh my God!" Laura exclaimed. "Then the gang IS up on this side of town. And they probably got Chalky and your friend Jack." She looked back in the direction where the rider had gone. "But why's he riding into town alone? Where're the others?"

"Maybe they're already IN town," Will answered. "Didn't the sheriff say he was worried they'd be coming to get their friends out of jail?"

Laura nodded. "So, Sheriff Bullock, Mister Roosevelt and Bill are going the wrong way —or they're going right into a trap at the Andersons' ranch." She spun around and ran back into the woods, returning and half-dragging Star by her reins. She gave Star a reassuring pat, clamped her left foot into the stirrup and swung up on the little mare's back.

"That's the main road into town," she said, waving back at the place where the rider had gone past. "You remember how we came out?" Will nodded. "Okay, then drive back in the same way, and don't stop for anything. Just get right on down to the Sheriff's office and let them know what's going on out here."

"What about you?" Will was puzzled by her instructions.

"I'm going back and warn the others."

"What?" He looked at her with amazement. "How do you plan to do that? You might be riding right into the rest of the gang if you go back. You can't just go back!"

"I have to do something," she said. "Somebody has to do something and we can't wait until we go all the way into town and then have to go all the way back out again. It'll take too much time. I have to try to help my friend."

"B-but..." Will stammered, "...you're a girl!"

"Glad to see you noticed," she gave him a disparaging look and he shrunk back further on the buggy's seat. "There's hope for you yet even if you are... just a kid." She added the last part in a semi-mocking tone, and he reddened and sat up straighter.

"I'm not just a kid!" he said indignantly. "I'm just ... worried that you'll get yourself hurt, or somethin'. And you're not the only one with a friend out there. My friend Jack is out there, too, you know? What about him?"

"Yeah, okay," she replied. "But don't...worry about me, I mean. And you gotta think that your friend is okay. So for now, the best thing is to just get this body into the Sheriff's office and tell them about Chalky's horse and that outlaw we just saw, and what we think's going on at the Anderson Ranch. And...just...tell them everything! Okay? Now get moving."

Will nodded, a miserable look on his face. Laura turned the horse away, started back to the road, then stopped and wheeled the animal around to ride back to his side. She pulled back on Star's reins and the horse blew out an exasperated snort at the constant changing of what her rider wanted her to do. Laura reached over and gave the animal another reassuring pat alongside the neck.

"Listen, if you see my sister tell her not to worry. Okay? And don't let that girl that's traveling with you try to come out after her boyfriend either. We got enough people in trouble out here and we don't need any more. Not her, not you, and definitely not my sister. Best thing everyone can do is stay where the Sheriff and his deputies can keep everyone safe."

"Okay," he said. He extended the rifle. "But you should take this."

She stared at the rifle as if unsure. She reached out, took it from him, and slid it into Chalky's scabbard. "Thanks," she started to pull the horse back around. "And be careful, okay?" She clucked to Star and they galloped away.

"Okay," Will said to the disappearing rider as he picked up the reins, "but I still don't see what you think you're going to do by goin' back?" He flicked the reins and the horse and buggy headed over to the road. Will reined in where the main road resumed and looked at the disappearing cloud of dust where Laura was riding away.

"Oh yeah," he half-shouted in her direction, "and Lil is NOT Jack's girlfriend!" He sat looking at the fading dust and thinking about what he just said. "At least I don't think she is." He looked back up the road, then spoke to the horse, a perplexed expression on his face. "Why do you think she thinks Lil is Jack's girlfriend?"

The horse snorted in response, anxious to move on and get back to her stable. "Yeah, that's what I say too," Will agreed. He shrugged and looked up the road one more time. "Boyfriend, girlfriend, sheesh!" He flicked the reins again and the buggy started rolling.

*****

After cresting the hill on the main Hot Springs road, Jake Curley turned off and rode due west, following the ridgeline toward Hot Brook road. Finally reaching the road, he started easing his way toward Bradley Flats heading back southeast into Hot

Springs. The sound of some sort of rig approaching caused him pull up and move his horse off the trail into the pine trees dotting the rugged hillside.

"Someone coming," he half-whispered to his horse, rubbing the big red stallion with his left hand as he pulled his pistol free with his right. "Steady boy," he said softly as the sound grew louder, joined by the sound of women's voices. They stood quietly, the horse's ears twitching as he listened to the horses approaching. Curley sucked in a deep breath and tried not to breathe hard as he held tight to the reins. The women's voices now filled the afternoon air and a four-passenger carriage pulled by two big bay horses rolled into his line of sight on the narrow road.

A buxom, copper-haired woman with a big feather-covered hat and extravagantly ruffled blue dress was driving. Seated alongside her was a trim, well-dressed middle-aged woman with brown hair and a fashionable suede traveling jacket and derby-style hat. Two younger women, clad in bright green and mottled purple dresses with garishly matching hats, were leaning forward from the back seat carrying on an animated conversation with the women in front. Jake exhaled, urged his mount forward and raised his free hand as he prepared to call to them.

Then, thinking better of calling to them, he jerked the reins across the horse's mane and galloped toward them from his hiding spot. As he rode up beside them, the gun still in his hand, both of the younger women shrieked. The well-dressed woman also looked alarmed, but the flouncy-dressed driver just grinned and pulled the team to a stop.

"Jake Curley as I live and breathe!"

"Gracie!" Curley reined his horse alongside the carriage. "Been a long time. Wasn't sure it was you. You've changed." He tilted the gun toward her ample cleavage. "Well, maybe not that much," he laughed and holstered the weapon.

She joined his laughter, half standing and leaning out to embrace him, her breasts nearly falling out of the opening in her dress as she did so. He grinned at her reaction and leaned halfway down off his horse to return her hug. The two younger women, reassured that their mentor knew the man, sat smiling prettily as if waiting for introductions. The outlaw sat back up on his saddle, barely glancing at the girls as he pointed to the other woman in front. "Who ya got there?"

The fashionably dressed woman reached up and touched the brim of her hat. "Mollie Previn. Grace and I are connected from earlier days—up in Deadwood."

"That so?" Curley said. "Working partners, or just friends?"

"Both," she answered.

He nodded knowingly and gave her an appreciative look. "Thought I might be meetin' you down by that caretaker's hut in hot brook canyon, Grace? Didn't expect to find you ridin' way out here. Might've missed each other completely, you know?"

"Maybe. But we had ourselves a situation, so to speak, and we needed to get out of town. Figured you had to be comin' in this way to get over to that hut. So we just started drivin'." She held her arms wide. "Guess it weren't too bad a plan, right?"

"No, guess not," he said, "but I was kind of hopin' you'd be able to help me out IN town. My man told you what happened, right?"

"Yeah."

"Well?"

"Well, we couldn't wait. If we didn't get out of town when we did, we maybe wouldn't of got out at all, if you know what I mean?"

"Yeah, I know how that is," Curley replied. "But I'm in a bit of a fix. Gotta get me a doctor AND see about gettin' a couple of friends out of the Hot Springs jail. That still down along the river in the Lower Town?"

"Yes, and the Doc's office is over that way, too."

"Well, that's good news," he said, more to himself than to the women. "Got a couple of boys waitin' at that hut, so I need to meet up with them and head on over. There's some more of our boys coming up Fall River Canyon, so we should be in good shape to get McCarty's brother out of that Podunk jail.

"Get them, get the Doc, and head back out to where McCarty is waiting, and then maybe I can get back together with you." He looked over at Mollie. "So, you knew Grace back in her Deadwood days, huh? You said you was partners?"

"For a while," Mollie answered.

"Not for long, though," Grace interrupted. "Mollie met the man of her dreams and they went off back to Chicago to live happily ever after." She gestured back toward Curley. "Jake here is the brother of Charlie Curley," she added. "You remember him Mollie?"

Mollie nodded. "Charlie Curley? No foolin'? I heard he had a little unfortunate run-in with a lawman down around these parts. That so?"

"Yeah, that's so," Curley frowned. "I still got a little 'debt' to settle up with that Sheriff that shot him if I ever run into him again. But I heard he retired and moved away, so maybe that's all water under the bridge." He stared off at the woods for a few seconds before looking back at the women. "So what brings you back to the Hills?"

"The 'Happily' part ran out of money," she replied. "And my 'Ever After' part thought we'd come back and get some more. Trouble is, my dream man seems to have run out of time before I could find exactly where it was that he hid a bunch of gold."

"Gold? Here? Around Hot Springs? Ain't no gold around these parts. They found a few nuggets back in the '70s but all the gold's up around Deadwood."

Mollie and Grace exchanged a knowing look and Grace gave her a little nod.

"Well, not all," Mollie said. "You ever hear the story about Lame Johnny?"

"Lame Johnny?" Curley half-snorted in derision. "That guy that got hisself hung? That's an old wives' tale. Weren't no real gold." He looked intently at Mollie, then back to Grace. Both women just stared back in return. "Wait. Was there?"

"Listen, according to Mollie's dear husband, he was in cahoots with Lame Johnny and that wasn't just no story; they had some REAL GOLD. That's why Mollie and her old man came back. He told her it's hidden in a cave up in the hills north of Hot Springs."

"So then why ain't he here with you, lookin' for the gold?"

Mollie and Grace exchanged yet another look as the two younger women sat silently, looking uncomfortable.

"Well, that's the thing," Mollie said. "He up and got himself shot before we could do very much lookin'."

"Shot?" Curley replied. "He going to survive?"

"Not really," Mollie answered. "Let's just say he's out of the picture." She shrugged.

"That's why I was excited to hear from you," Grace said quickly. "I sort-a figured that you and me...and her..." she paused and looked back at the two younger women "...and the girls here, a'course. We could all work together to re-locate that gold, especially since you know these southern hills so well." She gave him a flirtatious smile and leaned forward again. "I think the two of us, especially, have always worked well together Jake. Don't you?"

Jake settled back and wiped a trickle of sweat from his brow. He lifted his hat so that the leather thong holding it slipped down lower on his neck, then pushed until it dropped onto his back allowing the light breeze to blow through his thinning hair. "How much gold we talkin' about Grace?"

She turned back toward Mollie.

"My old man said it was maybe a hundred thousand back then, so probably worth a lot more by now," Mollie said. "He said that's what he and Lame Johnny and their gang took from the robbery."

"Gang?"

"Don't worry none about them," she answered. "Everyone's dead. My old man and his girlfriend were the only ones got away and she got herself shot up in Deadwood before he met me. And now he's gone too. So, if we find that gold, it's ours to split. Simple as that."

"And he's dead? You're sure of that?"

"Yeah, I'm sure. I shot him myself. We were in that Wind Cave and it seems like his plan was to shoot me and make me disappear." She held her arms out as if encircling the others in the buggy. "After we had our little confrontation, I got ahold of Gracie and she and these nice girls of hers came out to that cave and helped me move his body into a place where we thought he'd be safely hidden."

"Before he told you where to find the gold?" Curley chuckled. "I'd say that warn't to smart of you."

Mollie settled back on the seat. "Like I said, it seems like he had other plans for our so-called 'partnership.' I think he was kind of figuring that he'd be the one doing the shooting and I'd be the body hidden in the cave. Then he'd go pick up all that gold and start over." She tapped at her handbag. "He forgot I like to carry a little popgun with me...for emergencies and such."

Curley gave her a bemused look. "Must be a helluva popgun. So why Wind Cave? Ain't that some sort-a tourist place these days?"

"I didn't know that," Mollie answered. "When he said we were going into the cave, I thought that's where the gold was hidden. But then when we got down there and I asked him about it, he said it was hid in another cave."

She gave a little sigh. "Then we had our little face-off, and I couldn't very well get him out by myself. So I went back into town to get Gracie to help me."

"Me'n my girls were up there a couple weeks back for a little tour—just to see what all the excitement is about," Grace interjected. "When we got back in there a ways, this girl guide that was showin' us around, she pointed at this one opening and said that that was the 'unexplored region' and it would be a long time comin' before anyone got on back there. Then she told us they'd be closin' down the cave for a while until the owners got back from a big trip out East.

"When I heard about Mollie's little problem...well, hidin' her old man's body in that part of the cave just seemed like a real good solution. Especially since his body was already down there in the first place!"

Curley blew out a long slow breath, extracted a pouch of tobacco and some thin papers and started to roll a cigarette. "So I take it Wind Cave *ain't* where that gold is hid?"

"No," Mollie answered. "Alexander—that's my old man...ex-old man—he said he and Johnny hid it in another cave, one up northeast of there. A place called King's something. King's Ridge or King Canyon maybe. Trouble is, we don't have no exact location. That's when Grace told me about you." She pointed at him. "You need money. We need a partner to help us find THAT cave. You interested or not?"

"Yeah, I'm interested," Jake said. He tamped the tobacco onto the paper and licked the edge, getting it ready to roll into a cigarette. "Look, I gotta go get Doc McCarty's little brother out of that Hot Springs jail. Once I do that, I'll have plenty of time. Where's a good spot?" He lit the cigarette and blew out a long stream of smoke.

"How about by Wind Cave?" Grace said. "Ain't gonna be no one out there with the place closed down." She pointed up the road. "We can follow this road out a few more miles, then cut back to the northeast on the Pringle trail. Should take us right into the back side of Wind Cave. Right?"

He nodded.

"We'll wait for you there."

Curley tapped an ash off the end of the cigarette. "That'll work. Once I get everything wrapped up in town, I'll plan to meet you there. But, before I go, tell me one more time about what your old man said about that gold."

CHAPTER TWENTY

It was just after noon and hard on the heels of Nellie and Bat's discussion with Sheriff Akin when the Whites arrived at his office with the news about Sallie's bathhouse encounter. After one more awkward disclosure to Sallie about her true identity, Nellie sat down and waited for the couple to share their newest information.

"And that's all I heard Sheriff." Sallie stood back from the desk and crooked her hand into William's. "But a young black waiter at the Evans, Joe Hayden, he told us just before we came over here that he was pretty sure the woman I heard Mollie talking to was named Grace Franston."

"Grace Franston? The Madam?"

The Whites nodded in unison.

Sheriff Akin leaned back in the swivel chair behind his desk. "How in the world is she involved?" He shook his head slowly, then stood and held out his hand. "Okay, thank you both for coming in to let me know. Are you headed back to the hotel?"

"No, I've got a buggy and we're driving out to Cascade Springs for some of the water treatment," William replied.

Akin returned to his chair. "Sure, water there is great, too, and it's a beautiful resort, just a bit out of the way." He nodded. "Safe travels and thanks again folks."

The Whites turned back toward Nellie and Bat. "What will you be doing?"

"I don't know?" Nellie answered. "The Marshal's probably going to stay on here for a time. Where did you say the girls went?"

"Annie invited them to come over to the Chautauqua to see how they do their preparations for the exhibition. And, when we get back we want to go on over and see the show. Will you be returning to the hotel? I'm sure we'll be back by 4 or 4:30; 5 at the latest. We could all go down there together."

Nellie nodded. "Perhaps. But, if I'm not at the hotel, I might already be down there. So, why don't I just plan to meet you there?" She smiled and took Sallie's hand. "I'm sorry about my earlier deception, and I'm glad that you're not upset with me. I promise to be more forthright with you from now on."

Sallie stepped forward and gave Nellie a hug. "I forgive you, but as reparation, I demand that you share the inside scoop from your most harrowing tales. Then you'll not only be forgiven but also be my friend for life."

"Deal!" Nellie answered, hugging her in return. She went with them out onto the walkway in front of the building and waited as they climbed into the buggy that William had rented for the afternoon.

She waved as they reached the end of the street and headed out on the road toward Cascade Springs and walked back into the Sheriff's office just as Masterson finished saying something that had the sheriff looking perplexed.

Akin settled back into his big chair and grunted. "I don't like it," he said. "Too many chances of McCarty's men riding in here and hurting innocent folks in the process." He waved his arms around. "This look like a secure building to you?"

Masterson shook his head and Nellie nodded in agreement. "But what else can we do?" Bat asked. "You try moving these prisoners, where you going to put them?"

"Well, it ain't common knowledge yet, but the County's been building cells in the bottom level of our new courthouse up by the Evans Plunge pool. When they was diggin' down into the rock to stabilize the building, they ended up with quite a hole in the ground, and Judge McGraw told me that they kind-a figured they'd need a safe place to keep prisoners during trials and such. So they started building some cells. Probably be our next jail."

He took out a pipe and tamped it full of tobacco. After getting it lit, he puffed twice and pointed the stem back over his shoulder. "Up on that end of town, as you probably already saw, it's a lot tighter space to get in and out of. And, on top of that the new courthouse is solid stone. It's almost like a small fortress.

"Besides, most of the town's going over to the Chautauqua show tonight, so that should leave this part of town pretty much deserted. If any of McCarty's gang get this far, they'll find an empty jail and no one around to hurt."

Nellie walked over to the window and looked out at the wide streets of Hot Springs' Lower Town where the wooden jailhouse was integrated among a scattering of new homes and businesses—everything from a livery and blacksmith shop with an adjoining corral, to a dry goods store and law office building. A huge lumberyard with a sign declaring it to be "C.T.C. Lollich Lumber" stood straight down the street.

Wagons and horses stirred up small clouds of dust as they crisscrossed up and down the main street. Groups of children raced past on the wooden sidewalks after coming down the hill from the new stone school building looming above the intersection that separated this flat expanse of the community from Upper Town. That section, as Akin said, had been built along the narrower riverside section that housed the bathhouse and spa, Evans Hotel, Union Depot and Evans Plunge swimming arena.

"It definitely could be a problem for you trying to defend against an outlaw gang here," she agreed. "But how are you going to move the prisoners without everyone in town knowing something's up? I thought you wanted to not panic anyone? Don't you want to wait until it gets darker and folks have gone to the show?"

Akin blew out an exasperated sigh. "Hell, I don't know what I want to do. Outlaw gangs just don't ride into Hot Springs on a regular basis." He tapped the wooden wall with his left hand. "What I do know is that I don't think these walls would be much help if we was surrounded in a shootout, so we gotta get moved."

He stood and walked over beside Nellie, gesturing toward the street. "It'd be great to think we could stay right here and ask those good people out there to help set up a defense. And I know damn well that those folks would get their guns and help in a minute if those outlaws rode in. But look at all those kids," as if on cue, a group of children raced by the front of the building, laughing and shrieking. "This is a young town. Half the people here are school-aged kids, and they make better targets than helpers."

He stared back at the street. "Even so, I wish we could pull a Northfield, Minnesota on that bunch of thugs."

"Definitely worked there," Nellie smiled thinking of the story of how a few years earlier the Northfield townspeople rose up and drove the feared James-Younger Gang out of their community.

"Yeah, but like I said, I'm afraid for our kids," Akin said. "If everyone comes runnin' to our rescue with guns blazing, we're gonna end up with a bunch of casualties and a lot of 'em are going to be kids." He paced back toward the cells. "So, we gotta get these prisoners moved, even if we have to scare our townsfolk in the process."

Bat joined Nellie at the window and eyed the bustling street scene, jabbing his thumb toward a bright red stagecoach-style rig pulled by four white horses going past. It was loaded with men and women in traveling clothes. On its side were the words: Hot Springs-Cascade-Wind Cave Excursions. 25 Cents.

"Gene, come and look at this." The big man lumbered over beside them and Masterson nodded at the red carriage. "Maybe we could use something like that to move the prisoners? Who runs that rig?"

"The Evans," Akin replied as the carriage reached the intersection and met a big closed-in square wagon being pulled by a team of Belgian draft horses. The wagon, labeled "Fine Mineral and Soda Waters—Minnekahda, Cascade, Kidney Springs—Riordan Bottling," rolled on in their direction. "Wait, by God!" the big Sheriff exclaimed, half-turning and slapping Bat on the shoulder. "Not the excursion stage; we can use the water wagon!"

He grabbed for the front door, stepped out onto the boardwalk, and signaled toward the driver.

Bat gave Nellie a blank look. "What the hell's a water wagon?"

"Sheriff Akin!" The driver, a jovial man with a heavy black mustache and thatch of dark hair sticking out from under the brim of his hat, reined in his team as he greeted Akin. "When'd you get back? Thought you retired?"

"I am Archie, can't you tell?" Akin waved toward the door. "Good to see you again. You mind gettin' down and comin' inside for a couple minutes? I got a little proposition for you."

Riordan set the wagon's brake and climbed down, pulling the right-side part of the reins along with him and looping them over the hitching post in front of the building. His team impatiently pawed at the dirt and shook their heads, rattling their elaborate harnesses in the process.

Accepting a handshake from the Sheriff, the driver removed his hat and slapped dust from it as they walked into the office where Nellie and Bat stood waiting. Akin pointed at deputy Charles Roe, who was emerging from the cells after checking on the prisoners. "You know Charley?" The wagon driver smiled and nodded before shifting his gaze to the two strangers.

"These folks are here on 'official' business to do with a couple men we got locked up in back. That's what I need to talk to you about."

Riordan stepped forward and held out a hand. "Archie Riordan," he said by way of introduction as Masterson grasped his hand in return. "I got the bottling works here in town—mineral water, soft drinks and such." He eyed Masterson's U.S. Marshal badge. "Used to be in the law enforcement business myself. I was the town marshal over in Buffalo Gap for a few years. Had me a hotel there, too." He glanced over at Nellie as if wondering what type of law enforcement she might be in.

"Riordan? I saw a drug store along the river that went by that name," Nellie said. "Any relation?" She extended her hand to him.

He grasped it in return. "Yep, that'd be ours, too," he grinned. "Wife Lulu's helping run it while I make water deliveries. Both these businesses beat the hell outta tryin' to maintain the law. Hands down." He reached over and playfully tapped the Sheriff on the arm. "Sorry Gene, no offense intended."

"None taken," Akin answered. "This here's Nellie Bly, and that big ugly cuss is Bat Masterson."

Riordan looked impressed. "No foolin'?" He eyed Bat's badge again, before shifting back to Nellie. "Nellie Bly? You mean that newspaper woman?" She nodded and he gave a low whistle. "Guess I better watch my P's and Q's huh?" He plopped the hat back on top of his unruly locks. "So why you all wantin' to talk to me? Can't think that you heard about my stellar law career over to the Gap." He chuckled.

Akin waved at a chair by his desk and Riordan sat down.

"We need you and your wagon to help move the prisoners," the Sheriff began. "I don't want this to be general knowledge, but we're thinkin' that some of their friends might be makin' a move to try 'n spring 'em outta here. I want to move 'em up to the new courthouse," he glanced back out the window, "without gettin' everyone all riled up. You know what I'm sayin'?"

"Sure," Riordan answered. "And you're askin' at a good time. Been delivering for the past four hours, so the wagon's darn near empty." He looked around the office. "You couldn't use six cases of mineral water, could you?" He grinned again. "We get them off and that wagon'll be cleaned out and ready to roll."

"Put 'em over there," Akin replied, pointing at the far end of the room, "and send me the bill."

Riordan nodded.

"Thanks Archie," the Sheriff nodded at the back door. "I'm thinking we can get the prisoners out the back there—along the river side. Got three of 'em, but two are wounded. One'll need to go out on a stretcher, but the other one ought ta be able to walk. Should be enough room to maneuver, don't you think?"

Riordan stood and walked over to the back door, looking out at the alley-sized street running behind the building. "Easy," Riordan said. "I'll unload those water cases and move the rig."

"I'll help you," Bat grabbed his bowler hat off the rack and started for the door.

"We can both help," Nellie added, moving toward the front door ahead of them. She stepped out onto the walk just as two dust-covered men, riding hard, reined in in front of the Sheriff's Office. She recognized one as Pete Lemley, the Sheriff's deputy they'd met earlier, but on closer inspection she could see that the second one actually was a woman. A pair of pistols were strapped in the front of her saddle and a large double saddlebag was strapped just behind.

Both of them jumped down and looped their reins onto the hitching post alongside the reins from Riordan's team. Nellie stepped back, holding the door open for them to come inside.

"Got a big problem Gene!" Lemley panted as he and the dusty woman rushed into the jail. The woman shifted nervously from foot-to-foot while Lemley took a tin cup off a shelf and went to the water bucket near the entrance to the cells. Pulling out a dipper full of water, he gulped it noisily, then sloshed some water into the cup and handed the dipper over to her. "You tell him Nellie."

Nellie Bly was startled to hear her name and stood speechless, unsure of what she should do or say.

"He means Nellie Ryan, here," Akin said, seeing Nellie Bly's reaction. "How ya doin' Nellie? Saw Postmaster Stanley this morning and he told me you were still goin' strong." He grinned at her, but when her serious expression didn't change, he gestured at the others. "Miss Ryan's our lady mail carrier extraordinaire. Been ridin' the Fall River-Cascade mail route for years. Keeps us posted whenever she spots anything that don't look right." He shifted his gaze back to Ryan. "So, what'd you see?"

Nellie Ryan finished taking a big drink, eyed the empty cup and then started talking. "Sheriff there's a pretty suspicious looking bunch about halfway up the Canyon. I was out on my deliveries and saw them camped down by the big trestle."

"You sure they was up to no good? Maybe they're just a bunch of cowpokes."

"Nope, they had lots of guns and not much to give 'em the look of ordinary cowboys, if you know what I mean?" Akin nodded and looked over to Pete, who took the cup back, re-filled it and drank again before speaking.

"We ran onto Nellie about two miles down," Pete said. He stopped and glanced nervously around, unsure if he should continue.

"You both know Archie." Akin pointed in Riordan's direction. He nodded toward Nellie Bly and Bat. "And Nellie Ryan, this here's another Nellie—Nellie Bly; and Marshal Bat Masterson. They're all working with us, so Pete just go on ahead with your report."

"Boys and me were figuring to set up down at the Narrows," Lemley continued. "Figured no one'd get past us there. Whether they're come in along the river or up on the ridgeline, you got both trails covered at that spot. But after we met up with Nellie, I sent the boys over by the Carson's Notch Bridge, and

Nellie and me hightailed it back here to let you know what was goin' on."

"There's five, maybe six of 'em," Nellie Ryan continued. "Probably six. Like I said, they got a lot of guns; rifles and pistols. They didn't look like they were in any big hurry though. They were taking their time cooking something. That's how I first saw them—saw their campfire smoke and was thinking there might be some sort of forest fire going on. Otherwise I probably wouldn't have even gone over that direction."

She stopped and shrugged. "I heard about that train robbery just before I rode out, so when I saw that bunch, I just sort-of put two-and-two together about who they might be."

Lemley set the dipper down. "Any more of the Home Guard come in?"

"No. And I don't know who can even make it on short notice like this." Akin paced anxiously, coming around the desk and peering at his pocket watch.

"We head right back out to Carson's Notch we should be able to keep them from coming any further—at least not without a helluva fight. Might even be able to get the drop on 'em and bring 'em back nice and peaceable like."

Nellie Ryan pulled off her dusty hat and drew her forearm across her brow. Without the hat, she appeared surprisingly young—maybe in her early to mid-30s. Nellie Bly could see that this other Nellie was very fit and probably very feminine once she changed out of her cowboy's garb.

The mail carrier slipped her hat back on. "You want me to come along?" she asked. "I'm not a bad shot, you know, and I'm guessing you don't want me going back out on my route."

The Sheriff shook his head in response. "Thanks, Nellie, but no. You go on back to the Post

Office and secure those mailbags. Oh, and tell John I said he should give you the rest of the day off WITH pay for doing your civic duty."

She chuckled at that. "Yeah, I'm sure he'll be givin' me a huge bonus for THAT." She chuckled once more, straightened her hat and walked out. Seconds later, the door re-opened and she looked back in. "Did you say Nellie Bly and Bat Masterson? Seriously?"

Nellie and Bat nodded.

"Okay. Just checking that I heard you correct." She gave them a little smile and ducked back out.

"Gene, do you think any more of your Home Guard are going to get here? Or are we on our own?" Masterson asked. Akin shrugged in response.

"Sheriff, we can't wait for them," Lemley interrupted. "We gotta go back right now. Anyone shows up is just gonna have to ride out and join us as soon as they get here, because if we don't go now, we'll be too late. If that bunch gets past the Notch they'll be up alongside the Seven Sisters with nothing in front of 'em but the south valley and a clear road into town."

"What's Seven Sisters?" Nellie asked.

"Series of hills that start at the entrance to Fall River Canyon, but they run out toward Cascade Springs," Lemley said. "It's what we call the south entrance into town."

Akin looked around and signaled to Charles Roe. "Well, there's three of us to get out to the Notch if Charley rides with us. And with the two boys already out there, we got 'em about fifty-fifty. Plus, they don't know we're there. That's worth a couple more right there, ain't it?" He nodded at the door. "You boys get your horses and bring mine around. We better go."

He watched as Lemley and Roe headed outside before turning toward Masterson, Nellie and

Riordan. "If you three are willing to move these prisoners and hold down the fort until Chalky, Bullock and the rest of them get back from up north, I'd be much obliged."

Not waiting for a reply, Akin glanced once more at his watch. "Chalky and that Oklahoma fella oughta be gettin' back any time now, too, so they can give you some reinforcements. And Chalky knows all the ins and outs of that courthouse, since his old man's been helping build it."

He walked over to the gun rack by his desk. "I don't know how long it'll take Bullock and the others to get back with that body, but that'll give you more guns, once they arrive. You can keep the body there, too, until we get back to town."

He looked at Riordan. "And Archie, if any more of my Guardsmen show up, you tell 'em to hightail it on out to the Notch." He reached up and took a rifle out of the three-gun rack, opened a box of shells, loaded it and handed it over to the wagon driver. Reaching into the desk drawer he pulled out a badge and tossed it to Riordan.

"You are hereby deputized. So, get your wagon ready and start moving them prisoners." A flicker of a smile crossed Riordan's face as he checked the rifle and walked out the door.

Akin turned to Nellie. "Miss Bly..."

"I told you," she interrupted, "Nellie."

He made a harrumphing sound as he swung around and started pulling a second rifle from the gun rack. "All right...Nellie. I need you to go over to Doc Jennings' office and have him come back with you. If we're moving wounded prisoners, I want to make sure we don't kill any of 'em in the process. The Doc's office is straight up this street to where the road runs down from the schoolhouse. From there you go over to the right about half block." She started for the door. "You okay with all this?"

"Yes, I'm good."

"You know how to shoot?"

His question stopped her with a hand on the doorknob. She looked back over her shoulder. "Yes," she said. "And I'm not afraid to if I have to."

The Sheriff placed the loaded rifle on his desk. "Okay, this one's yours. Soon as you get back." She nodded and hurried out, pulling her hat down tighter. The door slammed shut and quickly re-opened as Riordan came rushing back in.

"Archie? What's going on?"

"You'll want to see this," Riordan said, jerking a thumb over his shoulder. Akin followed him to the door, looked out and grinned. Sitting next to Riordan's wagon were half-a-dozen men, armed and ready to ride.

He turned back to Masterson. "Well, Bat, things just started to get a little brighter. Step on out here and meet some of my Roughriders." Lemley and Deputy Roe rode up from the side of building, leading Akin's horse and nodded happily at the sight of the Home Guard members.

Sheriff Akin took the reins and climbed up on his mount. He tipped his hat to Masterson and started to turn the horse away, but reined in and turned back. Reaching into his vest pocket, he pulled out a key ring with two keys on it and tossed it to Bat.

"Just about forgot this. Small one opens the Courthouse door; bigger one is for the cells. Good luck."

"Yeah," Masterson answered. "You too."

CHAPTER TWENTY-ONE

Jack coughed and wiped his arm across his mouth, pushing on a boulder with his right arm as he braced his left leg with the left arm and staggered to his feet. "Is that running water I hear? I'm really getting dry. Probably should've drank something before we left the house."

He had just rolled part way down a steep draw after falling on one of the slick pieces of shale blanketing the hillside. Irene half-slid down the incline to his side as he struggled to stabilize himself. She slipped her arm around his waist as he regained his balance. He stared back at the path, turning quickly as the hot sun nearly blinded him. "Guess I should've taken my hat, too," he mumbled. "Stupid."

"I didn't give you much time to think about anything when we went out that tunnel," she answered. "It's as much my fault as yours."

She swung around and pointed down the hillside. "You're right, there's a stream at the bottom of the hill. At least you'll be able to get something to drink." She looked around. "I was hoping we might've met up with my husband by now."

Jack hobbled a few steps further. "Maybe he's coming back another way?"

"Maybe?" Her face clouded for a few seconds as she stared at the empty horizon. Turning to face him, she touched his head and pointed at his left leg, covered with dirt after his fall. "How's your head? And your leg?" She took his left hand, still wrapped with the piece of sheet, and turned it palm up. "And what about your hand?"

"I'll make it," he grimaced. "Got a headache and did something to my ankle, but I'm sure it'll be okay. And I don't want to think about my hand right now. I'll keep it wrapped. Come on, we better keep moving. Where we going?"

Irene looked back up the ravine. "Once we get all the way down, we can follow that streambed. I think going right leads back toward the Martins' Ranch; and left," she stopped and looked to the northwest. "I'm not sure. Maybe it winds back through King's Canyon or Red Canyon—around toward Wind Cave. I've never been either way. But, we should be able to find help no matter what direction we go." She eyed him nervously. "It's going to be a long way—at least a few miles no matter which way we go. You sure you can walk?"

Jack glanced at his left ankle. "I can make it." He tested the ankle and pain seared through his entire leg. He glanced over at her and gave her a half-hearted smile. "Hurts a little, but I can walk." He stared back up the hill behind them. "Sooner we get away from this hill the better, especially once they find out we're gone. I think if they catch up to us ... this time they won't waste any time tying us up. I'd rather deal with a sore ankle than a bullet."

She nodded and started moving again, easing down the steep incline toward the trees lining the streambed. Jack grimaced again as he continued following, half sliding along on his butt as he slipped and sat down hard. Suddenly Irene held up a hand and crouched behind one of the wild rose bushes that had appeared as they drew closer to the water. Jack slid further, sitting completely down as he reached her side.

"What is it?" he whispered, reaching down and grasping the handle of the pistol he had taken from Georgie.

"Horses coming," she said. "From the right up above the streambed. Can't see 'em, but I can hear 'em. Can't tell how many."

She barely had the words out of her mouth when the sound of galloping filled the air to their right. He scrunched down tighter behind the bush, barely breathing. Then the sound dissipated and it got very quiet before they heard a snort and one sharp whinny.

Irene edged up and peered intently through the top branches toward the sound of a single horse advancing toward them. "Oh my God! I don't believe it!"

"What?" he hissed.
"It's El Kebir."
"El what?"
"Kebir. He's a wild stallion running these parts. Paul's had to chase him off before. We thought he might've died." She looked back upstream. "He's getting old; and mean. Been around here for as long as we have and he was here when we first arrived."

Jack exhaled slowly, then got onto his knees and joined her in looking over top of the bush. A startlingly large white stallion was coming toward them. Suddenly, he stopped, snorting a challenge. "What the hell? Is he challenging us?"

Irene crouched back down. "I don't know? He's acting crazy. But how could he even see us here...?"

Her sentence was cut off by a sharp neigh, then a series of shrill, deep cries. Jack looked back in time to see the huge horse stamp a forefoot, his nostrils flaring before he reared up and pounded down with his both front legs again and again, neighing angrily in the process. After nearly a minute of this, he stepped back, pawing at the ground and still snorting. Appearing appeased by the results of his actions, he turned sideways, his magnificent body rippling in the late afternoon sun. Looking back up the hillside behind him he raised his head and gave two neighing calls.

Almost instantly the summit of the small hill was darkened by a group of shadows, which quickly turned into a herd of horses. Jack sucked in sharply at the sight.

"Our mares," he choked out. "I'll be damned." He sat back down and Irene knelt beside him.

"What do you mean?" she asked, confused by his reaction. "I just told you El Kebir's a wild stallion from here. That would be his herd."

"Now, maybe," Jack agreed. "But earlier today they were ours." He quickly explained about what had happened and how the mares had escaped from the train. "We were bringing them to the Martins," he added. "That's why Chalky and me rode out there; to tell them that their mares were gone because of the train robbery." He peered around the bush as the noise of the herd intensified. The mares were moving past, heading upstream and stopping from time-to-time to sip water as the stallion roamed around them—defending and organizing them at the same time. He nuzzled the grey mare that had been the herd's leader and she whickered in response.

"Wind's from the southeast," Irene said as she watched the herd over Jack's shoulder. "That's why he didn't smell us. Once they get past, though, he'll know right away that there are people nearby; otherwise maybe we could catch one of your mares to ride."

"Naw, they're brood mares. They're not broke to ride. And a lot of 'em are with foal."

"Wonder where he's taking them?" She pulled the branches of the bush apart for a clearer look at the horses moving past below them. Her action caught the eye of the stallion, which turned sharply, snorting and emitting a series of five or six warning sounds. The mares quickly bunched together and started moving faster up the streambed as the stallion rushed in Jack and Irene's direction, neighing loudly to challenge whatever had caught his eye.

"Stand up!" Jack ordered. He grabbed her hand and together they half leaped to their feet directly in the charging stallion's path. The sudden appearance of two humans caused the horse to skid to a stop, its full mane flying as he reared up. "Yah, yah!" Jack yelled, keeping the pistol at ready as he waved his other hand. Irene quickly joined in, ripping her apron free and waving it in the air. El Kebir whinnied another challenge at them before backing away toward his newly claimed herd.

As the mares galloped upstream the stallion whirled around one more time and sent a piercing high-pitched cry at the humans as if daring them to follow. In a few more seconds all of the mares were out of sight and he raced to join them. The sounds of the herd's departure dissipated as Irene and Jack exchanged an astonished look.

Irene headed toward the stream and stopped where the stallion had reacted so angrily before summoning the mares. "Well, this explains what he was doing before," she said, pointing at a spot just below a shelf of rock jutting out of the hill. There, mangled almost beyond recognition, was the carcass of a huge rattlesnake.

Jack reached her side and eyed the snake. "Whew, good thing El Kebir got here before we did. I hate snakes. And remind me not to actually try to fight with that horse if we get into another confrontation, okay?"

He re-holstered the gun and hurried past the dead snake as fast as his leg would allow. Splashing into the clear-running stream, he dropped to his knees and bent to the water. Cupping some in his right hand he drank noisily. Irene joined him and took a few hands-full before splashing water onto her face and neck. The water was cold despite the hot sun. Jack sat back and unwound the cloth from his damaged left hand unveiling a series of angry red gashes on the palm.

He leaned forward and thrust it into the rushing stream. "I can't believe how good that feels," he sighed.

"We need to keep moving," Irene urged, nervously looking back up the hill. She grabbed the piece of sheet and soaked it in the stream, then nodded at his hand. "Let me."

He held the hand toward her and she quickly wound the wet cloth around it going in both directions and knotted it on top of his knuckles.

"Okay?"

"It's good," he responded, flexing his fingers while eyeing her handiwork.

"We should go."

"Yeah, I know," he answered, groaning slightly as he stood. "Downstream or up?"

She shook her head. "If they trail us this far, they'll probably think we went toward the Martins'. It's downstream and easier walking."

"So we oughta go up. Right? Besides with all those horse tracks, it'll be hard to see ours."

"Can you walk it?"

"Yes." He turned his back so she couldn't see the agony on his face as he took a couple steps. He glanced back at the hill where long shadows stretched toward them. "How long until dark?"

"I don't know. Five hours." She walked past him downstream for half-dozen steps, and then veered out into the stream, holding the bottom of her skirt up as she went across to the other bank. After taking a few more steps to where a dwarf cottonwood jutted sideways out into the water, she disappeared over the topside of the tree trunk before reappearing in the middle of the stream again walking back in his direction.

"What are you...?"

She gestured at her footprints. "Go like I did...downstream a bit then back here in the water. But stay along that side and don't get in the water until you get to where those rocks are blocking the bank. If they follow us here, they'll see right off that we were headed downstream and figure we had to get in the water because of those rocks."

Jack hobbled along the bank, reached a large boulder pile that had formed from a rockslide and splashed down into the stream. The cool water was soothing on his throbbing ankle. He turned and sloshed back upstream. Irene already had regathered her skirt around her waist and was wading ahead. The water was running about a foot deep and about five to six yards across except where it gushed through narrower tight spots like that created by the rockslide.

They passed a bend and the stream widened out, dotted with dozens of tracks from the horse herd. Ahead of them the red canyon walls soared up on either side and the rose bushes and dwarf cottonwoods gave way to more ponderosa pine—some growing seemingly right out of the big boulders that had tumbled off the canyon walls toward the water.

"We need to keep following the horses' tracks," she said softly, waiting for him to catch up as she paused to scoop up a drink of water with her hands. "I'm thinking El Kebir knows the fastest and easiest ways in and out of this canyon." Jack nodded as he also reached down for more water.

Irene slogged on, staying about 25 yards ahead and never leaving the middle of the fast-rushing stream. From time-to-time the back part of her skirt would slip down into the water and she'd impatiently tug at it. Finally, she pulled it forward and tucked it into her waistband, exposing the white skin on the back of her thighs and calves. Jack's first reaction to the exposure had been shock, but after nearly an hour of constant numbing movement he paid little attention, choosing instead to concentrate on carefully placing each step with his injured left leg so that he wouldn't fall.

A large black and white bird swept over them heading downstream as the sound of the rushing water intensified. A red squirrel appeared and chattered a warning as Irene navigated past another sideways growing tree and disappeared from Jack's sight. He had a sudden panicky feeling but resisted the urge to call out to her—just in case someone might be within earshot. Ducking under the branches of the half-fallen tree, he grabbed hold of a branch and leveraged his way forward past where the stream gushed through a fissure formed by two large slabs of rock that had fallen together across it.

Now the banks of the stream were gone and with it the hoof prints of the horses they had been following. The only passage was in the waterway where he could faintly see one or two prints rapidly being washed away by the water's force.

Jack stepped through the natural archway and stopped. "What the hell?" he said to Irene, who was standing still on a flat rock shelf and looking back toward him. She turned and took a couple more steps along the shelf, her skirt still tucked up around her waist. Jack walked on in silence until he reached her side. The red-gold canyon walls towered above them and stretched out majestically toward the west.

"This might seem like a dumb question, but where's the water coming from?" he asked.

On their left was an expansive rock wall that appeared to be colliding with another wall coming at an angle from the right. At the point where the two walls met, they formed a sharp L-shape that swept out toward the canyon's main floor. A roaring waterfall appeared to be miraculously gushing out of a seam formed at the junction of the L. Beyond it was nothing but a solid rock wall.

Picking their way along the shelf, they reached another slight incline and Irene scrambled up over the top. Finally seeming to remember that she had her legs uncovered, she tugged at her bunched-up skirt and let it fall back to her shoe tops before holding a hand out to Jack.

He extended his injured hand and involuntarily cried out as she grasped it and pulled while he braced himself with his good right hand and pushed forward. Stepping up beside her he stared at the flat expanse of hard, empty canyon floor stretching out toward the sun and appearing to collide with another solid rock wall a couple miles distant.

She gestured at the spot where the water was erupting, creating a misty cloud and a series of small rainbows in the dying sunlight.

"I can't tell at this angle whether the water's coming up out of the ground or down from a higher point along those walls." She looked around and back up into the canyon. "Wonder where El Kebir took those mares?"

As if on cue, a wet horse's head materialized out of mist alongside the gushing stream.

"What? What in the world?" Jack sputtered.

The mare snapped around at the sound of his voice and whinnied a sharp warning. In seconds, more heads popped up alongside her followed by their bodies.

"There must be some sort of hidden protected area back there," Irene said. She started forward. "Come on, let's check it out."

At her movement, the horses began milling around and one-by-one started leaping across the stream toward the expanse of open canyon floor. Jack and Irene watched as the lead horses disappeared for several seconds and then, like magic, reappeared racing toward the northwest.

"Come on," Irene ordered as she moved toward the remainder of the herd. Jack stumbled along behind her. They made one final small climb and found themselves next to the roaring water, which was not erupting outward but, instead, pouring down out of a crevice about a dozen feet above them.

As the last of the mares splashed through the stream and out onto the flat, the magnificent old stallion stepped from behind the cascading water, shook himself and neighed another challenge at the intruders. Jack and Irene stood frozen as he spun around, jumped the running water and galloped after the mares. In less than a minute they had encountered the herd, lost the herd, and now faced what looked like a water source that was foaming out of solid rock.

"Where was he hiding?" Jack asked.

"I don't know. I didn't even know this place existed," Irene replied.

They cautiously advanced along the wet rocks, finally stepping behind the falls. There, completely hidden and sloping gently away from them, was the entrance to a very large cave. Irene stopped but Jack advanced further, trying to adjust his eyes to the semi-darkness.

"This is weird," he said, turning toward her. "Looks like there's a fence in here built out of logs and rocks." Irene came forward and cupped her hands around her eyes to get a clearer view of a defined rock wall splitting the cave into two spaces. A gate-like structure made out of logs was lying half-broken on the right-hand side.

Jack nudged her and pointed to the left. "That look like some sort of torch?" She stared at where he was pointing and saw a heavy stick with one end wrapped in dried grass, twigs and some sort of fabric hanging from a cutout in the wall. Jack walked over and pulled it loose and eyed it for several seconds before reaching into his right-hand vest pocket and retrieving a couple of stick matches.

"You never know?" he said, half-shrugging at Irene's amazed expression. "Had a foreman once who said to always carry matches." He pushed one back into the pocket, draped the end of the big stick over his left arm and swiped the remaining match on a rock. The match head's light, tiny as it was, still seemed to double the size of their visible surroundings. He slowly moved the flickering flame toward the stick's wrapped end. It was so dry it caught almost instantly, causing him to drop the match in surprise. He struggled to re-balance the torch so it wouldn't burn his arm.

Irene hurried over and grabbed at the end of it to help keep it from falling, while Jack crooked his bandaged left hand and forearm under the stick's center.

"Aaghh!" he gasped. She eyed his badly swollen left hand, with which he was clearly unable to grab the torch. She held on with both hands and continued to stare at his damaged hand. "We need to treat that," she nodded at the bad hand as he finally got a grip on the torch with his good right one.

"With what?" he asked, as he grasped firmly on the middle of the stick and pushed it back and up toward the notch where it had been resting. Together they fitted it back into the space as it continued to flare up.

The growing light illuminated two distinct rooms. To the left, where they were standing, appeared to be a corral with room for 25 or 30 horses. Old dried droppings were interspersed with fresh manure from the herd that had just been there. On the right, a smaller space, set off by the rock wall and rotted logs, looked like living quarters.

Black soot had stained the cave walls and a makeshift rock fireplace had an iron strap across the top, as if designed to hold a cooking pot. Rotted ropes, rusty cans, crinkly dried straps, a couple of leather boots, whiskey bottles and piles of rotted bedding littered the space, and yet it seemed to have an order to it.

"Looks almost like whoever was here before was kind of expecting to return," Jack said.

Irene nodded and gestured toward the far wall. There, crumpled in a broken heap stood the remains of a two-wheeled buggy and three large cast-iron boxes. Battered locks dangled from the front of each and the tops were flung open.

As they moved cautiously through the debris, Irene reached down and picked up a tin-pan lamp with the remains of several half-burned candles. Breaking two of them free, she walked back to the torch and held them up to the fire.

"Here." She held one out to Jack and dipped the other back toward the tin lamp, igniting a couple more candles soldered to the base by the old melted wax. Moving over to the twisted wreckage, Jack knelt by one of the iron boxes, first holding the candle inside, then moving it to read some writing on the outside. He emitted a low whistle.

"What are they?" Irene asked.

"Empty strong boxes." He stood up. "The lettering on them says Property of Homestake Mine."

CHAPTER TWENTY-TWO

Just as Nellie reached the intersection below the schoolhouse hill and prepared to turn up the street toward the Doctor's office, a two-passenger buggy hitched to a red-brown gelding rolled to a halt a few feet ahead of her. The driver pulled back on the rig's brake and stepped down directly into her path.

"Ah, there you are Miss Cochran. I heard you went out headed toward the Sheriff's office, so I thought I'd take a drive in hopes that we might cross paths." Robert Seaman doffed his expensive silk top hat and gave Nellie a slight bow

"Oh, Mister Seaman! You startled me."

"Sorry. I didn't intend that." He looped one of the horse's reins over the first hitching post and stood holding his hat in front of him, balancing a silver-tipped cane beneath it and looking contrite. "What I intended, actually, was to find you and make an apology for my earlier boorish behavior at the hotel."

He bowed slightly. "I also wanted to ask if you might like to attend that Chautauqua show this evening." He paused as if expecting an immediate response. When she didn't speak, he stammered. "I mean...with me?"

Nellie reddened. "Oh. I see."

"And I also promised you a visit to a shop to replace that ruined dress of yours. I've located the best dress shop and tailor in town. It's a place called Holmes', located quite close to the hotel. I spoke with Mister Holmes and his wife and they said if I could bring you by, they could take your measurements and get started on the pattern of your choice immediately. They did seem to be quite accommodating if I might say so myself."

He looked pleased by his initiative. But as Nellie hesitated again, he quickly added, "Or we can go directly to the Mercantile store. It's Fargo Mercantile and Millinery and I've discovered that they, too, have a very fine array..."

"Mister Seaman..."

"Robert," he said, slipping his hat back on and continuing to look pleased with himself.

"Robert," Nellie said, a slightly exasperated tone in her voice. "It's not that I don't appreciate this, believe me. But right at this moment I am on a very important and urgent mission to find Doctor Jennings' and get him down to the Sheriff's office. Now, if you want to walk along with me to the doctor's office that would be fine. It's right up this street and very close by. We could continue our conversation as we go. Otherwise, I'm afraid I must excuse myself and hope we might talk later...perhaps back at the hotel."

As before, Seaman appeared startled by her forwardness in how she addressed him, particularly since she was once again letting him know that she wasn't going to be doing something just because he asked.

"Of course," he finally said, stepping forward to offer her his arm as she turned to her right and started up the street in the direction of Doctor Jennings' office building. They walked several steps before he said, "Do you prefer to be called Nellie or Elizabeth?"

Nellie reddened again. "Look, I'm sorry I deceived you about that," she began. He held up a hand to stop her.

"I'm not upset. I understood your earlier explanation and it really doesn't matter that you were traveling incognito. I just want to be sure that we're on the proper footing here and I call you by the name you most prefer. So is it Elizabeth or Nellie?"

"Well, everyone calls me Nellie," she said, "except for my very closest friends and family who know my real name." She glanced up at him, still holding his arm. He was looking straight ahead as they walked and she was struck by the kind look on his face as a woman with two small children met them and passed. He reached up with the hand holding his cane and tipped his hat to them.

"I think I would prefer that you call me Elizabeth."

His eyes crinkled slightly at her response and she saw him form just the smallest of smiles before he turned his head. She blushed again at being caught looking up at him, and quickly turned her own face forward.

"Very good...Elizabeth. I think that's what I would prefer too." They took a few more steps before he spoke again. "Why are you going for the doctor? Is it something to do with Marshal Masterson?"

"No. Well, yes." She stopped and faced him. "Robert, I need to share some things with you. Things have been happening with those outlaws that tried to hold up the train, and on top of that some things have been going on with those people whose room you were in back at the hotel—the Previns."

He frowned. "What 'things'?"

"There's been a murder and the Sheriff and Marshal Masterson think the dead man might be the husband of the woman who was selling you that antique gun. And now they think there's some tie-in between her and the gang that attacked our train." Speaking quickly as they continued walking, she gave him a rundown of all that had transpired, ending with the decision to move the prisoners in case the outlaw gang rode into the community.

"So right now I need to bring Doctor Jennings back to the jail so he can insure that the prisoner being transported by the Marshal is okay to move to the courthouse. This is probably way beyond anything you want to have to deal with but, unfortunately, it's sort-of what usually seems to happen to me when I get involved in my investigative reporting assignments."

She paused and took a deep breath. "Not that this is a reporting opportunity by any means. That's not why I'm involved."

He smiled. "I see." He nodded at the door to the Doctor's office. "I think we should get inside and get that Doctor down there, don't you?" He reached out and opened the door. "And Elizabeth, I want to help. I lead a pretty boring life most of the time, while your life seems to be filled with excitement ALL of the time. I wouldn't mind having that kind of experience…at least for one day…with you, I mean, if that's okay with you?"

She had started inside and now stopped at his remark and turned back to face him, looking up into his eyes. "Yes," she said. She reached over and took his left hand. "I'm not certain why, but I feel like I want you to experience that with me, too."

"Okay." He took his hand from hers and turned away.

"But...where are you going?"

"To get the buggy," he answered. "When it comes to excitement these days, I'm much better at it when I can ride."

She burst into laughter at his remark and hurried inside while he briskly walked back toward the rig.

*****

Lil and Minnie shared gasps of delight as they reached the edge of a towering rock wall overlooking the Chautauqua Park and stared straight down at the twin-spired Pavilion, its colorful banners flapping from the poles that jutted from its rooftop.

"Wow, this is amazing!" Lil exclaimed.

"See, I told you it would be," Joe said. "Ever since Mister Cross hired me to come help him do some of his photos up here, I've been coming back on my own just for the view." He paused and spread his arms wide as if encompassing the beauty of the Park, which was filled with evergreens, golden-leaved aspens and a riot of fall wildflowers fully in bloom.

After spending about an hour with Annie Oakley and Buffalo Bill, including watching Lil shoot her new rifle for Annie's approval, Bill had suggested that Joe take the buggy and drive the girls up to the overlook, a spot to which he had taken his famous visitors on their earlier tour of the community.

At first, Lil had objected, saying she didn't want to miss a minute of the excitement in the park, but both Annie and Bill had insisted, assuring her that it would be well worth the girls' time to take in the view from above.

Minnie grasped Lil's hand and edged further out onto the rim of the cliff. "The river runs right down below us, alongside this cliff," she said. She pointed past the far side of the Pavilion where members of Sousa's brass band were moving around some chairs on the band shell and tuning their instruments. "And right there by the band is where it comes back out and turns toward the town. That must be the bridge we came across earlier."

A covered wooden bridge, its far side obscured by the white limestone cliffs that formed the backdrop to the peaceful park's setting, jutted across the point where the waterway turned left. The visible side of the bridge opened toward them onto a dirt road that skirted the flat area alongside the Pavilion and continued northwest. At a spot where another limestone wall defined that side of the park it rejoined the stream and both road and stream disappeared up into the hills.

"Where does the river start?" Minnie asked as she stepped back beside the others.

"It's not really the river," Hayden explained. "Mister Cross said that there's called the Hot Brook. It starts way up in the Bradley Flats out northwest of town and runs in from there and on down toward the Evan's Plunge where it connects up with the Cold Brook." Joe looked pleased with himself as he spouted the information. "And those two running together—Hot Brook and Cold Brook—is what makes up the Fall River itself." He smiled triumphantly.

"Tell us again—just who this Mister Cross?" Lil asked.

"Oh, sorry. He's a photographer. He's got a studio down on the Minnekahta Street by the Evans Hotel. He wanted to take my portrait one day—me'n some of the other waiters. And we just sort-a hit it off. Next thing I knew he was askin' if I wanted to earn some extra cash by helpin' tote his equipment and such. He wanted to come on up here and do some shootin' of the scenery; things like that." Once again, he spread his arms to encompass the surroundings and swung around from east to west.

"And look!" He pointed excitedly toward the next segment of the cliff jutting out to form a second promontory point. There, just across the chasm between the cliff sections, a man was maneuvering a large camera on a tripod. "There he is!" Joe waved, cupped his hands around his mouth and yelled. "Mister Cross! Hello!"

The photographer, who had just flipped the big camera's blackout cloth over his head, pulled his head from under the cloth and looked around. Joe waved again, and the man pulled out a long tube, pointed it in their direction and put it up to his face. After a few seconds, he lowered the device and waved, gesturing for them to come over to join him.

"I think he wants us to come over there," Minnie said. "Should we go?"

"Yeah, come on, let's go!" Joe was already moving back up the slight incline leading away from the cliff's edge and over toward a spot where the two promontories came together. "It must be an even better view of the park from where he's at or he wouldn't be settin' up there." Minnie looked at Lil and she shrugged.

Together they hurried after him, their button shoes kicking up pine needles. Joe turned around as he reached the spot that connected the two cliffs. "I forgot to warn you," he said. "Two things. First, there be timber rattlers up here, so keep a sharp eye, just in case." The girls looked around nervously at the admonition, certain that the snakes must be hiding behind every rock.

"What's the second thing?" Lil asked.

"Graves," he said solemnly, and pointed over to his right. Dotting the softly sloping hillside were dozens of gravesites, some with wooden crosses and others with small semi-circular headstones. "This area over here is a cemetery, too, so don't be steppin' on nobody's grave."

He walked on and Lil fell in behind Minnie so they could walk single file past the graves.

"Look," Minnie said. "Lots of little kids buried up here." She pointed first at one stone, then another, then at two of the crosses. All showed names and dates of children under age five—and three were under age one. Lil stepped beyond the first few graves and looked at some of the others. One appeared to hold a mother and her child.

"Almost seems like more kids buried up here than adults. Do you know what happened?"

Minnie nodded. "Probably from either the smallpox or diphtheria epidemics in the '80s. Hot Springs and Custer City got hit real hard when they went through. Don't know why, but Buffalo Gap got spared. I remember my folks saying that one epidemic came one year, and the other one the next, but I never thought much about it 'til now." She stared thoughtfully at the many graves. "Lot of these kids buried here would be about our age by now."

Lil involuntarily shivered despite the warm afternoon sun, and threaded her way around the graves and back to the trail Joe was following through the pine needles and sagebrush. They moved on silently until suddenly the photographer and his huge tripod loomed before them. The big man gave them a welcoming smile.

"Didn't expect to see you up here, sir," Joe said, accepting Cross's handshake and then turning back to the girls. "These here are my new friends, Minnie and Lil."

"Lil Marr," Lil said, tentatively extending her hand to the older man while staring at his camera.

"W.R. Cross." He smiled again and jerked a thumb back at the camera. "Nature and Portrait photographer."

"I'm Minnie Thompson," Minnie offered her hand. "What's the W.R. stand for?"

"William Richard, but you can call me Bill." He gave her a surprised look as she screwed up her face at his answer. "Did I say something wrong?"

"No...uh...well, it's just that a friend of mine earlier today told me that everyone of any importance these days is named William, Will or Bill, and I told him that was crazy. But since then almost every man I've met, except for Joe, has been just that. It's too weird." She sighed and Cross chuckled at her answer, took off his floppy hat and wiped his brow.

"That's probably a bit of an overstatement," he laughed again, "but I'll have to agree that there are a lot of us around." He waved the round tube he was holding out toward the Park. "Joe showing you the sights."

"Yes sir," Minnie replied. She nodded at the tube. "What's that thing?"

"Oh." He held it up with both hands and offered it to her. "It's my own concoction of a telescope." She took it from him and turned it over. It was a dull grey in color, about two feet in length with a center piece that allowed one end to slide into the other, thus extending another foot. "Go ahead, take a look down at the park. You can focus by turning the big end and moving it out or in, depending on how much of the scene you want to see."

She turned toward the Pavilion and band shell, which now were further to her left, and aimed it down, focusing as he had suggested. The band members, small and bug-like before, popped clearly into view and she could see Sousa shouting something from his podium. The middle-aged man she had seen meeting with Joe at the Evans' Dining Room was walking among the musicians handing them sheets of paper. Then he walked back to the podium and handed one to Sousa.

"Wow! Lil you gotta see this." Minnie passed the scope over to Lil and stood back as Lil took a turn and also gasped in appreciation at the view through the tube.

"My camera can take in a panoramic view, or I can focus it down on particular spots out there, depending on what I want to do," he said. "It's a Sanderson Universal Swing Front," he proudly explained. When he saw the blank look on the young peoples' faces, he quickly added. "It's like the Kodak, only a lot bigger and more powerful."

They all nodded at the mention of the trendy Kodak name and eyed the big camera that had a long flexible bellows and very black focusing cloth on the back. "I can look through my scope, decide how close I want to have the photo, and then get under the cloth and move the lens in and out to where I want it." He gave a little sigh. "Don't even have to get out from under the cloth to turn the lens. Amazing new technology."

He pointed back at where his horse was grazing, tied to a small tree at the entrance to the promontory point on which they stood. In the small square wagon hitched to the horse was a big box filled with other equipment. "Not that I don't like Kodaks. Been carrying the flat folder version with me, too. In a pinch I don't even need a tripod with that one, and I can carry it with me out on my bicycle, too. Got schooled on it when I visited the Eastman Company in New York last summer.

He gazed longingly toward the East as if thinking about that trip just as Sousa's musicians began playing a tune. Joe clapped his hands in surprise as Lil pulled the telescope back up to gaze down at the brass band in action.

"Listen to that would ya. That there's our new song!" Joe exclaimed. "Mine 'n Mister Metz's. That there's 'Hot Time'." Minnie, Joe and Cross all strained to listen as Lil kept her eye on Sousa directing the band. The crisply dressed conductor waved his baton to stop and the music ended as abruptly as it had begun. Lil could see him holding up another paper and as the members began pulling a new sheet onto their music stands, he turned and smiled at Metz, nodding as he said something about the first song.

A sudden movement to their right caused both men to turn back to the east where the front side of the Pavilion opened to visitors. Sousa pointed and Lil moved the telescope in that direction as Buffalo Bill and Annie Oakley emerged from the entrance and strode over to the band shell to shake hands. They stood chatting and Sousa gestured toward Metz and put a hand on the Minstrel Show leader's shoulder. As Buffalo Bill extended his big hand toward Metz, Annie turned and gave the band members a small wave and they responded with applause.

"What's going on?" Minnie asked, trying to make out who was doing what on the floor of the Chautauqua grounds.

"It's Annie and Bill!" Lil exclaimed, handing the tube back to Minnie. "They're talking to Mister Sousa, and the band's applauding them." She waved her arms wildly hoping to get Annie's attention.

"I don't think they'll see you unless they're looking for you," Cross said. "That scope makes everything look like you can reach out and touch it, but they're still a long ways off." He pointed toward the far end of the park. "Look out there, beyond where the road goes and you can see way up toward the caretaker's cabin. Even though it's a long ways, the scope brings it right up close." He took the tube and looked off in that direction. After focusing it, he handed it back to Minnie. "Take a look. You can see some riders over there getting saddled up."

Minnie looked through the scope. "Wow," she breathed. She handed it to Joe, who stared off at the area Cross was indicating. He grinned at the view before transferring it to Lil. "Here Lil, you look."

Lil gave up trying to attract Annie's attention and took the tube, stretching it out and looking up the canyon. "Can you see them?" Joe asked. She shook her head and lowered it to see where he was pointing, then raised it again.

"Oh, yeah, now I do. Three men." She moved the end of the tube to bring the focus in tighter and gasped.

"Good, ain't it?" Cross beamed at her reaction, but when Lil lowered the scope her face had turned pale and she was shaking. Cross reached out to grab the scope and Minnie took her friend's arm.

"Lil, what's wrong?"

"We need to get back down to the Pavilion, right now!" Lil said, already moving up the slope toward where Joe had parked the buggy.

"Lil?" Minnie hurried after her as Joe gave Cross a confused look, then started after them. Minnie caught up and touched Lil on the shoulder. "What's going on?"

"Those men with the horses," she said. "I'm sure they're some of those robbers. From our train."

CHAPTER TWENTY-THREE

Twocrow rode nonchalantly along the ridgeline trying to appear uninterested in the ranch stead below. He expected either a dog to bark or someone to come out to study him, but after a few minutes it was clear that neither was going to happen. He eyed the terrain stretching out in front of him and saw where the ground dipped off slightly to the south before continuing east in the direction of Buffalo Gap.

Guiding his horse in that direction he rode into a dry arroyo and lost sight of the ranch buildings. A grove of poplars and willows framed the trail and swept up toward the ridgeline overlooking the ranch. He urged his horse into the cover of the trees, jumped down and tied the animal to one of the branches.

Taking the rifle, he moved cautiously up the hill. The sky brightened as he neared the top, and he dropped down and crawled to the edge. Below him, Paul Anderson's horse-drawn wagon clattered out of the west-side draw and rolled toward the back of the barn. From his perch, Twocrow could see Bullock hunkered down behind the rancher grasping his rifle in both hands, but Roosevelt was nowhere to be seen. Twocrow's hands were shaking as he pulled the rifle up and inched forward against a fallen log.

Suddenly, a brightly clad rider with very white leggings galloped over the lower level ridgeline on the main trail approaching the ranch stead from the southwest. The rider pulled up, took in the scene of Anderson's wagon moving toward the barn, and quickly resumed riding toward it. He sucked in sharply. The rider was Laura.

"Hello!" Her voice filled the air below him as she waved toward the wagon. Anderson reined in his team and half-stood in front of his buckboard's seat as Bullock squeezed up tighter behind him to avoid being spotted. As Laura galloped on toward the wagon, Twocrow watched in horror as two heavily armed men edged out the front of the barn and started making their way toward the corner where the wagon Laura was approaching. Laura's path to the wagon and the point where they would emerge were now on a direct line.

A small upper-level door on the back corner of the barn swung open and Twocrow watched as the barrel of a rifle emerged. It was clear that both Laura and Anderson were going to be in this gunman's direct line of fire.

Twocrow started to rise, forgetting about his nervousness. "Laura!" Twocrow shouted. "Oh, no, no! Laura! Stop! Go back!"

He settled onto his left knee, the shaking in his hands intensifying as he pulled his rifle up to his shoulder and sighted first on the two moving men and then back on the upstairs door. "Shit!" he said as he watched the gunman's rifle extend further out of the barn door.

"Stop!" Anderson shouted at Laura, holding both arms up in a stop position just as the first of the two men on the ground rounded the corner. The man raised a pistol and fired a warning shot into the air.

Laura screamed and tried to rein in her pinto mare as the gunman sprinted toward her and snatched at Star's reins. She pulled the horse back and tried to turn away, and the outlaw dropped the rein and grabbed her right leg instead. Laura jerked the reins back harder and fought to get away. Now the second armed man came past the barn's corner aiming a rifle at the rancher and gesturing for him to put his hands up. The little doorway on the barn's upper level swung completely open and a man poked his head out over top of the gun barrel and took aim at the struggling girl.

"No you don't, you bastard!" Twocrow exclaimed. The shaking in his hands stopped as he sighted on the man in the doorway. But before he could do anything, a piercing yell cascaded down from the northwest side of the barn causing both him and all three gunmen to look in that direction. Anderson also jerked around as a bespeckled rider came charging over the hill yelling again at the top of his lungs.

"Roosevelt!" Twocrow exclaimed as the rider galloped wildly down the hillside that ran between the road and the draw from which the wagon had emerged. The buckskin-clad deputy yelled a third time, even louder, as he rode head-on, his horse's reins looped loosely around his right arm and his big rifle cradled over his left as he sighted down the barrel and fired at the man next to the barn.

The wood just above the man's head splintered at the bullet's impact. The outlaw swore loudly and dropped to his knees. In response, the man in the overhead doorway swung his rifle toward the charging rider and Twocrow reacted, snapping off a shot in the outlaw's direction.

Roosevelt's big hunting rifle boomed again as the young Indian chambered another shell and pulled his own rifle back in line for a second shot. But before he could fire, the man's rifle barrel bobbed and fell to the ground. The gunman started to turn, a surprised look on his face, and then he tumbled head-over-heels out of the doorway sending up a puff of dust as his body struck the ground.

The man pulling on Laura now pushed her leg away, looped Star's right rein around his wrist and jerked it down toward him. The little horse staggered and stopped fighting the rein as the gunman dropped to one knee, pulled a pistol from his belt and aimed under the horse's neck toward Anderson.

Twocrow cried out a warning. "Anderson! Watch out for the shooter by the horse!"

The gunman fired, Star neighed loudly at the explosion, and the big rancher jerked violently backward and dropped into the buckboard. Almost instantly the empty space where Anderson had been standing was filled again as Bullock leaped up behind the back of the seat and swung his rifle into position. Still holding Star's rein, the gunman pulled back, using Laura and Star as a shield between himself and the Sheriff.

Bullock held his fire as the outlaw leaned forward under Star's neck and popped off a round in the sheriff's direction. Still yelling full-throat, Roosevelt galloped past the buckboard and fired again at the man on his knees next to the barn. The man rolled away and scurried back around the corner and out of the line of fire.

As her attacker tried to pull a third time on Star's rein, Laura kicked out at him and pulled down on the horse's left-side rein, trying to jerk her sideways and away. But the gunman fought back, pulling harder on the rein in his hand. He started to swing his pistol toward her, and then froze. Slowly, he let the rein drop free and stepped back, both hands partially raised, the pistol still in the right one. Laura had her rifle aimed directly at his head.

She waggled the rifle barrel up and down and the outlaw raised his hands higher. As he did so, sunlight glinted off his gun's barrel and directly at Star's face. The little horse gave another frightened whinny and shied away, nearly unseating Laura in the process. She let the rifle slide along her right side and struggled again with the left-hand rein.

Seeing the horse's reaction, the outlaw swung his gun arm down to fire and a pair of shots rang out in response. He stood aiming at Laura for a few more seconds before his knees buckled. He staggered, dropped the gun and fell hard, face first into the dirt.

Smoke wafted from the barrel of Bullock's gun at the front of the wagon, while up on the ridgeline Twocrow lowered his rifle and took a deep breath, inhaling the fumes coming from his own just-fired weapon. Star whinnied loudly as the body of the man fell beside her and she continued backing rapidly away as Laura fought to get the loose right-side rein back in her hand.

Tossing her rifle aside she finally grabbed both reins just as Roosevelt galloped up next to her and reached over to get a hand on Star's halter. The little horse fought against the stranger's hand until Laura leaned far forward across the mare's neck and spoke to her while Roosevelt kept his bigger horse plastered up against them.

At last, Star snorted twice and stood quivering as Laura kept up her soothing talk in the horse's ear.

Seeing his companion lying motionless, the remaining outlaw tossed his gun forward and eased out from the corner of the building, both hands in the air. Bullock jumped down from the wagon and walked rapidly toward him, rifle leveled and ready to fire. Behind him, Anderson got to his feet and climbed back onto the seat, gathering up the reins in the process. He had a gash across the corner of his forehead and he swiped away blood as he drove forward.

"Whoa, whoa, whoa," Bullock held up one hand toward the rancher, while still keeping his rifle pointed at the outlaw. "Where do you think you're going?"

"For my wife," Anderson said, getting ready to snap the reins again.

Bullock shook his head, pointed at the outlaw, and gestured at the house. "Who's inside?"

"Doc McCarty, Georgie and the sodbuster's wife. And a couple of hostages—deputies from town, I think. One of 'em is pretty bad shot up. Doc, too. He's hurt pretty bad."

Bullock signaled for Anderson to get down and waggled his rifle in Twocrow's direction motioning for him to ride down. The young Indian stood, waved back and headed toward his tied-up horse. Roosevelt said something to Laura, passed her the reins to his horse and dismounted, walking around to check the body of the man on the ground. He picked up Laura's rifle, handed it up to her and got back on his horse, pointing toward the back of the barn.

They rode over together as Bullock pushed his prisoner ahead of him in their direction and Twocrow made his way down the slope and across the main trail. "Sorry about that cut on your forehead Anderson," the Sheriff said. "Figured I'd best pull you down out of the line of fire so you wouldn't get shot. You okay?"

Ignoring Bullock's inquiry, Anderson stood beside his horses staring past the corner of the barn toward the ranch house, a distraught expression on his face. "What about Irene?" He turned and grabbed the prisoner and slammed him against the back wall of the barn. "All right you bastard. Did you hurt my wife?"

"No, no! We didn't do nothin' to her. She's inside takin' care of Doc and them others." He had a frightened look as he warily eyed the angry rancher and looked to Bullock and the others for help.

"What do you mean?" Roosevelt asked as he finished giving Laura a hand down from Star's back and came toward them. "Who's inside?"

That's what I'm sayin'," he responded. "Doc McCarty's in there, and he's pretty bad shot....and so's that young deputy. And the other deputy, he was out cold from the knock on the head Charley give'm." He glanced over toward the house. "And...and your wife, she was helpin' fix 'em all up and get 'em fed. Things like that."

"Who else you say's in there besides McCarty?" Bullock was checking his rifle as he spoke and nodded to Twocrow as the young man rode up on the same path the wagon had followed. He was leading Bullock's horse behind him. He dismounted and looped both horses' reins around the back of the buckboard.

"Nice piece of shootin' from up there, Bill. Thanks." He gave him a wry smile.

Twocrow nodded in response and walked hurriedly over to Laura's side. "Laura?" he was shaking again as he gave her a questioning look before emitting a squeak of surprise as she threw her arms around his bare shoulders and hugged him hard.

"Thank you!" she said. She hugged him again and he looked around, embarrassed. Roosevelt grinned and tipped his hat in the young Indian's direction.

"Like I said, there's Georgie," the outlaw continued, ignoring the exchange between the young people as Anderson still stood directly in front of him with his fists clenched.

"He part of your gang?"

"Yeah. Can't figure why he didn't come out of there shootin', though...him'n Doc both? Especially when this whack-o came ridin' half-crazy from out of the hills." He stared fearfully in Roosevelt's direction.

Roosevelt chuckled at the description of himself as he joined Bullock alongside the buckboard and eyed the ranch house. "What do you think, Seth? They might've thought we had more men than they could see; especially with young Bill there firing from up above. You think they're going to use Anderson's wife and the others as some sort of shield?"

"Maybe," Bullock said as he reached over and pulled Anderson toward them and away from the gunman, who looked visibly relieved to have the angry rancher out of his face. "Tell us more about that hidden tunnel into the house. Can we get around there without being seen from the front of the house?"

"Sure." He pointed toward a small hill behind the house. "On the other side of that hill's where it comes out into a little cave we call our icehouse. When we built the house, we dug a tunnel down into that hill and connected it into that cave. Not much of a cave, I suppose, but it was the perfect size for keeping ice and other supplies and things. Took us dang near a whole year to get that tunnel dug and then we connected it through the pantry. It's got a back door off the hillside."

"Draw it out for me," Bullock said, kneeling down in the dirt. "Bill. Go take that rope off my horse and get this one tied up." He pointed back at the outlaw who hadn't moved but was still looking anxiously around.

Twocrow walked over for the rope, while the sheriff looked at Laura, pulled out his pistol and handed it to her. "If he moves, you shoot him," he said loud enough for the man to hear. "Got it?" She nodded and leveled the gun at him with both hands.

He turned back to Anderson. "All right, then. Now draw me a picture of that icehouse and tunnel and let's go in there and get your wife."

CHAPTER TWENTY-FOUR

The water wagon passed the Evans Hotel and creaked on up the cobblestone street toward the new County Courthouse. As Archie Riordan guided his huge team into the alleyway that led to the new stone structure's backside entrance, two boys came bounding from the edge of the river and scampered laughing and yelling directly in front of the big draft horses, causing them to shy away and jerk hard on the wagon in response.

Riordan hauled back on the reins and spoke to the team, and they eased back onto the path as the wagon rocked violently.

"Damnit Archie, I said we got to keep it slow and on the level!"

"Sorry Doc!" Riordan yelled back over his shoulder. "Just a couple of kids in the way. Should'a been on the lookout."

Inside, Doctor Jennings pointed toward the bottom of the litter holding Frank Pasch's bandaged body and Nellie grabbed onto the man's feet and shoved them back over to the middle of the device.

Masterson, seated on two water crates stacked in the back corner, half-swung his rifle as a signal to the other two prisoners to stay put, even though both of them were handcuffed to a support bar running across the wagon's inside front end.

Jonas McCarty scowled and raised both hands as far as the handcuff chains would permit. Next to him, Jeremy Franklin, his arm bandaged, sat quietly staring through his chains at the floor.

"Good thing you've got that rifle, Marshal." Jonas smirked at Nellie over the top of Jennings' hat as the doctor leaned closer to Pasch's face to listen to his breathing. "Otherwise me'n Miss Bly here might be gettin' ready to have ourselves a little party." He chuckled and made a kissing sound as Nellie glared in response.

Robert Seaman, seated on an empty water crate behind Nellie and holding the rifle that had been assigned to her by the sheriff, started to stand with one fist clenched. Nellie reached back and put a hand on his and nodded back at the crate.

"Good idea," McCarty growled. "Best to keep your grandpa seated if he wants to stay healthy." He chuckled again as Seaman's face reddened. Nellie let go of Pasch's feet, satisfied that he was staying stable on the litter, then sat back upright on the crate that she was occupying.

"It is a good idea," she agreed. She glanced back at Seaman. "Robert happens to be the head of a steel works company, and he can bend a steel rod with just one hand. I'd hate to see what your neck would look like if he got hold of it with both hands."

Seaman smiled at her remark and McCarty's face darkened in anger. But before he could say anything more, Masterson chambered a shell in his rifle and eyed the two outlaws in front.

"I was thinking it might be time for a little peace and quiet in here in case the doc needs to hear if your pal's heart is still beating." He lowered the rifle so that it was aimed directly toward the front of the wagon and right at McCarty's chest. "It'd be too bad if all this yammerin' you're doing riled up the horses again and caused my rifle to go off—accidental, of course."

The wagon rolled to a stop and they could hear Riordan climb down while his horses alternated between snorting and stamping. The back door of the wagon popped open and the water works' owner's unruly shock of hair appeared first, surrounded by a halo of late-afternoon sunlight that streamed in behind him.

"We're here," Riordan said. He pointed at Pasch's body. "Hand that end of the litter on out to me and then you can jump down and take the back end." His directive seemed aimed at Masterson, although he didn't speak to anyone in particular. Doctor Jennings half-stood and moved to his side of the litter while gesturing to Robert to grab the other side. Together they started sliding the litter toward Riordan while Masterson kept a wary eye on the two outlaws chained up front.

"Get that rifle on them before I put mine down," he ordered, pointing at the rifle that Robert had placed on the seat behind him as he moved to help with the litter. Nellie reached around, picked it up, and aimed it at McCarty's chest.

"You sure you know which end of that thing to point before pulling the trigger?" the outlaw smirked. Nellie quickly chambered a round in response and held the rifle out in front of her.

"I think so," she said, partially inclining it toward him as she studied the weapon. "Maybe I should just pull the trigger and see what happens." The smirk on his face disappeared as he eyed the rifle. "You know," she said, turning toward Bat and inclining the rifle even further in McCarty's direction,

"When I was getting ready to travel to Mexico to do a story about the smugglers there, my editor thought I ought to have some shooting lessons. He spent a lot of money to teach me how to aim quickly and..." an explosion filled the space as the rifle went off and McCarty's hat went flying.

"Ooops," she said, turning the rifle sideways again.

"Jesus Christ lady! You could-a killed me!" McCarty shrank back against the wagon's front wall while Franklin, still chained next to him, sat unmoving and still staring down, although Nellie saw just the slightest flicker of a smile cross his face.

Nellie swung the rifle back at McCarty and chambered another round. "I could have," she answered. "Guess it's a good thing I know which end to point before pulling the trigger." She exchanged an amused glance with Masterson while Robert gave her a look of wonder and shook his head in admiration. They continued moving Pasch's body out the back and Doc Jennings climbed down to help stabilize the litter. Masterson jumped down next and then Seaman slid his legs over the back edge and eased down to the ground.

A clattering noise caused them all to look up the hill past the Evans swimming center as a one-horse buggy handled by Will Rogers rolled toward them. The young cowboy drew back on the reins and pulled his horse to a stop alongside them. The buggy swayed violently at the sudden stop and the wrapped body directly behind him strained at the ropes holding it in place. "Marshal! Didn't expect to find you way up on this side of town."

"Rogers?" Masterson said, pushing back on his hat as he eyed the young man. "What's going on?" He stepped toward the buggy and looked up the street behind him. "Where's all the rest?"

"That's sort-of a long story," Will said, shifting back on his seat and setting the brake as he did so.

"Give us the short version," the Marshal replied, waving toward the litter. "You can do it while you're giving us a hand moving this man inside." He pointed up at the new stone structure that still showed signs of construction and digging around the outside.

Will jumped down and hurried over, joining Riordan at the foot of the litter while Masterson and the Doctor stabilized the front. Nellie slid out of the back of the wagon, handed her rifle to Seaman, and dropped lightly to the ground.

"Will? You okay?" She glanced toward his buggy. "Where are the others?"

"I'm fine," he answered. "And everyone else is still out there. "But, Marshal!" Will said hurriedly, the edge to his voice causing them to stop moving the litter and wait for him to finish. "One of them robbers that was on that train this morning came riding into town from up on this side. Laura and me, we saw him when we were about two miles out. He rode right past us. Figure he's gotta be here by now."

"Alone?"

"Yeah. He was one of them riding on our train car when we got stopped."

Talking quickly as they moved the litter inside, Will filled them in on the trip out and back and about finding Star untended along the road, then watching the outlaw ride past them. As they walked back outside, he pointed at the wrapped body tied on the back seat of the buggy. "So, I ended up with him and everybody else is still somewhere out there by that rancher's place."

"Okay." He handed his rifle to Will and turned to Riordan. "You see any solo riders might've looked like what Rogers was describing ... when we drove up this way?" Riordan shook his head. "Can't figure he'd come into town on his own, so maybe he was meetin' up with some of the others." He stood contemplating the options as Nellie left Seaman guarding the prisoners and walked over to join them.

"Besides this road that Rogers just drove in on, are there any other ways into town from up this direction?" the Marshal asked.

Riordan pointed past the courthouse. "Road running up behind here, past the Evan's Plunge, splits off straight north and northwest. North fork follows the Cold Brook, and the northwest one comes in by the Chautauqua Park. That'd be the Hot Brook."

"And that's where all them folks are settin' up for tonight's big to-do?"

Riordan nodded.

Masterson pointed at the body in Will's buggy. "Okay, let's get him inside and then Will, you drive with Nellie and Mister Seaman on over to the Chautauqua and warn them about that rider. Probably not much chance he'll come that way, but we might as well be prepared." He turned to Nellie. "Talk to Cody. He'll know what to do."

Nellie turned to the buggy and began undoing the ropes holding the wrapped body in place. Bat put a hand on her shoulder and she looked back at him. "And get anybody who doesn't need to be out in the open back out of the way. Okay?"

"Okay."

"And hurry."

She nodded.

Riordan joined Seaman at the back of his wagon. "What about these two?" He pointed toward the inside of the big transport.

"I'm not messin' with 'em now," the lawman replied. "Lock it up and come inside to help. I'm going back inside with Pasch. I don't want to leave him unattended."

"But we can't...I mean...just leave them out here. Can we?" Riordan stammered.

"How many padlocks you got?" Bat asked in response as he moved back toward the courthouse.

"A couple."

"Good. Slap 'em both on that back door and then get inside to help me as soon as you can. And don't forget your rifle."

*****

"The passage seems to keep going," Jack said, eyeing the way the torch flickered and moved as he held it up. "There's a little breeze coming from somewhere." He held the torch higher in his good hand and swung it around to display mostly solid rock walls in every direction. "But even if it goes on, it looks like the passage gets really narrow. I don't think I could get through it on this bad leg. Maybe you could go on without me?"

Irene sank down on a small rock ledge. "Or we could just stay here," she replied, "and then see about slipping back out into the canyon once it gets dark."

"Maybe," Jack contemplated the options. "But if we stay here and the gang figures out where we are, we'll be trapped. And I figure we're out of chances with them. They'll just shoot us and leave us in here to rot." He pointed back in the direction from where they had started their trek toward the back of the cave. "And, as we saw, not many visitors ever find this place."

She put her face in her hands and took in a deep breath. "Look, I don't think we should split up. We should go back to the entrance and try to go out in the canyon now, while it's still light." She nodded at his injured ankle. "But, it's going to be painful...and slow...walking with that sprain."

He hobbled a couple of steps closer to her. "I've been thinking about that. There's a lot of stuff back at the entrance that we could use to brace it. I was out on a roundup once where one of our men broke his leg. Some of the guys got the bones lined up and put a splint on it, and he was able to get around pretty good; even got back up on his horse. You think you could help me fix it up like that?"

She gave the ankle a skeptical look followed by a small smile. "Sure. I'm a rancher's wife. Haven't you heard? We can do anything." She snorted as she said it and Jack chuckled.

"You know what? After watching you in action today, I believe you could."

She stood up and moved up close to his left side, wrapping her right arm around his waist. The action startled him and Jack half-stepped away before being stopped by the force of her strong arm holding on to him.

"Give me that torch," she said, holding out her left hand. "And put your arm over my shoulders."

He did as directed.

"Now, use me as your left leg and try to keep as much weight off it as possible while we walk back to the entrance. Okay?"

He breathed in deeply and took in the smell of her body—a mix of cooked food, sweat and even a hint of some sort of soap. He grasped tightly to her shoulder. "You smell nice," he said, instantly embarrassed that he had confessed that to her under these circumstances.

She leaned back and looked up at his face, now just inches from yours. "Good to know," she answered, then wrinkled her nose. "Wish I could say the same about you but I'm afraid you've gotten pretty ripe. If we had better circumstances and more time, I'd say we should both stand under that waterfall and get ourselves cleaned up proper."

He could see in the flickering torchlight that she was blushing and now it was his turn to snort and hers to laugh. Then they both grew sober and started shuffling back toward the sounds of the falling water and the entrance to the cave.

*****

Roosevelt leaned over the edge of a water trough and sighted his big rifle in on the ranch house doorway. He silently signaled to Twocrow, who was standing at the northeast corner of the barn. Twocrow signaled back that he, too, had the doorway in his sights. Behind him the now-trussed up outlaw sat quietly alongside the wall of the barn.

Laura leaned in close to the Easterner's shoulder while staying out of sight behind the wooden trough. "What if they put the hostages out in front of them? Or what about Mister Anderson and Sheriff Bullock? What's going to happen when they get inside?"

Roosevelt pushed back on his wire-rimmed glasses and slightly turned toward her, keeping his rifle at the ready.

"Lots of questions, and my answers are all the same, 'Wait and see.'" He jerked around as Twocrow whistled sharply and waggled the barrel of his rifle at the house. The front door had cracked open and someone was looking out. "Looks like the waiting part might be ended," he muttered. "You stay close to the ground, even if you have to wreck that pretty dress of yours."

"Oh, poo!" she exclaimed, flattening down on the ground behind him and edging through the red dirt around the corner of the trough in order to get a clearer look at the door. She still had her own rifle and now she slid it forward and joined in aiming at the door.

Roosevelt chortled at her response but kept his own weapon sighted in.

"What's that?" Laura looked up at him for an answer.

"Looks like a flag of truce," Roosevelt said as a broomstick with a white dishtowel attached poked out the door. Slowly the doorway opened wider and then a man emerged carrying the broom. The late-afternoon sun flashed off an object on his vest and the horses tied up behind them whinnied nervously in response.

"It's Sheriff Bullock!" Laura started to get up on her knees as she spoke.

"Stay down!" Roosevelt commanded. She dived back into her prone position, re-grasping her rifle as she dropped.

"Seth! You okay?"

Bullock waved the makeshift flag. "We're good," he called back. "But it's not so good inside. Got one dead, one pretty bad wounded, and another one tied up tighter'n bull's ass in fly time."

Laura stifled a laugh at Bullock's description and looked over toward Twocrow, who also had a hand to his mouth trying not to laugh. More movement at the doorway caused them both to pivot back toward the house and Anderson emerged, pushing a thin man with his hands tied and his feet bare. Bullock waved for them to come in and they hurried forward, rifles still at the ready.

"One dead?" It was Roosevelt's first words as they approached the house. "Is it the dep…?"

"No! He's hurtin' pretty bad, but he ain't dead. Looked dead, but he's still got a pulse. We're going to need to get him into town as soon as possible if he's going to make it." He nodded to Anderson. "Go get your wagon over here right away." The Rancher roughly shoved the prisoner out of his way and strode toward his wagon.

"It's McCarty that's dead," Bullock continued. "Looks like he just laid down on their bed and died. Theodore, I know you got some medical knowledge, so I'd be obliged if you took a look at the boy and see what you can do." Roosevelt gave a quick nod and ducked into the house.

"So where's the others—Anderson's wife and that cowboy out of Oklahoma?" Twocrow was looking past the Sheriff into the house as he asked the question.

"No idea," Bullock tossed the broom and towel aside. "This guy says they got the drop on him and left him trussed up, blindfolded and bootless. He thought that young deputy in there was dead, and he didn't know his boss was the one that had succumbed instead."

Twocrow looked up to the hills on the east side, behind where the storage cave exited off the back of the house. "If they wanted to cover their trail, they probably headed due east for one of the creeks—maybe the Beaver or Lame Johnny," he said. They both run just east of here and that's gotta be the way they headed or we would've spotted them on the way in."

"How much ground they gotta cover to get to them?"

"Probably two miles. Pretty rough ground, though, even on a horse let alone on foot."

"You know it?"

"Yeah, I've been over it a few times." He put a hand on Laura's shoulder. "Both Laura and me have. We used to go riding together out of the Gap, and that's an area that we sometimes tried." Laura nodded in agreement.

"The Lame Johnny Creek's probably closest, but more straight east," she said. "Beaver Creek would be the main one that empties out past Buffalo Gap. The town I mean. From here, I think once you reach it you could follow it on down to Martin's Ranch. If they knew where they were headed, they'd probably go that way first." She looked at Twocrow for confirmation. "And there's French Creek, too—but that'd be way more north. Runs all the way out from Custer City, I think."

Twocrow stood staring at the hills to the east. "You know there's lots of other smaller creeks and streams that run into those main ones too, and lots of box canyons. If they got turned around they might be followin' one of them right into a dead end." He turned back to Bullock. "They could be anywhere. Big country out there."

Anderson pulled the wagon up to the door and jumped down.

"We're thinkin' your wife and that Oklahoma fella headed east and maybe will try to follow one of the creeks. She know much about them or that area? Beaver Creek or Lame Johnny?"

"A little, I guess?" He stared off in that direction "It's kind of off our land and a little harder to travel. Me'n my boys have been out there once or twice, but we usually don't go that way with the wagon or the buggy. Still, she knows about Beaver Creek because we've been down to Martin's Ranch a few times and talked about how it runs all the way past our place down to theirs. She'd probably try for Beaver Creek. I'm not even sure she knows where Lame Johnny runs. Even me and my boys, we never follow it."

Roosevelt emerged from the house and shook his head. "Wound's pretty bad. He got some good bandaging on it, but he's lost a lot of blood. We need to get a move on if he's going to survive."

Bullock stroked the corners of his mustache. "Okay, we got to do some decidin' here." He pointed at Roosevelt. "Theodore, I want you and Anderson to go into town. Go get that prisoner from the barn."

Roosevelt headed off in that direction as Anderson whirled around to face Bullock with an angry look. "Mister Anderson, I know that's not what you want to hear, but it's the way it's gotta be. You're the only one knows how to handle this rig and we gotta get these prisoners into town and try and save that boy's life."

He pointed at Twocrow and Laura. "Now these two young folks know this area, too—maybe even better than you. So the three of us are going to track down your wife." He walked over to the still-tied outlaw, slouching down against the corner of the porch. "Georgie? That what you said your name was?" The thin outlaw nodded. "Was she hurt? The rancher's wife?" Georgie shook his head. "How about the other one? The cowboy?"

"Bad crack on the head. I thought he was out cold. I don't know how in hell he got loose." He shook his head. "Oh, and his one hand was pretty cut up." He jerked his chin toward his left shoulder, which had a smeared stain on it. "That's his blood, not mine."

Bullock pulled him upright and pushed him toward the wagon. "Okay, get in there now and be a good boy, or I'll make sure that some of your blood gets on that shirt, too. You understand me?"

Georgie nodded again and struggled to roll onto the back of the wagon without the use of his still-tied hands. Bullock reached down and grabbed one of his legs and half-lifted, half-pushed him face first onto the flatbed. The outlaw slid up against the wagon box's side as Roosevelt emerged from the barn pushing the trussed-up outlaw ahead of him. He guided him to the rear end of the wagon and Twocrow moved over to help load him in.

The outlaw angrily looked Twocrow up-and-down. "Keep your hands off me you dirty Indian!" Twocrow stepped back, stunned by the reaction. Laura stepped forward and wrapped both arms around one of Twocrow's.

"That's probably a good idea Alv...Bill." She hugged him tightly to her side. "You might catch something touching HIM," she half-sneered as Anderson walked around and roughly pushed the outlaw onto the back end of the wagon. Laura pulled Twocrow toward the house. "Come on, we need to help Sheriff Bullock move Chalky out here." Twocrow gave a disdainful glance back over his shoulder then followed Laura inside.

"Anderson, tie those two up to the sides of the wagon while we bring out the boy," Bullock said. "Theodore, keep that bear-shooter of yours primed and ready."

Roosevelt tipped the corner of his hat, cocked the rifle and held it at the ready as the rancher climbed up beside the two outlaws and bound each of them to opposite sides of the wagon. After several minutes, Bullock, Laura and Twocrow emerged with Chalky's body swaddled in sheets and blankets and wrapped tightly onto the top of the kitchen table, which had been broken off of its legs to form a makeshift litter.

Anderson eyed what used to be his table and the bloodied bandages and sheets wrapped around Chalky and extended his arms to take him onto the wagon. Laura and Twocrow stabilized the back end, while Bullock clambered up and took the litter from them as they edged it toward the wagon box's front end. Maneuvering the litter past the outlaws, they laid it crosswise just behind the seat. After making sure it was secure, Anderson slid over onto the seat and took the reins. His team stamped nervously, waiting for him to drive.

Roosevelt handed his rifle to Bullock, climbed onto his horse, took the weapon back and gave the sheriff a small salute with his free hand. Bullock nodded in response.

"All right, then. Let's go!" Roosevelt commanded, and Anderson clucked to his team and shook the reins. The wagon lurched forward rapidly increasing speed as they headed past the barn and back on the path leading toward Hot Springs.

"You think Chalky'll make it?" Twocrow asked.

"Gotta think so," the sheriff said. Then more to himself, "Always gotta think so."

They untied their horses and mounted up. "You sure you're going to be okay riding with us out here?" Bullock asked Laura as she pushed at her skirt and once again stuck her frilly bloomer-covered legs into the stirrups as she prepared to ride. Both the skirt and the bloomers were rapidly losing their luster from her riding and time spent crawling in the dirt.

She pulled Star's head around and the edges of her skirt billowed up at the movement. The horse whinnied nervously. "This damn thing!" she muttered. Grabbing the bottom front edge, she lifted the skirt up in front of her and ripped it straight down the middle, then tucked the sides in under her legs.

"Don't worry about me." She started Star moving, leading the way up the hill on the east side of the house. "You coming?" she half-shouted over her shoulder.

Bullock exchanged an amused look with Twocrow. "Guess that's a yes," he offered.

Twocrow shrugged. "Yeah. That's my Laura," he said matter-of-factly as he made a clicking sound with his tongue and snapped his horse's reins to start after her. Bullock turned in his saddle to check on the wagon, watched it crest the far hill to the west and disappear, then urged his horse into a gallop and hurried to catch up with his young companions.

CHAPTER TWENTY-FIVE

Sallie White held tightly onto the side rail of the buggy seat with her right hand
and clamped down on top of her bonnet with her left, struggling to keep it from blowing off as William drove swiftly toward Hot Springs.

"Nice of that Pierce fellow to direct us over this way," he spoke loudly to be heard over the noise of the buggy, the horse's hoofbeats, and the wind whistling past them as they drove. He gestured to his left. "Pierce said if we go up over this hill it'll take us right down onto the back road leading into the Chautauqua. The girls will sure be surprised to see us get back there so quick."

The Whites had driven southwest through Alabough Canyon to Cascade Springs where Sallie drank deeply from the warm mineral spring gushing out of the side of the canyon wall near the four-story sandstone-sided hotel—which was remarkably similar in style to the much larger Evans. After a short rest that included the hotel's famous sandwiches and tea, they headed out, explaining that they needed to meet friends at the Hot Springs Chautauqua in advance of the evening's big show.

"You should take the 'westside' route back in," Edwin Pierce, the hotel proprietor and Cascade's self-appointed mayor told them as they turned the buggy around. "You can connect with the Edgemont Road and come right down past Chautauqua Park. It'll save you some time AND having to drive all the way through town."

He tipped his hat and smiled broadly as the Whites exclaimed about how thoughtful he had been. "Glad you feel that way. Always happy to be of assistance and I hope you'll tell all your friends back in Kansas about Cascade when you get back home. And thanks again for coming out our way."

Now, as they drove, William peeked at his pocket watch and had a broad smile of his own. "I feel like we're going to get there in time to watch some of the preparations by Annie and Buffalo Bill."

Sallie, who was feeling a bit woozy from the rapidly rocking buggy, gave him a half-hearted smile in response, keeping her teeth clenched tightly while fighting the urge to vomit.

"Look, there's another buggy," William pointed as a buggy carrying several brightly clad women emerged on the hilltop ahead of them and rolled along the ridgeline heading west. "I'll flag them down and we can make sure we're on the right trail."

He half-stood and waved his hat while urging his team to an even faster pace as they raced toward the women. "Oh, William..." Sallie started, before jerking her bonnet from her head, leaning forward and vomiting into its top. White gasped at her reaction and immediately pulled back on the reins, slowing his team as they continued on course to intersect with the other rig. He pulled to a stop and leaned down to help her.

"I'm so sorry," he spoke quickly. "Here, let me help you down." He jumped to the ground as the other buggy headed toward them and also slowed. The woman driving yelled a loud "Whoa!" to her own horses as they pulled alongside.

"Everything Okay?"

White kept his hands on his wife's waist and helped her down. "My wife's not feeling well," he explained. "I think a few minutes out of the buggy will help." He gave the other woman a grateful smile as she handed him a heavily perfumed hankie, which he used to dab at beads of perspiration that had formed on Sallie's forehead. "Is it far from here into the Chautauqua Park? We can rest there."

"No, not far at all. Right girls?" The woman opened a pastel parasol to shade herself from the hot afternoon sun as she spoke to two young women in the back seat of her buggy. Her other passenger, riding beside her, sat quietly, not speaking and looking uneasy at the encounter. White glanced at her, looked back at Sallie, and then did a double take and looked again at the second woman.

"Why Mrs. ... Previn, isn't it?" He put one arm around Sallie and half-turned toward her, doffing his hat with his free hand.

The woman looked surprised. "Have we met?" As soon as she spoke, Sallie registered a strange expression at the sound of her voice but said nothing.

"Not formally, but I saw you at the Evans Hotel. We're staying there, and I was ... with Marshal Masterson and the others when there was that mix up at your room earlier today. I was in the hall." He nodded to her. "William Allen White. And this is my wife Sallie." He glanced back at her and at the ruined bonnet, which he now took away from her and placed on the ground next to his buggy. "Who, as I mentioned, is not feeling very well."

Sallie managed a weak smile but still did not say anything.

"Girls, give the poor woman some of our water," the feather-laden driver, who was wearing a very revealing dress, spoke again to her two younger companions. She made no move to introduce either herself or the others, one of whom stood, climbed down and walked to the back of their buggy. In seconds, she emerged with a jar of water, which she brought over to the Whites. Unscrewing the top, she held it out. William took it from her and helped Sallie take a few sips.

"Thank you," he said, giving her back the jar. "Are you ladies traveling far? Over to Edgemont, perhaps, or up to Cascade? Sallie and I were just there and it was delightful."

"No, just up to a spot in the hills that Mollie wants us to see. Then, hopefully, we'll get back to town in time for the evening's events at the Park." She smiled sweetly. "It should be quite a time from everything I've heard!"

The more she spoke, the more ashen Sallie's face became and she put a hand up on her husband's shoulder as he started to respond. "Can you...?" He turned toward her as she spoke and saw just the hint of a signal to stop talking in her eyes. "Can you help me up and then we should go back to town before I get any worse?"

White glanced across at the four women. "Ladies, I don't mean to be un-civil, but I think I need to get Sallie into town." He turned back and put his arm around her shoulders, feeling her trembling slightly as he steered her over to the edge of the buggy and held her by the waist as she climbed up onto the seat. Several strands of her hair fell into her face, but she ignored them and pointed at her bonnet. "Is it ruined?"

He stepped over to pick it up, but the woman with the water jar retrieved it first, stared at it with a screwed up expression and then gingerly dangled it in his direction. "Smells pretty bad," is all she said. He started to reach for it, but the woman driver snapped her parasol shut, leaned forward and snagged the edge of the bonnet with the umbrella's tip.

William gaped at the exposure of her ample cleavage as she continued to lean forward with the bonnet on the parasol's point. With a grin, she sat back in her seat and swung the bonnet back toward her younger companions. They shrieked and held up their hands to stop it from landing on them, but the buxom driver deftly flipped the bonnet out into the sagebrush that was growing almost onto the dirt road.

"Jemmie, give me yours." She dropped the front end of the still-closed parasol back over her shoulder and waited as the woman who had remained seated undid her bonnet's strings and placed it on the tip.

The driver swung it around and dropped it into William's hands. "Leave it at the front desk of the Evans when you're through. Tell 'em it's for one of Grace's kittens." She smiled sweetly. "They'll know who to keep it for, won't they dear?" She peeked back at Jemmie who was helping the other woman back into the carriage. The younger woman just shrugged and settled back on the seat.

"Oh no, I couldn't," Sallie began before Grace snapped the parasol open again and swung it up in the air.

"Oh yes you could!" she said with a no-nonsense sound in her voice. She dipped the bright parasol to the west. "Besides, sun's starting to go down, and we'll be headin' more north than wes..."

she abruptly stopped speaking as Mollie's hand reached out to grasp her forearm. Grace glanced at the intruding hand and up at Mollie's face before registering awareness of what she was doing. She swung her gaze back to the Whites. "You just take Jemmie's bonnet and be on your way now. Glad to be of service."

As Sallie started tying the bonnet into place, the buxom driver folded the parasol and handed it to Mollie.

"So, I'm on the right road back toward the Chautauqua?"

"Yes. Just follow the road along this ridgeline and right down into the canyon. You'll go right to the park."

"Much obliged," William said, settling onto the seat and picking up the reins.

"Hope to see you this evening back at the Chautauqua," she said, giving William a wink as she picked up her own set of reins and flicked them to get her team underway. The buggy jumped forward and the two younger women grabbed frantically at the sidebars as it picked up speed and headed west over the hill.

William shook his head and chuckled. "Well, I don't believe I've ever..."

"William, that was the woman's voice I heard in the baths at the hotel," Sallie cut him off as she leaned across his body and watched the buggy disappear. "Both voices—that woman driving and the passenger. They were the ones talking about the body."

"You're sure?"

Sallie nodded. "Positive."

"Well, then that definitely means Mollie Previn knew something about her husband's death before we went to her room," White mused. "And if that's the other woman's voice you heard, then this

Grace person and the other women riding with her must be involved too." He helped Sallie sit back. "Nice hat," he chuckled again, "and ooh, plenty of perfume on it, too."

She pulled the bonnet off her head and swatted him on the arm. "Just get back into town," she said as she returned the hat to her head and tied it into place. "And stop driving like a maniac. I want to live long enough to tell Marshal Masterson and the Sheriff what we just saw."

*****

Joe was driving faster than he ever thought he could and Minnie and Lil were tightly hanging onto the buggy's side rails with one hand and their hats with the other. The buggy came careening down the trail from the overlook and nearly collided with Will's rig as it came across their path headed toward the Chautauqua.

Joe pulled back sharply on the reins as Nellie, seated directly behind Will, screamed and pulled her arms up defensively. Seaman, who was sitting to her left, wrapped his arms around her and pulled her up and over his body just as both rigs lurched to a stop, each horse neighing loudly at the near collision.

Minnie and Lil exchanged shocked looks at how close they'd come to catastrophe. Then everyone started talking at once. Nellie leaped to her feet and held both arms up. "Stop! Stop!" she shouted. "One at a time." She pointed at Joe's buggy and all three occupants started talking at the same time before Lil grabbed Joe's shoulder with one hand while placing her other hand in front of Minnie's face.

"The robbers!" she blurted. "They're coming into town from the back side of the Chautauqua Park!"

Will leaned back on the seat, holding tightly to his nervous horse's reins. "Yeah, Laura and me saw one of them already. He was coming in on the Wind Cave Road. It was one of those men from the train."

"That's who I saw over west!" Lil exclaimed. "One of the men from the train, and he was with two others; maybe three."

Now it was Seaman's turn to speak. "Obviously there are two groups of outlaws coming in; one from this side, and one from the south side. We're going to have to warn the folks up by the Park and then get ready to defend the town." He pointed at the road ahead of Will. "Is this the right path over to the Chautauqua?"

All three young people in the other buggy said "Yes!" at the same time.

"All right then. Let's get up to the Park right away. Follow us. Will, get moving."

He half-pulled Nellie back into the seat beside him as Will slackened the reins and chirped to his horse. Still snorting from the near crash, the Bay jerked ahead, eager to keep moving. Joe reined his horse and buggy in behind and both rigs raced up the road.

Band members and a few city workers were milling around the big Chautauqua pavilion as the two rigs rolled into the clearing at the Park's edge. Buffalo Bill and Annie looked up from a conversation they were having with Sousa, started to smile but quickly sobered as they saw the worried looks on the faces of the buggies' occupants. Bill said something to the others and hurried over with Annie close behind.

"What's going on?"

"Some of the gang that held up the train this morning are headed into town from this end," Nellie spoke loudly as she climbed across Seaman's legs and started to get out of the buggy. Startled by her quick move, Seaman grasped her waist and helped her down. She gave him a small smile. "Thank you Robert," she smiled more warmly and his face reddened.

"The girls and Joe spotted them coming in from over there," Nellie said, pointing up the road going out of the far side of the park. "There's three for sure; maybe four."

"And there's another group down southeast, along the Fall River road," Seaman said. "Don't know for sure how many, but the sheriff and some of his men went out there to try to stop them before they get to town."

"So, we can't worry about them," the showman said, eyeing the road leading away from the park. "Seems like this bunch up here ought to be our primary concern." He turned toward the second buggy. "How long since you saw them?"

"Probably twenty minutes," Lil piped up. "They were getting their horses saddled. Up by a cabin of some sort."

"Caretaker's cabin," Joe inserted. "Remember when we drove up past it when I took you around earlier?" He directed the question to Buffalo Bill and Annie.

"I remember. That's pretty close to here," Annie said. She surveyed the park. "Even if they're just getting started, won't take 'em long to get here." She looked from one buggy to the other. "Any of you armed?"

"I've got a rifle. Sheriff gave it to me before he rode out," Nellie said, reaching back under the buggy's rear seat.

"There's another one here," Will said, pulling his rifle up into view. Annie nodded and looked at the second buggy.

"My rifle's still in the Pavilion," Lil said.

"That's right, of course it is," Annie said. "What's the gauge again?"

"It's a twenty-two," she answered.

Annie smiled. "Big enough if we're close enough." She pointed toward the road at the end of the park and then swept her arm toward the right, following the path being taken by the stream. She nodded to a rocky knoll at a spot where the river turned from the west and veered sharply north. Buffalo Bill followed her gaze and nodded.

"Okay, that's a good spot," he agreed. He turned toward Joe and the girls. "You take those three with you and head on over there. Let them come on through the park entry and wait for my signal. My hat goes in the air; you shoot. After that I want you to come on up toward me. And keep those rifles at the ready, but don't take any chances."

"Where you going to be?"

"Right here." He pointed to the road. He took off his broad-brimmed hat and eyed it wistfully.

Annie grinned. "Sure you want to use the hat? It's your good one."

Buffalo Bill plopped it back down on top of his head. "Yeah, don't I know it." He sighed. "Just do it, okay?"

He turned toward Joe. "Joe, you pull your buggy across at that spot, set the brake and then you and the girls go with Annie. Hurry!" As Joe started maneuvering his rig around the other buggy, Bill turned toward Will. "Once he gets his buggy in place, swing yours at an angle alongside. Make it look like you're parked here. Get your brake set and the horses unhooked. Take 'em over and tie 'em up by the pavilion, and then get on back here with me."

Sousa came across the divide separating the tent from where the two buggies were stopped and Bill turned to meet him. "Sousa, I know this is going to sound weird, and it might be dangerous...but I need you and your musicians to get back onto that stand as soon as you can and start playing—like you're still rehearsing for tonight. The louder the better."

Sousa looked confused by Buffalo Bill's instructions. Seeing the concerned looks on the others' faces, he turned back to Bill. "How dangerous?"

"I don't know. Some of those outlaws who hit the train earlier today are on their way into town." He waved toward the far end of the park. "Right through there. I need them to think we don't know who they are until they get up here to me. Then we're going to have ourselves a little chit-chat about what's what?"

Sousa stared across the park and gave a curt nod. "I'll tell the men." He looked at the others. "As Colonel Cody here knows, most of us are ex-Marines. We may be musicians, but we also know when we have to stand up to tyranny." He whirled around and marched off toward the Pavilion.

"Sousa!" The bandmaster stopped at Cody's command. "There's more. I need Miss Bly and Mister Seaman here to be there with you. Front row." He reached out and put a hand on Nellie's rifle. "With this at the ready. I'll toss my hat in the air; that's my signal." Sousa eyed the rifle and the determined look on Nellie's face, raised his right hand and snapped off a salute.

"Where did you say you're going to be?" Robert asked as Sousa resumed walking.

"Right here with young Will, set up between these buggies. Miss Bly, when I throw my hat, you need to jump up and aim that rifle at whoever is in front of me and fire a shot over their heads." He faced Nellie. "Make sure they see you so they know you've got a gun. Got it?" She nodded.

"What am I supposed to do?" Seaman said.

"Yell your head off at the band members to get down, or do whatever else you think will be a distraction," he paused. "Or, even better, whatever you think will make these outlaws think they're outgunned. Maybe we can get this thing stopped before there's any bloodshed."

"But..." Robert started. Nellie grabbed him by the hand.

"Come on Robert, use your imagination," she said with a twinkle in her eye. "Let's go!" She pulled him away from the buggies and they hurried toward the band shell just as Annie emerged from the Pavilion carrying two rifles. She handed the smaller one to Lil, said something to Joe and Minnie, and led them off toward the rock formation by the river.

CHAPTER TWENTY-SIX

"All right, Omohundro, you can do this," Jack spoke to himself under his breath and grimaced as he stepped gingerly across a dip in the pathway made by the exiting herd of horses. They were about a mile from the mouth of the hidden cave. Irene had helped him negotiate the slippery rocks in and around the cascading waterfall, but from that point on he had been determined to walk alone. Now they were approaching a narrow trail along the canyon's east side, and as he made the step across the gap, he slipped sideways and cried out. Irene leaped forward to grab him around the waist and prevent him from falling.

      She leaned hard into his side until he was stabilized again. She peered down at his injured leg, which was solidly braced with two smooth branches wrapped tightly with pieces of the rotting rope that had been on the makeshift corral inside the cave.

      Jack nodded. "I'm okay. Let me give it a try."

She released him and moved back and he stepped forward, stopped and stepped again. He reached a rock outcropping and put his injured left hand out for more stability.

"Well?" she asked.

He glanced back over his shoulder. "Not too bad. I can wal..." he half-slipped yet again, this time with his good foot as he stepped ahead. He spun around, caught himself on a rock outcropping with his right hand, and re-stabilized himself on the splinted leg.

She hurried up beside him and wrapped one arm around his waist. "Like it or not, I'm helping you until we get out past these rocks."

He gave a nervous laugh. "At least the splint is strong; that leg held up real good."

"Sure. But you've got to watch your step from here on out." She pointed at his good leg. "You hurt that one, too, and we might as well forget going anywhere."

They hobbled along together, like participants in a slow-motion three-legged race, eyeing the horses' tracks, which appeared to be going straight toward yet another solid canyon wall now mottled by the final rays of the descending sun.

"Seems weird that the horses went this way," Jack waved his good hand at the wall that was looming ahead of them.

"El Kebir has to know the best way out of this place," she puffed, half-directing Jack's footsteps as she struggled to help him squeeze between two big rocks at a point where the trail narrowed even further. "Trust me, we need to see where their trail leads." They emerged from the rocks into a small glen fully bathed in the dying sunlight. She nudged his body to the left. "The trail goes this way and we can just try to foll..." She stopped abruptly and leaned away from him, her arm slipping from his back and falling limply onto his forearm.

"What?" Jack had been looking down, doing his best to place his footsteps carefully and ease Irene's burden in helping him advance. As her voice trailed off and she grasped his arm. He stopped too, raising his head as he spoke.

Ahead of them, half-a-dozen men holding rifles stood in the shadows of the canyon wall facing them, not more than a hundred yards away.

Irene looked up at Jack, trying to keep calm even though her trembling hand told him she was far from it. "Indians, I think."

Jack nodded. "They look different from the ones I know in Oklahoma and Texas."

"They're Sioux. They go past the ranch sometimes, but never so close as this." Jack felt her grip tighten as one of the group waved a rifle in the air. The men started forward and Irene flinched and pulled down. "We should get down, back behind the rocks." She took a step back, half-turning his body in the process.

I'm sorry, I..." he moved uneasily on his splinted leg, but tried to stay as erect as possible without showing any weakness. "I can't. My leg won't go."

Irene released his arm. "Give me the gun." She held out her hand and he pulled it from his holster and handed it over. She faced the on-coming men, starting to raise the pistol as they came out of the shadows into the shaft of sunlight that bathed the ground between them.

"Don't shoot!" a shadowy man in the lead shouted. He raised his left arm as he yelled and a bright flash glinted off his chest, accenting the shape of a star. A young woman hurried up beside him.

"Mrs. Anderson? Is that you?" she called. "It's Laura Thompson. I'm from Hot Springs. We're here with Sheriff Seth Bullock. We're here to take you home."

*****

Laura's, Twocrow's and Bullock's horses had picked their way down a steep slope leading to the river, all three riders holding back on the reins to keep them from going faster and possibly falling.

Twocrow, in the lead, held up his right hand and pulled his horse to a stop with his left. Laura and the Sheriff reined in beside him and Twocrow pointed toward a flat area off to their right where two large hawks appeared to be fighting over something on the ground.

"Hey!" he shouted. His horse snorted uneasily but held his ground as one of the big birds flapped its wings and rose skyward. The other stayed perched where it was as if daring the intruders to interrupt what it was doing. Satisfied that they weren't coming his way, he dipped his beak, tore at the thing on the ground and raised a piece of it into the air and gulped it down.

"What is that?" Laura asked, pointing at the hawk's meal.

"Snake. Big rattler I'd say. Looks fresh, but I doubt the hawks killed him."

Bullock nodded his agreement. "Something else got him, that's for sure." He half-stood in his stirrups and stared down the rest of the slope to the riverbank. "Something went through here not too long ago. See how some of those plants have been torn up."

"Deer maybe, or horses?" Laura asked.

"Not unless they were wearing boots," Twocrow interjected. "See there." He gestured at a spot that flattened and then took a sharp drop off. The heel mark from a boot was clearly visible. He clucked to his horse and continued down to the river's edge where several more boot and shoe prints were interspersed among hundreds of hoof prints.

Twocrow climbed down and studied them, looking first upriver, then down. Laura slipped off her horse and joined him, crouching by the water's edge.

"You two read sign?" Bullock asked. He stayed up on his horse and peered toward the river.

"Some," Twocrow answered.

"No, not really," Laura added.

Twocrow pointed up the river. "Yeah, but even Laura could tell you that a big herd came through here not long ago and headed upstream. And the people that came after them went the other way. I'm going to take a quick look." He dropped his horse's reins and followed the trail downstream to where the rocks narrowed on either side. He went into the water, ducked under the rock overhang and moved out of sight. Within seconds he popped back through the narrow spot, his rifle at the ready and a worried look on his face.

"What'd you see?" Bullock asked.

"Company."

"Who?" the Sheriff asked, shifting in his saddle and unsheathing his own rifle as he spoke.

Before Twocrow could answer, an Indian stepped into view behind him. Twocrow kept moving slowly toward his companions as one-by-one six more Indians emerged along the riverbank. Dressed in leather leggings and wearing moccasins, they all were carrying rifles and knives and two had bows and quivers of arrows as well. Three wore makeshift cotton or linen tops, but the others were naked from the waist up, including the tallest one, who appeared to be their leader.

They stopped and eyed Bullock and Laura suspiciously. Somewhere out of sight they could hear the men's horses snorting and softly whinnying. Laura edged forward to Twocrow's side.

The hawk screamed at the sight of these newest intruders and rose up with the remains of the snake tangled in his claws, flapping upstream with his prize.

Startled, the men crouched and pointed, and one cried out "Cetan!"

"Sintehlahla," one of his companions said, gesturing with his rifle at the flying bird.

Bullock shifted his rifle to his left hand and dropped his right hand onto the butt of his pistol. "No, wait! They're just talking about the hawk and the snake." Twocrow said through clenched teeth, a warning look in his eyes. "I still know some Lakota. We should see what they want."

The tall leader awkwardly took a step forward along the bank, stopping in a spot illuminated by a patch of sunlight. A yellow feather twisted into his long hair glinted as it shifted from both his movement and a slight breeze that kicked up and wafted over them.

Twocrow handed his rifle to Laura and turned back to the men. "Han," he said, nodding in the direction of the rapidly disappearing hawk. The tall Indian turned slightly to his men and spoke quietly. They relaxed their weapons and shuffled backward as he, in turn, came closer to where Twocrow was waiting.

"Hau, kola," the tall man said.

"Hau, kola," Twocrow answered.

"Iya woyaglaka he Lakhotiya?"

"Han." Twocrow looked back to Laura and Bullock. "He said do I speak Lakota and I said yes. "

"I thought you told us you forgot all your Lakota?" Laura said, a big note of disbelief in her voice. "It just came back to you? Just like that?"

"Sure....well, sort-of."

The Indian gave Twocrow a quizzical look. "Lakhotiya? Na English?" the man said.

Twocrow nodded. "Hau. English. Na Lakhotiya..." he paused and waggled his hand to signify that his Lakota was limited.

The tall man grinned at the response and let his rifle stock settle onto the ground at his feet. Leaning the weapon against his body he extracted a stained sheet of paper from inside a leather pouch around his neck. He held it toward them. Twocrow exchanged another look with his companions and Bullock nodded at the paper. "Let's see what it is?" Before Twocrow could react, Laura hurried forward and reached for the paper in the big man's hands.

The Indian looked shocked at her sudden response and half-thrust the paper at her while quickly stepping back as if fearing that she might try to touch him.

Laura surveyed the paper and looked back at Twocrow.

"It's a letter from the Indian Agent on the Reservation. It says Chief Yellow Feather—that must be him—and members of his Band have permission to leave the Reservation to hunt and fish in the Black Hills."

The man watched their exchange and pointed at the letter. "Good?" He asked. He pointed at himself. "Mitakuyepi." He paused and stepped ahead holding out his hand again. Laura looked at the paper and handed it back to him. He touched the letter and pointed again at himself. "Miye...wiyaka zee." It sounded like Me-yea, We-yah-kah Zee. He pointed firmly at his own chest, and back to the letter.

"Yes, that's him." Twocrow exclaimed. "Miye weyaka zee ...Yellow Feather." He pointed at the Indian. "You? Miye weyaka zee. You...Yellow Feather?"

"Hau. Good." The man nodded and smiled. "Good."

He turned abruptly at the sound of a horse approaching and the rest of his men stirred uneasily, relaxing again as an Indian rider came over the edge of the hill and skidded down toward them in the same fashion Twocrow, Bullock and Laura had done shortly before.

The rider slid off the horse's back, leaving him to drink from the stream, and walked over to his chief. He pointed at Laura and spoke quietly to his leader. Yellow Feather shifted to give the man room beside him and the other man spoke, startling them by speaking in English.

"Who are you?" he asked.

Twocrow made quick introductions and the man turned back and translated. He pointed at Twocrow. "*You* are Two Crow?"

"Han. Yes."

At his response, the chief stepped past Laura and put his hands on Twocrow's shoulders. "Tiospaye. Cinkse, Ise Mato. Quick Bear." He smiled broadly and patted the younger man's shoulders. "Oyate." He said. "Lakhotiya." Twocrow inhaled sharply.

"He says I am the son of Quick Bear of The People. The Lakota. I am 'family.'"

"Ise Mato," the man repeated to Laura and Bullock. He signaled to the English-speaking man to come up beside him. He said something and the second man nodded.

"My chief says Quick Bear was great leader for our people." He pointed at Twocrow. "This his son."

Yellow Feather and his translator walked back to re-join their group and stood talking with them as Twocrow moved up next to Laura. She took his right arm in both of hers, seeing that her friend's eyes were glistening from hearing the praise for his dead father.

The English-speaker turned back from the others.

"My chief asks where you go?"

Speaking in both English and his broken Lakota, Twocrow explained what they were doing, ending by pointing at the footprints made by two people after horses had gone through. He pointed downstream and at his eyes. "Did you...see anyone?" he asked in Lakota.

Yellow Feather spoke again, looking behind him before sweeping his arm upstream.

Twocrow looked puzzled.

"What'd he say?" Bullock asked.

The young Indian turned toward the Sheriff. "He says their footprints go downstream, but they did not. They have gone upstream."

Bullock looked upriver. It was clear that the river wound toward a canyon wall, before going out of sight.

"Where does the river lead?" he asked.

Twocrow turned and asked, and the man spoke again.

"He says to a place where the canyon walls turn red and a cave hides behind the water."

*****

The Indian hunters had retrieved their horses and led the way up and around the formidable rock wall onto a hidden switchback trail. Eventually the switchback opened onto a wider trail heading into the heart of a red-walled canyon. It was there that they emerged to the sight of Irene and Jack hobbling toward them.

"So that big scar-faced dirt bag that was holding us hostage—he's dead?" Jack asked with undisguised contempt, interspersing his words with an occasional grunt of pain as Laura and Irene re-bandaged both his makeshift splint and wounded hand with strips of cloth from Laura's petticoat. "We thought it was Chalky had died."

"No," Bullock answered. "That young deputy is hurt bad, but he's alive. At least he was when Anderson and Roosevelt took him into town. And now we have to figure out how to get back into town, too—as quick as we can. That other guy you said was there before. That Jake. Laura and your friend Will spotted him heading into Hot Springs. He must be trying to get those prisoners free."

Jack nodded. "That sounds right." He looked to Irene for confirmation. "We heard them talking about getting Scar-face's brother out of the jail. Jake said he'd be meeting some of their 'boys' out on the edge of town." He stopped, thinking about what they'd heard. "Since Will went in, wouldn't he have warned the Sheriff?"

Bullock nodded. "Hopefully. But I think we need to get back. And soon."

He walked to the English-speaking Indian and pointed at the crevice from which they'd just come into the canyon. "Is that our best way out?"

"Hiya. No."

"No?" Twocrow interrupted, stepping up beside the Sheriff. "Tokiya la hwo? Where do we go?"

"Past the...cave," the man replied, struggling as if searching for the right words.

"But we just came from the cave," Irene said. "It's not fast that way at all, and you have to go on foot along the river."

"Yeah, *that* can't be the best path out of here," Twocrow agreed, gesturing in the direction from which Irene and Jack had come.

The Indian shook his head and pointed opposite, up the canyon. "No. Not past the Bad

Medicine cave. Past cave home of Wakan Tanka. Wakan Tanka. Great Spirit cave."

"What?" Twocrow stepped back and looked with disbelief in the direction the man was pointing. "Wind Cave?" he said. "There? From here? But how? It's too far."

The man shook his head emphatically. "Hiya. No! Not far. Close." He spoke to Yellow Feather and swung his right arm in a half-circle. "Yes. Close. Hidden trail." He looked to Yellow Feather again for the leader's okay to continue. The chief nodded and said something. "Our chief say, we lead you. Then you follow the white man's road to Minnekahda."

"Minnekahta? In Hot Springs?" Laura asked, listening to the exchange.

"No. It means the place of hot waters. Hot Springs. The city." Twocrow was concentrating hard on every word the Indians spoke in their native language. Yellow Feather spoke again to his companion and touched his chest.

The second Indian spoke. "Our chief says we take you, but then must hunt." He spoke directly to Jack and Irene. "You have been in bad medicine cave behind the water?"

They nodded.

"Bad cave," he shook his head. "Stay away."

Jack looked to Bullock. "You're from Deadwood. We found old ore boxes in there—from the Homestake."

"What? Were they sealed?"

"No, broken open. Whatever was in them is gone."

"Yellow metal," the Indian inserted, listening to the two men. "My people find. We take. We give..." he paused and switched to Lakota.

Twocrow listened intently. All right, I think I know what he's saying. "He says Wakan Tanka, the creator, put the yellow metal in the earth to protect the people and the sacred Black Hills. When it was taken away, Wakan Tanka was sad, and angry, because his protection was stolen."

He said something to the man, who spoke again. "Mazaska zi. Inyon maza zi. Heyapi Wakan Tanka…" He continued on, gesturing widely with his hands as he finished. Twocrow nodded and turned to the others.

"He said Wakan Tanka was sad, and angry, to see the yellow metal taken from the land and put in the cave, where it should not be. So he gave the cave bad medicine, and all the men who came there with the metal were killed."

The man listened to Twocrow's interpretation and interrupted him, pointing to the earth, saying something again in Lakota.

"He says 'The People took the gold away and returned it to Paha Sapa—the sacred Black Hills. Because the yellow metal belongs to the earth.'"

Bullock whistled as he looked around. "So they buried it out here somewhere, eh?"

Twocrow asked the Indian. The man replied in English. "Yes, in the red canyon."

Yellow Feather spoke again to Twocrow, pointing first to the east, and then at Twocrow himself.

Twocrow shook his head.

"Mitakuye Oyasin," the chief replied. "Mitakuye Oyasin."

He touched Twocrow's arm, turned and walked back toward his men. The younger, English-speaking man nodded and followed. Twocrow watched them go, a troubled look on his face.

"What is it?" Laura asked him, concern filling her voice as she watched his face. She grasped her friend's arm. "What did he tell you?"

"Their families are camped to the east, near the Mako Shika; the Bad Lands. They are very hungry, and some are sick," Twocrow said.

"But what was it he said last. Mitak...?" She struggled to say it.

"Mitakuye Oyasin?" Twocrow finished.

She nodded.

"It means we are related. We are family. And not just The People. All—people, animals, birds, trees, and plants...even rocks, rivers, mountains and valleys. We are all related and the chief says they are calling me home. I should return and be with my own people."

He paused as a fresh, cool breeze suddenly wafted over them. He turned into the wind standing mesmerized by the gentle whisper it created as it wafted across the canyon floor and through the tall grasses at their feet. "Listen. Did you hear that?"

"What?" Laura touched his arm. "What is it? What do you hear?"

"My name," Twocrow answered. He turned to face her. "The wind whispered my name."

CHAPTER TWENTY-SEVEN

The four outlaws rode casually into the west end of the Chautauqua Park and were greeted by the sound of a brass band playing and the sight of two unhitched buggies parked at an angle alongside the main part of the trail. A group of young people sat near the river on the open area's north end.

Jake Curley held up one hand and the riders stopped. "What do you think?" he asked. He took in the whole scene before re-focusing on the buggies ahead of them. "Kind of a weird spot for them rigs to be parked, ain't it?"

Tom Ketchum shrugged, while Arlie Posthus nervously rubbed his right hand across the top of the revolver dangling in the gun belt strapped around his waist. Harvey Logan, the fourth member of the group, sat stoically waiting for the others to decide the next move.

"Don't see anything wrong," he said. "That band sounds good, don't it? I thought you said they was having Buffalo Bill and Annie Oakley out here? What's going on now?"

"I don't know." Curley eyed the buggies. "Who's that by them rigs?"

As if in response, Buffalo Bill climbed up onto the seat of the buggy closest to the men and gave them a little wave. The outlaw who had been caressing his pistol gasped.

"Jake! That there's Buffalo Bill hisself!" Ketchum exclaimed. "I'll be damned. He IS here." He reached over and poked Curley on the arm. "You think he's got Annie with him?"

Curley stroked his moustache and took in the placid surroundings. "How the hell would I know? Guess we ought'a just ride on up there and ask." He looked around the park. "Harvey. You stay back here and make sure there ain't any 'surprise' visitors comin' out of them trees behind us. I'll give you a signal when it's okay to come on up." Logan reined in his horse as the others started forward, soothing the nervous animal that wanted to go forward with the others.

"Oh, and Harvey," Curley said, pulling his horse around as he spoke. "Don't be afraid to use that rifle if you see we need some help. Okay?"

Logan tipped his hat in response and took the rifle from its scabbard, laying it across the top of his saddle.

The trio rode forward and drew to a halt just short of where the famed showman stood facing them.

"You really be Buffalo Bill?" Ketchum asked excitedly before Curley could say anything. Curley glared at him and the man shrank back down on his saddle.

Bill smiled and took off his big white hat, making a sweeping bow in their direction. All three men's horses whickered nervously and pranced back at the motion. "At your service," he responded. "And who might I have the pleasure of meeting?" He held his hat in front of him, one hand on either side of the wide brim.

The band's music stopped and there was movement from the men sitting by the conductor. The men appeared to be putting their instruments into cases and talking among themselves while the conductor was bending down talking to the two people still sitting in front of him. Over by the river, the young people had gotten to their feet, eyeing the three horsemen.

"Jake Curley," Curley said. "And friends."

"You got Annie here with you?" Posthus interrupted. "We heard you was gonna be out here tonight—you and Annie." He spotted the look on Curley's face and the excitement in his voice ebbed. "Always wanted to see how good a shot she is, that's all," he muttered.

"Well, yes," Bill replied. "That's understandable. You know, I can give you an exhibition of that, right now!" His voice raised sharply as he said "now" and whipped his hat into the air.

As the hat soared skyward a shot rang out and just as it started back down it was literally slapped from the air as a bullet ripped through it.

The outlaws' horses whinnied and reared back as the hat dropped beside them, a large hole through its crown. All three men fought their reins while grabbing for their pistols. At that second, a sharp boom came from the area where the musicians had been playing. A woman there had jumped up, aimed a rifle toward them and fired. They heard the bullet go whistling past and gaped in surprise as all the musicians dropped in behind their chairs, formed a firing line, and appeared to raise weapons in their direction.

Buffalo Bill glanced back at the musicians, chuckled at seeing them in defensive firing positions, and pointed a finger at his hat lying in the dirt.

"My hat, which I was quite fond by the way, was just shot out of the sky by Annie Oakley herself." He pointed toward the young people where Annie was standing, smoke curling from the end of her rifle. "And her next shot won't be at anyone's hat, gentlemen, it'll be much lower."

He pointed behind him. "Those men you just heard playing that stirring march music; those are former U.S. Marines. Trust me, they may be musicians, but they KNOW how to shoot."

The group that gathered by the river started advancing toward them—two women in the lead, both carrying rifles at the ready.

"What the hell!" Curley exclaimed. He aimed his pistol at Buffalo Bill. "Call 'em off; all of 'em; or you're a dead man," he ordered. He glanced back over his shoulder where Logan was waiting, and raised his left arm. "And so far as having someone else who knows how to shoot, well I got some of them myself and they got rifles trained on all of you. So, I'd say we got ourselves quite a standoff here, wouldn't you?"

The rattling sound of a horse and buggy being driven fast filled the air and the Whites' rig raced around the corner behind Logan and nearly ran him down. The outlaw fought to control his horse, backing away toward the stream, rifle raised. His horse slipped on the edge of the bank and flipped Logan straight into the stream as the gunman fired wildly into the air. William pulled back hard and reined in the rig for a few seconds, eyeing the fallen outlaw. Seeing him sit up in the stream and start to reach for his rifle, William snapped the reins and raced on as Sallie clung tightly to the side of the seat, her colorful bonnet flapping in the breeze.

Curley swung sideways in his saddle to assess the situation, and Will jumped forward from the edge of the parked buggy and yelled "Hey!" Curley's two companions swung their guns in his direction and Curley, undecided about who to deal with first, half-turned his horse and aimed at the oncoming rig.

At Curley's shift, Buffalo Bill dropped into a crouch and raised one arm skyward while yelling "Annie. Now!" Curley glanced back over his shoulder as another shot rang out. His gun went spinning from the bullet's impact.

"Aaghh! Shit!" he yelled, grasping at his stinging hand. His companions gaped at their leader's reaction and began pulling back on their reins while aiming wildly in Annie's and Lil's direction, unsure whether to shoot or ride. Will leaped forward, spun his rope and neatly snagged the right front hoof of the horse nearest to him, just as Curley pulled his own horse backward, out of the way.

Ketchum's horse, caught by the loop, stumbled and its rider went sprawling directly into Posthus. Both men fell and Ketchum fired wildly into the air. Seeing his men on the ground, Curley shook his wounded hand, swore loudly and pulled his horse around. As his companions stumbled to their feet, the outlaw leader kicked his horse in its sides and galloped away.

Buffalo Bill stood again, now holding Will's rifle, and fired a shot into the air before aiming it directly at the two men still remaining. Seeing the rifle aimed at them, they slowly raised their hands.

In the background, Logan's horse whinnied as Curley rode past and the rider-less horse raced after the outlaw leader's horse, leaving the dripping Logan standing at the edge of the stream, rifle still in hand. Annie and Lil veered toward him and Annie fired a warning shot over his head.

Logan dropped his rifle and turned in the direction of Curley's and his retreating horses. Shaking his fist at them he yelled, "Thanks for nothin' you damn chickenshit!" He kept his hand raised and brought up the other as Annie and Lil reached him and pointed with their rifles for him to move toward the other men's position.

"Gentlemen," Buffalo Bill addressed the men in front of him. "We're going to show you a lot more of all of our shooting skills if you don't put those guns down and surrender right now." Ketchum started to bring his gun hand down. "Slowly." Buffalo Bill cautioned. Posthus looked nervously at his partner and followed suit. "Lay them down on the ground and get your hands back up."

Both men looked from side-to-side as if debating whether to run.

Bill jerked his left thumb over his shoulder. "You know, there's at least twenty more guns behind me, and those aren't just ordinary rifles. You try to make a run for it and they won't hesitate to drop you before you can get fifty yards. Like I said, those boys are ex-Marines."

Both men stared toward the band before carefully putting their guns on the ground.

Will flicked his rope and it came loose from the horse, which backed away unsure what to do. Ketchum glared at Will. Will reached up, tipped his hat, and spun the rope again, dropping it over the outlaw's pistol and reeling it back to himself before the man could react.

The outlaw gaped in amazement at the roping feat, and Buffalo Bill gave an appreciative whistle. "Pretty darn handy with that rope young fella." Will picked up the pistol and grinned.

Annie and Lil came up with the soaked Logan walking dejectedly before them. "Howdy gents," she said. She reached down and picked up Curley's smashed gun. "Too bad about your friend's shootin' iron." She kicked Posthus' gun over toward where Minnie and Joe had arrived, and Joe picked it up. He joined the others in covering the outlaw trio.

Annie turned the smashed gun over in her hands and spoke to the three men. "This is what happens when you point these things at other people. Don't do that no more." She chuckled and signaled toward the band shell. Nellie signaled back and started toward them with Robert and Sousa tagging along.

The musicians all stood but stayed by their overturned chairs. From his vantage point on top of the buggy, Buffalo Bill could clearly see that the bandsmen's "weapons" were only parts of their musical instruments. None appeared to have an actual rifle.

The Whites had driven off to the side of the road, and now they headed back toward the others, reining in their buggy alongside the other two.

"Well," Sallie said somewhat breathlessly, her cheeks flushed bright red. "I don't know about the rest of you, but that certainly got *my* blood pumping."

William and the others gave her a surprised look and Lil started laughing.

"Yeah," she said, still keeping the small rifle in her hands trained on the three outlaws. "Mine, too."

Buffalo Bill spoke to the outlaws again. "This city is noted for its posh accommodations, gentlemen, but I'm afraid you're going to find yours a little less 'accommodating'." He smiled and nodded to Nellie, Robert and Sousa as they walked up to the buggies. He looked back to the three captives. "By the way, 'Welcome to Hot Springs.'"

*****

"Okay, since we're here anyway, are you absolutely *positive* that gold ain't hid here somewhere? I'd hate to go lookin' all over creation for another cave and then find out later that somebody found it buried in this one." Grace Franston gave her traveling companion a skeptical look as Mollie Previn made her way back to their buggy after walking from the partially constructed Wind Cave Hotel.

The women had turned north after leaving their encounter with the Whites and driven over to Wind Cave from the west. As they passed the spot where the new visitor's hotel was under construction, Mollie noticed a pair of tin pail lanterns sitting by the building's walls and made Grace stop while she went to get them. She handed the lanterns to the two younger women riding in back, and pulled herself back up onto the seat alongside the Hot Springs madam.

"Well, I'm *pretty sure* that it ain't, and even if it's here, where would we look?"

"Then why in hell you want to get those lanterns if we ain't going in there to have a look?"

"Well if we find that other cave that Alexander said Johnny hid the gold in, then we're gonna need some way to light it up, ain't we? You saw how good these lanterns worked before when we were moving his body around, didn't ya? I'm just tryin' to be ready for anything—especially if we find another cave."

Mollie held her hands wide. "Besides, I think we ought to go down there one more time and check on his body." She paused for effect. "Whether you like it or not!"

"Waste of time if you ask me..."

"Well I wasn't askin', I was tellin'!" Mollie cut her off. "Look since his body's been found, they'll probably send someone out to take him back to town tomorrow. I want to be sure that we didn't overlook something he might've been carrying with him." She blew out an exasperated sigh. "I just figure we ought to check to be sure there ain't some sort of map or directions sheet—something, anything—that'll help us find that gold.

"Besides, even if there's no map or anything like it, I just want to be damn sure that there's nothin' else on him that can put his death on me." She paused. "Or on you either Grace. You got a hell of a lot more at stake around these parts than I do."

"Okay, okay." Grace blew out a sigh and sat back with a look of resignation on her face. "But you ain't even sure his body's still down there, are ya?"

"Well, that Marshal told us they found a body, and they thought it was Alexander. But they couldn't get into any of his stuff at the hotel until they brought him back to town and got him identified proper-like," Mollie answered. "I don't know about you, but to me that sounds like he's still down there, now don't it? *And* didn't you say we need to wait here anyway? To meet up with Jake? While we're waiting we might as well go back in there and check. Right?"

She looked back at the two younger women for confirmation but they both stared straight ahead, not speaking, as if afraid to dispute anything their madam might say.

Grace shrugged. "Okay, okay. We'll check. But *I* ain't goin' all the way back down in that hole. You take one of the girls and go if you're so hot and bothered about it. I'm gonna sit out here in the buggy and rest. And if you don't like it. Well, fuck you!"

"You know after I first met Alexander up in Deadwood and he learned Lame Johnny had been hung, he decided we needed to get out of the Hills and hole up for a while. He said that gold was so well-hidden nobody'd ever find it until he come back here himself. So we went off to Chicago and laid low with the money he already had from when he and Lame

Johnny split things up. We were there fifteen years, and all he ever talked about was US coming back and getting that gold. US!

"Damn it all," she bowed her head and sniffled. "I always thought we was lifelong partners and we'd get that gold from wherever it was hid and go on having a wonderful life together. I never thought he was gonna try an' kill me." She stopped. "Damn it all. Shit Grace. I loved him, you know?"

"Love." Grace snorted. "Waste of time, if you ask me. And, look what happened to the two of you. I rest my case." She started to pick up the reins, paused and looked at the pathway ahead. "You hear that?"

"No. What?" Mollie looked around. Just ahead of them was the entrance to the cave, now whistling slightly as the late afternoon air started rushing back in. Beyond it was a small knoll that blocked the view toward the primary road heading southwest toward Hot Springs.

She cocked her head to one side. "Nope, I don't hear any..." she stopped as the obvious sound of horses' hooves grew louder, moving toward them from the other side of the knoll. She looked back at the younger women again. "Now I do. Do you?" They both nodded and sat up straighter.

"That's gotta be Jake and his boys!" Grace exclaimed. "Thank God. Now he can go down there in the stupid cave with you and check your old man's body. Then we can get the hell out of here; maybe head on up to Custer City for tonight? Plenty of time to go looking for that other cave tomorrow."

She handed the reins to Mollie and stood up, cupping her hands around the corners of her mouth. "Jake!" she shouted toward the knoll. "We're over here! Over by the..." She stopped shouting and emitted a small shriek. Behind her both girls screamed and shrank back on the seat. Mollie just sat there, stunned by what she saw.

Ahead of them, riding around the side of the knoll, was a band of Indians. The leader of the group, a yellow feather dangling from his hair, jerked his horse to a stop, raised a rifle sideways in the air and glared at the women. Grace Franston emitted one more sound—almost like the squeak of an overactive mouse—and fainted dead away.

CHAPTER TWENTY-EIGHT

Gene Akin and his men picked their way across Fall River and up the bank onto a wide flat grassy area sloping toward them from the back side of nearby Battle Mountain. They reined in halfway across the open expanse as a rider crested the knoll directly ahead of them and galloped headlong in their direction.

A couple of his men pulled their rifles from their scabbards, but Akin held up one hand.

"It's Pelly," he said, naming one of his deputies who was supposed to be down at Carson's Notch.

The possé members held their position until the deputy got to them, his horse blowing hard. Pelly reined in alongside the sheriff and gave the others a small wave of his hand.

"What's up?" Akin asked, looking past the deputy toward the open space behind him.

"Where's Chris?" Pete Lemley interrupted, edging his horse up toward them. "He okay?"

"He's good. Still holding fast at the Notch, and John Hulme's there with him, too," Pelly answered. "After what John told us, we figured one of us ought to ride over and meet you before you got any further than this." He glanced around at the Home Guard. "Didn't expect you to have so many men with you though. Real glad for that." He grinned.

"So, why'd you want to catch up with us?" Akin was getting impatient.

"Well, old John was ridin' in from his place and instead of takin' his usual route, he decided to check on the new trestle and see how it was holding up. But when he got over there he said there was a real suspicious looking bunch camped out. When he told us about them, we figured it had to be that same bunch Nellie Ryan spotted earlier.

"Anyway, he didn't hang around to find out; just started for town before they could spot him. When he got to the Notch, a-course, we stopped him and he told us everything he saw. But here's the strange part; they wasn't makin' any kinda move toward leavin'. Fact is, he said some of 'em seemed to be sleepin'. Like they was waitin' on someone."

"Or something," Akin added, stroking the whisker stubble on his chin. He looked up at the sky. "Maybe they think it'd be better to come on into town around dusk. Or after dark. Easier for them; harder for us."

He turned in his saddle to look at Lemley. "What do you think Pete?"

"That sounds right," the deputy answered. He took off his hat, wiped his brow, and kept the hat in his hands as he stared off toward the river. "If that's the case, they're ripe for the pickin' down there by the trestle." He pointed his hat toward a gap that ran up across from where they were stopped and on up toward a small mesa along the other side of the river. "And that would mean we'd have time to take the high road over there. Maybe slip some of our guys in behind them."

Pelly nodded. "That's exactly what old John was sayin'. But he knew we needed to catch up with you before you got too far, or you'd waste a lot of time going on down to the Notch and then having to come all the way back to take the ridgeline." He swiped a hand across the top of his horse's head. "That's why I got sent to meet you. Got the best horse in three counties, you know?"

A couple of the other men chortled at Pelly's brag, and the deputy feigned anger. "Now, don't you go laughin' at my horse." He patted his horse again. "Maybe he ain't the sweetest looking nag, like old Chalky's pinto; and maybe he ain't the fastest like Pete's here; but he ain't too bad on a short run like this." He pointed back in the direction from which he'd ridden.

"And Chris is a helluva lot better shot than me. Plus you all know how good John can shoot." Several of the older men nodded knowingly. "Between 'em, we figured they could hold most anyone off while I skedaddled on over here to fill you in."

Akin nodded. "Yeah, you thought right. It's a good plan." He reached over slapped Pelly on the shoulder. "Damn good plan."

He turned back to the posse. "Charley?" he directed his remark to Chief Deputy Roe. "How long you think it'd take for you and Pete and some of the boys to take the ridgeline up across to the back side of that trestle?"

"I'd say, half hour," Roe answered.

"About the same for getting us down to the Notch from here?" he said it as a question to Pelly, who gave a quick nod of assent. "Okay, then here's what we're going to do. And if it works, we all ought'a be back to town in time for supper and tonight's Chautauqua show."

He gestured at Pelly and two of the other men. "You three ride with Charley and Pete and get below the trestle. Go to that spot right where the river bends back to the south. Easy to get down off the ridge from there." Roe nodded his affirmation.

"The rest of you come with me. We'll meet up with Chris and John and ride on down from this side."

He turned back to his deputies. "Remember, though, this here's Doc McCarty's bunch and he's one mean son-of-a-bitch. I don't figure he'll want to just put up his hands and play nice, if you know what I mean? I'll put these boys around this side in a semicircle, fire a couple of shots, and give McCarty a chance to make a liar out of me.

"But if that don't work, and you hear a BUNCH of shooting...well, you ride in on 'em full bore. One way or t'other, this here thing's going to be over today. And I mean for it to be over in our favor."

"Pelly, you want to lead the way on that 'flashy' horse of yours?" Lemley asked.

The deputy grinned. "Yeah, my old bones here'll be glad to take the lead." He looked around at the others. "Speaking of flashy horses. Where's Chalky and that pinto of his, anyway? Thought for sure he'd be ridin' out here for something as excitin' as this."

"I sent him out to Martin's ranch with a wrangler from the Oklahoma Territory," Akin replied. "Had some information on that train robbery for them. Something about a load of horses Martin was expecting." He looked around at the others. "And...well...you know Chalky ain't never been tested in a situation like this. Still just a young pup."

"Geez Sheriff, all he talks about is getting into some 'action'; showin' what he can do," Pelly answered. "He's gonna be pissed as hell that all he got out of this was a ride in the country to take care of some missing horses, instead of takin' down one of the biggest gangs in the whole damn region."

There were murmurs of agreement from the others and Akin nodded. "Yeah, I know. He'll be madder'n a wet hen. But all-in-all, I'm thinkin' it's for the best. Besides, I'm just the 'acting' sheriff, so he can be mad at me all he wants. I ain't gonna be here anyway. And he still will be."

"You did the right thing Sheriff," Lemley said. "Chalky's old man will probably sympathize with his kid, but privately he's gonna be real glad his boy ain't in harm's way. Chalky's a damn good kid, so I'm glad you put him out there doing something safe."

*****

Chalky was still unconscious, the sheet covering him coated in a light brown/red dust, as were the two outlaws riding alongside him in the back of the buckboard. Both were looking down, eyes closed to avoid the swirl of dust being stirred up by the wagon's wheels.

Anderson had been driving as fast as his big rig would stand and now it rattled ominously as he came barreling down the hill toward the new courthouse.

He pulled back on the reins and brought the buckboard to a stop. Ahead of him was a strange sight—Archie Riordan's water wagon rocking violently back-and-forth at the edge of the street running alongside the big stone building.

Roosevelt rode up and stopped next to the rancher, gesturing at the wagon. "What do you think is going on over there?"

"I don't know," Anderson answered, looping his horses' reins around the brake rod and climbing back over the seat to check on the wounded deputy. "But I didn't want my team getting spooked.

Besides," he knelt beside Chalky, "thought I should see how the kid's holding up."

The Water Wagon continued rocking violently from side-to-side, its team of huge horses nervously pawing the ground at their wagon's strange movement.

Theodore pushed back on his wide-brimmed hat and shook his head, emitting a slight gasp as the wagon tilted precariously at a 45-degree angle away from them and then rocked back hard in their direction. The big team shifted together trying to move away from their wild wagon, which seemed to have a life of its own.

Theodore's horse whinnied loudly and Anderson's big horses snorted in fear, shaking hard against their reins, stamping backward, and forcing the buckboard to jerk violently in reverse.

The makeshift tabletop litter holding Chalky shifted at the unexpected movement and Anderson grabbed for it to keep it in place. But the trussed-up outlaws sitting behind it both sprawled sideways at the sudden movement, and the one named Georgie had his arm wrenched sideways with a sudden pop. He screamed loudly as Anderson shouted "Whoa!" to his team.

Roosevelt reached over and grabbed at the team's reins, pulling back on them as tight as he could. The horses halted and shuddered again as Georgie emitted another loud cry.

At the noise, the rocking from the water wagon halted and the tentative voice of Jonas McCarty came from inside.

"Who's out there? Georgie? Is that you? Hey, Georgie, it's Jonas! I'm here. Inside the wagon."

Roosevelt and Anderson both looked at the injured outlaw, still moaning, just as the side door of the courthouse popped open and Masterson eased his way out, rifle at the ready. Seeing Roosevelt and

Anderson, he lowered the weapon, quickly snapping it up again as the voice from the water wagon resumed, this time louder.

"Georgie? What's going on? You come to break me out? Where's Doc?" The sound of a boot kicking at the inside wall of the enclosed wagon followed. "Get something to knock open this back door! Me'n Franklin are hooked up in here, but it won't take much to break the cuffs off. We been tryin' to tip the wagon so this rod holding us will slide out."

He stopped shouting, waiting for a response. Georgie, his arm still twisted sideways in an ugly fashion, only moaned.

Roosevelt climbed down from his horse, removed his rifle from its scabbard and walked across to the back of the wagon. He tapped loudly on the rear door with the rifle barrel.

"Georgie! That you? You there?"

"Your friend Georgie's here all right," Roosevelt called to the men inside. "But he's not going to be doing anything to help you get those cuffs off OR get you out of town." He turned and shouted over to Masterson. "Marshal! We've got a badly wounded man in there." He pointed to Anderson's wagon. "We need to get him a doctor."

Doc Jennings emerged behind Masterson, followed by Riordan.

"I'm a doctor," he said. "Who's hurt?"

"It's the young deputy, Chalky Burrell," Anderson called from his spot next to Chalky's side. Anderson looked across to where Georgie was still writhing in pain. "And one of the men who hurt him maybe needs a look-see, too." Anderson glared at Georgie and the other outlaw, who was leaning sullenly against the wagon's opposite side.

The doctor already was coming toward them and Anderson stood and reached down, offering a hand to Jennings so he could come up onto the seat.

"Get my bag Archie," Jennings called back to Riordan, who turned and hurried back inside.

Doc Jennings climbed over the back of the buckboard seat and jumped down beside the wounded deputy. Ripping off the dusty sheet, he put his hand alongside Chalky's neck to check for a pulse. He leaned in close and listened to the young man's shallow breathing.

"We need to get him inside right away," he said, turning sideways to look at the other two men in the back of the wagon. "That one," he pointed at Georgie. "Looks like a dislocated shoulder." He glanced down again at Chalky, a grim look on his face. He stood up and signaled to Roosevelt and Masterson. "I need you to come and help move him right now, men. No time to waste here."

Looking again at Georgie, he added, "But he can wait until later."

The water wagon started rocking again and McCarty's voice re-erupted. "Hey! You need to get us out of here! You just can't leave us; it's hot in here! There's no air!"

Masterson spun around, raised his big rifle and fired squarely into the middle of the wagon, ripping a large hole in its side. Both McCarty and Franklin shouted in surprise.

"There!" the Marshal yelled. "Now you've got some ventilation! So shut the hell up and sit your asses back down."

Roosevelt nodded approvingly.

"Well, Marshal, I know I've said it before, but I'll say it again," he was speaking as he helped Doc Jennings down and climbed up to help Anderson move Chalky's makeshift litter. "Bully!"

*****

Seth Bullock nervously eyed the four women they'd found in the buggy at the entrance to Wind Cave.

Mollie glared back at him and looked over at her traveling companions. The two young women looked frightened. Grace was reclining between them, leaning her head against a large boulder and taking slow deep breaths now that she had recovered from her fainting spell.

"Ladies, I'm sorry to have to do this to you," Bullock said. "But we're taking your buggy. We need to get back into Hot Springs as soon as possible. Up 'til now we've been forced to ride double and it's too slow." Bullock was holding his dark grey Stetson in both hands in an apologetic fashion, sliding his fingers in-and-out of the satin band that ran just under the sharply creased crown.

The two younger women ignored him and began dabbing a damp cloth on the forehead of their gaudily dressed older companion, while fanning her with a flat piece of wood they had picked up from the hotel construction site.

Mollie turned indignantly back toward the sheriff.

"That's ridiculous!" she said. "If you take our buggy, how are we supposed to get on with things? We were just visiting Wind Cave, and it's vital that I get to Custer City yet tonight." She waved toward the half-built hotel. "We can't stay here. What do you expect us to do—sleep in that lean-to?"

"Look, Ma'am, I'm real sorry," Bullock continued. "But there might be an outlaw gang riding in on the town, and we need to get in there to warn them."

He pointed over to the buggy. "And on top of that I've got two folks here who've had a real bad experience today, and one of them's hurt pretty bad. So, like it or not, I'm confiscating your buggy and you're just going to have to deal with it. Now, two of you can ride back into town with us, but two of you are going to have to stay."

He pointed an accusing finger toward her. "And, it seems sort-a suspicious to me that you'd be out here 'visiting' Wind Cave when it's supposed to be closed down." He moved his index finger in the direction of a sign that read: "Closed until September 20th."

She started to respond, thought about what the sheriff was saying, and clamped her mouth shut.

"How's your friend?" Laura asked, walking up from where she'd been helping Irene and Twocrow get Jack situated in the back of the buggy. She and Twocrow had been sharing their horses with Jack and Irene, slowing their progress considerably. Irene had re-examined Jack's hand and declared that he needed to see a doctor soon, even if it meant someone had to stay back while Laura or Bullock took him on into town.

Twocrow and the Indian who spoke English were engaged in an animated conversation behind her and now they, too, turned and walked to where Laura was standing with Bullock and the other women.

Mollie gave Grace a look of disdain. "She's fine!" she spat. Grace grimaced at the tone of Mollie's voice and waved feebly toward the Indian hunters who were standing nearby.

"It was just such a shock," Grace half-wailed, speaking in her own defense. "I was sure we were all going to be killed by those Indians."

A flicker of a smile crossed Laura's face as she exchanged a glance with Alvin and his Indian companion.

The English-speaker frowned at Grace's pronouncement before turning to Bullock. "We will go on to our hunt now," he said.

The sheriff nodded. "Okay. Good hunting," he replied. "And thank your chief for the help. I won't forget it." He turned and gave a small salute to Yellow Feather.

The chief raised one hand in response and climbed back onto his horse. His hunting group followed suit, but the man with Twocrow waited, resting a hand on the younger man's shoulder for a couple of seconds more and giving him a determined nod. Taking back his hand, he over to join the other hunters.

As the hunting party rode away, Twocrow watched them for a few seconds, a troubled look on his face.

He turned back as Bullock spoke to Mollie and the other women.

"As soon as we get back into town, I'll have Sheriff Akin to get one of his men to bring your buggy right back out to pick up whoever decides to stay. But I don't think you're going to make Custer City tonight." He pointed to the horizon. "It'll be getting dark in a couple hours, I think. You'll need to come back to Hot Springs and head up to Custer City in the morning."

Mollie bristled again at Bullock's pronouncement.

"Sheriff, I'm a respectable businesswoman, and you're ruining my plans for both tonight and tomorrow. If you think you and your 'friends' here have heard the last of this outrage...well, you're sorely mistaken, that's all I've got to say!"

Bullock clamped his hat back on and tipped the brim toward her. "Whatever, Mrs." He paused. "Or is it Miss? What'd you say your name was again?"

"Pr..." she started before seeing Grace move her hand rapidly back-and-forth in front of her body. Laura gave both women an odd look at the exchange. "Um. Fr..anston," Mollie finished. "Grace Franston."

"Grace Franston?" Laura sounded incredulous. "You mean...?"

"Yes," Mollie said firmly. "*That* Grace Franston." She glared at Laura. "And don't be making any high-and-mighty judgments young lady. We all can't be born with silver spoons in our mouths. Some of us have to find our own way to make a living."

"Well, I-I wasn't making any judgments," Laura stammered. "It's just I'd heard your name a few times and..." she glanced at the other women, back to Mollie, and swallowed. "Nice to meet you."

"Yeah, me too, I'm sure," Bullock added with a disdainful look at them. "But I'm still putting the law ahead of your 'business' needs here, so make up your mind who's ridin' back with us, and who's stayin' here 'til later, because we're on our way."

Mollie started to protest again but stopped as it was Bullock's turn to glare.

"Okay," she said, waving a hand at the others. "The girls will ride back with you and Gr...Lola...will stay with me. Won't you?" she added, looking at her buxom companion who now had the damp cloth lying across her forehead. The other woman responded with a dejected nod.

"Good." Bullock replied. He gestured to the two younger women. "Get on board ladies. We're leaving." He dismissively tipped the brim of his hat toward Mollie. "And thanks again for the use of your buggy."

CHAPTER TWENTY-NINE

The Evans Hotel's glamorous dining room had been opened just for them, and now the diners chatted around the oak tables, relaxed for the first time in 24 hours after dealing with the momentous events of the day before.

The town's jails—both of them—were filled to capacity with members of the McCarty/Curley gangs; some brought in by Buffalo Bill, some by Roosevelt, and the rest by Akin and his Home Guard, who had captured six by only firing a couple of warning shots. They had ridden up on them so quietly that Akin had abandoned his original plan and come right up to the edge of their camp before putting them under arrest.

To celebrate the capture of the two gangs that had been causing the region so much trouble, Akin told the Home Guard members to go home, get their families, and attend the gala Chautauqua celebration compliments of the Sheriff's office.

"Old C.S. is going to have a cow when he finds out I paid for damn near fifty people out of his budget," he half-laughed to the others at his table—which Theresa Evans was labeling "The Sheriffs' Table," since both Akin and Bullock, along with Roosevelt were seated there. She and Akin were "hosting" the table, which also included Irene and Paul Anderson, who had been "guests" of the Evans Hotel overnight.

"This place. It's so beautiful," Irene said.

"It's a lovely setting isn't it?" Nellie sighed pushing herself away from an adjoining table that she was sharing with Robert Seaman, Bat Masterson and the Whites. "Thank you so much for hosting us Mrs. Evans."

"It's the least we could do after you and the others here did so much to help our town yesterday. We're just glad you were here—for us. A night's stay and a few meals hardly seem sufficient to repay you."

Nellie smiled her thanks and glanced over toward the room's large center oval table where Buffalo Bill and Annie were regaling the people seated there with tales of some of their travels and past shows. Jack, whose hand and ankle were both heavily bandaged, shared one side along with Lil, the Thompson sisters, and Twocrow.

Across from them sat Will Rogers, John Philip Sousa, Minstrel Show owners Thomas Heath and James McIntyre, and their show's band leader Theodore Metz, who was ignoring Buffalo Bill and instead chatting quietly with Joe Hayden, who had just sat down next to him at the foot of the table.

Hayden had started the morning as a member of the serving staff, but Metz had spoken to Evans and insisted that the young black man be seated by his side. The playing of their new song "A Hot Time" had been wildly cheered at the previous night's gala opening of the Chautauqua, which had gone off without a hitch. Now that they had the tune in place, Metz wanted to work with Hayden on some more words to go with it.

The huge crowd attending the event—most unaware of the drama that had unfolded around them the previous day—seemed to justify Fred Evans' contention that "Folks don't mind paying a dollar if the entertainment is worth the price." Annie's shooting exhibition; Bill's storytelling; and the music of Sousa's musicians and the Minstrel Show's band had kept people dancing and cheering until late in the evening.

Fred Evans was not dining but instead had been moving among the guests chatting and answering questions while also discreetly signaling to the wait staff at just the right time to take away empty dishes and plates and replace them with yet another fabulous food offering or drink.

Fred stopped at the Sheriffs' table.

"How's Chalky?"

Akin grimaced. "Doc says it'll be touch and go for the next few days. But he's a strong kid, so I think he'll pull through. Doc says the bullet ripped him up pretty good. Ain't gonna be ridin' in any rodeos any time soon, that's for sure."

He pointed to Irene. "Thanks to Irene's good work on them bandages, he's still alive. Otherwise, he probably would've bled out." He nodded toward her and the others at the table all murmured their appreciation. She blushed and gave a small dismissive wave, but her husband wrapped an arm around her shoulders and gave her a hug.

"Did a real nice job on that Oklahoman's hand, too," Akin added, pointing over at Jack. "Doc said without your attention to it, he might've got a real bad infection in it. And that splint on his ankle was top of the block. He asked me if you'd like to think about doing some nursing for him."

Irene laughed at the suggestion. "I got enough to take care of just dealing with my family." She grinned at Paul. "I'm just glad we ran across those ladies out by Wind Cave so we could get Jack into town faster. Did they get their buggy back okay?"

"Well, that's a real strange thing," the Sheriff said. "I sent a couple of the Home Guard back out there to bring 'em into town and they weren't anywhere to be found."

He looked over to Bullock. "And I was really wanting to have a little talk with them,

too, especially after I spoke with Mrs. White over there and she told me about the conversation she overheard in the spa baths yesterday."

"What was that?" Roosevelt asked.

"Let's just say it had something to do with that body the young folks discovered in Wind Cave. Turns out it WAS Alexander Previn—his brother Paulus staying here at the hotel verified that. But, it seems like that woman who told you she was Grace Franston really might've been Mrs. Mollie Previn, wife of the man who was killed." They all gasped.

"And I'm surprised she took off, because now that we've properly identified her husband's body, she would've had access to those two large bags Fred was storing for Previn in the hotel safe."

He looked up at Evans. "You handed those off to his brother, I presume? Were they full of gold bars? Rumors going around had those bags being full of gold."

Fred Evans laughed. "No. No gold. No cash either. Mostly just business papers and clothing. Looked like he brought enough clothes along for an extended stay. Oh, and there were a couple of strange-looking maps that seemed to be hand-drawn by someone from around these parts."

"Why do you think that?" Bullock asked.

"Well, because they were drawings showing the area north and east of here. They looked old, too." He shrugged. "Who knows? And now we don't have Mrs. Previn to ask either. She had just joined her husband here two days ago, so maybe she decided to go back up to Deadwood."

"Deadwood?" Bullock said. "What for?"

"I guess that's where she used to live—back in the Gold Rush days. Paulus Previn said that's where she and his brother met in the first place, and she came out here a couple of weeks ago already to visit with some friends up there before meeting Alexander down here."

"So she was running around up in my neck of the woods first, eh?" Bullock said. "She wasn't trying to hide her identity before, was she?"

"No. So it seems pretty strange that all of a sudden she was puttin' herself out there as being someone else—especially right at the place where they found her husband's body. I'd definitely like to have a little chat with her about that," Akin said.

Laura stood up from the adjoining table and moved over to theirs. "Couldn't help but overhear you," she said. "You think Mrs. Previn might've had something to do with killing Alexander Previn?" She had taken a small notepad from her bag and the Sheriff eyed it nervously.

"You reportin' now?" he asked.

"Well, that IS what I do," Laura answered. "At the least I want to tell our readers about how weird the widow was acting before she disappeared."

"Does seem to be a bit of a mystery doesn't it?" Roosevelt said. He looked back to Akin. "You have any idea where she or her companion might've gone?"

"Like I was sayin', not yet. But don't worry, she can't stay out of sight for long, so we will." Akin nodded reassuringly and pointed to Bullock. "When you get back home, if you see her anywhere in your town, I'd appreciate you hanging on to her for a couple of days so I can meet with her and have that little chat I was talkin' about."

Bullock nodded and returned to his food.

Akin turned back to Laura. "As for your story, Miss Thompson, I think you can just say that the widow is still wanted for questioning." He tapped the notepad. "And be sure and say that you got that from the 'acting sheriff.' Anything 'official' has to wait until C.S. gets back."

He nodded over to Bullock and Roosevelt. "Oh, and be sure to give my thanks to our friends from the Northern Hills." He looked from Roosevelt to Bullock. "You two going to hang around here for a few more days now that Bat won't need your help getting his prisoners on down to Denver?"

With the gang in holding cells and McCarty dead, Masterson had joined them for breakfast with the news that the Denver Marshal's office had arranged for Army troops to come to Hot Springs and help transport all the prisoners. So there no longer was any need for secrecy in transporting Pasch or any of the others. He expected the soldiers to arrive on the next day's train.

"No, I think we're going to go back to our original plan for why Theodore came out here in the first place—to do a little antelope hunting and some fishing before he has to get back to the big city," the Deadwood sheriff replied.

"But we might try and stop off at Wind Cave first," he added after taking a sip of coffee. "Going in there after Previn's body kind of got our interest up, right Theodore?"

"Yes, indeed, and young Mister Twocrow said he'd be willing to take us back on an 'official tour' before we head out. It seems like a fine opportunity to see one of your local treasures. Besides, I don't know when we might get back this way—at least that's the case for me."

"Speaking of treasure," Theresa spoke up. "I find it fascinating Irene that you and Mister Omohundro found some empty Homestake Mine chests in that hidden cave. Fred says you learned from those Indians that the gold that was in them might still be buried somewhere out there?"

Irene half-nodded as if unsure what to say.

"That's what the Indian who spoke English told us," Bullock answered. "But who knows whether he fully understood us, or we were correctly understanding him? One thing I do know is that a lot of gold was stolen from a Homestake shipment a while back, and so far as anyone knows it was never recovered. Maybe that was it."

"Yeah, maybe," Akin said. "I'll send some men out that way in a couple days and see what they can find. But, I ain't holding my breath that they'll find anything Theresa. Who knows? Stranger things have happened, that's for sure."

Harry Clark came in and whispered something to Fred Evans, who got a startled look on his face.

"What is it?" Theresa asked. "Good morning Harry." She beamed at the young man who was both the head clerk and her son-in-law.

Clark smiled back at her. "Morning Mother Evans," he said. "I came in because I think we have a bit of a problem with a couple of Indians out in the lobby."

He was interrupted by a disturbance at the dining room entrance from the lobby. Evans started over just as two middle-aged Indians, one wearing buckskins and a leather band around his head, and the other dressed in cowboy garb stepped past head waiter Sam Bass and walked into the room.

They looked around and pointed to Buffalo Bill, who jumped up and smiled.

"Friends," he called to them, stepping away from his table and rushing past Evans over to the entryway. He clapped the buckskin-clad man on the shoulder and turned toward the room as Evans came up beside them.

"Everyone. This is my good friend Short Bull." He turned toward Evans. "Fred, if you don't mind, I'd like to have him and his companion join us for the rest of the meal. You DON'T mind, do you?"

Evans looked nervously at the others as if expecting some sort of complaint, but getting none he nodded and said, "No. Certainly." He held out his hand. "Gentlemen. Welcome to the Evans Hotel."

Short Bull gave his hand a suspicious glance and nodded in response. He gestured toward the other man.

"This is Chief Kicking Bear. We came for Buffalo Bill. To sign for his show."

Buffalo Bill smiled. "Fantastic!" He looked around. "I have many Lakota in my show," he explained. "Sitting Bull himself was in my show, you know?"

"My uncle," Short Bull agreed. "Great leader. He spoke well of you." He pointed to Annie. "And her. Little Sure Shot." He smiled at Annie. "We watch you shoot yesterday. My uncle would have smiled. Your skill remains."

"I was sorry he was killed," Annie said. "But I'm glad you are here." She stood. "Will you join our table?" McIntyre and Heath both stood and offered the two Indians their places, moving to a smaller table nearby. The waiters hurried to bring more food for the two new guests and to start new plates for the Minstrel Show leaders.

"You speak good English," Jack said from across the table as the two men sat down. "Where did you learn?"

"In prison," Kicking Bear answered matter-of-factly, picking up a piece of bacon with his fingers and popping it into his mouth. He swallowed the bacon and continued. "We were with Sitting Bull when he was killed. We said things in our own language that did not make the White leaders our friends. They thought we wanted more fighting. They put us in the Army prison."

He looked around. "We don't want to fight any more. We will do what you do. Go where you go." He picked up a piece of bread. "Eat your food."

He swept his arm up and down on the clothing he was wearing. "And wear what you wear." He frowned. "But I think if Buffalo Bill takes us, I will not wear White man's clothing. It scratches."

Those around the table laughed lightly at the remark, but he just frowned once more.

"Why do you want to go with Buffalo Bill?" Jack asked.

"Pay is good," Short Bull answered. "My uncle and others from our tribe who have gone say he is a good man." He shrugged. "We can see many places. Eat well. People will scream at us, but...better than staying on the reservation."

Jack nodded. "Yeah, or on a ranch in Oklahoma Territory, especially when you want to see the world."

"Speaking of that, when are you heading back to the Territory?" White asked from the adjoining table. "We'll be taking the train back to Kansas City in a few days, and we'd love some traveling company." He nodded toward Lil and Will. "Your friends can come with us, too. We'll show you the big city before you have to go on home."

Lil and Will both grinned at the suggestion, but Jack looked pensive before finally speaking.

"Thank you Mister White. That's nice of you, but I'm thinking of asking Mister Cody here if I might tag along with him for a while."

Lil gasped.

"Jack? What?" Lil seemed flabbergasted by Jack's remark. "What're you talking about? I thought you were coming back to Oklahoma with me...uh, with us?"

"I might just be a wrangler, but I've been studying on things like sharpshooting and bulldogging," Jack said. "And thanks to your dad, I've learned how to manage money and things. Anyways, I'd like to spend some time with Buffalo Bill and Annie—if they'll have me—and learn more about their show; maybe even get my own Wild West Show goin'," he grinned at Buffalo Bill. "But, don't worry, sir, I won't steal your thunder." He chuckled and pointed at Rogers. "Hell, maybe even young Will here'll want to come work for me, if he gets his ropin' under control!"

"I'm a damn good roper an' you know it," Will sputtered.

"I'm just teasin' ya pal," Jack smiled. "But you do need to do a bit more growin' up before you can come with me. Okay?"

"What else will you have?" Short Bull said, his voice muffled as he wolfed down more food. He swallowed, took a sip of water, and continued. "Buffalo Bill, he's got raiding —that's what my uncle and his friends did; pretended to be raiders," he looked proudly around and everyone nodded. "You need Indians?" He looked at Will. "You are Indian, yes?"

"Cherokee. Half." Will said. He laughed. "I can be both a cowboy AND an Indian." The rest laughed at his remark and Will pointed to Twocrow, who along with Minnie and Laura had moved over toward the door getting ready to leave. "Maybe you should have Bill Twocrow in your show?"

Twocrow looked startled at the suggestion, and Laura even more so. They glanced at each other.

"You think I should go along with Jack?" Twocrow finally stammered.

"Or Buffalo Bill?" Short Bull spoke up. "Why not? Earn money. See things. You can come back to your family. Or to her if that's what you want." He pointed to Laura as he said it, and she blushed.

"Oh! Alvin...I mean, Bill, and me...we're just good friends. Like brother and sister." She brushed against his arm. "And I've got my writing. Bill ... understands."

Twocrow patted Laura's hand and looked toward Buffalo Bill and Jack. "Maybe someday I might think about coming with you," he said. "But right now, I've decided to go to Yellow Feather's camp and see how I can help my people. I need to figure some things out—about myself."

He said the last words directly to Laura, who stared into his face and slowly nodded.

"All your people could go with you. To the show," Short Bull said seriously. "Good for the show; good for them. A show from the West needs Indians."

Minnie reached out and put her hand on Twocrow's arm. "If you go. I'll come and write about you." Laura sucked in sharply at her sister's comment. "What?" Minnie said, at Laura's reaction. "You're not his only sister, you know? And I'm a good writer, too. Besides I don't want to stay at Buffalo Gap, and there's nothing for me here in Hot Springs." She squeezed Twocrow's arm. "I'll go write about Alvin." She held up a hand as he started to say something. "And, I don't care, I'm not calling you Bill."

"Yeah, maybe I should just go back to being Alvin," he gave her a wan smile as he looked around the room. "Too many 'Bills' around here, anyway."

Everyone laughed and Lil spoke out.

"Look 'Coz' if you're going to be writing about people in Wild West Shows, then you better not forget to write about me. I'm planning to be just like Annie someday."

"Okay by me...'Coz'," Minnie giggled.

"I want to learn about that kind of shooting myself," Jack nodded. He looked over to Buffalo Bill. "I heard my old man was a dang good shot. You knew him, right?"

"Look, anything you want to know about your Pop, you can ask me," Buffalo Bill replied. "I'm not afraid to admit that I probably wouldn't have even started the Wild West Show without him."

"So, then those stories I heard about him? They're true?" Jack said, sitting up straighter.

Bill nodded. "Every word. Me'n your old man, we started the Scouts of the Prairie with Ned Buntline back in Chicago in '72. He and I went there lookin' for work and Ned had this idea about having us do things in the theater. Kind of a *little* Wild West Show." He chuckled. "Man, this big hat I wear, the buckskins, that was stuff your Dad did.

"People thought I was good looking, of course," he smoothed back some of his long golden hair and ran his fingers through his beard. Annie laughed, and Bill gave her a mock glare.

"Anyway," he continued, "Jack, he was the one everyone liked best. He was impressive and he looked like a real cowboy hero. On top of that he could shoot and rope. Everyone loved Jack." He leaned back and stared thoughtfully. "They broke the mold when your old man died. Terrible loss."

Jack cleared his throat. "Well, thanks for telling me about that Mister Cody. I appreciate it.

Like I said, if I can get some learnin' about sharpshooting and things, I'd like to do something like you've been doin'. If you don't mind?"

"Well, course not," Bill answered. "It might soon be time for me to ease up a bit, anyway. Maybe I'll retire to my ranch. New blood's needed in this business all the time." He smiled and gestured toward his shooter. "If I retire, Annie could work with you."

"No!" Lil spoke up. Everyone stared toward her. "I-I mean, there won't be a spot for Annie in Jack's show. He'll have me."

"What?" Jack smiled. "You?"

"Yes, me!" she said indignantly. "If you're planning to start yourself a Wild West Show, Jack Omohundro, then you're going to need a sharpshooting gal to help headline your show—just like Annie done for Bill. And I plan on that being me!"

She swept her hand toward the ceiling. "Can't you see it? Lil Marr, all-American cowgirl. I can ride and shoot, and you know I ain't afraid of nothin'. And, well...", she paused as if thinking about what to say next, shook her head and grabbed his wrist, just above the bandaged hand.

Jack flinched but didn't pull away. "And well...what?" he asked.

"And, well, I'm tired of you thinking of me like a little sister." She pulled his head toward her and tentatively kissed him. Leaning back she gave him a questioning look as the others broke into laughter at the surprised look on Jack's face. He took a deep breath, nodded ever-so-slightly, and tilted his head toward her while reaching around with his right arm and pulling her closer. Then he kissed her again as the rest of their group switched from laughter to cheers and applause.

Lil grinned and Jack blushed as they finished the kiss and turned toward the group. She looked to Annie. "Will you teach me more about shooting?"

Annie grinned. "Sure thing, sister. You want to start today? I'm going to be practicing down at the Chautauqua again. Everybody was so complimentary last night that we decided to do one more show before we hit the trail. I could show you some more things to work on."

Lil squealed and jumped up to give Annie a hug.

Will got to his feet. "Too dang much huggin' and kissin' goin' on around here. Could make a fella downright sick to his stomach if you ask me."

"Yeah, well who's asking?" Lil turned and kissed Will on the cheek and he made a sour face, pretending to pull away and work with his ever-present rope—even though the others could see he was blushing a deep crimson.

"You're darned good with that rope, young man," Buffalo Bill spoke up, hurrying to mask Will's embarrassment as he nodded at the lasso in Will's hands. "You wouldn't be interested in doing some cattle droving on your way back to the Territory would you?"

Will stood up straighter. "Maybe," he said. "Who needs drovers?"

"I do," Cody answered. "Got a herd out by my ranch in Nebraska and just sold 'em off to a rancher down near Oklahoma City. If your friends don't mind leaving you with me, I'll set you up with a horse and supplies and pay you a dollar a day to help drive 'em on down there."

Will looked stunned. "No fooling? How many days you think it would take?"

"Probably around six weeks," Cody said. "Plus, it's going to take a few days to get everything ready to go. But you should be back in the Territory by end of October."

The young cowboy glanced over at Jack and Lil.

"Sounds like too good a chance to pass up," Jack said before Will could even ask. "I'll send a telegraph to your dad and get his permission. I can't imagine he'd stand in the way of doing something like this." He smiled. "And once you get back home you can tell everyone you been working for Buffalo Bill Cody. Who knows, you might end up getting into the show business field yourself someday."

Lil giggled at Jack's statement, but Will looked thoughtful. "Yeah," he said, lightly twirling the rope. "Maybe so."

Jack stood, hobbled over to Will's side and clapped him on the shoulder.

"Listen Will," he said, "first things first. You help get that herd down to Oklahoma, and then you spend a little more time working on your roping and riding skills, and maybe think of something else that might make for a good act. Once you get that all figured out, you come and find me." He looked at Lil. "Us...wherever we might be. Who knows, maybe we'll get an act together that'll have Mister Cody here quakin' in his boots."

Buffalo Bill guffawed. "Well if you're as honest and entertaining as your old man was, then I might be at that. As my friend Wild Bill used to say, 'We'll just let them chips fall where they may.'"

CHAPTER THIRTY

"What's the plan now?" Bat asked Nellie. "You still going on to Denver?"

They were standing together in the lobby near the Evans' entryway. Bat was waiting for Sheriff Akin to join him and head back to the jail. Bat had just received a second telegram from Denver, this time explaining that the Army unit was being dispatched from Fort Laramie to help transport the two gangs back to Denver. He would stay with the troops until the transfer had been completed.

"Yes, I'll go down there in a few days," Nellie said. "But I still have a week or so here relaxing in the spas. And I'd like to go do a tour of that Wind Cave. After talking with the others, it sounds amazing. Alvin Twocrow offered to take The Whites and me up there tomorrow before they have to leave for Kansas City. And before he heads out to join his tribe."

As she was speaking she was looking out of the corner of her eye over his shoulder toward where Robert Seaman was talking with Fred Evans and two other men—one of who looked like he, too, had come from back East. The fourth man appeared to be a rancher.

The Marshal glanced back to see what Nellie was looking at and gave her a little grin. "Seaman seems like a nice man," he said.

She blushed. "Yes. Amazingly we've found we have a lot in common—way more than I was expecting; I mean, given the difference in our ages. I don't know? We just seem to be..." she paused as if thinking of the right word. "Kindred spirits, I suppose." She stepped back a bit and smiled as Seaman came walking toward them, the other men trailing along.

"Marshal," he said, extending his hand to Bat. Turning to Nellie with a shy smile, he added, "Hello again...Elizabeth." Releasing Masterson's hand he reached over to take hers, turning toward his companions and not letting it go. "Mister Evans was just introducing me to a couple of the other guests, and they said they'd be honored to make your acquaintance." He looked back at Masterson. "Both of your acquaintances, of course."

"Oh, of course!" Masterson chuckled. "I'm sure my name was right up alongside Nellie's when they asked for the intro."

"Actually, it was," spoke the man who definitely looked "Eastern" with his stiff high-collared shirt and tie, thinning hair neatly trimmed and combed back, and the latest style in gold, wire-rimmed glasses. "Back in New York, where I'm from, we have a great respect for Old West lawmen like yourself." He smoothed back the edges of a full, drooping mustache and extended his hand.

"Charles Rushmore."

"Bat Masterson," the lawman replied, involuntarily reaching up to smooth his own bushy mustache as a reaction to the other man's move.

"Charles is quite the local celebrity," Evans said. "Seems they've even named a mountain after him." Both Rushmore and the other man laughed.

"I'm a local," the second man said, extending his own hand to Masterson. "Ted Brockett. I do some ranching up near Keystone, north of here. Charles has been coming out every year for about a decade now to do some hunting with me. So, last year when we were trying our luck over by Slaughterhouse Rock, we thought maybe we'd rename it Mount Rushmore."

Rushmore laughed again at the reference. But the others remained quiet.

"Local joke," Brockett added quickly since the others weren't laughing. "But the name's sort-a stuck."

"Yeah, nobody knows ME, but everybody knows my mountain," Rushmore said. He gave Nellie a warm smile, too. "But I'm sure my fame, unlike yours Miss Bly, will be fleeting. A hundred years from now I'm sure everyone'll be back to calling it Slaughterhouse Rock."

Brockett grinned. "Maybe. But Mount Rushmore has kind of a nice ring to it, too, don't you think?" He said the last to Nellie and she nodded.

Both men now looked expectantly toward Nellie, waiting for their introduction. "Oh," Seaman said, seeing their reaction and finally releasing her hand. "As you've heard, this is local rancher Ted Brockett and this is Charles Rushmore from New York City." She extended her hand to Brockett first and then over to Rushmore.

"What is it you do back in New York, Mister Rushmore?" she asked. "And what brings you to Hot Springs?"

"I'm an attorney," Rushmore said. "Got started coming out here to the Black Hills in the mid-80s to check on some claim titles, and like Ted says, I've been coming back for some hunting almost every year since. Black Hills is one of my favorite spots. This time around Ted and me thought we'd try our luck down in these parts."

As she spoke, Nellie casually reached back and looped her hand around Seaman's left arm and looked up toward him with a warm smile.

"Well," she said, "good luck with your hunting. If you're staying here at the Evans perhaps we'll see one-another again?"

They both nodded and following Nellie's lead, Seaman tipped his hat to them.

"Now, Gentlemen, if you all will excuse us, I'd like to take Elizabeth over to the local mercantile. We have a dress to purchase."

"Good shopping," Bat said. "Sounds like a painful excursion if you ask me." They all laughed. Bat looked toward the desk as Sheriff Akin started toward them. "Time for me to go." Masterson tipped his bowler hat to everyone and hurried over to join the Sheriff. The two men stood together looking at a sheet of paper Akin had brought with him.

Nellie and Robert turned toward the door just as Masterson and Akin started out, and the Sheriff stepped back and held the door for the couple. As they exited, a gust of wind whipped across the veranda and blew Nellie's hat off. Robert hurried to gather it up and she gratefully accepted its return and pulled it firmly back in place.

"Sorry folks. You have to watch out for those gusts of wind around these parts," Akin said. "You both have a real nice day."

"Yes, I'm sure we will," Nellie replied, re-taking Seaman's arm and giving it a squeeze.

"Hell of a thing." Masterson said, watching the couple as they walked arm-in-arm up the street.

"What's that?" the Sheriff responded, already looking back at the paper in his hand.

"Oh, nothing," the Marshal continued, hanging onto his own hat as they started in the other direction, headed toward the courthouse. "Just commenting on the wind."

THE END

AFTERWORD

Facts, fiction and other historical stuff

And The Wind Whispered is a novel based on historical happenings and people. While some of the characters (and their names) are fictional, many were real people. Some of the events depicted in the book actually occurred, while others, including the conversations and interactions among the characters, are depictions imagined by the author.

Nellie Bly was the pen name of Elizabeth Jane Cochrane, the pre-eminent investigative reporter of her day, who had covered the great Columbian Exposition in Chicago in the fall of 1893 where she met representatives touting the Black Hills as a new vacation paradise. In the fall of 1894 she traveled to that region, meeting Robert Seaman, nearly 40 years older than her, on the trip. They were married in the spring of 1895, and after his death in the early 1900s she managed his business holdings for many more years.

Nellie gained fame for her record-breaking 25,000-mile solo trip around the world in just 72 days, taken as a "challenge" to surpass the 80-day record by Phileas Fogg, a character in Jules Verne's best-selling book *Around The World In 80 Days*. Nellie met Jules Verne in France while on her 72-day trip. Her journey was one of the great travel achievements of its time, for both the "quickness" of the trip and the fact she was a woman.

Often willing to put herself in dangerous situations to "get the story," she went "undercover" to write exposés on the terrible conditions in some New York mental institutions and factories. A pioneer in her field, she launched a new kind of investigative journalism still practiced by many reporters today.

William F. "Buffalo Bill" Cody – founder and owner of the world-famous "Buffalo Bill's Wild West Show" – and his protégé and sharpshooter Annie Oakley were often in the Black Hills, including in 1894 for a shooting exhibition at Hot Springs' Chautauqua Park. Cody, who first gained fame as a buffalo hunter and scout for both the U.S. Army and the railroads, owned a ranch in Western Nebraska where he raised and trained many of the animals used in his famous show, which he started in the 1880s. Today, Buffalo Bill's ranch, located outside of North Platte, Neb., is a living history state park and includes many historical exhibits about him, Annie, and the show itself.

Cody cast many Lakota tribal members as performers in his show, including Chief Sitting Bull, Chief Kicking Bear, and Short Bull. The latter two joined the show after coming from an Army prison at Fort Sheridan, Illinois, where they were sent after Sitting Bull's death in the early 1890s. In 1896, Kicking Bear was one of three Lakota leaders chosen to represent the seven Lakota tribes at a meeting in

Washington, DC, to present grievances to the Bureau of Indian Affairs about the appalling conditions on the Reservations. Besides his friendship with Cody and Annie, he had a close friendship with the famous Western artist Frederic Remington.

Bat Masterson was a famed lawman known for his long-range shooting skills and his feats of strength (he once unseated an outlaw by grabbing him as he rode past and pulling him from his horse with one hand). Masterson was sheriff of several Kansas communities (including Dodge City) in the 1870s and 1880s. After moving to Denver in 1888, he served as a part-time U.S. deputy marshal and as a security officer for the railroad, helping "clear the track" so that a train taking Nellie Bly from San Francisco to New Jersey to complete her "Around the World" trip could move unimpeded through Colorado and Kansas. Bly was behind schedule when the train trip began, but a "clear track" put her days ahead by the time she arrived.

While continuing to bring several notorious outlaws to justice as a part-time lawman, Masterson also was developing a sportswriting career. As his writing fame grew, he moved to New York City in 1902 to work as a full-time sports writer and to collaborate on adventure articles about the Old West. He worked as a columnist and editor for New York City's *Morning Telegraph* until his death in 1921.

Cowboy and showman Texas Jack Omohundro met Lil Marr, daughter of an Oklahoma rancher, in the early 1890s. He, Lil and Will Rogers, whose family had a longtime friendship with the Marrs, took a herd of horses from Oklahoma to the Black Hills in the early 1890s, although the exact date was not recorded. This depiction in the novel is the "imagined" time for their journey since it was widely assumed that he and Lil met with Buffalo Bill and Annie Oakley for advice and counseling while on their Black Hills trip.

In the late 1890s, Jack started "Texas Jack's Wild West Circus," modeled after Buffalo Bill's show. Lil became both Jack's common law wife and his show's sharpshooting showstopper. The show ended in 1905 when Texas Jack died from malaria while on a trip to South Africa.

Jack's other claim to fame was that his father, also known as Texas Jack, helped Buffalo Bill start "Scouts of the Prairie," a precursor to the Wild West Show. Cody spoke fondly of Texas Jack and the key contribution he made to "The Wild West Show's" origins.

Will Rogers, born to a prominent Cherokee Nation family, began his own show
business career as a trick roper in Texas Jack's show in 1902. After accompanying Jack and Lil on their trip to the Black Hills, Rogers got a taste of cattle-droving by helping take a herd south to the Oklahoma Territory.

By the 1920s and '30s, Rogers was one of America's most-loved and best-known celebrities. He gained fame as a stage performer, humorist, writer, social commentator and motion picture actor, a career that spanned more than 30 years. His writings were seen in newspapers around the world, and he appeared in more than 70 movies. Often referred to as "Oklahoma's Favorite Son," he died tragically in a 1935 plane crash.

Theodore Roosevelt became President of the United States in 1901 at the age of 42 – the youngest person to ever hold the Presidency. Lauded as one of America's greatest presidents, he moved from his native New York to live and work in the Badlands of

North Dakota in the early 1880s and traveled several times to the Black Hills. In 1892, while serving as U.S. Civil Service Commissioner, he visited South Dakota's Indian Reservations and said: "The wretchedness of life on the Pine Ridge (just east of the Southern Black Hills) has stayed with me since my visit there." He was empathetic with the plight of the Native Americans and strove to improve their living conditions during his presidency.

He returned to the Black Hills in early autumn, 1894, to meet and hunt with Seth Bullock, longtime sheriff of Deadwood, who first met Roosevelt in 1884 and quickly formed a friendship that would last throughout their lifetimes. "Seth Bullock is a true Westerner, the finest type of frontiersman," Roosevelt wrote. In 1898, Bullock served as a Captain in Roosevelt's "Rough Riders" regiment during the Spanish-American War. Roosevelt's leadership and courage in the war resulted in his being awarded the Congressional Medal of Honor, the nation's highest military award. In 1906 he became the first American to win the Nobel Peace Prize. In 1939, Roosevelt was enshrined as one of the four faces on Mt. Rushmore National Monument.

Roosevelt appointed Bullock in 1902 to serve as Forest Supervisor of the Black Hills National Forest, which included supervision of Wind Cave and its surrounding prairieland. And, in 1903, Roosevelt established Wind Cave National Park under Bullock's supervision. The Bullock Hotel, which he founded, still operates in Deadwood, where Bullock is buried in Mt. Moriah Cemetery near the graves of Wild Bill Hickok and Calamity Jane.

In 1919, Bullock oversaw the building of Mount Roosevelt Friendship Tower near Deadwood, dedicated on July 4 of that year as a memorial to his friend's life and a place where people could view the wide-open spaces that both he and Roosevelt cherished.

Separately and together Bullock and Roosevelt played a major role in the history of the Black Hills. Both men died in 1919 – Roosevelt in January, and Bullock in September.

The name "Rough Riders," adopted by Roosevelt for his Regiment during the Spanish-American War, is credited to many different people, including Buffalo Bill and Southern Black Hills lawman Gene Akin.

In 1890-91, Akin started the Battle Creek squad of the Home Guards, which he called "a rough-riding cowboy militia," to help protect homesteaders along the western side of the new state of South Dakota.

Akin first gained acclaim in the late 1880s by killing two notorious outlaws – Frank Diamond and Charley Curley. That started a long feud between him and the rest of The Curley Gang, a Southern Hills outlaw gang depicted in the book. In real life, the gang aligned with the larger "Doc" Middleton Gang terrorizing Northwest Nebraska and the Southern Black Hills. The McCarty Gang in the book is modeled after the Middleton Gang. Both gangs met their demise during an encounter with Akin's Home Guard and other law enforcement officers from the Black Hills and Northern Nebraska.

John Philip Sousa and his band were playing in South Dakota in 1894 when they were invited by hotelier Fred Evans to come to Hot Springs to relax in the warm waters and perform at the opening of the city's refurbished Chautauqua Park. Sousa's "Liberty Bell March" was wildly popular and he was in the process of writing what would become his signature song, "Stars and Stripes Forever." Fresh from a career as Marine Corps officer and band director, he often performed a stirring "opening" song for his shows that the U.S. Navy had adopted as its official anthem. It was called "The Star Spangled Banner."

Sousa's frequent use of the anthem helped inspire widespread public enthusiasm for adopting it as the U.S. anthem, but it did not officially become the U.S. anthem until 1931.

William Allen White was a Pulitzer Prize-winning writer, editor, and publisher, who started his career at *The Kansas City Star* in 1892. He was married to Sallie Lindsay in 1893. In 1895, he purchased his hometown newspaper, *The Emporia Gazette*, in Emporia, Kansas, following a vacation the previous fall to the Black Hills. White developed his idea of the small town as a metaphor for understanding social change and for preaching the necessity of community. He was a great admirer of Theodore Roosevelt, having first met him while traveling in the Black Hills. He hosted him in Emporia as well as visiting him at the White House after Roosevelt became President.

Theodore August Metz, band leader for the "McIntyre and Heath Minstrels," said he met Joe Hayden in Hot Springs where the Minstrels were performing and where Hayden was temporarily employed at the Evans Hotel. "A Hot Time in the Old Town" is an American ragtime song, composed by Metz with lyrics by Hayden. Their song, finalized in 1895 and widely distributed in 1896, became one of America's most popular, and was a particular favorite of American military forces, including Theodore Roosevelt's Rough Riders, during the Spanish-American War.

Laura Thompson and her sister Minnie were nieces of *Buffalo Gap News* editor Col. "Jack" Thompson. Both young women were accomplished writers and reporters. Laura's story about a group of women "cowboys" who brought a herd from Denver to the Black Hills, and her writing about a riding exhibition by young Black Hills women willing to ride "astride" instead of sidesaddle (as most "ladies" of the day rode), made news reports throughout the region. Laura and Minnie were influenced by the writing and reporting of Nellie Bly, and Laura supposedly traveled to New York City in 1895 to meet with Bly and interview Theodore Roosevelt — although no formal record of her supposed meeting with Bly or the story about Roosevelt has been found.

Joshua Dickover, Fred Evans, and Archie Riordan were all Hot Springs community leaders. Dickover, who served as the city's first mayor, had a key role in encouraging Evans, founder of both the Evans Hotel and Evans Plunge, to run as his successor.

A businessman and entrepreneur, Dickover became mayor in 1890 when Hot Springs was establishing itself as a growing tourist destination. He was instrumental, along with Evans, in attracting two major rail lines and many important investors to the community in the city's developmental years.

Evans was a wealthy businessman who had made a fortune as a streetcar owner and then teamster, transporting supplies to growing Black Hills communities in the 1870s and 1880s. He came to Hot Springs to develop the natural warm water springs as a new playground for the rich, establishing both the Evans Plunge covered pool, and the Evans Hotel and Spa, which included baths and access to the restorative waters of nearby Kidney Springs. He was elected mayor following Dickover's endorsement and served one term in the mid-1890s.

The Evans Hotel was one of the most luxurious in the Old West and was residence for many rich and famous travelers. Evans spared no expense in setting up his hotel, including installing elevators and electric lights, and an elegant dining room with crystal chandeliers and an African-American wait staff. The hotel, on the national register of historic places, was restored in the 1970s and today is a retirement center.

Riordan was a town marshal and hotel owner in Buffalo Gap before moving to Hot Springs, where he opened and operated both a successful bottling company and a drug store. His leadership helped establish Hot Springs as a business center for the many surrounding communities, and he also played a lead role in developing tourism both in the city and to nearby Wind Cave, particularly during his years as mayor.

Elected to three terms, Riordan was known as one of the city's most popular community leaders and best-loved mayors.

William Cross devoted decades to photographing the Black Hills and the nearby prairielands and his work has been widely lauded by historians and artists alike. For a time he also traveled and took photographs in other parts of the country. But by the 1890s he kept busy in Hot Springs, where he spent time on landscape photography and compiled a sizeable collection of Black Hills Views. Cross operated a photography studio on Minnekahta Avenue for two decades until his death from pneumonia in 1907. Among his early 1890s photographs is a scene taken from the cliffside overlooking Hot Springs' refurbished Chautauqua Park. It shows the park's large wooden Pavilion and band shell built alongside the stream flowing through the park.

Alvin McDonald, his brother Elmer, and father J.D. did most of the early exploration of Wind Cave. During the fall of 1893, J.D. and Alvin traveled to the Columbian Exposition in Chicago to promote the cave. On the trip Alvin caught typhoid fever and was never really well again. He died that December at the age of 20.

Exploration and tours of the cave's passages continued and wooden staircases were installed. A hotel was built near the cave entrance and a daily coach provided rides to the cave. On his visit there in 1894, Roosevelt called it a national treasure that should be maintained for all Americans. And, in 1903, true to his beliefs, he established the cave and its surrounding hills and prairie as a national park.

Alvin "Bill" Twocrow was not a real person, but his character represents the many young Native Americans who strove to make better lives for their families and the people of their tribes. They became integral parts of the fabric that made up communities such as Hot Springs, Buffalo Gap, and the surrounding region. Many Lakota, including entire villages, joined both Buffalo Bill's and Texas Jack's shows as a way to earn money for their families and their tribes.

The genesis for the Twocrow name grew out of the author's family's friendship with a young Native American named Albert Twocrow, a Hot Springs resident who often spoke proudly of his heritage. He asked that we remember that his people were there first, and that the Black Hills always holds a sacred spot in their hearts and minds.

The Andersons are not a real family, but the characters represented by Irene and her husband Paul are composites of the hard-working ranch and farm families who settled in or near the Black Hills after the initial euphoria of the Black Hills Gold Rush days of the late 1870s had subsided. They still make up a major and important part of the region. Many rural Black Hills area families trace their heritage to families that came to the region in the 1880s and 1890s, some of who married members of the Lakota nation.

Deputy Chalky Burrell was not a real person, but is a composite of the young men who not only helped ranch and farm the land but also served their communities as law enforcement officers, community volunteers, and builders. He also is representative of the men who made up Gene Akin's roughriding "Home Guard."
	Pete Lemley and Charles Roe, his fellow deputies in the story, were real lawman. Lemley eventually became known as "The Badlands Fox" for his stealthy tracking skills and ability to outsmart the outlaws he was tracking. Lemley, Roe, and Riordan, and even Roosevelt – who served for a time as a deputy sheriff in North Dakota – often spoke of the invaluable help and dedication of young cowboys like Chalky, who helped make the region safe for their own generation and many more to follow.

Nellie Ryan was one of the first female mail carriers, not only in the Hot Springs area, but also in the West. She delivered the mail on horseback to rural Hot Springs-area patrons for more than 25 years. She was noted for her riding skills, and her perserverance in "delivering the mail on time and in good condition" regardless the weather conditions she might encounter. Nellie and other rural mail carriers were known as "unofficial deputies" for local law enforcement agencies, helping keep an eye out for their rural friends and neighbors and making reports to lawmen whenever they spotted "suspicious characters" traveling through the region.

Charles Rushmore was a New Yorker who first traveled to the Black Hills in 1885 to check titles to properties for an eastern mining company. He returned each fall for many years to hunt big game.

On one such trip in the 1890s, accompanied by Ted Brockett of Keystone, Rushmore asked the name of a nearby rocky craig and was told that it was called Slaughterhouse Rock. Rushmore joked that his annual treks to the Hills had earned him the right to have the mountain named after himself. "So just for the hell of it," Southern Hills rancher Jerry Urbanek claimed, "the locals started calling it Mount Rushmore."

When sculptor Gutzon Borglum began carving his famous faces on the mountain in 1927, Rushmore donated $5,000 – the largest individual contribution to the project.

El Kebir was a real, "cantankerous and somewhat vicious," Arabian stallion brought to America in the 1880s by a French immigrant rancher living near Buffalo Gap. El Kebir escaped and roamed the Southern Black Hills for many years, eventually leading a herd of wild mustang mares. Descendants of those wild crossbred horses and wild mustangs can still be seen at the Wild Horse Sanctuary south of Hot Springs.

*****

The Missing Gold and "Hideout Cave"

In September, 1878, a robbery of the Homestake Mine's transport coach – nicknamed "The Monitor" because of its extra armament – netted the Lame

Johnny Gang about $27,000 in cash, considerable gold dust and small gold nuggets, some jewels, and over 700 pounds of gold ingots.

According to the robbery's victims, four men and a woman carried out the heist at the Canyon Springs relay station and escaped with several Homestake Mine strongboxes.

The woman and one of the men rode north, while the other three robbers went east toward Buffalo Gap. Within weeks, four of the five were dead. A possé killed two of the robbers and captured Lame Johnny. Lame Johnny said the way to find the hidden gold was to start from a three-trunk cottonwood tree and go up through the buffalo gap. He led the possé to the tree, but then had second thoughts. After refusing to say any more, he was hanged.

A couple weeks later, the woman believed to be from Lame Johnny's gang was shot and killed at a Deadwood brothel while trying to sell some of the stolen jewels. Her male companion disappeared and was never found.

Decades after the robbery, a Southern Hills rancher's wife searching for a lost cow stumbled upon a well-hidden cave near King's Ridge. She said it was set up inside like a hideout, including a falling down makeshift corral. Among other items she saw were rotting empty strongboxes. No one ever found the cave again, and some speculate that it collapsed in upon itself, obscuring both the cave and its entrance, when an earthquake rattled the region.

Some Lakota tribal members share stories from their ancestors about boxes of yellow ore being discovered in a "spirit" cave. Since yellow is sometimes depicted as the color given by the Great Spirit to protect Mother Earth, the Lakota returned the ore to the earth.

The 700 pounds of gold ingots – worth millions today – have never been recovered.

For those interested in the search, you might start at a three-trunk cottonwood tree that still stands at the entrance to the buffalo gap, where the wind whispers through its leaves.

ACKNOWLEDGMENTS

This book is dedicated to my wife Susan, whose love, support and unwavering belief in me and encouragement for my writing has made this work move from an idea to a reality.

Special thanks to Joe and Karen Muller of Hot Springs, S.D., for their help in finding and providing resources about the era; "finding the locations;" and "walking the grounds" with us during research on the book, its locales, and in locating background information on its characters.

Thanks to Carolyn Amiet for her editorial expertise and support, and to Dave & Cathy Sorenson for their review of the manuscript.

Thank you to the Fall River Historical Society and, especially, Colleen Waxler, who assisted in locating resources about 1890s Hot Springs and Fall River County.

And, thanks also to the Hot Springs Library staff and *The Hot Springs Star* for information found in their archival materials about the era and the people who made the news during the community's early days.

ABOUT THE AUTHOR

Born in Minnesota, Dan Jorgensen grew up on a South Dakota farm/ranch and attended a one-room country school as an elementary student. He was the first member of his family to attend college, earning degrees from South Dakota State University. He has had a long career as a writer, educator and public relations specialist, winning awards for his feature stories and in educational p.r., marketing and public affairs. While working for colleges and universities occupied most of his time, he also spent a number of years as a feature writer and editor at several newspapers sandwiched around creative writing that started with his first novel, *Killer Blizzard*, written while he was working and studying creative writing at Colorado State Univ.

In addition to writing many hundreds of news and sports articles and features, both as a journalist and in public relations, he has authored six books, three songs, and a one-act play and is working on a number of other creative pieces. He also writes the daily blog, *A Writer's Moment*. Since the 1990s he has combined his work experience with teaching journalism, public relations, and writing at the collegiate level.

A frequent presenter at conferences and panel discussions, he has spoken on "Storytelling – From Journalism to Creative Writing," "Telling an Effective Story," "Effective Communication," and "Crisis Communications."

Dan and his wife Susan (Brandt) live in Broomfield, Colo., where he writes for *Broadlands Living* magazine and does project work and teaching at area universities. The Jorgensens have two adult daughters and three grandchildren.

Among the professional organizations with which he is affiliated are Council for Advancement & Support of Education (CASE); The National Association of Science Writers; Kappa Tau Alpha (the national journalism honorary); Sigma Delta Chi; Veterans of Foreign Wars; and Rotary International.

Previous Works

Novels

Killer Blizzard
Sky Hook
Dawn's Diamond Defense
Kelli's Choice

Non-Fiction

Family Hiking Trails in South Dakota
Jargon, The Book

Plays

The First Day

Anthology Inclusion

A Farm Country Christmas

MORE GREAT HISTORICAL FICTION FROM BYGONE ERA BOOKS

Immortal Betrayal
Immortal Duplicity
Daniel A. Willis

Primitive Passions
John N. Cahill

Kilpara
Patricia Hopper

The Harlot Saint
Susan McGregor

Bittersweet Tavern
S. Copperstone

CPSIA information can be obtained
at www.ICGtesting.com
Printed in the USA
FSOW01n0439150416
19231FS